Dangerous Pilgrims

Dangerous Pilgrims

Lawrence Swaim

ROUNDFIRE BOOKS

Winchester, UK
Washington, USA

First published by Roundfire Books, 2016
Roundfire Books is an imprint of John Hunt Publishing Ltd., Laurel House, Station Approach,
Alresford, Hants, SO24 9JH, UK
office1@jhpbooks.net
www.johnhuntpublishing.com
www.roundfire-books.com

For distributor details and how to order please visit the 'Ordering' section on our website.

ISBN: 978 1 78535 474 8
Library of Congress Control Number: 2016935420

A CIP catalogue record for this book is available from the British Library.

Design: Stuart Davies

Printed in the USA by Edwards Brothers Malloy

"And I remain unmoved—and yet, and yet,
These Christs that die upon the barricades,
God knows it I am with them, in some things."
Sonnet to Liberty
Oscar Wilde

Chapter One

In 1982 I drifted south into Mexico, bound for the regions of war and revolution.

I went to Mexico City first, taking a job with an American wire service. It was there that I began to hear the stories about Guatemala. What made these stories special was that they were about a place that was extraordinarily beautiful, by all accounts, but also extraordinarily dangerous—there was a brutal civil war under way there, which had been going on for a decade or so.

I asked my editor if I could travel to Guatemala as a stringer, a journalist who is not on regular salary.

"I know I'll get paid only for the stories you use, and that you may not even use my stuff very often," I said. "But I really want to write about the civil war and the political situation in Guatemala and everything else going on there."

He looked at me as though I was mad.

"People don't want to read about civil war in Guatemala," he said. "Most North Americans don't even know there *is* a civil war in Guatemala, and they probably don't want to find out. Trust me on that."

"There are plenty of other things I can write about."

"Maybe, if they're colorful and reasonably interesting, and have a good human-interest angle," he said. "Not using your stories won't be any problem for me, pal. It's just that I can't pay you very much for the stories I *do* use."

"That's okay."

"How's your Spanish?"

"Good."

"Can you live off what you make?"

"Probably not."

"*Probably not.*" He looked at me. "Do you have money?"

"I don't have a trust fund."

"Any money saved up?"

"Some."

"And you still want to do it?"

I shrugged.

Something about my shrug irritated him. "What's that for?" he demanded. "What the hell is *that* supposed to mean? I ask you if you want to do something, and you shrug your shoulders?"

"You don't like the shrug?"

"Fuckin' *aye*, I don't like it. It's disrespectful—disrespectful of me, disrespectful of the situation."

"I'm saying yes. That's my way of saying *yes*."

A strange look came into his face, a look that contained contempt, but also some sympathy. It was the kind of sympathy one might have for a sick dog, but the very fact that I had inspired any feeling at all in such a rude substance-abusing nihilist greatly impressed me.

"This thing, it's a little crazy, what you're doing," he said. "I mean, it's my responsibility to tell you that. Anybody who goes to Guatemala now as a stringer is either crazy or suicidal."

"Would you say I'm clinically insane?"

"Certifiably so."

"Sanity is highly overrated," I said.

"Guatemala's pretty rough territory right now," he continued, as though repeating a memorized speech word-for-word. "It's just a very dangerous place, man, especially for somebody going there alone; a stringer who isn't going to get paid that much."

"I know."

"I mean, if you value your life—"

"I know."

He was still looking at me. "Do you have some contacts in country?"

"A few."

"Okay," he said, sighing, "I'm gonna ask you again, and then I'm gonna give up. Are you sure about this?"

"Sure," I said.

His eyes narrowed.

"You're not just saying this for some kind of stupid effect?"

"I don't think so."

"I don't think so," he said contemptuously.

Then he looked away from me.

As he did so, a kind of distance came into his eyes, as though he were in an entirely different place, one that no longer included me. I had seen that look once before, when my wife told me she was leaving. He'd edited me right out of his copy, clean out of whatever story his life was telling him. To him, I was already dead—I no longer existed. It was then I knew that I really had to go to Guatemala.

Once in Guatemala City, I took up residence on a leafy side street in a fashionable neighborhood, not far from an office of the same wire service I'd worked for in Mexico. Most of the embassies were located in this neighborhood, including the American embassy. I boarded with a family of civil servants named Santos, who rented me a room in the back of their cavernous apartment and allowed me to put my food in their refrigerator.

Each night I joined the Santos for a dinner prepared by the matriarch of the family, a grizzled woman in her fifties. The family consisted of her and her husband, three aunts, and several children of widely varying ages. The Santos had lost a son in the demonstrations prior to the Olympics in Mexico City in the late 1960s; the son had been studying art at the university, they said, and had been shot dead at the Plaza de Tlatelolco while trying to shield his girlfriend from the bullets of soldiers firing automatic weapons.

The family had been in endless litigation about it ever since; and I was led to believe that one faction in the Mexican government had actually decided, for whatever murky political reasons, to pay reparations. But just four months before I arrived, the Santos' attorney had skipped out to Zurich with assets belonging to several of his clients, including the family's settlement money.

The various members of the Santos family were in shock.

It had taken them years to accept the death of the son, who was by all accounts an aesthete and nothing even remotely like a political activist; the loss of the money that would have gotten their younger children through university, and perhaps into the professions, had the effect of causing them to feel the loss of their martyred son all over again—this time unmitigated by even the prospect of compensation.

"Que lastima," they would say softly, shaking their heads, *"y que talento.* What talent he had."

"Lo siento," I would say. "I'm really sorry."

Later on, I discovered from contacts in the American Embassy that the son's death had been nothing like the family said it was. Far from sheltering his girlfriend from the bullets of Mexican cavalry, he was a compulsive gambler who had been murdered by gangsters in Guatemala City. Furthermore, it had been the government of Guatemala that the family had sued, since the gangsters were on the payroll of the Treasury Department; and the family's prospects for compensation, it was suggested to me, existed mainly in their own minds.

The tale of the Plaza de Tlatelolco martyrdom in Mexico was a benign fiction invented to protect the mother and the younger children from the truth, apparently. Their attorney had indeed absconded with money belonging to the family, but it was mainly from the sale of real estate and had nothing to do with compensation for any wrongful death—except, again, in the minds of certain family members.

The family lived in threadbare gentility (the government was sometimes more than a year late paying their salaries), and the evening meals were tense, silent affairs—except for Saturday night, when dinner was served quite late and always ended with everyone getting completely smashed. On Saturday night, anything could happen.

One of the things that happened regularly on Saturday night was that I was challenged and teased because I was from the United States. The United States seemed to be disliked by everybody across the political spectrum in Guatemala, from the far left to the murderous far right. *"Soy Canadiense"* had saved the lives of many an *Estadounidense* in a threatening situation, according to the journalists that I talked to; but with the Santos family, I refused to pretend that I was a Canadian.

"What are you doing in Guatemala?" family members would ask me.

The tone was playful, but the question was always the same and the tone challenging, which made it seem both more and less than a joke.

"I'm here to write about Guatemala and the things that are important to the Guatemalan people," I would usually answer.

"What kinds of things?"

"You know, the way people live their lives."

The family members would smile. "This country is full of poor people. How can you make money down here?"

"Ah," I would say, "but you are Ladino people, people of the upper classes, people of quality. You're not poor."

"Do you think we will give you money for saying that?"

"I don't need money. I am a poet. The spiritual things are important to me."

The family would roar with laughter. "Yes, of course—spiritual things! ... *Cosas espirituales!"*

The idea of a North American concerned with spiritual things was so amusing that it would usually take several moments for them to calm down. It did not correspond with any of the images that the family had assimilated from American television, American movies, and certain Americans they had encountered.

"Truly. *De veras.* It's only the higher things that interest me."

"Like the prostitutes and the drugs," one of the sons said daringly, but already the family was too drunk to care.

"I see women only as creatures of beauty, like the beautiful nudes that one sees in the great paintings of history."

"And the drugs."

"Never. I will strike every person trafficking in drugs—I will strike them in the face."

Since only one son spoke good English, we always spoke in Spanish. My accent—and the outrageous things I said—made them laugh.

On one particular Saturday night, they started speculating loudly about why I—an *Estadounidense* who was probably secretly rich—had come to Guatemala; and then proceeded to argue among themselves about the relative verisimilitude of the stories they had concocted.

"He is a hippie," one of the daughters insisted. "Why else would someone from his country come here? They like to travel. They come here to have an exciting educational experience."

"No, no, no," her mother drunkenly protested. "Look at him. Where is the long hair? And he doesn't even like drugs."

"That's what he says."

"He is a *turista.* Surely he is a *turista,* not a hippie."

"No, he is a businessman. Someday he will set up the headquarters of his business, and he will be rich and famous. He'll give us all jobs, and pay us on time."

They laughed.

"I think he is a missionary from a North American church. Soon he will get up on the table and preach."

There was a slight pause, and then the mother said crankily, "You should respect all religious people if they are sincere, even if they do unusual things."

"But he is not religious."

"How do you know?"

On this night everyone was quite drunk, and one of the sons said something careless.

"He is a *subversivo*," the son said at one point, his face red with drink. "He's looking for the ghost of Che Guevara. He wants to study *el proceso revolutionario.*"

The table got quiet.

"Is that what you are?" the drunken son asked softly. They all sat waiting to hear what I would say.

I had also had a great deal to drink, and I decided to make them as uncomfortable as they had occasionally made me—to pay them back for all the silly taunting things they had said to me and teased me about during the drunken dinners on Saturday night. I knew they were Catholics, so I decided to use that.

"I am exceedingly interested in the new liberation theology," I said. "I want to meet priests who are preaching social justice to the people. I want to meet nuns who teach the people to question the authority of the government in *comunidades de base* in the highlands. I want to meet *delagados de la palabra* who teach the people to fight for the Kingdom of God on earth. Only by doing that, and only by living with the Indians in their impoverished homes in the poorest parts of the mountains, can I truly understand *el proceso revolutionario,* and look deep into the hearts of those who have taken up arms to fight injustice in the government."

There was a very uncomfortable silence.

"Could you introduce me to any subversives?"

I looked from one horrified face to another with a big smile on my face.

"Could you?" I asked again. I turned to Alejandro, the son who had started the whole thing. "Surely you, of all people, realize how important it is to understand the rebels' side of the story."

His father crossed himself and cleared his throat.

One of the daughters was shaking her head. "You shouldn't

talk that way," she said, her voice almost a whisper. "*No digas nadie.* It's not a joke."

Her eyes were frightened.

By this time the family had begun to realize that I was deliberately needling them; but I had done it in such an alarming way that they were in no hurry to laugh. Instead, the mother at once began to talk animatedly about something else. The others followed her lead; but after that night they never teased me again, probably to eliminate the possibility that I might again speak so lubriciously about so delicate a topic at the dinner table. Even drunkenness was not, I noted with a certain satisfaction, a sufficient prophylactic against the fear and disorientation inspired by a stranger speaking so openly about the civil war in their country.

The office where I worked in Guatemala City was even more relaxed than its affiliate in Mexico City. I could walk to the office from my room with the Santos, and I was able to set up a schedule on a weekly basis. I was particularly good at rewriting certain kinds of copy, so I was put to work on stories submitted by my employer's sizable stable of stringers. Stringers, I should explain again at this point, are simply freelance journalists. Since they are not on salary, they receive no benefits—not even a free burial if they are killed.

They are often in harm's way, at least in a war zone; and since they are paid only for those stories that are actually used, their pay is minimal. Yet there has probably never been a war or revolution in modern times that has not attracted a sizable contingent of these amazing people. Apparently there is something about death, destruction and organized mayhem that they cannot resist—or perhaps they simply enjoy writing about it, subjecting its unruly violence to the discipline of something as impersonal as daily journalism.

Since I was good at rewriting, I was greatly beloved by the

stringers in the field. My specialty was piecing together a story from various pieces of information and making a coherent whole out of it. Many stories went out under the bylines of stringers that were in reality almost entirely written by me. For this reason the management of the wire service was open to my idea of taking a turn at field reporting.

So I began to write the occasional Guatemala story.

The bureau chief was a fallen Mormon who was extraordinarily sensitive to any story that questioned or focused on American support of the dictatorships then flourishing in Latin America. These kinds of stories he labeled "advocacy journalism;" as far as I could tell, that meant any kind of reportage that raised questions about American foreign policy in Latin America.

Once a wire service got a reputation for "advocacy journalism," he told me, daily journalism in America would drop it like a hot potato. Responsible North American news agencies did not go out of their way to do that kind of investigative reporting, not when the subject being investigated was American foreign policy in the Third World. Latin American governments supported by the US might indeed engage in torture, murder, imprisonment of dissenters, and systematic sexual abuse of females; but it engaged in them only as useful adjuncts to the winning of the Cold War.

Not only did my boss dislike stories about North American influence in Latin American politics, this same bureau chief did not like stories about Latin American politics at all. What he *did* like were stories about *futbol,* which he featured early and often in his dispatches—the more violent the story, the better. The assorted drunks, journalists and maniacs who assisted him referred to him as the "soccer editor."

He did not seem to mind.

I wrote a tongue-in-cheek and somewhat scurrilous piece about a North American seeing his first soccer game at the

National Stadium in Guatemala City (during which the Guatemalans in the stands chased the referee out of the stadium and tried unsuccessfully to set his car on fire). I wrote the National Stadium story entirely from material given to me by two stringers, and from a couple of phone interviews with people who had seen the melee. During this time I also wrote a series of cultural pieces about the arts and crafts of various Guatemalan Indian groups in the highlands, and a very nice piece about a couple whose child was flown to a hospital in Miami for emergency surgery.

In all fairness to my bureau chief, the other Americans who worked with him did not find his dislike of "advocacy journalism" all that objectionable. Following the money and looking for scandal was all very good back home in the States; after all, it got Pulitzers for Woodward and Bernstein, not to mention contracts from major Hollywood movie studios. But this was Latin America, and it was a different game—there were national security considerations here.

And it was dangerous. Journalists were getting killed.

Better to keep your peace, said the old-timers. Drink the cheap beer and get yourself a good-looking girlfriend; save the incendiary stuff for the book you would write someday.

And so I saved it, "the incendiary stuff."

But—lo!—the incendiary stuff took on a life of its own. It took up residence in my body; and in the years to come, it gave me, with its murderously smoldering fires, stomach ulcers, asthma, and a perennially sour disposition; and became, like all things born and nurtured of bad faith, the stuff of truculent, nagging, restless dreams.

In time I discovered that there was only one group in Guatemala City from which I could consistently get reliable information about human-rights abuses. This was the Roman Catholic Church, which was apparently the only institution in Guatemala that was capable of occasionally criticizing the government without being driven completely underground. The main human-rights group set up by the church was staffed by two Jesuit priests and some volunteers, but it collected information from all over Guatemala. I ended up spending a fair amount of time at their first-floor office, located on a side street in a poor neighborhood.

I got to know a few academics at the university, but with them I had the same problem as I had with the family Santos: I did not correspond to their conception of a typical North American, and therefore they had trouble sizing me up. Most Guatemalan intellectuals were not particularly enthusiastic about talking to American journalists in any case, since we were often assumed to be in the pay of the CIA. There were many quizzical and anxious looks, many heads shaken and much looking out the window. I was told many times that I was in a situation that I could not possibly understand, a situation that was much more dangerous than anything I could possibly imagine; either they saw me as excessively clever, or excessively naïve, or simply one more wraith lost in the minefield of competing paranoias that was Guatemala in the early 1980s.

Perhaps they sensed a certain recklessness about me, which could have suggested the presence of a death wish.

Since most Guatemalans—and not only the intellectuals—could not understand me or my motives, they were consequently afraid of the dangers that I might pose to them. In retrospect, that was a perfectly logical thing to feel. The one common denominator in every interaction was danger. I sometimes felt like everybody in Guatemala had a kind of internal fear meter that went from low to moderate to moderately high to extremely high, depending on every word that was spoken during a conversation, including the most innocuous words.

Adding to the paranoia was the fact that there were hundreds of foreigners in Guatemala City.

There were scores of NGOS—non-governmental organizations—many funded by the United Nations, others funded by international charitable organizations large and small. By the late 1970s and early 1980s, the NGOs had found themselves in an extraordinarily vulnerable position. By that time the Guatemalan military had decided that *any* effort to improve the situation of the Indians in the highlands was *de facto* proof of revolutionary intentions.

Most of the NGOs tried to develop lines of communication with indigenous contacts in the highlands, but trained staff from outside the country—relief workers, teachers, medical staff and others—had begun to stay away from the villages, particularly when it seemed that military operations might be a possibility.

Many of the best NGOs had already left Guatemala, and others were looking for a way to extricate their personnel until things calmed down. That might have been one reason the Guatemalan intellectuals found me so unfathomable—what was I thinking, coming to their country, when so many people were getting out?

I hung out from time to time at one of the disreputable bars favored by American journalists, which was located in the hotel where many of them stayed. The American journalists told me the things to watch out for.

Vehicles with four-wheel drive were widely used in Guatemala, and trucks or vans with tinted windows often belonged to security forces and were to be avoided (the same was true for vehicles with no license plates containing three or more men). Individual army officers could be bribed, but a small gift (a pen, a lighter, a small hardbound notebook) was probably better than money—with a money bribe there was always the possibility of offering too much or too little, and injuring someone's pride.

Many of the American journalists I met had convinced themselves that the death squads and massacres by the army in the highlands were an outcome of obscure but irresistible forces in Guatemalan culture, and therefore inevitable; others saw them as outbreaks of mass hysteria that could be more properly studied as abnormal psychology than as stories appearing in daily journalism in North America. One way or another, most of the American journalists had convinced themselves that the killing of civilians was not something that was in itself newsworthy. It was indeed a reality in Guatemala, but not something that could be made explicable in ordinary human terms to the readers of daily newspapers in the US. And writing too much about civilians getting killed by death squads and soldiers could be labeled "advocacy journalism," whatever that was really supposed to mean.

One evening I was walking down the leafy street in the quiet neighborhood where I lived, heading toward the apartment of the family Santos. It was the best time of day in Guatemala City. The horizon was a lovely high-octane pink in the west, the sky a cloudless blue; the heat rising from the streets was as palpable as vapor from a steaming pot. I had not heard any shots fired anywhere in the city all day.

Coming down the street was a car, moving slowly. It was coming toward me. I understood that I should be apprehensive, although the car did not have tinted windows.

The driver pulled over and stuck his head out the window. It was Alejandro Santos, the young man who had asked me if I was a subversive during the Saturday night meal in his family's apartment. "Hey, spiritual guy!" he said. *"Norteamericano! ...* I want to talk to you about spiritual things... *Cosas espirituales!"*

"Alejandro?"

"Come on over here, man. I want to talk to you."

Sitting next to him in the car was a woman. I could not see her very well, but I could see that she was quite dark, and that she wore dark glasses. There was a powerful latent energy about the woman; she sat very still in her seat, like a rabbit ready to bolt if there were any wrong moves.

I strode over to the car. "What's happening?"

He had spoken to me in Spanish, and I answered him in the same language. I spoke in what I hoped was a friendly tone.

"There is someone that I want you to meet," he said.

"Thank you."

"This is Sofia Mendez."

I leaned down to get a better look at the woman.

"My name is Maitland Sutterfield," I said in Spanish. "I'm from *el norte*. Please excuse my accent."

There was a pause, and the woman leaned in front of Alejandro and stuck her hand out the driver's-side window. I took it and was surprised to see how firm her grip was. Because of the dark glasses she was wearing I could not make out her face very well; but I saw that she wore designer jeans and a fitted blouse, and was therefore not a peasant.

"I'm very glad to meet you," she said in Spanish.

I nodded sharply. We continued to speak in Spanish.

"Do you want to meet a priest who knows about spiritual things?" Alejandro asked.

"What things?"

He glanced quickly in the rearview mirror but continued to smile. "The spiritual things you talked about last Saturday. About the poverty in the highlands. About the priests who preach social justice. About the people who are fighting against the government in the revolution."

"Yes, of course I want to know about those things," I said. "I have to write about every point of view, if I want to write fairly about the situation in Guatemala."

"You don't have to explain everything to me."

"Okay."

"But you should talk to Sofia."

"I would be delighted to talk to Sofia." I went around to the other side of the car in order to see her better, and put on my brightest smile. "Do you have time to talk now?"

"Yes."

"Is there a place where we can talk?"

"There is a place two blocks from here."

"Take me there, and we'll talk."

Sofia glanced at Alejandro, and he nodded in a somewhat impersonal way, a nod that was almost a shrug; and I saw that she did not belong to him in any important personal way. I was surprised but also quite touched at the help I was receiving from Alejandro.

Sofia got out of the car and closed the door.

"Thank you," I said to Alejandro.

"There's nothing to it," he said. "You are an unusual American. You are the only *Estadounidense* who knows who Angel Austurias is." Miguel Angel Austurias was a well-known Guatemalan author, the only Guatemalan to have won the Nobel Prize for Literature. "Only a poet or an author would know that. That's why I'm helping you, spiritual guy."

"I won't forget this," I said.

"It's nothing."

He drove slowly away, glancing back once at us in his rearview mirror.

The woman stood beside me on the sidewalk. She tilted her head in the direction of a business district a few blocks away, and we set off together.

"What is your name? Tell me again what your name is."

"Maitland Sutterfield."

"I have never heard that name."

"The first name is the name of an English historian. The second is a family name."

"Will you write your name for me?"

"Of course, if you will write yours for me."

She nodded in the same impersonal way that Alejandro had

nodded to her before. Her manner seemed casual, but at the same time, there was something extremely calculated about the way she moved and talked. She reminded me of an actor playing a role. She was trying to make some kind of impression, but one that I could only figure out later, after observing her awhile.

She looked over her shoulder to check out the street behind us, and did so very quickly; I had the feeling that she was seeing more—or at least looking for more—that I could imagine. Apparently there was no danger. She signaled for me to follow her, and we walked toward a block with several small businesses.

We went to a back table of a cafeteria with large plate-glass windows facing a small park. Sofia sat with her back to the wall, looking in the direction of the windows. I assumed she was looking at the drunks in the park across the street; but later, after I got to know her well, it occurred to me that she was probably checking out the plate-glass windows. The people I interviewed in Guatemala were always checking out the ways they could be shot at.

Sofia did not take off her dark glasses; and that, with her dark skin and a couple of pieces of expensive jewelry, gave her a certain regal quality.

"Write down your name," she said in Spanish, "and also your telephone number."

I wrote my name and number on a piece of paper.

"You can keep this," I said, handing the paper to her. "Do you have a telephone?"

"You can reach me through Alejandro."

"Yes, one could do that." I was somewhat disappointed. I preferred to keep Alejandro out of it as much as possible. "Do you speak English?"

"There is no need to speak English. We are in Guatemala and you speak Spanish. Therefore let us speak Spanish."

"But if there was a need to speak English, could you do so?"

She betrayed no sign of irritation or defensiveness, but simply said nothing. Peasants sometimes did this when they didn't want to answer a particular question; I concluded that although she was not herself a peasant, she had lived among them.

She looked down at the piece of paper with my name written on it. "Maitland Sutterfield," she said.

She pronounced it *Maylon Sooterfailed.*

I repeated my name several times, and we took turns saying it.

After a few moments had passed, she wrote her name on a piece of paper, with a number after it. "You can leave a message for me here."

"Is this the number of a friend?"

"It's a human-rights organization with French staff. There are also some Belgians who work in this office."

"Do you work with them?"

"Before, in another time, I worked there." She paused. "There are other places where you can call me. I think I will give you another telephone number, after we have talked some more."

"Please. I would greatly appreciate that."

"Would you?"

"Yes, very much."

She took off her dark glasses.

Sofia was a short woman with black eyes and black hair, which made her look like a woman from India—Bombay or Calcutta, perhaps—with rather Caucasian features; she wore her jewels very much the way a North American woman might have done. I could see now that the designer jeans and the blouse were very well cut. Her hair was simple but also cleverly done, and had clearly been cut by a professional.

I, on the other hand, had gone for six weeks without a haircut, and wore a t-shirt with the word *Adidas* on it. Beside her, I looked positively disreputable.

"What do you want?" she asked suddenly in Spanish.

"I want to learn about Guatemala."

"Why?"

"I think Guatemala has something to teach me."

"You can learn about Guatemala, but you may not like it."

"I'll take my chances."

"I thought Alejandro said you were a German."

Alejandro had no reason to say that; furthermore, I was reasonably sure that he had mentioned in her presence that I was an *Estadounidense*, a person from the United States. "No, of course I'm not a German—I'm from San Francisco, in the state of California, which is on the west coast of the United States."

"Most white North Americans do not speak Spanish."

"I'm different."

"You are a journalist?"

"Yes."

"From the United States?"

"I already told you that."

She was testing not only my bona fides but my temperament, I decided; my ability to take the curve ball and step up for the next pitch.

"*Estadounidense*," she said.

"Yes."

I got up and bought some beer, which I drank from the bottle. At her request I bought Sofia a Diet Pepsi, which she drank from the can with a straw. We sat drinking silently for a while. Sofia continued to look often at the windows.

I continued to look at her.

She was short, had a thick waist, and her breasts were small and her hips large. There were moments when I had no trouble envisioning her as a peasant woman in a highland village, carrying water or washing clothes. Her skin was so dark that when her hands moved, the white skin in the crooks of her fingers flashed in the yellow glare of the cafeteria's fluorescent lights.

Yet her manner, the way she moved and postured herself, was very much the manner of an upper-class woman of the Ladinos, which is what people from the traditional land-owning class called themselves. She spoke and acted with the unmistakable decisiveness—no, the entitlement—of an educated, upper-middle-class professional woman.

"Why did you come here?" she asked me suddenly. She was staring steadily at me through her dark glasses.

"I came here to find out about Guatemala."

"Why? Who told you to do that?"

"Nobody told me anything. It was something I wanted to do."

"Why?"

"I want to write about Guatemala."

"Perhaps you are a tourist," she said.

I found that quite irritating. "Why do Guatemalans think every North American has to be a tourist, a hippie or a missionary?"

"Because they come and they stay awhile, and then they leave. We don't have a lot of time to find out about them."

"Perhaps, but I'm a different kind of tourist than you are used to. I have no money to spend. I want only to learn about Guatemala."

She looked at me a long time.

"Why?"

"As I said before, I want to write about it."

"But you are already writing about it for the American newspapers."

"I would like to write a book about Guatemala," I said.

"Because you can make money writing about us?"

"No."

"Then why? Why would you write a book about us?"

"Because I can put things in a book that I cannot put in American newspapers."

There was a long silence. The white undersides of her fingers flashed brightly as she casually manipulated the straw of her Pepsi.

"What kinds of things?"

"I would like to write the truth."

"The truth?"

I decided to put a few cards on the table—I was tired of playing games with this strong woman. "It is a very difficult thing, writing about Guatemala for American newspapers. There are many things that the American reader cannot understand. We must be careful not to frighten or depress the American readers, because they are sensitive. I have to be careful not to write too much about politics, and that is not easy in a country where everything has been politicized, and where politics is a matter of life and death."

"What do you mean?"

"When I do a story about a crafts cooperative in the Mayan highlands, I must leave out the fact that the cooperative has been organized by a priest specifically for survivors of a massacre by government troops. When I write a piece about a clinic run by a church, I must not dwell too much on the fact that the people using the clinic have been forcibly removed from their village. Nor must I seek to verify the rumors that are circulating about the Argentinean and Israeli intelligence officers who are said to be advising the Guatemalan military, since the governments of Argentina and Israel are close to the United States.

"Needless to say," I continued, "I must not refer too often to crimes of torture, murder and rape committed by the Guatemalan army, the security forces, and the various right-wing militias and death squads that are intermittently funded through the American Embassy. I must not talk about how the money is dispersed, and which case officers in the embassy handle the money."

"You do not mention this in your newspaper stories?"

"No," I said, "and when women report that they have been raped by government forces, I generally don't mention those reports in the stories that I write. As my editor has pointed out, it is simply their word against the word of the soldiers involved. When people report finding family members mutilated in horrible ways, I philosophize about how cheap life is in Latin American countries. When people talk about friends who've suddenly disappeared or been killed by death squads, or tortured to death by the security forces, I write about people being 'caught in the crossfire' between Marxist fanatics, on the one hand, and a faceless but patriotic army on the other—an army with an odd and seemingly persistent inability to stop accidentally killing civilians on a daily basis."

I paused for a moment. Sofia was sitting very still, listening.

I continued: "When I hear repeatedly of villages in which the people have been systematically slaughtered by government forces with machetes and machine guns, apparently right down to the last woman and child, I make no reference to these cases—or at most, I refer darkly to unconfirmed rumors. Sometimes I throw in a few gratuitous references to the human sacrifices practiced by the ancient Mayans, by way of educating the American reader as to why there always seem to be so much violence against civilians in the area."

"I see."

"In all cases the basic operating rule is this: I have been discouraged from writing regularly about crimes alleged to have been committed by government forces or right-wring paramilitaries, because it might turn out that they are being funded by the United States. This has to be avoided at all cost, because such stories might identify the writer as a practitioner of 'advocacy journalism.'"

"What is that?"

"According to my boss, it is journalism that contains unfavorable information about the foreign policy of the US in Latin America."

"What if the stories are true?"

"It is especially embarrassing when the stories are true."

"What will happen if you write too many stories like this, and you refuse to stop?"

"Remember the Dutch journalists?"

The army of El Salvador had recently killed four Dutch journalists and then invited all the foreign journalists in Central America to San Salvador to view their mutilated bodies. The American embassies in both Salvador and Guatemala were delighted, although publicly they expressed pious disapproval. The Dutch journalists had been about to interview some left-wing activists that the military junta in San Salvador—and their friends in the United States—did not want them to talk to.

Sofia sat looking at me for a long time. I was amazed at exactly how black her eyes were. "Do you want to meet a priest working in the highlands?" she asked.

"What kind of priest?"

"The kind of priest who preaches social justice. The kind who preaches that we must start building the Kingdom of God here on earth. He is a new kind of priest who teaches that the poor have human rights, just like the rich Ladinos."

"Such a priest might be dangerous," I said.

"Do you want to meet him?"

"Yes, I would like very much to meet him."

"Would you write something about him?"

"Yes, probably—liberation theology is an important movement in Latin American Catholicism, and I would greatly appreciate the opportunity to find out about it. But I will be careful to use fictitious names for everyone I interview, and to conceal completely anything that might be used to identify this man."

She smiled suddenly and unexpectedly. I had not seen her smile yet, and I was surprised at the playfulness of it. She was smiling at me in a rather patronizing way, as though I was an imaginative but difficult child.

"You find me amusing," I said.

"Does that bother you?"

"Not as long as it makes you smile. What is it about me that you find amusing?"

"Maybe I will be in your book."

"I suppose what I'm doing *might* seem a bit unusual," I said. "What do you call a man like that, a stranger who comes to Guatemala to write a book about your country?"

Sofia glanced down at the piece of paper upon which I had written my name and my contact information.

She was still smiling.

"I call him Maitland Sutterfield," she said.

"Who?"

She said my name again.

Again she pronounced it *Maylon Sooterfailed,* and she continued to do so for as long as I knew her. I was delighted by the way she said it, but considering how good her English turned out to be otherwise, I had to wonder if she pronounced it that way on purpose.

Chapter Two

Sofia met me at dawn, and together we waited at a ramshackle bus station on the outskirts of Guatemala City. Our driver let his ancient diesel engine idle for a good ten moments before he would let anyone on the bus; then—seconds after we had gotten on board—we jerkily departed the station, heading toward the mountains. There were only three of us on the bus; Sofia and I were bound for a village in the highlands, about forty miles away from the capital. Our objective was to make contact with the priest she had told me about; the priest who ministered to poverty-stricken peasants and preached social justice.

"You will like this man," Sofia was telling me over the low roar of the bus. "I'm sure you will want to write about him."

She was speaking to me in Spanish; so far she had rarely spoken in English, even when I had. Hadn't she spent some years studying in the US? I made a mental note that perhaps she felt there was something wrong with speaking English in Guatemala.

"Why do you think I'll like this priest you are so enthusiastic about?" I asked.

"He cares about the poor. And he speaks out about the poverty of the Indians in the highlands." She thought about it for a moment. "He cares about the people enough to tell them the truth."

"What *is* the truth?"

"The truth is what God wants for people here on earth."

"How can you be sure what God wants for them?"

"The people read the Bible together in small groups and then talk about it; each group is called a *comunidad de base,* a base community. In these small groups the people decide for themselves how to apply the Gospel to their everyday lives." She paused. "God has a special love for the poor. He wants them to have better lives, to have enough to feed their children, and to live without fear."

"It would certainly be good if people had these things."

"God wants us to start building the Kingdom here on earth. Then He'll finish what we have begun."

I had heard about the *comudades de base,* the base communities, in some of the material I had read about liberation theology. They reminded me of the cells or small discussion groups of the political left, particularly the Marxist-Leninist groups—except that followers of liberation theology talked about a practical applied Christianity rather than socialism as a means for achieving social justice.

"Is it a good thing to encourage desperate people to believe that they can have these things? Aren't you afraid that you might be raising peoples' expectations unrealistically? And should one encourage the poor to believe that God is on their side?"

She looked up at me, searching my face with her eyes.

"Who else is on their side?" she asked.

"Nobody, I guess, except people like yourself."

"Yes, but I do not have the power to change people's hearts. Only God has that power."

"You are already changing me with your enthusiasm. Is it permissible to be inspired by you as well as by God?"

Something in the deadpan way I said this made her laugh.

Her laughter was spontaneous, like a child discerning some naughty double meaning in the casual remark of an adult, overjoyed with the sheer fun of sharing it with someone who might find it as darkly serendipitous as she did. It also occurred to me that she might be flattered but embarrassed by the suggestion that I found her manner inspiring.

"Is it a good thing," I asked again, "to have God on your side?"

"How could it not be?"

"Well, it seems to me that in a place like Guatemala, having God on your side could be downright subversive, and therefore dangerous."

She laughed again but looked quickly away. "Many things are dangerous. But danger by itself is not a good reason to—"

"Do something?"

"Or not do it."

At that time danger meant little to me personally because I had not yet been required to live with daily fear. But it was a perfect standard for the way one behaved toward others: one did not, nor did one ever, have the right to put others at risk. I believed that to be the basic operating rule in Guatemala. Sadly, I did not ask Sofia how she felt about this rule; nor did I understand how important it could be to observe it in my own life.

Anyone who has traveled in Central America knows the disabling combination of terror and boredom that awaits the innocent pilgrim who travels by bus. The roads were full of potholes, and the bus rarely went more than twenty miles an hour. Instead of three hours to reach our destination, it was more like eight; and in addition to frequent stops to check out problems with the bus engine, we were stopped at two checkpoints by soldiers. At one checkpoint, the driver simply wandered away and didn't return for an hour and a half.

The bus climbed steadily; several times I was sure that we would plunge over cliffs into the mountain gorges below.

The fear must have shown on my face.

"Are you afraid?" Sofia asked me.

"Terrified."

We had taken seats near the back of the bus. Dust blew in from a broken window in the front.

"How about you?" I asked.

She murmured something I didn't quite hear before closing her eyes. In a moment she was asleep.

She murmured continuously to herself as she slept. I could make no sense out of the things she said—perhaps she spoke in an Indian language, or perhaps the language of sleep, her sleep.

She wore nondescript trousers that were rolled up at the ankle, and the bright stitched *huilpil* of the highland Mayan women, except that hers had been tailored so that, although it was loose and richly embroidered, the sides were completely closed. She wore no watch or earrings; yet there were, as before, unmistakable indications of her affluent background. Her trousers were old but clean, and apparently made from some kind of khaki; furthermore, the crease had been ironed (a dead giveaway, that). Her hair was unadorned, but she had a gorgeous haircut, and her black hair was shining in a way that a peasant woman's never would – its sleekness bespoke a diet with daily protein. She wore battered-but-expensive boots for walking, and there was even a small chain around one wrist.

We headed deeper into the mountains, and the roads got worse.

More than once the bus almost took us plunging into various mountain gorges. But it gradually dawned on me that I had little control over the situation, since I was not driving the bus; it followed, therefore, that one could be terrified for only so long. After that, one became fatalistic—which is not, I hasten to add, exactly the same as becoming reconciled to one's situation.

Finally all I cared about was emptying my bladder.

Sofia touched my arm as the bus slowed down. The bus stopped at a small clearing by the side of the road, and we gathered together our things and disembarked. There were some shacks on one side of the clearing, and just enough signs of previous habitation to make me suspect that people had once lived here. Sofia and I stepped down from the bus as the driver watched us with what appeared to be undisguised loathing.

"I am about to die," I announced sleepily. "My bladder is going to explode inside my body."

Sofia smiled. "There," she said, indicating a thick jungle on the east side of the clearing.

"Where?"

"*Dondequiera*. Anywhere."

It was not unusual to see men urinating in public in Latin America, even in Mexico City; women pretended not to notice. In the *cantina* I frequented in Guatemala City, there was no bathroom, and men left the bar to urinate against the side of a brick wall. The urine collected in a trough at the bottom and drained into a nearby canal.

"*Con tu permiso,*" I joked weakly.

"You don't need my permission."

I headed for the tree line. One moment I was in the clearing; the next moment I was in an almost impenetrable wall of vines, brush, and foliage. I had not yet discovered that one usually had to use a machete to make space in this kind of jungle, and also frighten away the snakes. But I soldiered stiffly on until I was engulfed in it.

I urinated, and the relief was immeasurable.

When I emerged, I saw Sofia on the other side of the clearing under a tree, reading a small New Testament.

"You must be careful of snakes," she said. "A friend of mine was bitten by a snake in that very spot."

A horrible picture formed itself in my mind of a man loosening his pants, only to be bitten in some private place. "Is that true? Was a friend of yours really bitten there?"

She looked away to control her laughter. "No," she said finally in a very small voice.

"You're laughing at me."

"I'm sorry."

But I didn't mind, because of what I saw in her face, which was amusement. That was good—anything that could help me ingratiate myself with her was good.

Sofia went down on her haunches beside the tree under which she had been standing. In a moment she had dozed off. I got out of the sun and put my own back to a nearby tree, and after a few moments I had also drifted off to sleep.

I did not ask who we were waiting for.

When Anglos wait, they do so impatiently—they fidget, they complain, they indicate in a variety of ways that the world should share their anxiety. When Central Americans wait, they do so intensely, silently and reverently, with something a little like ecstasy. They focus their energy on the waiting itself, rather than the thing for which they're waiting.

Is it entirely coincidental that the Spanish verb *esperar* means both to wait and to hope?

We were about halfway up the mountains that made up this part of the Guatemalan highlands; but here, in the lower highlands, it was very hot. I took off my shirt and let the sweat roll down my body. I paced around the clearing fitfully, unable to sleep.

After about an hour, a dark, small man wearing a wide-brimmed hat came hesitantly out of the tree line about a hundred yards away. Sofia woke up instantly. She stood up and started toward him; I trailed some distance behind. When we reached him, he and Sofia exchanged greetings. He glanced at me once before quickly fixing his eyes firmly on the ground.

"This is Miguel," Sofia said.

I introduced myself in Spanish. Miguel looked alarmed and moved quickly away, up a path that led into the jungle.

"What did I do?" I murmured to Sofia.

"Nothing—he's just afraid of you."

"Why?"

"You're North American. And you raised your voice."

"I didn't mean to."

"I know."

We fell in behind Miguel and started up the path.

"But this Jesuit priest you've been telling me about—isn't he also from the United States?"

"Yes," she said, "but Padre Julio went to seminary in Spain, you see. A lot of the Jesuits around here are Spaniards, so the people are used to priests who speak with that accent."

"Miguel seemed positively terrified."

"He doesn't know why you're here."

"I'm not completely sure myself."

"Do you want to go back?" she asked sharply.

I gave her one of the little zingers I used with sources. "Even if I did want to back out of this interview," I said, "you probably wouldn't let me—I'm up here because of you."

"What do you mean?"

"You want me to interview this priest you know, but you're not doing it as a favor to *me*, are you? You want the world to know what's going on here in Guatemala, how the government and the army are hurting the people…and that I can understand; but let's face it, you need me just as much as I need you, or perhaps more. Am I right?"

I said this softly, but with a certain emphasis. Sofia watched me solemnly, waiting respectfully until I was finished.

"Yes, yes. Of course."

She turned and walked away.

She was already several yards up the trial before I saw her struggling once again to control her laughter.

We started up a path, Miguel leading the way. Sofia pulled a couple of sweat-stained canvas hats from her knapsack to protect us from the sun. We took turns carrying the knapsack, which was full of medicine; Miguel stopped at a turn in the trail and took a bag of rice from where it had been secreted in the crook of a tree, throwing it over his shoulder. After a kilometer or two, he stopped to rest. I took the bag of rice from him and put it over my shoulder.

From some hiding place in a cleft of rocks he produced a machete, and when we started again he began to hack expertly at the underbrush that grew up around the trail.

We were climbing steadily.

"How much further do we have to go?" I asked Sofia.

"Un pequito mas."

"How many kilometers?"

"Eight. Maybe nine."

The sun was absolutely overwhelming. "Do you mean to say that we're going to walk nine kilometers in this heat?"

"*Seguro.* Come on."

We walked for what seemed like hours. I sometimes suffered from asthma at the higher elevations, so I had brought a fair amount of asthma medicine for myself; but my symptoms were not bad on this day. After a brief wheezing spell at the beginning, I got a second wind.

We walked for a long time along a deep gorge.

On the other side of the gorge were three brightly dressed women walking lazily along a path. All wore *huilpil* open at the sides. All had baskets on their backs with what I imagined was kindling wood, and they were accompanied by children. The children stared at me as though I had just arrived from another planet. The women kept their eyes firmly on the ground; one of them spoke sharply to the children, but they could not take their eyes from me. I was probably taller and whiter than any human being they had seen for a long time.

"How come you didn't tell me we were going to walk this far?" I asked.

Sofia stopped walking for a moment. "If I had told you how far we had to go, you probably wouldn't have come."

"How do you know I wouldn't?"

She did not reply immediately. "You're a North American," she said finally, "and you're the first journalist to come up here."

I decided to tease her a little, as she had been teasing me. "I have more courage than the other North Americans. Is that not true?"

"*Chico,* that is clear," she said, again holding back the laughter.

"You have a great deal of courage."

"Or perhaps..."

"Perhaps what?"

"Perhaps I'm simply crazy, like most North Americans."

She laughed, which is what I wanted her to do. "Yes, of course you are *un pequito loco*. Why else would you be here?"

When she said the word *loco,* I saw our guide Miguel smile a few steps ahead of us on the trail.

We stopped to pick up a second bag of rice that had been hidden in some rocks; Miguel carried it, while Sofia continued to struggle with the knapsack. "He doesn't seem tired," I complained to Sofia when we had fallen far enough behind Miguel to be out of earshot. "He has incredible energy for a man his age."

She glanced back at me, then at Miguel ahead of us in the trail. "How old would you say he is?"

I am notoriously bad at guessing ages, but it seemed he was at least in his middle forties. "I don't know. Forty-five? Fifty?"

"Twenty-eight. He has five children."

Miguel's face was a mass of brown wrinkles, and his ankles were so thin that they looked deformed. "Impossible," I said.

"No," she said, "this is the way they live. Does a journalist want the truth? Well, here is the truth."

We resumed our upward hike.

"Are they all like that up here?" I asked.

"All of them." Across a gorge three scrawny trees were filled with ugly black birds with white legs. They were zopilotes, the Guatemalan vultures, and they were watching us intently. "The men in the highlands don't grow much taller than five feet four or five. They die in their forties."

"Why?"

"The people here are chronically malnourished. They work on the big coffee plantations and also try to raise a little corn in their milpas, their private cornfields. But even in a good year most of them can't raise enough to feed a family."

"How much do they get paid for their work on the plantations?"

"They receive almost nothing from the plantation owners. The wages aren't enough for one person to live on, much less a family."

Rising from the gorge beside us was a light mist, just enough to scatter the area with what seemed to be hundreds of tiny rainbows. The rainbows were luminous and multi-dimensional and seemed separate from the mist, like holographic images.

"It's hard to believe that Miguel is only twenty-eight," I said finally to Sofia. "I'm not surprised to hear that people in the Guatemalan highlands are undernourished. But it's still hard to believe, when you see it with your own eyes."

"There's been at least one Indian uprising up here in the highlands every fifty years," Sofia said. "The Indians here have been virtual slaves in their own mountains since the arrival of the *Conquistadores*. People like Miguel have never had enough to eat." She motioned toward the vultures that sat on the trees across the gorge. "See them? The zopilotes eat better than Miguel and his family. And they always have."

We passed some women and children on the trail; all the women were dressed in bright *huilpils* and single-colored skirts. The women were as small as our guide Miguel, except for a certain broadness around the hips that bespoke childbearing. They were completely astonished to find me in their world, a towering white man, sharing the same path on which they were walking; they stopped dead in their tracks to stare at me. As soon as I made eye contact with them they hurried onward, convulsed by barely suppressed giggles. Thirty or forty feet down the trail they began to twitter like sparrows.

"What language are they speaking?" I asked Sofia.

"The eastern dialect of Kekchi."

I had been led to believe that people in this area spoke another Mayan-based Indian language. "What are they saying?"

"They are saying that you're so tall, I'll have to build a special house for you."

"Why would you build a house for me?"

"They think I'm your wife."

"So, when will my house be ready?"

"You can build your own house, *companero.*"

Even Miguel laughed at that.

A moment later we were approached by another group of women carrying wood on their backs and shoulders. Sofia seemed to know them, and spoke to them for a moment or two. Her Kekchi did not seem to be particularly good; but the women with whom she spoke also knew Spanish, and they went back and forth from one language to the other.

After a moment we soldiered on.

We were supposed to be arriving at a place called Chapila. But in Guatemala things were often not what they seemed, so I was not surprised when Sofia told me that there were actually two villages with that name: Chapila Chica (Little Chapila) and Chapila Grande (Big Chapila).

Chapila Grande, or Big Chapila, was at the end of a wide path that forked off the main trail to our left through a shadowy and partially overgrown gorge. The people in Chapila Grande had converted to Pentecostalism two years before, Sofia told me; a missionary woman from one of the Pentecostal denominations in North America had moved to their village last year and now lived with them. Straight ahead was Chapila Chica, or Little Chapila, which was where the mission of Father Julio Domingo was located. Both villages had traditionally been Catholic, and Little Chapila had remained so after the villagers of Big Chapila had converted to Pentecostalism.

In a few minutes I could see Little Chapila ahead of us.

The village that gradually came into view consisted of three buildings, which I knew without being told were a church, a school and a clinic. It looked more like a small compound than a village because most of the people lived at some distance from the buildings at the center. I saw a group of Indian women waiting patiently in a line in front of a low building at the left.

"That's the clinic on the left," Sofia said. "Off to the right is the school. The church is in the center."

"Somehow I knew that the church would be in the center."

She clucked in mock amazement. "What an intelligent man you are."

"You are an intelligent woman to realize that."

I liked teasing her. Sarcasm can often be the purest way to express affection, and also the safest, since within certain limits it can be practiced by people who have the most superficial kinds of relationship. And at this point that seemed important to me—I wanted only the kind of relationship with Sofia that would help me complete the book I wished to write, and nothing more.

The women gathered in the courtyard of Chapila Chica stopped what they were doing and stood gaping at us. In the midst of the women was a tall, handsome priest with olive skin and thick white hair. When he saw us coming he stopped what he was doing and stood waiting with his hands on his hips. He had a confident and subtly prepossessing way of smiling, reminding me of the older players one sometimes saw on TV in the popular Latin American *telenovelas*. Sofia waved once, but the priest did not return the wave—instead he smiled and nodded slowly, waiting patiently for us to come to him. As we got closer I saw that the priest had piercing chestnut-colored eyes, a medium brown that turned out to be partly gray—horse chestnut, as my grandfather would have said.

"Hola," Sofia called out.

The priest smiled but said nothing. He was looking intently at the backpack she was carrying.

Our guide Miguel put down his bag of rice, leaning it carefully against a wall of the church building. He strode directly up to the priest without saying a word; the two men embraced, kissing each other on either cheek. Then Miguel removed himself to the far side of the group of women and began to furiously manipulate the handle of an ancient pump; when it began to draw water, he poured some into a tin cup and drank long and mightily. The ground around the pump was muddy; he shucked off his sandals and stood in it barefoot while he drank, his feet making damp sucking sounds when he moved.

When he was through he handed the cup to the priest. The priest put the tin cup under the pump, and when it was full he handed the cup to me. I had never tasted water so delicious, nor had I realized how thirsty I was—nor had water ever felt so good splashing down my neck into my shirt.

The priest drew a second cup and handed it to me. When I was finished, I handed the tin cup to Sofia.

The priest pumped and she caught the water in the cup. She drank it while the water was still drawing and energetically pumped a second cup with no difficulty. While she drank the second cup, her eyes seemed focused on something in the sky, but when she was finished, her eyes slowly focused on me.

She smiled at the priest and gestured toward me. "This is the man I was telling you about. *El periodista.* The journalist."

"Maitland Sutterfield," I said, stepping forward.

"Much pleasure in knowing you," the priest said in Spanish. *"Mucho gusto."*

He extended his hand. *"Me llamo Padre Julio Domingo."*

"Mucho gusto en conocerle."

He asked me to repeat my last name.

I took a wooden clipboard he was holding and carefully wrote both my first and last names on the margin of a list of medicines clipped to the clipboard. "Maitland Sutterfield," I said again, this time slowly and with emphasis on the consonants.

"There was a famous British historian named Maitland," the priest said in perfect English. "He wrote a book on the history of common law. I read one of his books in seminary. There's also an English family with that name; they were in the British Foreign Service."

I tried not to show surprise. "Yes, I know. That's why my father gave me that name."

"How did he know about them?"

"During the Second World War my father did some liaison work with the British. My father was a bit of an Anglophile—perhaps a bit too much of an Anglophile, in fact."

"Too much?" The priest smiled. "Did his colleagues call him a snob, then?"

"More than a bit. How did you know?"

"My father was in the Spanish Foreign Service, and I got to recognize the type very well. There are many Latin Americans who cannot wait to tell anyone who will listen that their grand-parents were born in Spain. Just as there are Latin Americans who identify with Spain, there are Americans who identify with the British."

"Not so much anymore, thank God."

Actually, my father had worked throughout the Second World War in liaison with one of the British intelligence services, but I didn't want to say that. It would have sounded unnecessarily dramatic, especially in a country torn by civil war.

"Where did you learn English?" I asked politely.

"In private Catholic schools in Washington. My father was the ambassador to the United States from Spain, and before that he was working in the embassy, so I was just another American kid during the winter. In the summers, my father would take us back to Spain. But I always thought of America as my home, much to my father's annoyance; my only concession to him was to study for the priesthood in Spain. Today, of course, I think of myself as a citizen of the world, trying to build the City of God wherever I am."

"Is it possible to build such a city?"

"If we begin, someday God will complete the work."

"How will He do that?"

"In ways we cannot imagine."

Out of the corner of my eye I saw Sofia Mendez watching us and smiling. "Don't you get curious about what the City of God will look like, once God gets around to completing your work?"

"Sure, but that's the sin of pride. We're always looking for guarantees, because we're human. But the whole point of faith is precisely that we *don't* have any guarantees. Or rather, our guarantees come from God, but that is entirely different from the kind of guarantees the world can give us."

"Spoken like a good Augustinian."

He smiled and turned away briefly to talk to one of the women standing nearby, speaking rapidly in what seemed to be fluent Kekchi.

His olive skin had been burnished into a rich golden brown in the Guatemalan sun. His beautiful smile, while a definite asset, did not quite offset a certain ironic undertone in his voice. He made eye contact easily and wore his dusty vestments like armor. If forced to guess his age, I would have said he was in his early fifties.

"How do you want to be addressed?" I asked him in English, after he had returned to Sofia and me.

"Addressed? Are you going to send me a letter?"

"No, I mean, what should I call you in everyday conversation?"

"My name is Julio Domingo."

"What do the people here call you?"

"Padre Julio. Many call me Padre and leave it at that."

"I'm a very liberal Anglican, but Padre Julio sounds okay."

"Call me Julio if you feel like it. After all, we're from the United States; so it's only right that we should call each other by our first names. We'll be the *Estadounidense* in this part of the Guatemalan highlands—the North American caucus, as it were."

Thereafter he spoke in Spanish to Sofia, and almost always in English to me. Even when I used Spanish, he answered me in English. It was not until later that it dawned on me how much, having lived in the US, he must have missed using American idioms.

He took us inside the clinic, which was smaller than it appeared outside. There were two large windows covered by thick screens on both inside and outside. Above a work table next to one of the windows he had nailed several racks of carefully labeled cubby-holes. The cubbyholes had been made from discarded plastic containers.

There had once been a doctor who visited Chapila Chica regularly, but according to Padre Julio, he had retired and left Guatemala. Padre Julio knew which people needed medications and continued to deliver them; they would continue with this arrangement until they could get another doctor to visit them regularly.

"There are some medicines that need to be delivered immediately," he said, consulting the list on his clipboard and rummaging through another list in a box under the table. He murmured the names of the medicines according to their American brand names. "I'm not going to use the antibiotics unless there is real infection involved—danger of infection alone is not enough to justify using them."

"Where do these medications come from?"

"From the United States."

"Were they sold directly from the pharmaceutical companies?"

"Some of them were."

"How do you know if they're any good or not?"

He shrugged. "I don't, but what choice do we have?"

"May I come with you while you deliver the medications?" I asked when he had finished arranging the medications in his backpack.

"Of course."

I looked around for Sofia. Padre Julio smiled. "If you're looking for Sofia, she's probably down at the river."

"Should I let her know that I'm going with you?"

"That's probably not necessary."

Julio shouldered the backpack, and we set out together.

We got on a path that led further up the mountain, then dropped into a long high valley overgrown with trees and tall bushes. The path we were on looked as though it had been cleared recently, but it was sufficiently overgrown that I was careful to let him indicate the way. He had many questions. What did Americans know about the civil war in Guatemala? What did I think about the political situation?

"I am not a particularly accurate historian, at this point," I said. I thought it ironic that he wanted information from me. "Surely you know more about what's going on in Guatemala than I do. That's why I'm here, actually, to use you and Sofia as sources."

"Yes, of course, of course; but there's a difficulty in my situation. I know everything that goes on in this village, and in this part of the Guatemalan highlands. You, on the other hand, must know a great deal more than I do about what the American people think about us here in Guatemala. You have been in the United States recently, and you've talked to other North American journalists." He adjusted the strap on his backpack. "Why don't we make an agreement? You tell me what you know, and I'll return the favor."

"Sure."

We walked around a long curve in the path without saying anything. I heard something rustling in the underbrush, close to the ground.

"Even here," he said, "it is often quite possible to be too close to the situation to see the big picture. All villages have the same problems, but at the same time every village is different."

"But you know a great deal about the life of the Indians in the highlands."

"I can tell you what I know. The rest you can find out for yourself."

"As for the American people," I said, "they know a little about El Salvador, and since the victory of the Sandinistas they know that there was a revolution in Nicaragua. But I must tell you that most Americans have no idea that there is a civil war going on in Guatemala."

"And the death squads and the massacres?"

"They don't know about them."

He stopped in the middle of the trail to look at me. "How does the American government get money into Guatemala?"

"According to rumors, there are people in the Argentinian Embassy who give it to the right-wing paramilitaries, and the station chief in the American Embassy gives it to the politicians on the US payroll."

"Is there any chance of getting that into the press in America? Surely the intellectuals and the churches, at least, would object to the fact that the American tax dollars are bankrolling a bunch of murderers."

"All the American people know is that Ronald Reagan is a nice man who makes them feel good. They are happy that in the United States even an actor can be president."

Padre Julio chuckled. "Yes, exactly. Even the Europeans say that."

He was not surprised about the media blackout on covert US support for the paramilitaries, and saw in it no sign of a media conspiracy. It all came back to the self-willed innocence of the American people, he said—they simply weren't interested in hearing anything that made their country look bad, as though by knowing the truth they might be driven mad, or their dreams corrupted in some way the human mind could not yet imagine.

"I personally don't think that the news services need to be *quite* so overprotective of American sensibilities," I said. "As for armed revolution in Guatemala, I don't see anything good coming out of it. Nor can I see anything good coming from the Guatemalan government. They are both evil."

Julio smiled and shrugged. "I only know what I am supposed to do as a priest."

"Which is?"

"To provide religious training and spiritual guidance, to celebrate the sacraments, and to help build the Kingdom of God."

"Would you be likely to build the Kingdom through what Sofia calls the *comunidad de base*, the Christian base community?"

He was surprised. "Yes, yes it is."

"Are you shocked that I know about it?"

"I'm surprised that any North American would even be interested in such a thing. I suppose I'm a bit impressed."

"The two big US newsmagazines have run stories on liberation theology in Latin America, as have most big-city newspapers. Liberation theology is well known among North American intellectuals, and even among some Catholic laity, although most of them would probably not agree with it."

We finally arrived at the place where the medicines were to be delivered. It was a hut made of concrete blocks; an obese woman with three children huddled in the narrow door. Julio gave the woman the medicines the children were supposed to take. He talked to her a long time, giving her detailed instructions—what dosages the children were to take, how often, what side effects to look for, and so forth.

The woman seemed to listen intently, and nodded often.

Later, as we took the path back to Chapila Chica, I asked him, "Do you think she will remember to give her children the medications?"

"I don't know. If she does give her children the medicine, she may not dispense the right dosages at the right time." He smiled bitterly. "I've had trouble with that woman before. She believes that the North Americans are trying to kill her children for their body parts. It's a form of hysteria that is very common in these mountains. And since I speak English, she thinks I'm working with them."

"I've heard some of the same stories myself."

"She may think the meds are poison. She always agrees to administer them exactly as I tell her to; but after I'm gone, I've heard that sometimes she throws them away."

"Can't you talk to her about this?"

"I've tried. Nothing will change her mind about the North Americans killing babies."

"So why waste the medications?"

He hesitated. "That's a hard question to answer."

"Give it a try."

We walked on in silence for some time.

Then he said, "Maybe the mother will never give the children the medication, but if her children see me there often enough maybe *they'll* follow my instructions someday. Or if not me, someone like me."

"You can't be sure they'll take the medications, but you give them medicine because it is better than doing nothing?"

"Exactly." He sighed. "Crazy, isn't it?"

"Not really; actually, it's rather pragmatic. It's exactly the kind of pragmatism that I wished I possessed, but don't—a pragmatism based on what people can become."

He looked at me and smiled.

"How would *you* handle it if you were me?"

I thought about it. "First, I'd be pissed off at such a stupid peasant woman. Then I would congratulate myself for seeing through her particular pathology. Of course I wouldn't give her any medication, because I'd refuse to waste my time on her. And then afterward—"

"Yes?"

"I'd probably feel guilty and disappointed that I hadn't taken a chance."

We walked several minutes without saying anything.

"Does it make sense to you, then," he asked, "what I am doing up here in these mountains?"

"It makes sense, but over the years it must be very lonely."

"Not doing anything would be lonelier."

"Well, that depends," I said.

But he was, of course, absolutely right.

Since my divorce I had been in a cold and disconnected place. I hated the world; but I had no desire to replace it with a spiritual kingdom. What I really desired, I think, was its extinction by fire. In the meantime there was increasingly little in my heart and mind that could sustain even a respectably ironic view of life, much less benevolent attitudes toward life itself.

But maybe Padre Julio had some new plan for balancing ice and fire—some novel technique, some fresh idea.

Which was, I thought, exactly why I was here on this trail in the Guatemalan highlands. I wanted to bask in Padre Julio's reflected warmth, even if it could be proven for all time that love and justice did no good, and never had. Likewise I wanted to share the warmth Sofia Mendez evidently possessed. I still knew the difference between justice and injustice, good and evil, but precisely because I had nothing of their hope or faith, I longed to bask in their glow, no matter how they generated it.

That night Sofia Mendez and I slept in the empty schoolhouse. The long tables and benches that the children had sat on during the day were pushed back against the wall. We slept in two hammocks hanging from the roof beams, which Sofia showed me how to hang. We slept in our underwear, undressing in the darkness after blowing out the three candles that sat in the corner.

Under and around us we heard the scuttling of lizards and many other tiny creatures—*animalitas,* little animals, Sofia called them—on the rough splintery planks of the schoolhouse floor and walls; but the darkness in which the scrambling occurred was dense and soft. There were flying cockroaches, but in the enveloping black darkness of the night they rarely deigned to fly. It felt heavenly, to be held in the fetal sway of the hammock, to relax in the bunched-up sleeping position I had preferred as a child.

I was exquisitely tired.

"You're crazy, you know," I murmured into the darkness as I hung in my hammock. "You call *me* crazy, Sofia, but it's you and Julio Domingo who are crazy. The peasants of the highlands will not make the changes in Guatemala that you think they will. You'll be lucky to survive the civil war, much less create a just society."

There was a pause.

I could hear Sofia breathing very evenly. When she spoke again, her voice was thoughtful, almost pleading. She started to go back and forth from Spanish to English. "You know what it is like to live here. The government kills us like we're insects. Sometimes you have to fight back. Sometimes it's better to die than to live with such fear."

"Even if you're going to lose?"

"We're not going to lose."

"What if you do?"

"It's still something we have to do."

There was nothing more to say about it. There was a long pause.

"Anyway," she said, "you're the one who's crazy. You don't even have to be here. Yet here you are."

"Yes, here I am."

All was silent except for the sounds of the little animals scrabbling about, and the occasional rumblings of our stomachs.

"Is he a communist, your Julio Domingo?" I asked in the darkness.

"No."

I had the feeling that she had been expecting the question.

"Some kind of Marxist, at the very least," I insisted.

I could hear Sofia breathing in the darkness, hanging not more than four feet away from me in her hammock. There was always something different about sharing close space with a woman, at least until one got used to it.

"No," she said finally, "he simply believes in Christianity the way it should have always been practiced, but usually isn't."

"It's a bad time to have dangerous ideas. There's a civil war going on."

"Can you blame the people for rising up against the government?"

"No, of course not, but the rebel leaders *are* Marxists."

Her hammock creaked slightly; I assumed she was shrugging defensively. "Padre Domingo cannot do anything about that—he does not support the rebel leaders, or their program. He simply wants justice for the poor. That is part of the work of a priest in Latin America."

I sensed that she'd had this conversation before.

"Is Father Julio affiliated to organizations that have been declared illegal?"

I heard her sigh in the dark.

"Yes. But you cannot write about this."

"This is all deep background, all off the record."

"Padre Domingo is the local treasurer of the United Committee of Farm Workers."

La Comite Unida de Camposionos was a peasant's cooperative, a mildly reformist organization that struggled for more money and better conditions for the peasant farmers. But in the Guatemala of the 1980s, it was seen by the landowners as anything but reformist; it had been outlawed by the government and was generally referred to by them as a front for the Marxist guerillas. Whether it had moved that far to the left, I didn't know.

"Don't tell anyone what I have just told you about Father Domingo and the *Comite,*" she said. *"No digas nadie."*

"Everything I hear from you is off the record."

But why had she decided to trust me with this information in the first place? Maybe it was something that Julio Domingo wanted me to know. Or maybe it was because Sofia had brought me to Chapila Chica precisely to introduce me to someone struggling for social justice who was not associated with the armed opposition, but was radical enough to qualify as a member of the opposition. I suspected that this was something Sofia thought Padre Julio wanted me to know.

"I promise you," I said as formally and as solemnly as I could, "that I will tell no one about Padre Julio's affiliation with the United Committee of Farm Workers. If he brings it up, I'll discuss it with him directly."

"Thank you."

I felt a blessed sleepiness, a floating, sweet kind of fatigue. It was as though nothing in the world could hurt me; I had not felt this way in a long time.

"Why do you trust me?" I asked. "What you just told me could get both of us killed. Not to mention Padre Julio."

"You are a journalist."

"That by itself does not make me trustworthy."

"No. Not by itself." I could hear her laughing softly. Her hammock creaked. "Do you really want to know why I trust you?"

"Yes."

"I trust you because you are like a very smart child."

"I thought you said I was crazy."

"No, you are not crazy. *Inocente.*"

I couldn't remember if I had heard the word *inocente* before, or in what context. I thought it mean *fool;* but I wasn't sure.

"Inocente," she whispered.

Then I remembered—it was a word that Latin Americans used on Dia de los Inocentes, the Latin American equivalent of April First. Instead of shouting *April Fool,* the way North Americans did when they played an April Fool's joke, Latinos said *Inocente!* ...which implied not so much that one was foolish, but rather a dear little, sweet little child, blissfully unaware of the world's dangers and impediments; therefore forever at risk.

Inocente, she whispered again.

And sleep came.

I awakened only once to walk down a path to empty my bladder in the bush. I was completely alone on the trail, listening to the sound of my urine splashing down through layers of underbrush.

From far away I heard it, as I stood there urinating, the rustling of a large animal in the deep brush. But I felt no fear—I had chosen this quest, hadn't I? I had selected this Central American adventure on the computer menu of my own rude North American needs, and then made it happen in real life; it was a movie of my own creation, and I could therefore not possibly be in danger. I was the star of my own screenplay, filmed in the living colors of my own fantasy; and I was therefore completely protected.

If you wrote your own script and produced the film yourself, you were spared from having to do the life-threatening stunts, weren't you? Wasn't that in the contract of every good Californian?

When I awoke at dawn, Sofia was already gone. I made my way a quarter mile down a faint path to an ancient outhouse, a two-seater with one seat much smaller than the other, and no door on the front. There were pails of water sitting outside the schoolhouse when I returned, and some crude wooden stalls; I bathed myself along with several others in the pale dawn light. The sensual sleepiness I had felt the night before was still with me.

We ate rice and watery cornmeal, with one tortilla apiece.

Portions was strictly rationed; I was conscious of being hungry after the meal. I was also aware that I probably looked terrible, since a few days' growth of beard usually made me look like a combination of award-winning poet and deadly sociopath. At the same time I didn't give a damn *how* I looked—I was there to observe the people who lived in Little Chapila, not the other way around.

After the breakfast Julio Domingo came up to talk to me outside the dining hall. Sofia was nowhere to be seen. "I have some medical supplies that have to go to a family about three kilometers from here," Julio said. "Would you like to accompany me?"

I told him I would be happy to do so, if my asthma didn't act up.

He nodded. "Actually I'm taking meds to some kids who have severe respiratory problems. I have some steroid inhalers, by the way. Would you like to try one?"

"I have my own, thank you."

"That's good, because the inhalers I have aren't worth very much."

"Why is that?"

"These pharmaceuticals are manufactured in the United States. But if they sit on the shelf too long, they lose their potency. So the big pharmaceutical companies sell them in Latin America. Technically, it's against international law, but the North Americans do it anyway."

We packed two backpacks with medication and supplies and got out on the trail. Julio had a wide canvas belt with pockets that contained hard biscuits made from cornmeal mixed with water. He was ahead of me on the trail, keeping up a steady pace, using his machete on the underbrush.

Before we had gone half a kilometer, I started to wheeze.

"Are you okay?" he asked without turning around.

"I'm fine."

"Che Guevara also had asthma," Julio said cheerfully.

At first I thought nothing of Julio's comment, but as we continued to walk it began to make me uncomfortable. The asthma was upsetting me, and the reference to Che Guevara was a little weird.

"That was a damn silly comment, by any standard," I called out.

Julio looked back briefly at me over his shoulder. "Really?" His bright civilized smile did not waver. "About Che Guevara?"

"Silly and tasteless."

He stopped walking, and turned to face me.

"Why?"

"Che Guevara's dead, for one thing. And he caused a lot of other people to die with his reckless foolishness."

"Would you like to rest?"

"Yes," I said.

Nearby was a large outcropping of rock in the shade; I made sure there were no snakes around before I sat down. I was wheezing loudly from the combined effort of walking, talking and carrying a backpack. I wondered if Padre Julio often sat on this rock when he used this trial, since it was just the right height from the ground.

"Don't people have the right to die for a good cause?" Julio asked me after we had been seated awhile.

"It's better to live for one. And Guevara's cause wasn't good—it was a Stalinist fantasy."

"Granted. But aren't there situations where a person has to risk their lives for something even if they can't predict the outcome?"

"If that's what they have to do," I said, "then by all means let them do it; but they should do it alone. They don't have the right to take other people down with them, people who don't have the intellect or the experience to know what they're getting into."

"Are you saying that it's okay for a person to be a martyr, if they're martyred alone?"

"Exactly."

"How is it okay?"

This subject matter made me uncomfortable. "Because if one dies alone," I said a bit weakly, "that way it's..."

"A personal choice?"

"Well, yes."

After a few moments my wheezing gradually subsided.

Despite his disavowals, I still wasn't sure that Padre Julio might not be a revolutionary of some kind, with all the fanaticism that would go along with that. It also occurred to me that he was doing a very good job of sounding me out about my politics.

If that's what he wanted, I wouldn't disappoint him.

"It would be criminal to support armed revolution in Guatemala," I said. "Criminal and stupid."

"Because the rich deserve to rule?"

"No, because the poor don't have the arms, the training, and the manpower to overthrow them. It would simply mean more suffering, more killing."

"What *do* you support?"

"I don't support anything. My fantasies don't take the form of political theater. I either like things or dislike them."

"What do you like, then?"

"I liked eating dinner last night. I liked sitting with you and the others in the candlelight." We had been joined by a few parishioners and their children for dinner. Afterward we talked about the problem of the peasants and then celebrated the Eucharist. "The candlelight made everything look like a dream; if I were a filmmaker, I would want to film that. But your Marxist rhetoric doesn't impress me."

"I'm not preaching Marxism."

"It sounded like it to me."

He shook his head. "I believe in Jesus, the son of a carpenter, who defied and was executed by the most powerful empire in the history of the world. We're here on this earth for a reason—and in part, we're here to build the Kingdom of God, or at least to lay the foundation; God will do the rest, in his own time, and his own way."

"But you're an activist of sorts, and as such, you may have to work with the Marxists. I'm sure you have some contact with them; perhaps you admire their courage. Some of their ideas and their rhetoric may have rubbed off on you."

"How would I come in contact with communists?"

"Have you ever heard to the United Committee of Campesinoes?"

"Yes, they're a good organization. What's wrong with that?"

"The government says they're led by Marxists."

"It was the Church that organized them. They had nothing to do with Marxism. Why must social justice always be Marxism?"

"The government sees them as communist."

"The government acts on the orders of the rich and the owners of the big plantations. This is simply the truth, and it would still be true even if Karl Marx had never lived."

He smiled and shrugged. The shrug was a thing of beauty, probably inherited from his father; the shrug of a Spanish grandee.

"Perhaps that is all true," I said, "but can't you see that resistance to the army is futile at this time?"

"The Kingdom of God is not just something that exists in Heaven; we are supposed to start working to bring the Kingdom into the world *now,* because that is God's will. And we have to do that even if it is dangerous."

"Where does it say that?"

He smiled. "Haven't you ever said the Lord's Prayer?"

"What are you talking about?"

"Thy Kingdom come. They will be done...on earth, as it is in Heaven..."

I suddenly felt that horrible sinking feeling in my stomach that occurs whenever one stumbles into an emotional logic that cannot be overcome with common sense. "I've never thought of the Lord's Prayer in that way."

I wondered how many other incitements to revolution could be found in the New Testament, not to mention the seemingly harmless prayers and collects of my own Anglican tradition, words that I had been muttering all my life out of sheer love for the sound of them.

All along some of them were incitements to insurrection.

"Just as God has a plan for personal salvation," Padre Julio continued, "God also has also a plan for the salvation of the world. I honestly don't know exactly when and how it will happen—I'm not a prophet who can predict the outcome of specific historical events. But somehow the Kingdom will transcend death, if we believe in Jesus and try to follow his example."

I sighed, and then laughed. "These are dangerous things you're saying, you know."

"Are you jealous?" He was laughing with me. "Do you perhaps find it ever so slightly attractive?"

"Perhaps."

"Or perhaps you are a disappointed idealist, who had a faith that didn't work out."

"Perhaps." I thought of marriage and divorce, *my* marriage and divorce. "To have the courage of one's convictions is easy," I said. "Having the courage of one's doubts, after one's convictions have been smashed, is the real trick."

Padre Julio turned to face me. "But if there is never any certainty in your life, how can you have a standard by which you can know and understand your doubts?"

Padre Julio's robust smile had not wavered, and he was clearly enjoying the play of wits; it was all rather sweet. But there was something about it that disturbed me. "People like you *can* be dangerous, you know, though of course you may not intend to be," I said.

"Like Che Guevara was dangerous?"

"Yes."

"Except that I don't believe in armed struggle, the way Che did."

"Perhaps you think of yourself as a kind of nonviolent version of Che. But the violence will happen, just as it did whenever Che was around. I mean, he wanted to overthrow capitalism, didn't he? So—"

"I don't want to overthrow capitalism," Padre Julio said. "I just want a better deal for the people who live in the highlands."

"The government would see that attitude as revolutionary."

"That's their problem."

"They have the guns and the money to *make* it your problem. And when they do, it will become a problem for everyone around you."

"Then you'd better run for your life."

"I can't run. My asthma won't let me."

He smiled his bright smile. "Just like poor Che, whose asthma also prevented him from running away when danger came at the last hour."

I was getting tired of his constant probing insinuations, the point of which I did not quite grasp. "Don't compare me to Che, not even for a moment," I said sharply. "To hell with Che Guevara, and every last one of his true believers and rich wannabe revolutionaries!"

There was a long pause.

"Why are you here on this mountain?"

I turned to face him. "Guatemala is a good example of how my country's foreign policy in Latin America is failing, and I'd like to write a book about it. Maybe by writing about it I can get some of my sanity back."

"Who or what took your sanity away?"

"My wife, when she left me."

He seemed impressed by that. "Where will you do your research?"

"Right here, if you'll let me. I'd like to stay on at Chapila Chica as a volunteer."

"How long?"

"As long as I need to, or as long as you want me to."

For the next seven months I worked as a volunteer at the mission in Chapila Chica. I told the wire service that I needed a leave of absence to write a book, but they kept me on as a stringer, inviting me to file the occasional first-person story at my convenience. Padre Julio and Sofia Mendez spent an enormous amount of time talking to me about the political situation in Guatemala, the history of the civil war, and the ongoing privations of the highland peasants, especially the local Kekchi-speaking Indians. Perhaps they talked so much to me because they were afraid they'd not see another journalist anytime soon; or perhaps they simply saw someone who would appreciate why their concerns had become so obsessive, and would listen patiently without interrupting.

Padre Julio did not once ask me if I considered the things he said to be off the record, which by itself was a remarkable omission; it was the first thing most people wanted to know when talking to a journalist. Probably he and Sofia knew from the beginning that I wasn't there only to write about their dreams and aspirations for Guatemala, not to mention the quality of the faith they avowed, but also to take up temporary residence in their worldview as a shared entirety—to explore its validity, partly, but also to personally test its ability to bestow life, death and working antidotes to the despair I felt. But Julio and Sofia tended to became so enthusiastic about their ideas for the future of Guatemala that they apparently failed to notice the full extent of my emotional brokenness—and that was fine with me.

They started by telling me the history of Chapila Chica.

Chapila Chica (Little Chapila) was separated from Chapila Grande (Big Chapila) by a path about two kilometers long, which ran along the side of a narrow gorge. Chapila Chica sought to keep the connection between the two villages alive, it seemed, more than the families living in Chapila Grande. The villagers in Chapila Chica took care to clear the trail with machetes at least once a week, and sometimes more; otherwise, they said it would quickly be overgrown by jungle.

The fifteen or so families of Chapila Grande had converted three years before to a rowdy and inelegant evangelical denomination, and a year after that to an even rowdier California-based Pentecostal sect. The people of Chapila Grande held almost nightly services to celebrate their newfound Pentecostalism, and they could often be heard in Chapila Chica singing their rather odd-sounding gospel music, like desperate American urbanites who had somehow wandered from downtown Detroit or Los Angeles into the Guatemalan highlands.

To the east of Chapila Chica was a hamlet called La Espina; to the northeast was the mountain Tzotzil Gapachula. There were several peasant families living on this mountain, some in caves and abandoned mineshafts, but they were seen only on market days. To the northwest was Finca San Diego, a large *cafetal*, or coffee plantation, run by family members of Felipe Maximiliano Morrano. Don Felipe had at one time been a local functionary of the Movimiento de Liberation National, an extreme right-wing party, but had suffered a stroke in 1978 while listening to the World Cup soccer playoffs; he had been confined to a wheelchair ever since. Further west was Finca San Mateo, a partially abandoned plantation owned by a Swiss who had used the land for cattle grazing.

North of Chapila Chica were the remains of two small

villages, Yalamboron and Tojobojoch, both of which had been abandoned after massacres by the Guatemalan army in the western highlands—there were rumors that the villagers living in those two villages had harbored surviving family members who were hunted by the army, and the villagers had been warned that they might be next. To the south of Chapila Grande was the village of Las Espantulas; connected to it was San Marcus, another village, and to the southeast was San Jose del Rio, the district market town.

The area around San Jose del Rio—including the village of Chapila Chica—was in the northern part of the Department of Baja Verapez, in the lower Guatemalan highlands. The peasants who lived here scraped by, tending their small plots of land and working most of the time at the coffee plantations. The area was thought by most people to be relatively free of guerrilla activity, and until recently none of the villages in the area, with the exception of Yalamboron and Tojobojoch, had any tradition of organized resistance.

But in Guatemala, things were not always as they seemed.

In the late 1970s, the Jesuit priest at the market town of San Jose del Rio had covertly organized an agricultural cooperative. Small groups began to meet in houses around San Jose del Rio to study the New Testament of the Bible from the perspective of social justice. At the same time, rumors began to reach people of death-squad killings and massacres of Mayan Indians who were involved in Church-sponsored rural cooperatives. In 1978, a massacre of more than a hundred Kekchi-speaking Indians in the town of Panzos was widely reported. Guerillas were known to be extending their influence among the Ixil Indians in El Quiche Department. In 1979 mass death-squad killings began in San Antonio Aguas Calientes and in many other places.

In 1980 the La Estancia hamlet in the western highlands was bombed, and its inhabitants scattered. Villagers were massacred in large numbers in Chimaltenage and Quiche throughout 1981.

In 1982 the army destroyed La Esperanza cooperative in the Ixcan, followed by massacres in both Alta and Baja Verapaz. The village of Totonicapan in Alta Verapaz was destroyed, and well over three hundred men, women and children were massacred at Finca San Francisco.

I shuddered when I heard of this last massacre. I had passed through the market town of San Jose del Rio at about that time, having gotten a ride there with a nervous group of Dutch rural-development advisors who were going to pick up one of their vehicles before leaving the country. I was looking for the priest of San Jose del Rio, with whom I wished to conduct an interview, but by the time I got there it was too late. The priest in question had disappeared two weeks before.

The mayor of San Jose del Rio, a staunch Christian Democrat, had disappeared at about the same time. On the wall of the shanty office near the marketplace where he had once worked, were pasted several pictures of *desaparacidos* (people who had disappeared, presumed killed by the army). Most of the photos had been taken from documents the local peasants were required to carry by the Guatemalan army. The death squads were thought to be coordinated from an army base east of San Jose del Rio called Zona Viente, although most of the soldiers stationed there had originally come from the army base at Copan in Alta Verapaz, to the north.

These disappearances were a shock to people in the area: such things happened mainly in the western highlands. The people around Chapila Chica were not thought to be particularly militant, unlike the Kekchi-speakers further to the west. Units of the Guerilla Army of the Poor (the EGP) were concentrated further west in Huehuetenango and northern Quiche; this was also true of ORPA, the Organization of People in Arms. (I had interviewed representatives of both groups in Mexico City.)

But neither organization had much to do with Chapila Chica, or the villages around it, perhaps because of Zona Viente, the army base east of San Jose del Rio—or perhaps because the area had always been sparsely settled. Since the evacuations at Yalamboron and Tojobojoch there had been a steady trickle of people leaving for the shantytowns around Guatemala City.

Nonetheless, fear of the army was still a driving force among the peasants in the area. The conversion to Pentecostalism by the fourteen families of Chapila Grande had occurred at least partly because of that fear. Avelino Calderon, the priest who had preceded Padre Julio at Chapila Chica, had served both villages and had been conspicuous as a human-rights activist; at some point the people of Chapila Grande had grown frightened of the possibility that the army might retaliate against them because of Padre Calderon's opposition to governmental human-rights violations.

There had also been rumors of vast amounts of money possessed by the evangelical American churches, especially those from California, and the dream of North American money was especially seductive. Since their conversion to Pentecostalism, the people of Chapila Grande had been patiently awaiting the arrival of North American capital. Sadly, the particular Pentecostal sect to which they had converted was so small and so poor that it could not even supply decent scholarships to youngsters in the highlands who had learned to read; but the people of Chapila Grande had not yet realized that.

Virtually all the families in the area were peasant farmers, growing corn, squash, chilies and beans on their tiny milpas. The men—sometimes the women and children as well—also worked as *jornaleros*, or day workers, at nearby coffee plantations. These included Finca San Diego, the plantation owned by the ailing political boss Filipe Maximiliano Morrano.

From before dawn to midday, the local Indians labored as plantation workers; in the afternoons they tended their milpas. The wages paid by Maximiliano Morrano were very low in the best of years, and in recent years had become almost meaningless because of inflation; and the milpas produced less each year, due to gradual erosion of the soil. Since the Mayan peasants had over a period of several hundred years been pushed ever further into the highlands, their milpas had become progressively harder to farm.

The single greatest change in the daily life of the peasants had been the formation, in the late 1970s, of the *Comite Unida de Camposinos*, or United Committee of Farm Workers. Supporters of liberation theology within the Catholic Church had been among its early organizers and supporters. The organization of the CUC had been followed by a staggering number of rural development cooperatives, some of which provided important marketing strategies for the peasants, and some of which provided the latest research on agricultural techniques.

Supported by the Catholic Church, various United National agencies, several NGOs and humanitarian groups (briefly including the US Agency for International Development), some of the rural cooperatives had begun to give the peasants the political clout to demand better conditions and better wages at the coffee plantations. The rural cooperatives were also the first organizations led by Mayan Indians that Guatemala had ever seen. It was the landowners' worst nightmare: the Mayan peasants were organizing, and this time they had significant support from abroad.

Since the time of the *Conquistadores*, the original Mayan inhabitants had been driven into the highlands, Sofia and Padre Julio told me, and there they had stayed. The plantation system had kept the upper-class Ladinos rich, but now the system was being challenged. The Indians had organized themselves into several hundred rural cooperatives, demanding higher wages, better conditions, and more-advanced agricultural methods. A real shift in the balance of power was a distinct possibility.

Then the land-owning Ladino class struck back.

The army, whose officers were almost entirely Ladinos, or

land-owning Guatemalans, began a campaign of state terrorism against the civilian leaders and organizers of the rural cooperatives; the government security services denounced them as communist-inspired. In the late 1970s, nearly seventy leaders of rural cooperatives were killed in the Ixcan region of El Quiche, in the Ixil Triangle; forty were killed in Chajul, thirty in Cotzal, and more than thirty in Nebaj. Any association with a rural cooperative, or any kind of rural development project, was enough to invite a massacre.

Some 250 rural agricultural cooperatives were declared illegal, the government declaring them the creation of Marxists. People who were suspected of being members were put on death lists, their names published in newspapers; those who did not leave the country or go into hiding were hunted down and killed by death squads, army patrols, or large-scale army operations. Crops were systematically destroyed in the highlands; the objective, quite obviously, was to terrorize the Mayan population, while at the same time starving it.

Soon the Mayan nation was suffering its worst catastrophe since its original defeat by the *Conquistadores.*

Luckily, Chapila Chica had been spared the worst of it: most of the killing was going on in the west, where the guerrillas were most active. But the war seemed to be moving closer; Avelino Calderon, the Jesuit priest who had preceded Julio in Chapila Chica, had been an impassioned and outspoken supporter of human rights. It was this that had caused him to be included prominently on a list of people marked for death in a right-wing newspaper. Calderon was eventually ordered out of the country by his bishop.

We were on the trail to Tzotzil Gapachula mountain when Padre Julio told me the story of Padre Calderon. We were delivering rice to a family on the far side of the mountain. "It is an outrage," Padre Julio was saying, "that the government can affect the assignment of priests by publicly threatening to kill them."

I set down the back of rice I'd been carrying. "There is another way to look at it."

"*Digame.* Tell me."

"As unjust as it clearly was, Padre Calderon was lucky to escape Chapila Chica alive; and his timely departure may very well have been the only thing that saved the peasants in the area from the massacres that were regularly happening elsewhere in the highlands."

"What do you mean?"

"By having the good sense to leave, Calderon saved the people living in the area from the prospect of dying with him."

Padre Julio smiled. "Many of the people around here saw his precipitous departure as cowardice, on his part and on the part of his bishop."

"Then they are fools. It wasn't worth dying for."

Padre Julio smiled again. "Then—what are *you* going to die for?"

"Why on earth do you ask me that question?"

"Isn't that why you are here?—if not to die, at least to risk your life in some heroic way?"

I was shocked that I was so transparent to him. Nakedness exposes who we are; transparency reveals what we're trying to be, and therefore our pretensions. Amazingly, Padre Julio had seen through me all along.

"Who says?" I demanded hotly. "Who says I want to die?"

"No one can say that you *want* to die. But I have the feeling that you came to Guatemala partly to put yourself at risk. Perhaps you wish to test yourself in some way."

"That's part of being a journalist."

"But why come to Guatemala in 1982, at the worst possible time?"

"People don't test themselves in the best of times, but in the worst of times, and in the worst places."

"I think you are also engaged in some kind of spiritual quest."

"Maybe," I said, "or maybe not. But my alleged spiritual quest has nothing to do with a metaphysical master plan, and everything to do with my own personality. So if I fail, my failure will affect me alone, and I won't take a bunch of innocent people down with me. That's a rather important distinction, don't you think?"

"But still," Padre Julio said with maddening deliberation, "you are apparently willing to suffer the same discomfort as the people who live on this mountain. You eat the same food; you sleep in a hammock, the same kind of hammock used by most of the people; you even suffer from the same respiratory problems. Some people would say this is a good thing, even if it happens for the wrong reasons."

"Does it qualify me for an extra crown in Heaven?"

He laughed. "What would you do with a crown, Maitland?"

"You believe in martyrdom, but not sainthood?"

"Something like that."

"You may have your martyrdom sooner than you think."

"What do you mean?"

"What do you think would happen if the army—or the civilian security forces—got the idea that you're some kind of organizer of the United Committee of Farm Workers, the rural cooperative most feared and hated by the landowners and their allies in the military?"

Padre Julio didn't seem too concerned. "They're probably too busy to worry about me. I doubt they'd even investigate it."

"What if they did?"

He thought about it for a moment and shrugged. "I suppose sooner or later they'd send someone out to kill me."

"Just like that?"

"Just like that."

"And what about the people of Chapila Chica—what would happen to them?"

I was thinking of the increasing incidence of massacres, in which the army shot all the inhabitants of entire villages. Padre Julio said nothing.

"Or are you going to say that it's all in God's hands?" I demanded.

I was surprised to hear more hostility in my voice than I had intended. "A lot of people use that as a cop-out," I said. "I mean, I suppose you could always use that as a cop-out."

Again he said nothing.

He put the sack of rice on his shoulders, and we started walking again. Then I heard him speak, and his voice was quite soft, as though talking to himself: "But it really *is* all in God's hands, isn't it?"

Chapter Three

I became a familiar face around Chapila Chica. During the week, I organized medications at the clinic and did other odd jobs for Padre Julio; but when Sofia Mendez was there I spent a great deal of my time with her. Each night I slept in the schoolhouse, scrunched in a fetal position in a hammock strung between two splintery beams. (When I wanted a firmer surface under my back, I made a bed from a tarpaulin and blankets spread over four wide benches that I pushed together.) Sofia also slept in the schoolhouse, ensconced in a hammock hanging from two beams not far from mine.

Sofia stayed three days a week in Chapila Chica, working for a British non-governmental organization that specialized in healthcare for women. Like most of the UN and private humanitarian groups, Sofia's NGO was terrified that their paid staff might be killed by government troops, since the army was inclined to consider even the most innocent humanitarian project as evidence of subversive intent. I made it a point to accompany her whenever she went out on the trails.

It was also my job each morning to battle a colony of snakes that lived under the village chicken coop. Several ancient chickens were kept in an old shed on a path that went to Tzotzil Gapachula mountain; and when they were not sick, these scrawny and thoroughly depressed fowls laid the occasional egg. I would arrive before it was light enough for the snakes to see very much, prepared to fend off the marauding reptiles long enough to collect whatever eggs the chickens had succeeded in laying overnight.

I would go to the henhouse and attempt to frighten away the snakes with my candle; I also found that stamping my feet vigorously would cause them to slither deeper into their lair under the floor. There were often no eggs—whether because of the delicate condition of the chickens or because the snakes had already gotten them, I never knew. The chickens were usually too debilitated to stand, and if they did they wobbled about in an alarming way. They sat looking at me accusingly as I waved my candle menacingly at the snakes; some of the snakes stared beadily back at me from a sagging cupboard on the far side of the coop.

I usually had to push the chickens aside to see if there were any eggs, and as often as not they would simply fall over on their sides and stay there, protesting weakly, making it necessary for me to put them back on their nests. If there *were* eggs, I would present them to the women who were already up and working by candlelight in the lean-to kitchen at the back of the church. If the woodpile was depleted, I would go up one of the many paths that led away from the village and gather firewood. Then we would stand around, three or four of us, shyly, not looking at each other in the predawn candlelight, while one of the women struggled to get a fire going. And then, when the fire was lit, we would all smile and rub our hands, and another day would begin.

There were usually morning prayers, which Julio said in both Spanish and Kekchi; afterward I would deliver medicines to people on the outlying paths for help the children who were in school with their lessons. There were only a few children in school at this time, since many of them were sick with respiratory illnesses.

Julio was forever dashing off notes pleading for vitamin supplements and various medicines; Sofia delivered these notes to the UN missions and non-governmental organizations in Guatemala City, but the medicines were very difficult to obtain—even the vitamins were in short supply. Later I learned that the army was carefully monitoring all medications, trying to keep them from getting into the highlands, where the armed rebels might use them.

I quickly learned the paths around Chapila Chica, and where those paths led. There was one that meandered eastward from the village and ended in the partially abandoned village La Espina; there were also the many paths northeast up into the wilds of Tzotzil Gapachula mountain, where some very old people and a few families lived in unbelievably primitive conditions. Since many families lived on or near this path, I traveled on it often, sometimes all the way to Finca San Diego, the coffee plantation to the northeast.

I spent a great deal of time explaining to people in Spanish and broken Kekchi exactly how the medicines were supposed to be taken, and how often. Like Padre Julio, I had no idea if they actually took the medications or not. Later I would sometimes come across certain medications I had delivered weeks before, still sitting around the concrete-block houses of sick people, medications that people had clearly not taken or even bothered to hide or throw away. But they always listened with enormous deference to my instructions, and invariably agreed to take the medicines in the future exactly as instructed.

The people of Chapila Chica were generally nice to me but also vaguely amused by my presence in their village. Often I noticed them smiling to themselves when I was around. I was clearly a human being just as they were, with characteristics similar to their own; at the same time, I was evidently not quite real, as though I had just stepped out of a photograph in a North American magazine. Nonetheless I began to fit into the routine of the village. The life was simple but full, and the things expected of me likewise simple; I began to experience an unusual but welcome sense of personal tranquility.

The thing that disrupted the peace of Chapila Chica arrived in the form of an unexpected government edict. Padre Julio announced it at a regular Saturday-night meeting of the *comunidad de base*. The government of Guatemala was initiating a sweeping program to organize *patrullas de autodefensa* (self-defense patrols) in villages throughout the highlands. Each patrol would have five or six people who would be would also be responsible for dealing with politically unreliable elements in the population.

Julio read the edict as it had been given to him, without commenting on it one way or the other. Chapila Chica would be required to organize a self-defense patrol.

The people at the base community meeting seemed stunned and uncomprehending. After the Eucharist, they filed out silently, not looking at each other. Sofia and I walked to the schoolhouse and prepared to get into our hammocks.

We talked softly in the darkness.

"So," I said, "what do you think?"

"The government wants us to be murderers like them. That's why they're organizing the *patrulla* in Chapila Chica."

"Clearly."

"Then we must pray for the strength to do what is necessary."

We shucked off our clothes and climbed into our hammocks.

I waited until the hammocks had stopped creaking before asking the obvious question: "What can Chapila Chica do about this government order?"

"We must resist, of course."

"You can't resist openly, Sofia. There's a civil war underway; they'll kill everybody and burn down the village and every house around here for ten miles, if you don't at least pretend to do what they want."

"The patrulla goes against everything we believe in."

"Let Padre Julio handle that," I said. "He's not just an intellectual and a priest, he's a Jesuit. He can figure out some incredibly nuanced rationalization for organizing a *patrulla de audodefensa*. The point is, if the Guatemalan army tells you to do something, you can't openly resist it."

There was a long silence.

"What does Padre Julio say about this?" I asked.

"What makes you assume I've already talked to him about this?"

"Have you?"

She hesitated. "Yes," she said finally.

"And?"

"So far he has no idea what to do."

But *I* did.

Not for nothing had I worked for newspapers in San Francisco: I knew public relations rather well, especially public relations in damage-control mode. The secret to good spin was to determine what was wanted, and then appearing to give it while actually not giving anything up.

I cleared my throat. "There's a way you can do what the army is asking you to do, and still not violate your principles."

"How?"

"Listen to what I say. Then tell Padre Julio about it."

"I'm listening."

Chapila Chica should agree to the government edict immediately, I said; furthermore, it should ask for someone from the government to visit the village as soon as possible. A *comandante* of the patrol should be chosen from the village, and five or six men should be trained. Everybody should appear perfectly willing to receive both arms and training from the government. At the same time, everyone in the village would agree at a Saturday evening *comunidad de base* meeting that they would *not* go on patrol and perform the military operations the government wanted them to do—especially, the people of Chapila Chica were not to be in the business of killing or intimidating those who opposed the government. With my help they would then get word to the two main rebel commands that Chapila Chica did not want to engage in combat with them.

I had already interviewed representatives of the rebel groups when I was in Mexico City, so it would be easy for me to use the telephones at the wire service in Guatemala City to contact them.

The good people of Little Chapila wouldn't support the rebels, but they wouldn't fight them either. They would go through all the motions of having a *patrulla de autodefensa* in Chapila Chica, without really doing the things that such a paramilitary formation was supposed to do.

Sofia's hammock was creaking slightly. "Good, good," Sofia was murmuring.

"Do you like it?"

"Yes, yes, that's good."

I could not see Sofia's face in the darkness, but I could tell from her tone that she liked the idea. I didn't think it was all that original, but I was delighted by the tone of respect that came into her voice. "Yes, that's just the way to handle it," she said. "Of course, of course."

"You don't hate me for suggesting this?"

"Why should I hate you?"

"My idea is morally ambiguous. You tend to see things in black and white."

She said something I did not catch, because her voice was muffled. Then I heard her murmur softly, "This idea is very helpful. *Muy practico.*"

"De nada."

"You are an intelligent man."

"I think it will work."

"Espero que si. I hope so."

The next morning she went to Padre Julio with the idea.

He accepted it almost immediately, probably because he had no choice but to go along with whatever the government said anyway; it was the only way he could remain in Chapila Chica. If Chapila Chica refused the government's edict outright, the army would assume that he had encouraged the people to do so.

The government stood to gain in many ways from the *patrulla de autodefensa,* the main one being that they would quickly find out which villages were loyal to the government (or sufficiently terrorized that they wanted to appear loyal). It was my idea that

Chapila Chica should appear loyal, and do so as soon as possible, while actually standing down from the civil war entirely.

If my brilliant idea didn't work out, I would to some extent be responsible—but of course, that did not occur to me at the time I was telling it to Sofia. I thought it would work, and I was so intent on impressing her that I gave no thought to the consequences if it didn't. And that, I have discovered, constitutes the basic economy of moral responsibility. One does not think about a past course of action when it turns out well; it is only when it turns out badly that one must reluctantly assume, or aggressively deny, one's own culpability.

Then one thinks about it a great deal.

I am not complaining about this: it is no doubt an inevitable and even practical arrangement—except for the victims, of course.

Padre Julio explained the new situation facing Chapila Chica at the next Saturday-night meeting of the *comunidad de base.* Chapila Chica would pretend to go along with the government's plan to organize a *patrulla de autodefensa*—otherwise the government was likely to destroy the village. But the people would not do the things the government wanted them to do. They would not go around killing or terrorizing people who were supposed to be rebel sympathizers. Instead they would get word to the rebels that the people of Chapila Chica did not want to fight them.

They would, in other words, practice a kind of covert civil disobedience. They would pretend to obey the government while agreeing in advance not to carry out any orders with which they did not agree.

There was not much discussion.

It was painfully clear that the people of Chapila Chica were happy that Padre Domingo had made the decision for them.

An old man raised a shaky hand. "Who will be the comandante of the *patrulla?*" he wanted to know.

Padre Julio shrugged.

"I have no idea," he said. "Does someone want to volunteer?"

"I do," the old man said.

Everybody laughed.

"Why?" asked Padre Julio. "Why do you want to be comandante?"

The old man smiled toothlessly. "I'm old and ready to die, so I won't be afraid."

The group was quiet, thinking this over. Would it work, to have the old man as the comandante? He would certainly be less likely to be corrupted; and even if he was, he couldn't do much harm—he could hardly walk, as it was. No, someone said, it would make the government suspicious. It would seem like Chapila Chica did not really care about the *patrulla*.

The toothless old man nodded, still smiling.

"No," said another man, "Juan must be the comandante. Juan knows how to fire a rifle."

Juan Delmonico lived with his wife off the trail to the main road. I had worked with him a couple of times in the communal milpa. He had a big nose, large ears and big eyes with impressive black circles under them; I always had the feeling that if he spoke with enough volume and conviction, he might sound like a stage actor. But he was habitually soft-spoken, so my theory was never tested.

"Yes," said another man, "Juan is the one to be the comandante."

"No!" a woman cried out sharply.

This woman turned out to be Juan's wife. The other women in the room laughed nervously, glanced away, and afterwards sat staring somberly at the floor.

"We'll discuss the role of the comandante at another meeting," Padre Julio said, a bit irritated. "If anyone would like to volunteer, please see me and we will talk about it. It will be a difficult job, but someone must do it."

Everybody was glum after the meeting.

Nobody wanted the *patrulla de autodefensia.* It was clear that the people had been hoping that Padre Domingo could find some way to make it go away. Everybody understood why a compromise had to be made, but nobody liked it. The civil war had come to Chapila Chica, and it had come in a way nobody would have predicted.

Sofia Mendez had now become my main source of information. Every journalist in a strange place recruits such a person, at one time or another. This person, which I have heard referred to as an "indigenous counterpart"—or more often, a "fixer"—is like oneself in many ways; but also different, in that he or she belongs to the indigenous culture and knows it well. The indigenous counterpart is often someone who wants to inform the world about the host country's needs and suffering, and would therefore like to manipulate the journalist into writing stories that reflect those concerns. Such a person therefore has a built-in incentive to help the journalist, if only to influence the way the news is reported.

This person will know whom to bribe and how much, which streets and neighborhoods are safe when there is civil unrest, which government officials make the best informants. Such a person might also have a rough idea of the petty rivalries current in the army, the civilian security forces, and the government bureaucracies; it is, after all, by playing on these same rivalries that one is best able to manipulate informants. The indigenous counterpart will also know enough about the hidden subtexts of public events to relate needed background to the journalist and prevent him from making egregious mistakes.

The journalist is also in a position to give valuable information to his counterpart. The journalist comes from outside the country he is writing about, and can therefore see the larger picture; that means that he can instantly spot winning strategies in the local political wars that might take the indigenous counterpart months or years to figure out. (Something similar to that happened when I advised Sofia about the *patrulla de autodefensa.*) Thus the journalist and his informant can develop an intense interdependency based on nothing more glamorous or charismatic than mutual survival.

As a result, it sometimes happens that a journalist falls in love with his indigenous counterpart. Usually this love is platonic, or perhaps metaphorical in nature (as when the journalist falls under the spell of the country he is writing about and wants that country to love him in return). Other times the love is literal, and sometime heartbreakingly sexual. There are powerful forces driving the journalist and his informant to see some higher wisdom in each other, and these same forces can drive them into each other's arms.

One of the main forces is often guilt, because the journalist usually comes from a rich country and the indigenous counterpart is struggling to save a poor one; there is therefore a staggering asymmetry of power in their relationship that acts upon them and binds them to historical circumstances that are beyond their ability to control.

Because of this, the journalist will often give money or other perks to the indigenous counterpart in a desperate attempt to make somewhat more equal what is inherently unequal. But the simple fact is this: despite the fact that they are both getting something from the relationship, the indigenous counterpart is never in control. It is the journalist who decides what to write, and his newspaper what to print; the counterpart can only try to imagine in a rough way what will best motivate the journalist, and then strive to manipulate events in that direction.

While I had concentrated on Padre Julio at first, Sofia Mendez had now become my indigenous counterpart, because there were things about Sofia that she seemed to be hiding, and I wanted to know what they were. My attraction to Sofia was not sexual, but situational, in the sense that I also sought something from Guatemala itself—some kind of special wisdom, some kind of transcendent experience that could overcome emotional pain; and my intuition told me that Sofia might help me find it. Little by little Sofia came to represent Guatemala in my thoughts and feelings because I could see that she was as obsessed by her country as I was.

If I could get to know her on some deeper and more intuitive level, I could know Guatemala better—or so I thought. This made me believe (at least in the beginning) that my relationship with her would work better if there were no flirtation or sexual attraction. Simply to be close to Sofia, to understand what drove her, would be enough.

After the meeting, Sofia and I came back to the empty schoolhouse to sleep. We stood together whispering in the darkness. I was suddenly struck numb by a weird kind of fear; and in that moment, for reasons that I will never understand, I asked Sofia, speaking in English, if I could give her a hug. At first she did not seem to understand. We had a candle but it was flickering out; and I was suddenly wary of the darkness.

So I asked again.

"Why?" she asked.

I thought I heard a catch in her voice. "I'm afraid," I said, "and I thought that might help."

"How?"

"I don't know—it would make me feel protective and strong if I could make you feel safe, and I could forget about being afraid. North Americans think like that."

She laughed.

As we were both standing there wondering what to do next, the candle went out, and all I could see was her after-image. I was already starting to feel like an incredible fool. It occurred to me that I had just managed to botch up a very necessary relationship with a primary source.

Sofia murmured something in the darkness that I didn't understand.

I jumped slightly. "What?"

"Do you still want to hold me?" she asked, to my great surprise.

"Yes."

"Tell me why again."

There was a faint hint of a suppressed laugh in her voice.

"People hug each other all the time in the US." I waited for her to acknowledge this reasonable and accurate observation, but she didn't. "Men do it to women, women do it to men. It's a sign of affection, of friendship."

"Amistad?"

"Exactemente. Amistad."

"Yes, yes," she said. "I like that."

And then she sighed, followed by a sharp intake of breath.

The sigh was the tip-off. Now I knew that she wanted to be held as much as I wanted to hold her.

"Yes," she said. "Friendship."

We were still in darkness, and my eyes were just starting to make out shapes. I took her gently into my arms and held her tightly for a long time. I felt her breasts flatten themselves against my body. She made no move to leave my arms; I leaned down to put my cheek next to hers. She smelled like salt and earth, and her hair smelled like baked bread; over everything was a faint trace of the body's perfume. In a moment she was breathing deeply, like someone going under hypnosis for the first time.

I breathed with her.

We breathed like two divers getting ready to go deep, deep under the waves. It was very exciting. I could see nothing of her, not even her face or hair; all that I knew about Sofia Mendez was what I could feel with my body. She was breathing very deeply, and each time she did so she pushed against my chest. I had a fantasy that her nipples were hardening like peaches growing in reverse, getting harder and harder with every second until they were the hard pit at the fruit's center.

Still she made no attempt to move away.

"Are you happy?" I asked. "I mean, does this make you feel safe? How does it make you feel?"

She tried to say something, but whatever it was came out as a breath-catching little squeak.

"Creo que si," she said finally. "I think so."

I let her go.

After a moment I embraced her again. Again she made no effort to resist or otherwise stop me. It was not a kiss, it was a hug; but she entered into it willingly and after a long moment the embrace belonged to both of us. It felt like a secret as soon as it happened, already something a bit clandestine. I could not stop myself from murmuring: "People would not understand it, if they saw us holding each other like this—"

"How could they see us?"

She said it briskly, but the huskiness was still there in her voice. I thought at that moment that I could have kissed her lips and gotten away with it, but I didn't want to take the chance of being rejected.

So after another hug I let her go.

It had been a powerful embrace. I was very aroused, solely from the excitement of holding her tightly in my arms; and I was careful not to let the lower half of my body touch her, because I did not want her to feel how much she aroused me. I turned reluctantly away from her and went to my slingshot of a bed hanging from the rafters, and quickly undressed to my jockey shorts, laying my clothes carefully over my boots with my back to her; and then slipped into my hammock.

I could hear her doing the same.

I was so aroused that I instinctively wanted to touch myself, but we were far too close in this space, and every sound seemed magnified a thousand times. I could hear Sofia breathing. She was still breathing deeply.

"Thank you," I murmured softly, almost to myself.

And after a very long time the answer came back.

"Why do you thank me?"

It was the whisper of a child.

"For being here," I said.

"Is that enough for you? Just that I'm here?"

"Yes."

She seemed to think about this a long time.

"Good," she said. "I'm glad it's enough for you, that I'm here."

Again I felt that I should refrain from saying anything that might force the moment; and this willingness to wait gave me an odd sense of control over my desire. I decided to go to sleep, since it was the only way to escape from my arousal.

Then I heard Sofia murmur something: *"Inocente."*

She whispered it almost soundlessly, as though to herself.

"You or me?" I said. "Who's the innocent one here? I need to know. We need to get this straight."

"Maylon Sooterfailed."

"No, not just you, more like both of us."

But she didn't answer.

Instead she repeated the single word that she had said before, *inocente*. She whispered it very softly. This word was clearly a powerful one in her vocabulary.

"No, no, we're all innocent in some way. It's not just me."

There was only silence.

I went to sleep, dreaming of the village of Chapila Chica, because it was now my dream capital, the capital of all the lands of my imagination. But even as I dreamed, I knew it would not stay peaceful forever, because there was a real village upon which the dream was based; and the real world would catch up with both the dreamer and the dream, as it always did.

The day after I held Sofia in my arms was Sunday, and I could not stop thinking about her. The church service wasn't a very impressive thing, lacking almost completely the drama of the *comunidad de base* meeting on Saturday night. During the liturgy, people went forward to "receive the host," as I had often heard my mother describe Holy Communion in the Episcopalian style; I sat stonily on my rough bench and affirmed nothing except my erotic fantasies. Only at the end of the service did Sofia glance quickly at me and smile, as she came back to her seat on the bench in front of me.

There was a second mass; and I stayed for that one too, again contriving to sit right behind Sofia. During the Peace the congregation turned to embrace the person sitting next to them. Sofia turned around on her bench to face me, and smiled; we both stood up, and she hugged me tightly.

"Thank you," I whispered.

I had the feeling that everyone was watching us.

I spent the rest of the day trying to deliver medicine to people who had not come to church. Sofia, on the other hand, helped Padre Julio pass out some vitamin packets outside the church. From time to time I heard Padre Julio patiently explaining how to open certain little envelopes of powdery Vitamin C, and how it worked to protect the body from sickness. People listened respectfully and nodded; I had the feeling that many of them would throw the packets away as soon as they could. In Padre Julio's voice I heard the despair of the teacher who knew the truth but could not give it away, much less convince those who needed it most to embody it.

The day went on forever, but finally night came.

As we always did, Sofia and I walked to the schoolhouse together; I was carrying only a single candle to light our way. Sofia was silent as I opened the door to the darkness where our hammocks waited. I was holding the candle; and once inside I set it on the counter that separated the main room from the rudimentary kitchen. I was thinking of how convenient it was that the candle had gone out the night before.

On an impulse I blew it out.

As I had the night before, I heard Sofia's distinctive sigh, followed by a sharp intake of breath. I stood beside her in the darkness. I stood without touching her for a long time, synchronizing my breathing with hers. There was a quarter moon and no clouds, so I could see the bare outline of her body—what light there was came in the window through the tree outside. She was evidently waiting for me to do something; and I felt that almost anything I did would be acceptable, as long as I was very gentle.

Again I took her in my arms and held her gently.

"I like doing this," I whispered.

She did not resist. I fact I felt her arms go around my neck. "I thought about you all day," I whispered.

I felt her tears against my cheek.

"*Si, yo tambien,*" she said. Both her voice and her body were trembling. "Me too."

I did not want tears, I had not expected tears to be any part of it, and I was irritated.

I whispered: "Why are you crying?"

"I'm not crying."

"Yes, you are; and it's way too early to be crying."

"But I'm *not* crying." Her voice was barely audible.

"Yes, you are," I said, "I can feel your tears on your cheek."

"They're *your* tears."

I took my hand and put it to my cheeks. And God help me, they *were* my tears.

"You see?" she said.

I was speechless.

But those tears, the unexpected shock of them, gave me permission to do the next thing that I did.

I went over to where the benches in the schoolroom had been pushed. I shoved four of the widest benches together to make a bed against the wall and put a tarpaulin over it, and then some blankets. I led her there by the hand, and she sat down beside me.

After I held her a moment, I gently pulled her down beside me, so that we were laying together.

She was breathing heavily. At the same time I could sense her struggling against some very real restraints inside herself. And I had to be careful not to rush anything, not to push too hard. I simply held her close to me.

I did not kiss her.

At that moment simply to hold her in my arms was enough. If I held her without kissing, it would not violate whatever private code she had devised for herself; and at that point I did not want any other kind of intimacy anyway. There was already almost too much passion between us, or so I felt.

At one point the lower part of my body moved against hers, and she must have felt my excitement. She did not stop me, but I could sense some hesitation. So instead of moving my body against her again, I stroked the black hair that fell down her back, gently at first then more rapidly.

Her body stiffened suddenly.

"What is it?" I asked.

She moaned, and her lower body moved.

Sexual passion had overtaken her, and it came to a climax; only then did I kiss her face and lips, more in astonishment than in hunger. I held her tightly as convulsions of pleasure passed through her body; toward the end her body jerked like a skewered animal. It crossed my mind that she might be dying.

Afterward I held her as she wept.

How long had it been since she had experienced a sexual climax in a man's arms? What smoldering banks of fire had lain within her, and how long? Simply holding each other had been enough to bring her to orgasm. I had not even kissed her on the lips until her orgasm had already begun. I had simply held her in my arms and stroked her hair.

And that was enough.

I knew that this power, whatever it was, came from within her and from the circumstances of her life, and not from myself; I was amazed and humbled. I did not even think about having an ejaculation. My body ached, and I already leaked enough fluid to father a regiment; but it was not necessary to have an ejaculation, it seemed to me. Her astonishing unbidden orgasm had been enough to satisfy both of us.

Sofia's father had been a Ladino, part of the traditional landowning classes, her paternal grandfather a German-speaking Swiss. Her father had been a coffee grower whose friends were German and Swiss and apolitical, interested mainly in quick money with which to finance their frequent trips to Europe. Sofia's mother had been Indian and very dark, but from a family that was considered Ladino because of the large plantations they owned. Her mother was noted for her head for business, and for her skills with herbs and various kinds of magical potions.

Sofia's father had died young, and Sofia had been raised mainly by her mother and her mother's retinue of *curanderas*, women who healed the sick with herbs, special prayers and sometimes by practicing the folk arts of magic; and by members of her mother's large and well-connected family. Because of her prowess with herbal medicine and rumors about her ability to cast spells (and also probably because of her two brothers, who were powerful businessmen in Guatemala City), Sofia's mother was able to hang onto most of her deceased husband's property.

I discovered that Sofia was a kind of closet intellectual, who among other things had once been involved in an abortive effort to organize a Guatemalan political party of the moderate left. (The idea had been to find an alternative to the Marxists, on the one hand, and work for genuine democratic reform on the other.) The leaders of this small social-democratic political party, which most notably included a former mayor of Guatemala City, had been killed by death squads; the party had voted to disband itself, and Sofia dropped out of political activism.

She claimed to have lived most of her life in Guatemala, the most notable exception being her college years, and a few years after that—about seven or eight in all—during which she lived in the US. It was nothing short of a miracle that she had survived so long despite her political involvement and her continuing opposition to the military dictatorship in Guatemala. From everything she told me, I guessed that she was in her late thirties.

Sofia indicated in indirect ways that there were friends of hers who were involved in various kinds of illegal political work or who had gone over to the armed opposition. That Sofia might herself be involved in some kind of direct aid to one of the rebel groups did not occur to me at the time.

I was aware, however, that there was a great deal about Sofia that I did not know. I was not sure, for example, exactly what she had done for a living most of her adult life. She had worked for various NGOs and humanitarian groups, and had at one time lived in Mexico City; during the 1960s she had gone to a prominent Catholic university in the United States, but apparently in a vague liberal arts program that had no occupational application that I could see. Then she had lived for a few years in the US in a women's commune, with women who were similarly interesting in religion and social justice. That was not consistent with most of the Ladino families I knew, whose children tended to become either well-placed professionals or complete wastrels.

At one point I asked her about it directly: "Why didn't you train for a professional career?"

"How do you know I don't have one?"

"You're not a doctor or a lawyer, or a professor at the university."

She laughed. "Just because I don't talk about it doesn't mean I don't have a vocation."

"Why don't you tell me about it now?"

But she wouldn't cop to me. "You wouldn't like it," she explained.

I had to settle for that. Although she would sometimes talk about her life if it illustrated some phenomenon common to life in Guatemala, she was noticeably reticent when it came to talking about her past, not to mention her personal aspirations for the future.

Gradually I came to believe that Sofia had lived off her family's money most of her life. Perhaps there was an arrangement similar to a North American trust fund, an arrangement that gave her a prescribed amount of money every month for living expenses. That would explain the lack of professional training and the dabbling in various kinds of humanitarian and charitable work. But I wasn't sure; clearly there were things about her life that Sofia was not ready to reveal to me.

Each night in Chapila Chica we lay together on our little bed of blanket-covered wooden benches and held each other closely. Sometimes we lay on a blanket over a tarpaulin, sometimes many blankets. It took Sofia a long time to even initiate a kiss. Then we began to experiment with different ways of making love.

She had strict rules: we could kiss and I could touch her breast, but that was all. We lay naked above the waist, but in underpants and panties. There would be no intercourse; once when I knelt above her, she pushed me away. (Also there would be no oral sex; when I tried to kiss her body, she screamed softly and put her hand over my mouth.) We lay side by side to kiss and hold each other tightly in our arms, and I would gently stroke her body, including her beautiful breasts and her stout but perfect legs.

When she reached a certain point, she would slip her hand inside her panties, and with enormous concentration bring herself to orgasm. She had to struggle not to moan too loudly, which made it all the more exciting.

We had been doing this for several nights in a row when she

hesitatingly touched my lower body. I was quickly aroused, but she withdrew her hand.

"No, *Chico*," she murmured.

"Why not?"

"Do it yourself. *Por favor*."

"You mean to have an ejaculation?" I was speaking in English, but I wasn't sure she knew that particular word, or would be comfortable saying it.

"La semilla," I said, "the seed?"

"Yes, the seed," she said, very excited, "I want to see it."

"You want to *see* it?"

Her lower body was already moving slightly.

It was pitch dark and I was holding her very close. We were both stripped above the waist and I could feel her breasts against my chest. Her nipples seemed rough and angular and hard; I touched them and they *were* hard, like the cranberries that one finds in the grass, the hard ones that electrify the palate but are impossible to swallow.

"You can't see anything in this darkness," I said reasonably. "Therefore, you can't really see my seed when it comes out."

"I can feel it," she said insistently.

"Is that enough?"

"Yes," she said breathlessly, "I want to feel it."

"I guess that can be arranged."

"What does it feel like?"

"The seed is a sticky white fluid," I said. "It's about the same chemical consistency as egg white."

"Yes, yes," she said excitedly, after considering it for a moment.

"If you want me to have an ejaculation, why don't you help me?"

"Do it!" she whispered. "*Hagalo*!"

Rather absentmindedly I began to move my hand.

"*Como eso*! Like that!"

So I continued.

As I built up to an ejaculation, she took me in her arms and held me, rocking me steadily back and forth. When the ejaculation arrived, she moaned deeply and opened herself wide to let the semen spurt on her open legs, although she instinctively covered the place where her two legs met with her hand. When the hot juice came out onto her legs she cried out and kissed me passionately.

And that is how she liked to make love.

She specifically liked for me to ejaculate on her thighs; and when I did, she would moan and give a little animal cry of victory.

At first I wondered what vagrant lover had taught her this strange way of making love. It did not occur to me then that she might have arrived at it on her own; but I now believe it was the Catholic in her that gave her this fascination with the life-giving seed that I spilled nightly. She did not want intercourse, but only to feel the hot seed upon her legs.

After I gave myself a release, she would often cry. The tears seemed to have less to do with sex, I suspected even then, that with the fact that she had never married and had children. The hot viscous liquid jumping onto her thighs was our ersatz family, our lost tribe; for that moment, perhaps, we both felt what conception of a child would be like.

Which made me long to plant my seed deep inside her, hurling it toward the eggs that carried her DNA perfect and complete, her personality past and present, everything she was or would become, the whole shebang; her eggs like cocked pistols waiting for the right moment, the right world, the right man.

It was wild, this mutual masturbation in the arms of a lover—it was exactly like being alone and very close to someone at the same time. It felt like the culmination of something that had been going on since my divorce, representing in absolute physical terms the psychic distance that had grown up between me and the world.

Yet it was precisely that distance that made sex with Sofia so good. Sex with Sofia had begun to feel like the ecstasy of mania, the hysteria of a religious visionary, the sexual equivalent of second sight. Instead of waiting until the hour of my death for enlightenment, all I had to do was lay in Sophia's trembling arms and compliantly put my seed wherever she told me to; and each ejaculation was stronger, each animal cry more triumphant, until my pleasure started to become an ecstatic kind of pain.

One night we were together, entwined in each other's arms and legs on our tarpaulin-and-blanket bed. My loins were spent, my body ached with pleasure.

Sofia was unusually quiet.

"I have a surprise for you," she said at last.

"What is it?"

"I love you," she said in English.

I could think of no reply. *Now she's gone and said it,* was all I could think.

"I'm sorry," I said finally, "but I don't know what to say."

"*Te amo. Te quiero.*"

She had gone and said the words.

I had been bushwhacked by love. Here in this strange place, in my pursuit of a fantasy (and my desire to find diversion from that same dangerous and time-consuming fantasy), someone had fallen in love with me.

"Well," I said, "in that case, I have something to tell you."

Sofia waited.

"I want to tell you why I came to Guatemala."

"You came to Guatemala to write a book."

"Yes," I said, "that is one reason, and a good one; but there is another reason why I came to Guatemala."

Here's what I told Sofia:

As weird as it might seem, I began my pilgrimage to Guatemala when I was a child.

Or at least I began preparing for it.

I was sick with asthma throughout the entire sixth grade, and spent almost the whole time flat on my back, wheezing like an old man at death's door. It was then that I began my preparations for the pilgrimage to the violent land of war and revolution. I read Sir Walter Scott, Edgar Allen Poe, Alfred Lord Tennyson, and every book about King Arthur that I could get my hands on, especially those about the Quest for the Holy Grail.

I also read *Don Quixote* in an excellent translation, thinking it yet another story about knights and chivalry. I understood in a vague way that it was a satiric indictment of some central blindness generic to idealism, but I nevertheless assumed that Quixote was essentially right, and the others in his world essentially wrong. Otherwise why had the book been about him, and not about Sancho Panza? (The possibility that Sancho's suffering might have been just as important as the colorful delusions of the old Don, did not occur to me at the time.)

I loved to read about the Quest for the Holy Grail, especially the story of Percival and the Waste Land; and during those long asthmatic days and nights I came to the conclusion that such a quest was likely to be my life's work. Already I was obsessed with the idea of getting the hell away from my family, and going on a quest sounded like just the ticket.

But there was more to a quest than just leaving home: one had to travel to some enchanted and endangered land, a magical but death-haunted domain. But simply going to an enchanted place was not enough, either. Once having reaching the assigned Place of Wonders, the questing knight was thoroughly tested. If he successfully accomplished certain feats of imagination and daring—if he passed the test, in other words—the Waste Land would be restored to life, and the knight would return to the real world with special powers.

I considered it inevitable that I would be tested myself in the same way; but I had no very great expectations of returning triumphantly with special powers, nor was that idea particularly attractive to me. What I *really* wanted was to die in the assigned Place of Wonders. The key to the fantasy was as follows: if one were killed heroically, it made no difference if one passed the test of imagination and daring. Disgrace was impossible. All you had to do was die while being tested, and *voila!*...you were automatically a hero, no matter what. You would also be dead, a not inconsiderable advantage in itself, considering the things that happened regularly to the living.

These fantasies of a heroic death were further elaborated by reading Hemingway's *For Whom the Bell Tolls* (while listening in my attic to endless repetitions of Ravel's *Bolero*, borrowed from my mother's record collection). I recognized in Robert Jordan, Hemingway's protagonist, a certain kind of modern Arthurian figure; a man who traveled to a strange and magical country (in this case, Spain) to fight for his beliefs, and uphold the values for which he was prepared to die. About those beliefs and values, Hemingway said very little; nor was Robert Jordan himself inclined to talk very much about them.

What was important was the fact that he died gloriously.

Perhaps Papa Hemingway glorified war without being aware of it, as some critics have charged. But I didn't come away from reading *For Whom the Bell Tolls* wanting to *make* war, particularly; I came away from the book wanting to *die* in a war—which is a much different thing, as even the most stringent critic would have to admit.

It did not occur to me at the age of twelve that it was possible to fail one's test of strength and daring in a Land of Wonders and to nevertheless survive, instead of heroically dying. Nor did it occur to me that after surviving, it might be necessary to wander for a very long time in the borderland between the Land of

Wonders and the real world, being a full citizen of neither. I did suspect that a great many good and deserving people—a majority of the human race, some would say—regularly suffer just such an ambiguous outcome. The heroic patriarchal tradition from Homer to Hemingway had very little to say about it; nor did I have enough life experience to imagine such an outcome on my own.

When I was thirteen, my asthma began to diminish.

Instead of asthma, I began to have recurring dreams of war. The people in these dreams spoke an almost unimaginably beautiful (perhaps liturgical) language, a language especially suited to love, to chivalry, and especially to heroic death. I increasingly longed to speak this mysterious language myself; but it was not until much later that I realized what language was being spoken.

I lived and worked in San Francisco for twenty years, engaged mostly in futile labor for a newspaper owned by political conservatives, in a city of anarchists; and during all this time I waited for the truth to come to me. For a long time I wondered if the magic language was the High German spoken by my German wife, or the fiery Yiddish she spoke when angry or inconsolable; but however important they were to her and to her world, I knew they were not the language I had heard as a dreaming child. I was attending the riotous wake of an Irish-American friend who had died on my birthday, exactly one week after I was served divorce papers; and it was there, suddenly, that it occurred to me, for whatever obscure reasons, the language the people in my childhood dreams had been speaking.

They had been speaking Spanish.

Whatever caused me to finally realize this, and why it took me so long to realize it, I do not know.

On another level, of course, I had always known it. Wasn't Spanish the language spoken by the characters in *For Whom the Bell Tolls*, and by its protagonist Robert Jordan, erstwhile antifascist and knight errant of Spanish republicanism? Wasn't it in Spanish that Jordan told his lover that the earth moved, when they made love? And wasn't it in that same Spanish language that the tragic but hilarious tale of Don Quixote had first been revealed to the world?

I simply hadn't connected it to the language being spoken by the people in my dreams.

But now I could, so I immediately began to teach myself Spanish. Within six months I was conversational in it; in a year I was fluent. It was an astonishing experience, especially since I had demonstrated no aptitude for languages before.

But now my divorce was full-blown upon me; and as I allowed myself to be divorced by my wife Liese, something inside me snapped. One day I woke up to find that I was quite mad. (I am not the first divorced person to whom this has happened.) In my madness I was more than ever haunted by the notion that I had to be tested in some foreign land, some Place of Wonders—and I assumed that it should be a place where people spoke Spanish.

Early I quit my pathetic newspaper job in 1982, sublet my apartment, and began my journey south, taking second-class buses as soon as I crossed the Mexican border. I left behind San Francisco and all the dreams that had been part of San Francisco. My 18-year-old daughter, my only child, had moved to a dorm in Berkeley and was attending classes at the University of California. Liese—now my ex-wife—was in Berlin, crossing into East Berlin at regular intervals to sing at a cabaret owned by a family member. I was alone in the world, driven by dangerous ideas of self-sacrifice and death, not to mention insane expectations of a private redemption.

Which was, God help me, the real reason why I came to Guatemala—to get out of San Francisco and come to a place where I could find whether I should live or die.

Sofia listened intently in the dark to everything I said.

Afterwards she said nothing for a long time.

Then she began to laugh hysterically, to the point where she actually lost the power of speech. Finally, with great effort, she was able to regain control of herself. "As a child you lay in bed reading these stories about knights and castles and ladies—"

"They weren't just beautiful stories," I said hotly. "They were, and still are, great works of literature."

"*Cualquiera*...you read them, and you imagined that you were like the people in the stories?"

"One or more of them, yes."

"And you came to Guatemala to make the story come true?"

"Apparently so, yes."

"How does the story end?"

"It's no longer a story. It's me, it's my life; I have no idea how it ends."

She shook her head in wonderment, but sadly, as though confirming a tragedy.

"You came here to die," she said. "You just said so."

I hesitated, but only momentarily. "Maybe. *Creo que si*. But it doesn't have to happen that way."

She thought about it, then shook her head suddenly, as though shaking an insect off her hair.

"*Inocente*!" she hissed. "*Inocente*!"

"I'm not always a fool," I said in English.

"I didn't say you were a fool." She sighed and put her forehead against my chest. "*Inocente*," she said softly, as though to herself.

"You make it sound like I'm feeble-minded, to be scolded, but also pitied and protected."

"Aren't you?"

"Maybe, but was not Don Quixote a hero?"

"Yes, in a book. But living in this world, he can be very dangerous."

"But wasn't he still, despite everything, a person of integrity?"

"Yes, of course—in the book written by Cervantes. Perhaps also in your imagination. But in Guatemala such a person is not reliable, and that is never a good thing."

She was right, of course.

I came to Guatemala to walk on the wild side, to look into the abyss; but I was battling so many demons inside myself that I couldn't see what was in front of my nose. I was a dreamer, but the whole world had become my dream, and no matter what I did, I couldn't wake up.

"You are quite right," I said. "I wish I could change things, but I probably can't. So you must be careful around me."

"Who else will love you if I don't?"

Everything she said was right, but I hated hearing it. "That's beautiful, but hardly complimentary. It makes you look good, and it makes me look idiotic."

She cocked her head: "Aren't you?"

"Yes, but—"

"Then I am a fool, too, for loving you."

Fools were not easily tolerated in Guatemala; but for my sake she was willing to be one.

"Why on earth don't you turn around and start running away from me," I asked, "and not stop running until you are in Guatemala City?"

"Do you really want to know?"

"I want to know."

"Because you make me laugh," she said, laughing.

For the rest of the night she could not stop laughing. She would doze off for a while, and then she would remember, and she'd laugh again. *I have given her a reason to enjoy this night*, I thought; and although it was my own craziness that was giving her such enjoyment, I was quite satisfied to go along with it. Providing her with free entertainment was the least I could do.

We were careful not to look at each other the next day when we were with other people, but I was incredibly aware of her presence. I could not wait to be alone with her that night. There was no meeting of the *comunidad de base,* and Padre Julio went early to his little office in the back of the church, where we could see a small kerosene lamp flickering. As we watched, the light flickered out. Padre Julio liked to go to bed early.

The moon was out, and as I carried our single candle to the darkened schoolhouse I thought I saw shadows made by the moonlight. I could hardly wait to hold Sofia in my arms and seek a release for the things that had been gnawing at my vitals all day.

I quickly shoved four benches together and spread the tarpaulin over them, and then three blankets. Before I blew out the candle I saw that Sofia was smiling. She took her time laying down beside me.

I took her into my arms and held her.

The liquid shock of sexual arousal hit me like a storm surge, carrying me into the world that we entered when we made love.

"How have you been?" I asked.

"*Bueno, Chico,*" she said huskily.

My hands moved slowly. Her breathing grew deeper.

We breathed slowly together, and again I felt like we were preparing to go underwater together.

"*Te amo,*" she murmured in my ear. "You know that, don't you?"

"Yes, you told me."

"Do you love me?"

"Of course I do. How could I not love you?"

It was not true, but the lines themselves were authentic, because they had been given to all men at the beginning of the world.

It was all very simple, so easy to understand.

"Do you?" she asked again. "Do you love me?"

"*Come no*?—How could I not?"

She laughed. "When you find out how, let me know."

"I promise you."

She laughed.

We stripped our clothes off and lay down again beside each other; but tonight was different. She unhesitatingly touched my body in the place where I was aroused.

"I know you don't love me, but I love you enough for both of us," she whispered. She breathed heavily, but her words were focused. "You think I am crazy to say this, but it's true."

"I don't think you're crazy."

"It's true, what I'm saying to you."

I knew it was, but it made me feel bad. So I said, "You are a beautiful woman—I can't get enough of you."

"I love you enough for both of us," she said again.

"Thank you for both of us."

This amused her, and she laughed. "That's all? That's all you want to say to me?"

Again she laughed; and with great affection she murmured, "*Inocente. Inocente!*"

A moment later she gently guided me to certain places where she wanted me to kiss her, and I did. I kissed her legs, her breasts, and other parts of her body. She entwined her hand in my hair and held onto it as though I might run away. My desire was overwhelming.

Tonight would be different. She wanted me inside her.

With her hands she began to guide me inside her. I did not mind that it was slow and she was very tight because the pleasure was so great. Even if I was only partly inside her when my sexual release came, my seed would know the way home.

I was moving inside her a little more, and she was very wet, but it was still difficult because she was so incredibly tight.

It occurred to me that I was hurting her.

At that moment she murmured with incredible urgency:

"*Hagala!*—Do it!"

"Sofia—"

"Do it!"

She grabbed my hips and pulled. She did this repeatedly, furiously pulling me into her, each time arching her back. *"Hagala!"* she panted into my ear; each time she pushed upward, I went deeper inside her. Because she was so tight, it occurred to me that she had not been sexually active for a long time.

I moved back and forth with endless little strokes until our bodies produced more juices, and now the flesh yielded ever so surely inward. So powerful was this connection that I did not have to move or even breathe, but simply clung to Sofia as she single-mindedly roiled up against me, panting and pulling; and then I was deep inside her, and began to feel the long conversion to pure sensation, the long tide that would take my travelers to the other side.

The pleasure was so overwhelming that I wanted to live there, and let the seed drip home over a period of days, weeks, and months—and in fact it did go on for a long time; then finally the wave exploded, and Sofia loosed a furious, triumphant sob.

It was a sob of childbirth and death, but also of victory, the culmination of a lifelong struggle. Through everything she kept telling me she loved: *"te amo, te amo, te amo, te amo, chico, te quiero—"*

And I died of pleasure.

It lasted a lifetime; and we slept the delicious sleep of the sated and the dead.

When we awoke, it was done.

Afterwards I lay beside her and wanted nothing more than to be silent; but there was something I had to talk about, something that wouldn't stop bothering me.

"I'm afraid I hurt you. I forced my way into you."

She didn't seem to understand.

"Thank you," she said.

"When we were having intercourse, I must have hurt you. I'm sorry I pushed my way into you."

"I told you to do it."

"I know; but—"

She nuzzled against me. "I felt you."

"But you were very tight—it was hard to get inside you."

"I'm sorry."

"It must have hurt you."

"Thank you," she said again.

This was not about pleasure and pain, as North Americans would have it; this was about sexual intercourse as a delivery system for getting the seed delivered despite all impediments.

"But you were very, very tight. I'm sorry if—"

"Why do you keep saying you're sorry?" She kissed me tenderly on the mouth. "I'm the one who is sorry. I'm sorry it was so difficult for you. *Yo lo aprecio mucho*."

"You appreciate it?"

"I love you. *Te amo*."

I wondered if I should ask the next question; but of course I had to. The body could tell me only so much. The rest had to come from voluntary disclosure.

"Clearly you have not been sexually active for a long time," I said as gently as I could.

"Sexually active? What do you mean by that?"

I explained in both English and Spanish exactly what that meant, and she laughed. I hadn't expected the laughter.

"When a woman is sexually active," I said, or something like that, "it is noticeable to her partner, because sexual intercourse is much easier. That is why I say you have not been sexually active in a long time, because your vagina is so small and so tight. A man has not been inside of you for a long time."

She giggled.

"No man has *ever* been inside me," she said.

It didn't occur to me to believe her. "No," I said, "you don't have to say that."

She shrugged.

"Tonight was the first time," she said very matter-of-factly. "I have never let a man inside my body before."

Had she specialized in giving her lovers oral sex? But if that were true, why had she declined oral sex with me? I decided to let her go on, just to hear what she had to say.

"Why *haven't* you ever had sexual intercourse?"

"I was not allowed to have sex with a man."

"Why not?"

"I took a vow of chastity."

"A vow of *what?*" I thought I wasn't hearing right.

"I was in orders for fifteen years," she said. "I took a leave of absence two years ago and didn't go back."

Now, of course, it was beginning to dawn on me.

"Orders?"

"Do you know what it means for someone to be in orders?"

"Sofia," I said, trying to stay calm, "are you telling me—"

"I was a nun in the Maryknoll order," she said calmly, as though talking about the weather. "Technically, I still am."

"A *what?*"

"A Maryknoll nun; I took a vow—"

"Did you say you were a *nun?*"

I was getting upset.

"Yes, what's wrong with that?"

"Nothing!"

"Then why are you angry?"

I was shaking my head: "Sofia, I can't really believe—why didn't you say something before? I mean, you should have said something!"

"I *am* saying something."

"You took a vow as a nun!"

"A vow of chastity."

"A vow of *chastity?*"

It wasn't as though she was active—she was on what amounted to a permanent leave of absence from the Maryknolls; but I was getting angry again. Partly it was because it had been so obvious, yet hadn't once occurred to me.

"Yes," she said, "and also a vow of poverty."

"And now, of course, the vows do not apply."

"Yes. I mean no."

"But why did you choose *me* to be the first man to make love to you in this way?"

"Because I want a baby."

"That's no excuse!" I heard myself yelling.

She laughed.

Then what she had just said began to hit me. "Why on earth do you want to have a baby with me?"

"I love you."

Of course, I thought.

The insanity of erotic love explained everything, for men as well as women. I could use the same defense myself, if I was ever called to account for what had passed between us—I would simply point in her direction and gibber like a monkey. Love was the great equalizer, an equal-opportunity madness.

"But I'm an *inocente*. Why would you want to have a baby with me? Aren't you afraid I might leave you?"

"You won't."

"Why wouldn't I?"

"You're an *inocente,* but also insane in a special way. You think of yourself as an honorable gentleman, *un cumplido caballero.* You even see yourself as a kind of *caballero andante*." She paused. "Would Quixote leave Dulcinea?"

"No," I said, "that would be out of the question."

So she had me.

"There must be other men who would make better fathers!" I said, once again genuinely upset.

"But you are the only man I have ever loved; therefore you are the only man who could be the father of my child."

I sat on the edge of our makeshift bed and took my head in my hands.

"I just wish you would have said something about being a nun," I said. "After all that celibacy, after all those repressed or suppressed feelings…and then I come along—"

"What do you mean?"

"It's almost like I caused you to leave a life of celibacy."

"You did," she said calmly.

"But you left the Maryknolls two years ago. You said so yourself."

"I had no reason to want a man until you came."

"See what I mean?" I cried. "See what you're doing to me? I mean, you were a nun for so long, and then *I* come along and I'm the first man you have sexual intercourse with you after you leave orders. And to tell you the truth, I'm not even sure you had sex *before* you were a nun—"

"I didn't. I was a virgin until tonight."

I was cursing softly.

"Can't you see what kind of responsibility this puts on me?"

"Yes," she said happily, glad that I could see the obvious.

"That's why you should have said something. I didn't know what I was getting into!"

"You didn't ask."

I was practically in a frenzy by now: "And that's all that matters, your needs and your feelings? The man's feelings aren't important?"

She thought about this for a moment.

"You showed me what your feelings were," she said in a low voice. "Every night you made your feelings clear to me—every night when you were laying with me in the dark."

"And that's why you didn't tell me you'd been a nun?"

"I didn't want to make you…to give you anxiety."

"Why?"

"I love you."

I told her that was crazy, that the two things had nothing to do with each other.

She turned slightly to whisper directly into my ear: "You did this thing—you started this thing. Each night you wanted more. You didn't ask me about my life. You simply wanted to do this thing. Isn't that right? So tell me yes or no, *Chico*. Did you ask me to tell you about my life first, before you kissed me and put your hand on my body?"

She was way ahead of me. I was trapped.

"No," I said.

"I did not do or say anything to stop you, but you started it, because you wanted me."

It was true.

I had entered into this animal thing with my eyes open; I wanted sexual pleasure, and I had gotten sexual pleasure.

And I would get more.

But—

"I still think you should have told me that you were a nun," I said weakly. "My God, the Maryknoll nuns are famous in Latin America. You're the ones who are always getting killed because the governments think you're a bunch of radicals."

"No importa."

"Of *course* your life is important, especially that part."

"Then why didn't you ask me about my life?"

"I thought you didn't want to talk about it." In fact she *hadn't* wanted to talk about where she'd been and what she'd done. "You were so damn evasive every time I asked you about it."

"But you made love to me anyway."

I sighed. "Yes, yes, I did, didn't I?"

I realized at that moment that of course Padre Julio must have known that she was a nun, or had once been; I wondered if he would have told me if I had asked him about Sofia's past. But I probably wouldn't have asked. That wasn't my style. I always wanted to find out on my own, in some kind of direct experience.

Now I'd pay the price.

Sofia was right about one thing: I couldn't leave now.

She had been a nun, and had waited all this time to be with a man. Not only that, she'd waited all this time to have a baby, and it was with me that she wanted to do this. She had also figured out my deepest secret: that although my life was a fantasy of death, it was also a fantasy of impossible personal honor. I may have been incapable of love, but still possessed—and was possessed by—a perverse kind of personal integrity. As it happens with most self-absorbed men, the real purpose of this trait was self-destruction—but if you knew it was there, you could use it for your own purposes. So this apparent whim of hers, this strange and unexpected biological need, had bound me to her with cords that couldn't be broken.

I *couldn't* leave her.

And she'd known that, she'd figured that out about me.

I had come to Guatemala to die in a Land of Wonders; but now I knew that Sofia Mendez would be choosing the exact nature of the wonders we would experience. For reasons I could never understand, nor had I even been given the chance to consider logically one way or the other before the fact, she had chosen me to be the father of her child. Was it simply because her desire to have a child had been building for some time, that it was some kind of irresistible instinct she could no longer resist—and that I had been available in this dangerous and embattled place, and been proven too weak-minded to resist? Ultimately, however, it was I who had initiated sexual intimacy between us; and no matter what else I thought or believed, that was where it all started. I didn't know why I'd found her so maddeningly attractive, and maybe it wasn't even important how much of it I could understand. I was connected to her, and she was connected to Guatemala, and now I couldn't leave either of them.

Chapter Four

Sofia Mendez and I continued to be lovers, but no longer was the object to make love in such a way as to avoid pregnancy—the object now, it seemed, was to get pregnant as quickly as possible. And I had no doubt that we *would* get pregnant, because it now felt predestined. It was as though Sofia and I were lost players who had wandered into a fateful place of personal theater, and were suddenly doing and saying things that had been written for us long before we were born. On the other hand, I was completely unable to think of myself as a parent, and Sofia's obsession with having a child seemed like a hopeless fantasy to me.

I tried to talk to Sofia once or twice about the *patrulla de autodefensa* that was being organized in the village, but she did not want to discuss it. All she could think or talk about, it seemed, was parenthood. She spent an inordinate amount of time with the mothers of Chapila Chica, talking nonstop about their children, their pregnancies, and their birthing experiences.

(Besides being a *curandera,* Sofia's mother had been a midwife, I now discovered.)

Although Sofia and I made an effort to be quiet when we made love at night in the schoolhouse, it was by now perfectly clear to everyone that we were lovers. Padre Domingo had a way of smiling sadly and giving his head a single shake that indicated that yes, he knew very well about Sofia and me; but he showed no inclination to talk about it with us. It was likely that he would eventually talk to us about marriage, I thought, but now was not the time for domestic planning. There were too many other things afoot, things far more dangerous than a secret love affair, for people to worry about two lonely people clinging to each other at night in a schoolhouse. It also occurred to me that Padre Julio might need us for something important in the future, something that might take us away from Chapila Chica.

The people of Chapila Chica were still concerned about the *patrulla de autodefensa*, but the five men who had volunteered for it seemed disinclined to think or talk further about it. In the meantime, there was an every-present feeling of danger in the air; but like the sexual energy between myself and Sofia Mendez, it was so omnipresent, so obvious to everyone, that after a time people no longer noticed it.

At first the sense of danger made me concerned for Sofia's safety. Then I found the danger exciting—it even made the sex we were having more exciting. But that aspect of our relationship had little to do with Sofia, and everything to do with my own death wish; the truth was, I was waiting for Sofia to explain with immaculate logic why I should give up the dream that had haunted me for so long, the dream of dying heroically in a Land of Wonders. Of course, this did not take Sofia Mendez into account as a person in her own right, but someone who existed solely to help me understand the meaning of the particular experiment in which I had gotten myself entangled. Guatemala was my laboratory, Sofia the subject, and I the sole beneficiary of the information gained—and if that is not exploitation, I would like to know what it is. But Sofia had turned the tables on me; it was now *she* to whom I was irreversibly connected, it was to *her* that my future was now in honor bound.

Furthermore the village of Chapila Chica had become special to me in a way that no other place in the world could ever be. Despite the fact that everything I felt about Chapila Chica related to my own dangerous dreams, the village had unmistakably, for just that reason, become my ultimate spiritual destination, my Latin Shangri La, my dream-driven Lambarene. Each night after making love to Sofia I had dreams that were vivid yet beautifully soft, lit up with a kind of North American Technicolor that suggested the clean and unambiguous pastels of a Hitchcock movie; the dreams themselves were deeply satisfying, almost as satisfying as the sex I was having. Although I could never remember the plot line when I woke up, it was almost always focused on the saving of a distressed woman's life.

It has been my experience that as soon as one achieves some hard-won insight or level of acceptance, new and entirely unforeseen complications begin almost immediately to manifest themselves. One of the most irritating complications was destined to be a man named Alan Klein, whom I met one day while working with a group of people in Chapila Chica's collectively-owned milpa. I was hoeing the ugly undergrowth that had sprung up, seemingly overnight, between the skinny rows of fragile corn; and like the others, I wore an old hat as protection from the ravages of the sun. But sweat poured off my hands in rivulets onto the handle of my short hoe, and from there onto the ground. If sweat could grow corn, I thought, there would be a bumper crop before the rainy season came.

I became aware that a tall, solitary man was walking slowly but purposefully up the path to the village. He was a fair distance away, but his mere appearance was a welcome opportunity to take a break. I tried to stand upright. Unfortunately, I tried too quickly, and the resulting back pain made me cry out.

This attracted the attention of the two men who were working with me. One was Miguel, the shy thin-boned man who accompanied Sofia and myself most weekends from the main road up the path to Chapila Chica with supplies. The other was Juan Delmonico, the man who had lately been chosen by Padre Julio to be the comandante of the new *putrulla de autodefensa.*

"We need to stop," I said, "We've worked enough."

"Are you hurt?"

"No, no," I said, "I'm just getting old."

He looked at me incredulously. Chronologically, I was older than he was, but he was stooped, and looked like a man in late middle age; I, on the other hand, looked like a gangly sophomore, albeit a sun-blackened one, on some North American campus.

"No," he said politely, "you are young; you know how to stay young."

He seemed about to ask my age, but instead turned to look at the man coming up the trail. The man was still about half a kilometer away.

"He's a stranger," Juan announced.

By that he could mean a stranger to the highlands, to this part of the highlands, or to Guatemala itself.

"How can you tell he's a stranger?"

"I can tell by the way he walks. He doesn't know the trail."

"Who would want to visit us?" Miguel asked. "Who in Guatemala would want to visit us?"

They laughed, albeit a bit edgily.

"Maybe he's lost," I suggested. "Maybe he's in the wrong country."

Suddenly Miguel turned toward Juan Delmonico. Something seemed to occur to them at the same time.

"La patrulla," Juan said softly.

"La patrulla." Miguel mouthed the words, nodding.

He made a vague commiserative gesture toward Juan, and turned away. It occurred to me that nobody had heard anything about the *patrulla de autodefensa* since a few ancient weapons had been delivered to Juan's house a couple of weeks before by an army patrol. Since that time the village had been waiting uneasily for some representative of the army or the government to arrive to talk to Juan about it.

"La patrulla," I murmured.

We turned back toward the solitary walker.

He was nowhere to be seen, having disappeared into a shallow gorge through which the trail to Chapila Grande passed.

"Desaparacido," I said, making a little joke.

The two men looked uncomfortable.

"No," Miguel said sharply.

In Central American *desaparacido* meant disappeared; and at this point in Guatemala's history it usually meant kidnapped by government forces, tortured and killed. *Desaparacidos* were people who were alive and well one day, and then disappeared suddenly and were never seen again alive.

"No!" Miguel said again, with unconcealed irritation.

Almost everyone in Guatemala had at one time or another seen the bodies of the *desaparacidos* lying by the side of the road, mutilated and carefully left where the maximum number of people could see them.

"Maybe this one will come back," Juan said.

"Then it will be a miracle," I said.

At exactly that moment the man on the trail reappeared.

"It's a sign!" I said triumphantly. "That means we should stop working."

We gathered our tools and took them to the village tool shed. It had collapsed a few weeks back, but we continued to store our tools there nonetheless. Miguel picked up one of the fallen walls and we quickly shoved our tools under it.

"It was the wind," Juan said by way of commentary on the collapsed shed, poking the fallen walls with his hoe. He added, "Nobody knew until the next day how strong the wind was."

We sensed, rather than saw, that the stranger on the path was pulling into hailing distance.

"Where is Padre Julio?" I asked Juan Delmonico softly.

"I think he's in his office."

Only when the stranger was less than a hundred yards away did we turn to stare at him directly.

"See how tall he is," said the peasant named Miguel.

"Very tall," said Juan.

This was a way of saying that the stranger was not Indian, probably not even Guatemalan, and certainly not from the highlands.

The man was athletic and carried himself like the kind of professional who might wear a briefcase and three-piece suit. He wore a backpack and khaki travel clothes that looked expensive, as though they might have come from a Tilly's catalogue, or perhaps one of the New York specialty shops.

"Hey there, people," the stranger called out.

He did not slow down, but neither did he hurry. When at last he came up to us, he made eye contact easily. He smiled boyishly, like a college student about to relate some particularly imaginative prank.

"Hey!" he said again as he came abreast of me. "My name is Aladdin, and I thought I'd just fly in on my magic carpet!"

I was taken aback by his remark and said nothing. "Some of my friends call me Aladdin," he continued, this time in English. "It's a stupid nickname from college. But I prefer Alan. Alan Klein."

He put out his hand.

"I'm Maitland Sutterfield," I said, taking his outstretched hand. "I'm a volunteer at Father Julio's mission. Welcome to Guatemala."

He smiled reflexively at the implied query about his tenure. "Oh, I've been here for awhile. I do a little contract work now and then for the American Embassy."

I'd been to the American Embassy and had never heard of any Alan Klein, nor had I ever seen him; and I thought I would have remembered his smile, which was ingratiating and calculating. That didn't mean he didn't work for them: perhaps he was a temporary employee, a consultant or a contract worker who did troubleshooting of some kind. If so, that didn't recommend him to me; I found the Americans who worked there rude and incompetent.

"You're working directly under the cultural attaché, I'm sure," I said, with what I hoped was a knowledgeable and worldly tone.

"Well, yes, but culture really isn't my beat."

"Nor mine," I said.

His eyebrows rose slowly. "But didn't I hear you were a

journalist? I always think of journalists as cultural workers of a sort. Don't you?"

I recognized *cultural workers* as a kind of awkward Marxist usage. *The bastard is trying to sound me out,* I thought. "Sometimes they are, sometimes not. I wouldn't use an expression like that in any case, because it sounds pretentiously leftwing, something some Maoist student might say. In any case, I'm not just a journalist, but also a writer working on a book."

Klein's eyes twinkled. "Aren't they the same thing, writers and journalists?"

"Hardly."

"But writers are definitely cultural workers."

"Most writers are barely literate."

He laughed with great relish, tilting his head back and closing his eyes. "I'll remember that," he said.

Klein turned to the others. They looked quickly down at the ground. After a moment, I realized that Klein was waiting for me to introduce the two men to him. There was a flicker of recognition on his face when I introduced Juan Delmonico.

"Bueno!" barked Klein. *"Mucho gusto en conocerle!"*

Juan shuffled his feet nervously and continued to stare at the ground. *"Mucho gusto,"* he whispered finally.

Klein smiled and said in Spanish. "You recognized my name."

"Si," Juan said.

"Did the soldiers tell you I was coming?"

"*Creo que si.* I think so."

"You think so."

"Si."

"But you're not sure."

Juan continued to shuffle his feet and look away. *Stand up straight!,* I felt like yelling at him, *Look Klein in the eye!* What I knew, and what Juan could not know, was that he had nothing to gain, and a great deal to lose, by being unsure of himself around this kind of North American. It had occurred to me that there was a good chance that Klein had been sent here by the station chief at the US Embassy, or one of his case officers. "You are to be comandante of the new *patrulla de autodefensa* for Chapila Chica," Klein said.

Juan nodded.

"How do you know about the *patrulla?*" I asked.

"I've been assigned to work with the *patrulla.* My expertise is in counterterrorism and counterinsurgency. My function is strictly informal, however. Juan Delmonico will be under the authority of Lieutenant Vincente Altamirano, of the army at *Zona Viente.*" He turned to Juan and repeated everything he had just said in Spanish.

And Juan turned and related everything that had been said to Miguel in Kekchi.

And Miguel looked at the ground.

I had heard rumors about American advisors working with the Guatemalan army and civilian security forces, although that was supposedly forbidden by the US Congress. Well, here was proof that American advisors were in Guatemala…what a story that would make, if I could find some way to get it into print at the *Miami Herald*! If not the breakthrough story of the decade, it would do very nicely until the real thing came along. I could imagine the headline: "US Advisors in Guatemala Defy Congressional Ban."

We began to walk slowly toward Chapila Chica, Juan and Miguel walking awkwardly ahead of us. "Maitland Sutterfield," Alan Klein was murmuring thoughtfully as he walked along beside me. "I'm glad to finally meet you. I've heard about you from people at the embassy."

"I don't know the people at the embassy that well."

"I'm sure," Klein said. He popped an American-style breath mint into his mouth. "What do you do up here in this village? You've been here awhile—a few months, anyway, right?"

"As a volunteer, I do whatever I'm told to do."

"What's in it for you?"

"I get a break from the real world, and maybe some material for a book. Anyway these people are pretty needy."

"Then you must be quite idealistic."

"I'd like to talk to you about your work," I said. "I may be a volunteer, but I'm also a journalist. And I know the US Embassy is not supposed to be helping the Guatemalan army."

"And so, you sense a story." He was smiling broadly. "Apparently your journalistic instincts are still intact."

"I certainly hope so."

"I'll talk about anything, anywhere, as long as our conversations are off the record," he said briskly. Klein was now all business. "So there it is. I'd be delighted to talk to you, but as deep background only."

"Agreed. Our conversations will be off the record until you say differently."

"Deep background?"

"Deep background."

But wasn't he afraid I might betray him and quote him anyway? He had no track record with me, no reason to believe I was trustworthy. He must have very good deniability, I thought, if he was willing to confide in a stranger.

Or maybe he didn't care. There were people like that in Guatemala, people who no longer cared about their careers, or even their lives. They made interesting sources but were rarely dependable.

"Deep background," Klein said again, taking great pleasure in the words themselves. "That's the best place to be, don't you think?"

Juan and Miguel continued to drift uneasily toward the village, Alan Klein and I following a few feet behind them. Even if Klein wouldn't let me quote him, maybe I could corroborate whatever he told me through another source—that way I could break the story without mentioning him or using any direct quotes from him.

"What would you do if I agreed to stay off the record, but quoted you anyway?" I asked.

"You wouldn't do that."

"You're right, I wouldn't. But suppose I did."

"You *really* wouldn't want to do that."

"Would I get whacked?"

He smiled. "Only if I knew I could get away with it."

It occurred to me that if I wanted to use him as a source, I'd better not get in a pissing contest with him. "Well," I said, "I'm glad you're willing to talk to me."

"I'm a great believer in freedom of press." He made no attempt to conceal his contempt. "What do you want to know about me?"

"Anything you want to tell me."

"I'm from Brooklyn—that's the place I know best. Are you interested in knowing more about Brooklyn, or about the CIA?"

Klein pronounced the acronym CIA as though he were saying *see-ya,* as the Latinos did. That was a tipoff that he was going to share whatever information he got here with the CIA station chief, if he wasn't already working for him. Walking ahead of us, Juan missed a step, but didn't turn around. "Why should I worry about the CIA?" I asked.

"You suspect I'm doing a little errand for them."

"That makes you an excellent source," I said. "You sound like a regular fount of information."

"I have to be."

"Because it's therapy for you?"

"Better than therapy, man."

"Is that why you're so interested that I'm a journalist?"

"There is a particular story here in Guatemala that the Americans should know about. It's their right to know, as I see it," he said. "And what they don't know about the US in

Guatemala could make the story of the century."

Was he talking about the same story I was thinking about?

If it was about the CIA going behind the back of Congress, it *had* to be hot, which meant I could take my place in the pantheon along with Woodward and Bernstein; I, a lowly stringer, a bottom feeder in the muddy pond of Latin American journalism, who hadn't filed a story in weeks!

"And no doubt," Klein said, "you would also like to know how I, a nice American boy from Brooklyn, came to be in Guatemala."

"How *did* you come to be in Guatemala?"

"All in good time, man."

"Whenever you're ready." Suddenly I felt exhausted, which is perhaps why I heard myself muttering weakly, "Your work must be very interesting."

"I get to meet some incredibly interesting people, really I do. That's the best part."

There was fair amount of self-deprecation in Klein's smile, as though he were inviting me to laugh at the easy familiarity of North Americans everywhere; but the smile was also a threat. *Yes,* it seemed to be saying, *we Americans are swaggering braggarts and sentimental fools; but we are also killers. Don't forget that.* Such a smile could come only from the world of Action Comics, John Wayne and western movies, the GI Joe universe of the American boy in a man's body.

But why was he smiling the killer smile at me? Who was I to him?

This was my first meeting with Alan Klein—and the one thing I knew about him was that he was a spook of some kind, most likely a contract employee for the CIA, although I wouldn't completely rule out the USAID. I decided to call him Alan, as he had suggested; I simply could not use a nickname like Aladdin, especially since it sounded so much like a code name. It sounded like some juvenile moniker he'd devised for people who longed to feel they were part of a cloak-and-dagger world of international intrigue; a code name he let them use, in the same way that policemen sometimes allowed cop buffs and small-time informers to wear guns and cop hats in cop bars.

But it all seemed a bit obvious, a bit much.

Almost surely, I thought, his oafish hail-fellow-well-met act was cover: if you thought someone a fool, you might be less likely to suspect betrayal or attack from him. I had already begun to wonder why Klein had come to Little Chapila, when there were villages all over the highlands where *patrullas* where being organized. And I sensed immediately the danger he might pose to Padre Julio and Sofia Mendez.

I had to protect Sofia; and I was in a good position to do just that.

All the more reason, then, to keep Klein close by agreeing to use him as a source; the more dirt I could get on him, the more I could threaten to use against him if I had to. At the very least, I thought, if things went south I would be able to provide Sofia and myself with enough time to run away. That was my thinking.

"I especially look forward to meeting your priest," Klein said as we trudged toward the schoolhouse. Juan Delmonico and Miguel were still walking silently a few paces ahead. "I've heard a great deal about Padre Julio Domingo."

"All of it good, I'm sure."

"Yes, very good. In fact, maybe too good. I have to wonder why a guy like him wants to be in a place like this."

"He's a priest—being here is part of his ministry. He carries a special burden for the suffering of the highland Indians."

Klein stopped and raised his eyebrows. "Special burden?"

"It's just an expression."

"A very distinctive expression."

In fact, I had heard Padre Domingo use it. "His interest is helping poor people. That's what he's supposed to do, give comfort to the poor and marginalized."

"Yes, but why here? Why now?"

"You will have to ask Padre Julio that...but I suspect because the suffering in the Guatemalan highlands is especially acute right now."

Padre Julio was just rounding the corner from the school. When he saw Alan Klein, a fleeting expression I couldn't quite read crossed his face; but almost immediately he smiled broadly and strode energetically to meet us. "Someone to see you," I called out.

Julio raised his eyebrows and continued to smile brightly. He did not take his eyes off Klein's face.

"Strangers are always welcome," he said.

There was no fooling around with nicknames when Klein introduced himself this time: "My name is Alan Klein. Please call me Alan. And you must be Padre Domingo."

"Call me Padre Julio. Welcome to Chapila Chica."

The two men shook hands. They were both smiling.

The stranger said something to Padre Julio that I did not catch. Julio glanced quickly at me: he was still smiling, but seemed on his guard.

"I see," Padre Julio was saying loudly, nodding. "Of course we can talk. You must stay for our midday meal."

"And after we talk, I'll talk to Mr. Sutterfield here," Klein said.

Throughout the meal, Julio seemed distant and preoccupied. I had no idea what the stranger Klein meant to him or what he was thinking. At the table were Juan Delmonico, Miguel, and some of the women; there was Julio, and Alan Klein, and myself. Most of the men in the village were working as day laborers at a nearby plantation.

Before the meal, Julio said a prayer while everyone held hands. The prayer was short and traditional. "Amen!" Klein said heartily after Julio was finished.

Sofia Mendez came to the meal late. When she saw Alan Klein, she grimaced for a fraction of a second, but he didn't seem to notice. Sofia studiously avoided eye contact with him throughout the meal and made a point of leaving early.

Although Klein didn't look at her directly—he was too busy talking to Julio about Guatemala's elusive national bird, the quetzal—I had the feeling that he was very much aware of Sofia's presence. In fact, I sensed that Klein was observing everyone very carefully, especially Padre Julio, Juan Delmonico, and Sofia.

"I hear you have Saturday-night meetings," Klein said in English to Padre Julio.

"Yes, we do."

"Do you discuss politics?"

"We discuss justice."

Klein's eyebrows shot up. "From what Christian teachings?"

"The New Testament."

"I can't believe that these people would be interested in political abstractions."

"Sometimes they aren't. But they can feel the pain that comes from intense poverty—you know, hunger, fear, and concern for their children."

"So does everybody else. Your point escapes me."

Padre Julio ignored this. "We discuss the problems that occur in people's daily lives."

"Including grievances against the government?"

"Including the grievances and privations and injustices that people here encounter every day, in every department of life."

"What do they expect to do about the grievances?"

Julio hesitated. "We live in hope of God's Kingdom. Jesus came to teach us a new culture, a culture based on love and cooperation rather than violence and deception. I don't expect you to approve, but I'm sure you can understand the basic dynamics."

Klein's eyebrows shot up. "Why shouldn't I understand. Am I

lacking in intelligence?"

"I didn't say that."

"Is it perhaps because I'm not Catholic?"

"I have no idea whether you're Catholic or Protestant, a Muslim, Jew, Hindu, Buddhist or a confirmed secularist. The most vocal opponents of Catholic liberation theology are other Catholics—mainly conservative Catholics."

"Tell me about this new kingdom you hope to inhabit. Does it exist in this world or the next?"

"Both."

Again Klein's eyebrows went up.

"That absolutely surprises me, Padre, because I would think that a Catholic priest would see this world as irredeemably corrupt. Isn't that the purpose of Heaven, to reward and ennoble people in the next world who have no chance for nobility in this one?"

"Yes, that is one of the purposes of the afterlife, but not the main purpose. The love of justice and loving-kindness must begin here, in this world."

"Do you really believe that justice is ever possible in this world, Padre?"

Julio laughed.

I knew him well enough by now to know that his laughter was usually sincere, but that he often used it to stall for time.

"Probably not," Julio said finally.

"Then why talk about justice, if it isn't possible?"

"Because God will finish in the next world what we begin now. The seeds of Heaven are planted right here in this world, and brought to fruition by God in his own time. That's how we build the Kingdom."

"In this village?"

Julio smiled, matching the stranger's smile perfectly in intensity. "Exactly."

"When?"

"Every day."

"Including today?"

"Especially today!"

"What about eternity?"

Julio wiped his mouth with a tortilla in the peasant fashion and moved his chair back from the table slightly. He looked at Klein as though taking aim at him. "Eternity begins now," he said, "or not at all. It starts now, in our own lives. Don't you think so?"

Klein said nothing.

Everybody knew that Klein's presence had something to do with the *patrulla de autodefensa.* Juan Delmonico ate silently and very slowly, chewing his food carefully. He avoided eye contact with others at the table, especially Klein.

I was amazed at the extent to which Klein seemed to be ignoring Juan Delmonico and attaching himself and his barracuda smile to Julio Domingo and myself. It was as though Juan Delmonico didn't matter to him, as perhaps he didn't. But to us, Juan mattered a great deal. He would be the comandante of the new civilian self-defense patrol; and as such he would be in a position nobody else in the village had ever been in before. He had the guns to be used by the *patrulla,* deposited at his house by sullen troops of the Guatemalan army just two weeks before. He would soon be under orders to an officer of that same army.

What would Juan be asked to do, and what would he be willing to do? We could not help but think about that. The guns, the very presence of them, had subtly changed everything in Chapila Chica.

After the meal, Klein glanced at the tin plates we had used. They were stacked at one end of the table. "Should I help clean up? Isn't collective work part of the great progressive tradition?"

"There is nothing necessarily progressive about washing dishes," I said.

"I was hoping you were going to politely decline my help."

I smiled.

Oddly, there was something I was starting to like about his unhinged and dangerous humor. "Cleaning up is not really a very big deal, as you can surely see."

"Can I be an honorary member of the Kingdom of Heaven, if I help?"

"Just help clean up, Klein. Virtue is its own reward."

But the women were already washing our thick dishes in water heated on the wood stove; so Klein and I folded the two tables and put them against the wall. When we were finished, we went outside and stood in the shade of the schoolhouse. Klein smoked an entire cigarette in silence, while I waited for him to talk.

"Where in hell is your goddamn padre?" he said finally.

"In his office talking to his catechists, I believe."

"I thought I made it clear that I wanted to talk to him. Having to wait like this pisses me off."

"Maybe he wanted to teach you patience."

"Fuck you, man. All of you."

"If Padre Julio said he'd talk to you, he will." At just that moment I saw him heading toward us. "See? Here he comes now."

Alan Klein turned toward me, smiling sweetly. "Would you please excuse us for a few moments? I mean, it'll be interesting to see what Padre Julio has to say about you."

"I hope you have more to talk about than me."

"I hope so too. Can you show me the path to Chapila Grande later?"

"Sure."

"Then we can talk about the big story you're going to write, with me as your main source."

Klein turned and went to Padre Julio, who was patiently waiting. He stood near the little wooden lean-to at the back of the church that was used as a combination office and sleeping quarters. He slept on an American army-issue field cot, which he kept folded in the closet during the day.

Klein disappeared into Julio's office. Both men were smiling.

Try as I might, I could not find it in myself to completely despise Alan Klein. He had a certain kind of criminal charm that I found comical, and I especially liked his Brooklyn accent. I had lived briefly in New York and had fond memories of Brooklyn. The first time I went there I observed a bit of folk theater that afterwards I never forgot:

Cabby stops at a red light, sees a little kid sitting on the curb.

Kid just sits there, doesn't say a word, he's singing to himself. It's driving the cabby crazy.

The cabby explodes: "What, I should give you a shiny new penny??"

That was Brooklyn, the place of the rough but kind-hearted cabby, the kid on the curb, the shiny new penny; not the real Brooklyn, but the Brooklyn of memory and American myth, the Brooklyn that only the dead know, Brooklyn as it should be.

So anybody with a Brooklyn accent got a pass from me, at least to some extent.

After Klein finished talking to Padre Julio, I went to the cabinet in the schoolhouse where I kept my things and got my canteen and filled it with water at the pump. As soon as it was full, I set out with Klein to the path that would lead us to Chapila Grande. The path dropped into the gorge on the east side of Chapila Chica. In about ten minutes of hard walking we got on the trail that led to the Pentecostal enclave of Chapila Grande, or Big Chapila.

I had no particular desire to see it myself—I thought of the noisy Pentecostals who lived there as gutless primitives pimping money from their North Americans brethren. Nor was I impressed with their belief that Jesus was about to return and establish justice in the Guatemalan highlands. Hadn't Jesus already died for them and left careful instructions for the way they were to live their lives? What made them think they rated a second visit?

"So," I said after we'd walked awhile, "did you talk about me?"

"Yes, but Padre Julio didn't have much to say about you. He said you were a dependable volunteer and on some kind of spiritual quest."

I didn't know what to say about that, so I said nothing. Instead I asked the question that had been bothering me since we'd talked earlier.

"Why did the US Embassy send an American to help these highland peasants form a self-defense unit? The US Congress outlawed direct aid to the government of Guatemala a long time ago because of human-rights violations."

"Nobody sent me here to organize anything," Klein said. "Juan and the other men of the village will be formally trained by a lieutenant from the army base at *Zona Viente.* I'm not even an advisor."

"Then what are you?"

"I'm here to evaluate certain assets in the villages before the training begins. Then I'll write a report about it."

"Do you have a title?"

He grinned. "Doesn't everybody? I'm an assessment analyst. I get paid by the Agency for International Development."

"I don't believe it will be good for Chapila Chica to have a *patrulla.* It would be better if they could stay out of the civil war entirely."

"They're already in it," Klein said. "Everybody who lives in Guatemala is in it, whether they want to be or not."

"The government kills people who simply want a better price for their corn."

Klein sighed. "The government is in a civil war. If the people of Chapila Chica don't support the government, they'll be resettled, or worse."

"Because they want a better price for their corn?"

"No, as a lesson to the other villages in the area."

"You would do that?"

"I don't do anything. It's all the work of the Guatemalan army. I just write my report."

"Then that makes you part of it."

Klein was walking slightly ahead of me. He turned and gave me a brilliant smile. "Would it make me less a part of it if I lied to you?"

He saw my thinking as silly and weak-minded, I could see that; he probably thought he was being generous to even talk to me, since he could so much more easily ignore me. *Unless he wants something from me,* I thought. I was curious about what that might be, but already I had a vague idea about his probable intent.

We walked without saying anything for several minutes.

"You should tell Padre Julio of the danger he's in," I said.

"I already did."

"I'm not sure I can add anything to that."

Klein affected exaggerated surprise: "I thought you wanted to talk to me off the record about my work here in Guatemala."

"Of course I do."

"Then you'll have to hear what I have to say about the future of Chapila Chica."

He had me, but I felt no resentment. Klein was so transparent in his attempts to manipulate people that it ended up being as comical as his Brooklyn accent.

"Go on," I said.

"I was hoping you might write a story about the formation of the *patrulla de autodefensa* in Chapila Chica. The creation of these self-defense patrols is a process that is going on all over the Guatemalan highlands, and the world should know about it.

Chapila Chica is a typical highland village. It would be a great story, appropriate for daily journalism. But something that could also lead to a book contract."

If he knew nothing else, it occurred to me, he knew how writers think.

"Have you discussed this with other people?" I asked.

"Let's just say that everybody I've discussed it with thinks it's an excellent idea."

"That being the case, could they get me a book contract?"

His eyebrows went up slightly. "I know you want to write a book about Guatemala, so you need a book contract, and probably an advance. These are things I can help you with."

I walked a few steps. "Who could publish the original story?"

"This is a story that takes a sympathetic look at a genuinely popular form of counterinsurgency—a policy that is, I might add, supported by your own government. And it's a first-person story by an American who's actually watching it happen. There's no reason why this shouldn't be a series appearing in one of the larger American dailies, or perhaps a single long story in one of the newsweeklies." He took his box of breath mints out of his pocket and popped one in his mouth without missing a step. "Don't worry about getting published. We'll see to that."

"Where?"

"Like I said, one of the big US dailies. *Miami Herald*. *Boston Globe*. Or a newsweekly like *Time* or *Newsweek*. Let us handle that. There are a lot of people we could call."

"Who's *we*?"

Klein tossed another breath mint into his mouth, raising his eyebrows slightly. It was clear he was not going to answer my question. We continued to walk in silence. The trail to Chapila Grande would be coming up soon at the end of the gorge.

"How much would I receive for my deathless prose?

"As much as you need."

"What makes you think it would be publishable?"

"We have an interest in making sure it gets into print."

At that point I remembered our previous conversation. "But what about the other story idea, the one about an Americans who is advising the Guatemalan military on counterinsurgency? I'd love to be that guy who breaks *that* story!"

"We'll get that published too," he said without missing a beat.

"Excuse me," I said, "but let me get this straight. When I speak of someone who is advising the Guatemalan military I am, of course, referring to you, because that's why you're doing regardless of your various disclaimers. So why would you go out of your way to get a story published about your activities in Guatemala? Aren't you trying to keep that a secret?"

He shrugged.

"What gets published, get published. Besides, after you break into one of the big US dailies with the *patrulla* story, it shouldn't be so hard to get the other thing into print. You just need someone to make the right phone calls for you."

"So," I said, feeling a bit faint, "you're saying that if I write a straight-ahead but rather bland *patrulla* story, we can work together on the story about your illegal activities as a counterinsurgency advisor in Guatemala?"

"How many times do I have to say it? Yes, I will absolutely work with you on both stories."

We walked in silence for several minutes. Klein was conning me, or trying to. He might help me get the *patrulla* pieces published, but when I wanted to write the story about his work in Guatemala, he would make sure it didn't happen. But what if I could write the advisor story without Klein's help, and trick him into corroborating certain key points?

Maybe I could get a piece into one of the left-wing British newspapers; something that didn't mention Klein by name. (Or maybe one that would.) Maybe then I could sneak a more-detailed piece about Klein into a US paper, referring to him by name and using attributed quotes. The fact that he was here at all was something the American people needed to know about. Once the story was broken, the press would want details—and as the reporter of record, I would produce them. Images of myself testifying in front of a Select Committee in Washington danced through my head.

"Why, exactly, do you want to give me this considerable break?"

For the first time since we started walking Klein turned to look at me. "I want to see something in the US press about counterinsurgency against communism in Latin America, but something positive, something from a North American eyewitness. We want a piece that shows the Guatemalan army winning the hearts and minds of the people."

"And not murdering civilians."

Klein got a pained look on his face. "They don't *always* murder civilians."

I sighed. "Did you talk to the station chief about this?"

"Actually, it was his idea."

"So why didn't he talk to me about it himself?"

"He has this crazy idea that you might misquote him. If he gets me to talk to you he has deniability."

"Well, yes," I said, "except that nobody in their right mind would be foolish enough to misquote a CIA station chief in Guatemala, if they valued their life."

"Do you?"

"Do I what?"

"Value your life?"

We had only been talking a few minutes, and Klein was already getting close to pay dirt. So instead of answering him, I made a show of looking around for the path to Big Chapila. Soon we would reach the last fork where the path to Chapila Grande cut off to the right: in a moment I would head back to Chapila Chica and let Klein go on alone. "What kind of angle do you want for this story?"

"Angle?"

"What kind of material do you want me to concentrate on?"

He thought about it. "Well, in Chapila Chica you have a bunch of people who have never fired a gun in anger, who are being trained to be militiamen in a paramilitary organization. What do they feel? Are the conflicted about it or do they accept it wholeheartedly? These are people who are fighting to defend their homes and families. There's something essentially compelling about that." He paused. "It would be extremely interesting to find out how the average Guatemalan feels about this, including those who maybe think of themselves as political progressives. I would imagine that they're terribly conflicted about this civil war."

"Such as?"

"People like the priest, Julio Domingo."

"Anybody else?"

"His friend Sofia Mendez. She wasn't born in Chapila Chica, so what's she doing here? I'd bet my bottom dollar she's an intellectual; and most of the intellectuals have been involved with the left at one time or another. Anyway, if I were you, I would concentrate on both of them. And of course Juan Delmonico. Interview him about his job as comandante of the self-defense patrol, and see if his heart's really in it, or it he's just going through the motions."

I stopped dead in my tracks. After a couple of steps Klein stopped and turned to face me.

"These aren't newspaper stories you want me to write," I said. "You want me to give you written reports about the people in the village."

Klein sighed.

"Look, chief," he said calmly, his voice low, "I really don't give a rat's ass, but I don't think you understand." He was still smiling. "Now, the way I see it, you have three choices. This part of the highlands is being watched very carefully; there will be military operations here before long. If you stay up here in this little village and do nothing, you may get killed and your friends may get killed. At the very least this village would be uprooted and resettled somewhere else. Or you can write the stories we want you to write, and you can stay up here with our blessing. We can try to protect everybody else in the village. Or you can get the hell out of Dodge, and stay out, and forget you were ever in Chapila Chica."

"What happens to Chapila Chica if I leave?"

"That's hard to say. They'll put more pressure on Padre Julio, and if he gets heroic and resists the pressure, it could go badly for him."

"And?"

"The village will be relocated. The houses will be burned, and the people transferred. Sometimes the Guatemalan army prefers to destroy the houses and the people at the same time. It has a way of getting the attention of the other villages in the area."

"If I stay and work on the story you want me to write, will you protect Chapila Chica from attack or relocation?"

"That's the deal."

"It's that simple?"

He nodded, smiling slightly. "That's it, pal."

We stood there, looking at each other.

His face was blank. He had said everything he needed to say with a minimum of overt bullying; for his part, he was probably unaware of having done any bullying at all. He was just doing his job, and giving me the facts about what the job included.

"Can you give me advance payments as I work on the story?"

Klein seemed surprised. "Of course," he said, "although I believe the usual arrangement is for the newspaper to pay you."

"It's easier this way."

"Okay, if you want it that way."

"What I really want to know," I said, "is why you're so concerned about Chapila Chica. It's just a tiny village on a mountain in the middle of nowhere."

Klein shrugged. "A test case. The *patrulla* idea isn't popular with the Guatemalan army. But the Americans really want this to work—popular self-defense is part of US counterinsurgency doctrine."

"So the North Americans are pushing the *patrullas*."

"Right. That's one of the reasons I want you to write the article. The American reader can identify with you."

"Thanks."

"Don't be so damn quick to thank me."

"Why not?"

He was looking at me sideways, like a boxer edging in for a jab. "We have our eye on certain things going on up here. There are medicines and other supplies getting through to the rebels, and we have to try to plug up any leaks that may have developed in the security picture. And Chapila Chica keeps coming up whenever we look at the security picture."

He was watching my reaction. I tried to keep my face completely still.

"I need to think about this," I said.

He smiled. It was the ugliest smile I had ever seen. Clearly he enjoyed threatening people.

"I'm honest with you," he said. "Why the fuck can't you be honest with me?"

It occurred to me that I needed to be very careful to say the right thing, or things might go badly for me.

I took a deep breath. "Sure, chief," I said, "I can write some articles. That's what you want, and I'll do it for you, and I'll give you the whole story. But believe me, you won't find anything bad about Chapila Chica. They're good people who just want to do the right thing. And if they get off on the wrong track, we'll work together to make sure they get back on the right track. There's no violence necessary, believe me."

Klein's nasty smile slowly faded away, and was replaced by

the warm, avuncular grin of the pal from Brooklyn. "You're good, Sutterfield. Just make sure you don't accidentally lie to me."

"I'll see to it."

Here's the way I saw it—or rationalized it:

Writing articles about Chapila Chica would be my way of protecting the village from harm.

It would be an effective way to protect Padre Julio and Juan Delmonico, and especially Sofia Mendez, my lover.

It would be an insurance policy for all of us.

If I didn't agree to Klein's suggestion, it would put the village at risk.

I would give Alan Klein information, but only things that I wanted him to know—innocuous things, nothing that would endanger anyone in Chapila Chica; I would be very careful to report only good things about Padre Julio, because it was clear that he was under suspicion as a rebel sympathizer. And I would be especially careful to report only good things about Sofia, my lover who wanted someday to be the mother of my child.

I would report only positive things about Sofia Mendez, but I'd do so indirectly, without going overboard or employing superlatives. Why was I so concerned about the tone I used in writing about Sofia? Because by now I suspected that it was at least possible that some of the medications she brought to the village were getting through to the rebels. I didn't know if that was true or not, or even what involvement Sofia might have if it was. Klein already suspected that she was some kind of intellectual with connections to the political Left. Given the fact that Sofia was already under suspicion, did I have any choice but to agree to Alan Klein's plan, if only to use my position to deflect suspicion from her? If things got too hot, I thought I'd be able to talk her into leaving Guatemala with me.

At the same time, I would get all the dirt I could possibly get on Klein. If Klein tried to double-cross me or the people of

Chapila Chica, I would collect enough incriminating evidence on his activities to take him down—or at least threaten to do so. If I actually had to act, I would start with the English and Irish papers, then call my contacts on the big American dailies. And Klein knew I could do that, or at least I thought he did. Anyway, that was my protection.

That was how I rationalized it.

I was not evil, it was the situation that was evil; I was just reacting to it as best I could, especially since I had to protect Sofia. And in the meantime—well, the story about what Klein was really doing in Guatemala was something the American people needed to know about, and it might be a historic opportunity for me. Here was a chance to document the flow of US dollars to the American Embassy, then out of the American Embassy directly to the death squads and the right-wing paramilitaries. What if I could get Klein to tell me how and when the money was transferred? What a story that would make, to catch the bagman at the very moment they handed over the cash!

Chapter Five

The system that Klein and I set up was simplicity itself. When I made my way to Guatemala City to get medications from the NGOs and the main church dispensary, I was in the habit of staying at a hotel with a cantina on the ground floor, where I often ate when I went alone; so I got in the habit of meeting with Klein in the cantina. To Klein's great irritation, I refused at first to write the *patrulla* story that he wanted. Instead I wrote several reports modeled on the chatty features that were then appearing regularly in the Sunday "Lifestyle" sections of most North American newspapers.

I wrote a story about Swiss medical students studying Medical Spanish in Guatemala; I also penned an inspiring story about a retired doctor and wannabe coffee grower who had self-published a book about the effectiveness of coffee in preventing colon cancer; and I contributed a piece about a paraplegic woman who communicated with the ghosts of people killed on the Pan-American Highway.

And I insisted that Klein pay me for each of these stories. I knew he would trust me more if he had to pay me.

Also, I needed the money.

About Chapila Chica I wrote only the most general things, or things that would deflect suspicion from the people I wished to protect.

In the first of these stories I was careful to quote Sofia Mendez as saying that priests should stay out of politics and leave the running of the world to politicians who knew what they were doing. To this I added some completely unpublishable deep background intended for Alan Klein's eyes only: I tried to create the impression of a talkative woman who had never been married, was full of gratuitous advice about how to catch a husband, a woman who could not quite manage her own life, and who was bristling with barely sublimated self-hatred. In other words, I made her out to be a middle-aged version of the classic maiden aunt, and a bit daft: but (and here was the point of the entire exercise) a woman who was for just that reason demonstrably harmless.

Above all, I portrayed Sofia as a woman who had absolutely no interest in social justice. (Which seemed to work: I noticed that Alan Klein almost immediately stopped asking questions about Sofia, concentrating most of his attention on Padre Julio.)

Padre Julio Domingo I portrayed as a kind of demented idealist in the great tradition of Miguel de Molinos, father of Spanish *Quietismo,* a theological system that maintained that Divine Grace came through passivity rather than active works. As I portrayed him, Father Julio was one of those indefatigable Jesuit intellectuals who had an opinion on everything and could read books in twelve languages, but who could not park a bicycle without detailed instructions. I also took special care to portray Padre Julio as a devotee of the works of Ortega y Gasset, and a political and social conservative, however benign and otherworldly.

I do not know whether Klein completely believed all this deep background or not, but my efforts to portray Padre Julio as a kind of conservative Quixote were so persistent, so dense, and so full of passion (and in an odd way so true to the philosophical side of Julio's nature), that even the most skeptical reader could not help but discern some element of truth in my portrayal. Far from being conservative, Padre Julio's political analysis of Latin America society was essentially Marxist, but his solution to the problems of poverty in Guatemala was not revolution, but a practical applied Christianity; nonetheless, I knew that many people would interpret that as a form of socialism, or at the very least a form of political radicalism, simply because it sought to improve the situation of the Indian peasants in the highlands. Furthermore, he was a covert organizer and main regional contact for a rural agricultural cooperative banned by the Guatemalan government.

Naturally I reported none of this to Alan Klein.

I hadn't seen Padre Julio do anything in his role of organizer, and I was determined to avoid first-hand knowledge of his association with the banned peasants' cooperative. The only reason that I knew about it at all was because Sofia had told me, and he had confirmed it indirectly in a conversation we'd had.

Almost everything I wrote about Julio Domingo I reported as an ongoing philosophical argument about the nature of life, in which I represented him as being a stalwart political and theological conservative, and myself as a cynical observer. Yet I threw in enough slices of real life—a dispute about cockfighting between Padre Julio and some peasants from the market town San Jose del Rio, for example—to give my portrayal of him the verisimilitude it needed to ring true.

Klein immediately registered his frustration with the lack of anything subversive in my portrayals of Padre Julio. "Good God, man," he said on our third meeting in Guatemala City, "is this all you can tell me about what's going on in Chapila Chica? So far you've given me absolutely nothing!"

"What do you want?"

"Real information, not your poppycock lifestyle fantasies!"

"Perhaps you're looking for information that's not there."

"It's there, and you know it's there."

We were meeting in the Cantina at the hotel where I stayed. Klein snorted and spread some handwritten pages I'd given him on the bar. He sat his wet beer bottle on the corner of one of the pages, creating a slowly spreading ring of water.

"What makes you think that a village priest in the Guatemalan highlands is necessarily subversive?"

"Don't get smart with me," Klein said.

"What if it's just a Guatemalan village with a medical clinic, and a priest, and a couple of volunteers?"

"You know what I'm talking about, asshole. What about Father Julio's ideas about social justice and the pedagogy of the oppressed? Don't you think I've heard about the things he says and teaches? He told me some of it himself. You might have to probe to get it, but I want some direct quotes about the things he does."

"What kind of social justice do you mean? Wasn't *Social Justice* the name of the magazine put out by Father Coughlin's followers during the 1930s?"

Klein cursed.

It was a game, and Klein knew it; but like any good spook, he kept the ball in play. It was the oldest strategy in the world. Ask enough questions, and eventually the person you questioned would give up something, something in the mind of the opponent would jar loose and he would inadvertently give it up.

But why wasn't Klein more interested in Juan Delmonico?

Juan was the man in charge of the *patrulla de autodefensa,* and therefore the main player in Klein's project. It was precisely Juan's motivation that Klein previously expressed the most interest in. Now he couldn't care less, it seemed.

"Don't you want to know more about Juan Delmonico?" I asked him directly in one occasion.

He shrugged and said: "What about him? I've had a fair amount of experience with the Indians in the highlands. They're all the same."

"How can you say that?"

"Easy, because it's true."

We left it there.

Klein's lack of interest was a nice break, at least at first, because now I didn't have to deflect suspicion from Juan Delmonico—Klein no longer sought information about him. But the whole thing was strange: wasn't Juan the comandante of the *patrulla,* and didn't the success of the *patrulla* depend to a great extent on him? It was becoming clear that Klein really wasn't interested in Juan Delmonico after all, but was actually after Father Julio Domingo. I had a very strong sense that Klein had something up his sleeve; but with him, you always had that feeling.

Two weeks later, when we met again in the same cantina, Klein's studied indifference to Juan Delmonico was gone. We were drinking cold beer straight from the bottle; the owner had withdrawn to the kitchen, as he always did when Klein and I were in his cantina. There were no other customers.

"So when was the last time you talked to Juan Delmonico?" Klein asked.

It was the first time Klein had ever directly asked me a question about Juan Delmonico. I took a long sip of cold beer before answering.

"Yesterday. We talked about the training he is getting."

"What did he say about it?"

"He talked about the lieutenant the army sent to train him."

"What did he say about the lieutenant?"

"He said they were getting along okay."

Juan had said nothing to me about the lieutenant, but I wanted to make him sound good. "Juan said the lieutenant was a very good communicator, and that they were all learning a great deal. Of course he didn't put it exactly that way."

"A very…good…*communicator*," Klein muttered contemptuously.

"I'm paraphrasing, man."

"What kind of weapons are they using?"

"I'm not sure. All I know is that they're old. Apparently the army had them laying around at the Zona Veinte base and didn't know what to do them."

"Why didn't you ask what kind of weapons the patrol is using?"

"I figured you already knew."

I'd seen the *patrulla* walking in single file down the trail carrying their weapons, with the tall somewhat imperious young lieutenant bringing up the rear, his burgundy-colored beret pulled low over his forehead. But I never thought to ask about weapons.

"So the weapons are old," Klein murmured, drinking from his beer. "How old?"

"So old that it probably doesn't matter. They could be Czech, I suppose. Or army-issue American. But whatever they are, they're as old as dirt."

"Kalashnikovs?"

"Hardly. I would have heard about it."

People like Klein often had an almost worshipful attitude toward the famous Kalashnikov, since it was a weapon that did not have to be cleaned—in fact people reported that it actually fired better when not serviced. It had therefore become very popular with armed groups that recruited peasants, since they were notoriously unreliable when it came to cleaning weapons.

Klein sighed.

"Along with the latest ordnance, I'm sure," he said.

"All I know about them is that three of them are single-shot rifles; the fourth is semiautomatic with a clip containing maybe fifteen rounds."

At least I had found that much out—I had overheard one of the men in the *patrulla* talking about it. There was no harm in passing that on. I did not doubt for a second that Klein already knew everything there was to know about the weapons.

"Juan must be pissed off by that."

"Not really. He's the kind of guy who is more than happy to make do with what he has."

"What makes you so sure of that?"

"That's my impression. I'm not sure about anything."

"Did you ever hear him complain about the quality of the

weapons?"

"No, not in so many words."

He sighed. "What about evidence of rebel operations in the area?"

"So far as I know, Juan and his men are not supposed to go out on patrol, but only defend the village. They're going to set up some kind of checkpoint on the trail on the far side of the villages."

Klein murmured something I didn't quite catch. I had the feeling that he thought the *patrulla* didn't venture out of the village enough.

"But Juan must hear things," Klein persisted.

"They're still setting up a regular watch rotation. One of the four men is supposed to stand watch between midnight and dawn throughout the week, with four extra men to spell them when they're sick or have family problem."

The four regulars of the *patrulla de autodefensa* so far were Juan Delmonico, Miguel, the guide who brought us up the path from the main road, a rotund man nicknamed El Gallo, who had once raised fighting roosters, and a wizened man I had never met, who lived on the farthest side of Chapila Chica.

They and some other were going to set up a small outpost that would serve as the checkpoint further up the path to Tzotzil Gapachula Mountain. Presumably if the village was thought to be under attack, the entire roster of men who had received training could set up an ambush on the trail, if it was being used by guerillas.

At least that was the official story.

In reality, the men of Chapila Chica had long since made up their minds not to fire a shot if they could help it.

"What about the people who use the trail?" Klein asked.

"Few people go past Chapila Chica. There's nothing past the village but the mountain. There's only a few people up there, and the people who live on the mountain almost always use the path that goes directly to San Jose del Rio, and usually only on market days."

Which was true, as Klein surely knew, if he knew anything at all about the villages in the area. But it was also true that the rebels would have to use the path to Chapila Chica if they wished to contact anybody in the village, and they might use a part of it to get to San Jose del Rio.

"Has Juan said anything about medications getting through to the rebels?"

"Nothing."

"Did you ask him?"

"Of course not." I laughed. "He doesn't even know about the medications, and certainly nothing about your suspicions."

Klein grunted. "Find a way to ask him. Keep him close."

"Sure," I said.

"Have you heard *anything* about the medications being smuggled to the rebels?"

"I only know about the medications that we use in the village."

His smile did not change. "What medications?"

"The regular medications for the clinic at Chapila Chica. *La clinica* is part of Father Julio's ministry to the village. It's certainly no secret."

"I know something about it, but I'd like to hear more."

I shrugged. "Well, I bring the meds up to the village every week, with a lot of other supplies. Father Julio keeps a record of all the people who need them, and I take a list of the medications we need and pick them up here in Guatemala City." I decided not to mention the fact that Sofia had accompanied me in the past. "I go to the church dispensary here in Guatemala."

"What dispensary?"

"Actually it's more of a warehouse. I'm going there tomorrow. You can go with me if you want."

"Tell me the name, just for the history books."

I gave him the name. "So I go there every week or so; I give them a list of the medication that Father Julio needs, and they give me the meds. I sign for them and put them in my backpack. Then I take the up the mountain to Chapila Chica. That's all there is to it."

"Who makes the list?"

"Padre Julio, of course."

I smiled and sipped my beer. It was important not to appear flustered. *Slowly,* I thought, *drink slowly.*

"And he gives you the list. Father Julio."

"Can you make me a copy of that list?"

"I suppose."

His smile did not change, but now there was a threatening tone. "Don't you bring the medications up there yourself personally?"

"Of course I bring the meds to Chapila Chica, but there's nothing wrong with that."

There was a pause.

"And I don't like your tone," I said.

I really didn't want to give Klein the list of medications, but I had to tell him something. While I pondered this, there was the sound of a woman yelling in the kitchen at the back, and we both looked up. The cantina's wife was giving the owner hell about something.

I decided to stall.

"Do you know what the Pentecostals in Chapila Grande believe? That just before the end of the world, all the Indians in Guatemala will convert to their church!"

He hesitated a fraction of a second. "Are we even talking about this?"

"I'm just telling you what they believe over in—"

"If you keep this up I'm going to knock you off that bar stool."

I ignored the threat. "A lot of evangelical Christians believe this, and so do the Pentecostals. They believe that the Indians of

Central America are one of the lost tribes of Israel, and that they'll all ditch Catholicism and come over to their side when the millennium arrives. So are you ready for the big event?"

Klein was looking at me incredulously. "I should just fucking kill you right now and get it over with. What the fuck are you asking me a stupid question like that for?"

"I thought you might be a great fan of religion."

"Yeah, and you're clinically, literally, whacko." Klein was shaking his head in exasperation. "Why on earth would anyone want to convert to Pentecostalism? It's not even a particularly attractive religion to begin with: I mean, all that cannibalistic blood-drinking and eating of the flesh, and being washed in the blood of a ram, of a lamb, or whatever the hell animal it is. I'd rather spend eternity as the only woman on a Greek freighter than sign up for that crap."

"There's a church right down the street, man. I can see you're ripe for conversion."

"Screw them, all of them…screw every one of their fucking Catholic and Protestant churches and all of their goddamn blood-fixated crucifixes and holier-than-thou fucking water and creeping Jesus priests and popes and arch-fucking-bishops of Canterbury!"

I was laughing—the guy was really funny. "Testify, bro!"

"Don't go too far, Sutterfield. You might need my help someday."

The hand that held his drink was shaking. I said nothing, and in a moment he continued. "I made up my mind about that fanatical crap a long time ago. All religion is bullshit, pure and simple. It's the same with politics."

"How long have you been aware of this?"

His voice softened. "I remember the exact moment when I realized it was all a hustle. I was twenty-two years old and fresh out of college. I remember the moment like it was yesterday."

"What happened to you?"

"My girlfriend dumped me for a multimillionaire, a goddamn boy wonder in medical research. They're still together, I hear—they have a big house down in Pacific Palisades, and a place in the south of France. She was religious, and I was religious at the time, and we were good together...but she just did what she had to do. I thought I was going to die. And then I said to myself, *Alan, you can either let this one kill you, or you can learn from it.* I decided to learn from it."

Although I thought I already knew, I asked, "What did you learn?"

"I learned that money is power, and power is the most important thing in the world. Everybody wants it. Some people can get it, and some people can't. The people who have it are reasonably happy, and the people who can't are resentful and unhappy." Klein paused. "Sometimes the people who can't get power invent a dream world where they can *pretend* they have power. Religion is one of the ways they do it. It's the same with politics."

"What's wrong with people who only dream about power?"

"They forget what reality is, they lose all their reference points, so when they start acting out their ideals in the real world, other people get hurt."

I immediately thought of Padre Julio. "Give me an example."

"Okay," Klein said. He drank deeply. "I'll give you a goddamn example: my father. He was a political idealist of the first water, a union organizer and a socialist, a local trade-union leader in a CIO union in New York, a guy who believed that the workers of the world could unite and create a new earth free of exploitation and nationalism and racism. And so he worked his goddamn tail off, organizing steel workers and garment workers and all the rest. And what happened? It didn't make the world a better place after all—and anyway all those workers he helped are voting Republican."

"That doesn't make him dangerous."

"Yes, it does. Because he was married to my mother, who had post-polio syndrome, and she needed treatment at a special hospital in Baltimore. But we could never afford to take her there because the workers of the world came first." His voice was amazingly steady and absolutely without emotion, so much that for a moment I wondered if he was making it up. "And that's not all—none of us kids went to a college that was worth a damn. We all had to work our way through state colleges. There was no money for us, because my father was too busy saving the world. People got hurt from all that idealism."

I kept quiet until I realized he wasn't going to say any more. "And you never hurt anyone?"

"Not if I don't have to." Klein finished off his drink. "Anyway, we're not talking about me, are we?"

"Of course we are."

"No, it's about you, pal. Because I hold the good cards."

He looked at me a long time, thinking.

"*Okay,*" he said finally. "It's about *both* of us. That's what this conversation is about—so let me tell you something interesting about you and me. There are a lot of people being killed in Guatemala. Right from the beginning I decided I would try to save your ass. I don't know why, but I did. Don't make me change my mind. Right now, it wouldn't take very goddamn much to make me change my mind." He smiled. "Remember that list of medications that we talked about ten minutes ago, the list that Padre Julio made out for you?"

"Yes."

"Get that fucking list of medications. Right now. Because if you don't, I'll take you up to your room and shoot you through the back of the head. Or I can kill you right here and drag your body out to the street and leave it there. I know the guy who owns this place, and it wouldn't surprise him very much."

"You're not even armed, man."

"I'm always armed."

"What's so important about that list of medications?"

"Get it."

I couldn't stall anymore.

I went up to my room and got the list of mediations, and I brought it back to the bar and copied it on a fresh piece of paper from my spiral notebook and gave the original to Klein.

I didn't even think twice about it. I had decided that handing over the list of mediations couldn't possibly get Sofia Mendez in trouble, or Padre Julio Domingo, or anybody else. On the contrary, by throwing Klein just this kind of useless information every so often, I could protect Chapila Chica more effectively. In any case, I was a little drunk from all the beer I'd been drinking, and I wasn't completely sure Klein wouldn't follow through on his threat and whack me out. He was starting to smile his ugly smile again, the smile I remembered from being on the trail with him, the smile that made him look like he was working himself up to some kind of violence.

This was Guatemala. You weren't allowed to miscalculate that kind of threat.

So I gave up the list of medicines; we continued to drink beer and Klein and I got drunk. He was very nice to me, paying for almost every round. The next day I went around to the various NCOs and warehouses I usually visited, and got the meds and the other supplies for Chapila Chica. I was surprised at how easy giving the med list to Klein had turned out to be. In retrospect, I wondered if signing off on the Faustian pact was like that: you thought of it in bombastic, Wagnerian terms, as something difficult and dramatic and accompanied by a lot of bells and whistles; but instead it turned out to be something very understated, but at the same time incredibly easy, because in the end it was an offer you couldn't refuse.

Sofia Mendez, I had to believe, was blissfully unaware of my dangerous games with Alan Klein, although she was smart enough to guess a great deal. But she had entered another world, and lived exclusively in a fantasy world difficult to imagine by anybody who has not shared his existence with a woman focused on what is politely called "the biological clock." Physically she lived in Chapila Chica; emotionally she was in the world of imminent motherhood, lost in her imaginings of the child that she believed was soon to take up residence in her body. She was in a frenzy of anticipation, so deep into the dream that nothing that did not concern her approaching pregnancy could really get through to her.

In time I found myself entering a dream world similar to hers, although my motives were different. I wanted to forget about Klein, and about the complicated situation in which I found myself, as well as the crazy place Guatemala had become. Luckily, my desire for Sofia had created a separate world—all I had to do to enter it was to be with Sofia, or to think about being with her. Instantly I would be transported to that world she was creating for both of us, a place that ran parallel to the real world and drew from it, but insulated from the real world's emotional pain. Just thinking about Sofia was enough to cause me to detach from everything around me.

Would we have a boy or a girl?

What would it look like?

All of which was crazy, since there was absolutely no evidence yet that Sofia was pregnant or even that she *could* get pregnant. But we were sure that she soon would be, because it was simply something that she knew would happen.

Our nights together had become more than two people having sex; the momentous sexual energy had a life of its own, a life that would live on in the form of the child we were creating, because it would live long after we died. It was more than just her racing heart or mine, or our whispered invocations of passion and the blessing of sexual release.

Given the choice between me and the baby we were creating,

I'm sure Sofia would have sacrificed me a thousand times over if it would have helped our child grow in her belly. Not only did I understand this, I would not have proceeded without it; this love was not about us, it was about something new, a new person coming out of this desperation in the lives of two strangers who had wandered into each other's arms.

But did I love Sofia?

What I loved now were my sexual complexities, which had been plunged into full cry. But because of their intensity, they promised some kind of personal transformation, some remaking of myself that might yet deliver me from myself, and from the world.

But did I *love* Sofia Mendez?

No, not yet, although I wanted to, but she already loved unconditionally the child that we labored to create together—she loved *a child that did not yet exist!* Because of that, I had allowed myself to hope that our child could deliver me from depression and self-absorption, and bring me to love again. So we waited for the arrival of the stranger who would show us, each in our separate ways, how to love in the way we wanted most—Sofia as a first-time parent, I as a crazy but still viable husband. Could we be blamed for hoping that this love child could make us better than we had been before? In the middle of the night we grappled with increasing desperation, dying in long shuddering moments that shook me to my marrow.

Afterward we were born again, brought back by the anticipation of the new life we were conceiving. The moment of completion was not far off; the arrival of the New Earth was at hand. All that was required was the arrival of the child, the True King for whom we longed, the sweet prince who would teach us how to love. Then we would live forever in a world that love alone could make.

However much I despised their religion, I was beginning to be fascinated by the way the Pentecostals of Chapila Grande sang their hymns. The hymn-singing almost invariably began as Sofia and I lay in each other's arms after making love; I often found myself waiting impatiently for it to begin, as we lay silently in the pitch-black schoolhouse at Little Chapila. The singing of the hymns usually came toward the end of the nightly services in Chapila Grande.

But why did I wait so intently to hear them? There in the darkness and silence of the schoolhouse in the night, lying beside Sofia Mendez, lost in our languorous world of post-coital dreaminess, there was nothing so important to me as hearing the distant singing of hymns in Big Chapila.

It made me insanely happy; why, I could not say.

But in the disturbing part was this: the singing made me happy in a way that seemed to complement my lovemaking with Sofia. The hymns seemed to carry with them some commentary on our sexual exertions: a commentary so apposite and so appropriate that it seemed to be meant especially for us.

Sometimes the pitch and volume of the singing would rise and fall as the sounds floated on the night breeze; other times I could barely hear the singing at all, as though it were distant echoes of people in another world. I felt safer and less lonely when the Pentecostals of Big Chapila sang. I had always felt that when people were singing, they were no longer required to deal directly with their most pressing problems; the problems might come later, but not at the moment when people actually *sang*, and certainly not at the moment when the secret sharer happened to hear whatever they were singing.

Magical thinking, I'm sure, but there it was.

Sofia was irritated by my fascination with Chapila Grande and the nightly Pentecostal *liederfest*.

"I can't believe that you find their singing enjoyable," she said as we lay listening after making love. "Do you really like it?"

"Very much."

"It sounds like North American spirituals. The singing of slaves."

"Well, yes, but slaves that want to be free. It moves me deeply. I don't know why, but it does."

Sofia sat up. "Did you know that sometimes they don't even know what they're singing about? That the people of Chapila Grande don't even understand the words of the hymns they've been taught?"

Astonishingly, the people of Chapila Grande had been taught to sing their hymns and gospel tunes in English, an astoundingly insensitive thing to do, by the standards of the Catholic Church and the more liberal mainstream Protestant denominations. But perhaps this Pentecostal gambit was shrewder than it seemed at first glance. Was it possible that the villagers of Chapila Grande saw the singing of hymns in English as the first payment, culturally speaking, on their eventual assimilation into the North American club of wealth and success?

"You're absolutely right about the *quality* of their singing," I said. "It isn't particularly good music. I'm the first to admit that."

"Then why do you like it?"

"I like to hear voices singing in the night. As long as people are singing, you may safely assume that the singers are alive, and aren't murdering their political enemies. The more unprofessional the singing, the more human they sound. And the more human they sound, the more…" I didn't know how to finish the thought. "They more alive they are, I guess."

Sofia was silent in the darkness for a long time.

Finally she asked me silently: "Have you forgotten what is going on in this country? Every day people are being killed and tortured and raped. How can the people of Chapila Grande follow the will of God without trying to do something about it?"

"I agree, but maybe they don't *want* to do anything about it—maybe they *can't*."

She sighed with exasperation. "Then why do they call

themselves Christians?"

"Because they practice a different kind of Christianity. They're waiting for Jesus to return to earth to fix everything."

"What will they do in the meantime?"

"They sing in order to get away from the world, to block it out, to escape from it."

Which was precisely the way I had always used Anglican liturgy, it occurred to me, to abolish the world for a few precious moments, to pretend that it had no power over me.

"I wish they'd go away," Sofia said with sudden vehemence.

"The people of Chapila Grande?"

"Yes. Every last one of them…and if they can't go away, I wish they'd at least stop singing."

I was shocked. "That village has been there forever," I said, "or at least as long as Chapila Chica. The two villages have had a relationship for at least a hundred years. Some people are related to each other by blood."

"The people of Chapila Grande gave up that relationship when they took money from the Americans and joined the California church."

"The American Pentecostals, you mean."

"The Americans from California, with their worship of money and their stupidity."

There was a long pause.

The singing from Chapila Grande began again, rising and falling slightly. They were singing a hymn I remembered from my childhood, a tune I'd heard at family reunions. But they sang it differently from anything I had ever heard.

"Okay," I said, "let's suppose the people of Chapila Grande left the highlands. Where would they go?"

"Let them go to California. That's what they really want, you know—they want to immigrate to California and meet some movie stars, and someday become rich and famous."

"They have just as much right to be here in the highlands as you do. And a hell of a lot more than I do."

"Just three years ago, they were part of us. But now they've been taught by their church to say that we're communists, and to hate us. They've been taught to lie about us to the government...they say we're under the influence of the devil."

"That is nothing but fanaticism, truly. But Chapila Grande is still important to this village."

"Explain that to me, please—why are they important?"

"They know we're here, and we know they're there. And that's why I like to hear the people of Chapila Grande singing in the night." I thought about it. "Why would they be singing if they didn't want somebody to hear them? No, they want somebody to appreciate them, and we're the only people around, so they *must* be singing for us."

She sighed and put her arms around my neck in the darkness, and drew me down onto her breasts. She spoke in precise, richly accented English. "*Chico,* you are a North American—you want everybody to be friends. You want the Guatemalans to be in a Hollywood movie. You want beautiful music in the background."

"Maybe. But you went to school in North America, and you have the same American passion for shortcuts and easy answers—I hate to say it, but in some ways you're a North American too."

She laughed. "*Si, Chico,* but I recovered."

"No. It's like alcoholism, you're always recovering."

We were silent a long moment: two lovers almost out of time, although we couldn't know it.

"I'm simply saying that for better or worse, Chapila Grande and Chapila Chica exist in the same country, and in the same world," I said. "There's a great deal that is wrong with Chapila Grande, but they like to sing, and so far as I can determine there's nothing wrong with *that*." I paused. "Maybe we ought to try singing a little more in Chapila Chica ourselves."

I had been told that Padre Domingo had once played a guitar

at mass, but he was tone-deaf and the experiment had been abandoned.

"All right, maestro, teach us how to sing."

"I will bring the people from Big Chapila here, and *they* will teach Little Chapila how to sing."

She sat up abruptly, our makeshift bed creaking.

"Are you crazy?"

"Yes," I said, "of course I'm crazy—*soy Californiano.*"

"And you, the Messiah from California, will lead us all to a grand reconciliation!"

"All I said was that maybe they could teach us how to sing."

On some level I actually believed that it *might* be possible that Chapila Grande could teach the people of Chapila Chica to sing, so that the two villages could sing together; and by singing together, to get along better.

Despite its commitment to the Kingdom of God, there was something a little grim about Padre Julio's village; something a bit too purposeful, too focused on a future kingdom of peace and justice that never seemed to arrive. Whereas there was something in the wild singing of Chapila Grande that was uncomplicatedly *in the moment*: and that was good, however cowardly and pathological their religion might be. In a strange way the two villages were witnesses to each other—each, in other words, had something the other needed.

But on this night Sofia was not in a mood to hear that.

"You're crazy," was all she would say. "You want this grand reconciliation between Chapila Chica and Chapila Grande just because you like their singing."

"I want to be happy, and there's something about the way they sing that gives me happiness."

Again she spoke in English: "Don't I make you happy, *Chico*?"

"Yes, of course."

"More than the singing at Chapila Grande?"

"Of course. But if the singing at Chapila Grande also makes

me happy, what's wrong with that?"

What Sofia could not see, I thought, was that the two villages were connected whether they liked it or not. Even if Chapila Chica were wiped out tomorrow, and every man, woman and child of us disappeared into a mass grave, the people of Big Chapila would remember us. Their memories of the connected histories of the two villages—even their complaints about our supposed radicalism and our complaints about their craven identification with the government —would witness to the fact that we had both existed side by side.

Furthermore, if the people of Chapila Chica were nice to their sister village, the less likely the people of Chapila Grande were to denounce them to the government.

And so, despite Sofia's growing irritation, I listened for the singing from Chapila Grande in the night; and although on some nights it was so faint that it was hardly more than shadow voices sung by shadows, I always heard it.

But I never heard the villagers of Chapila Grande speaking in tongues. They might have been doing it, but I never heard them. Ultimately, I came to feel that perhaps speaking in tongues was not quite the regular occurrence that Pentecostals claimed it to be—or that perhaps these particular Pentecostals in Chapila Grande suffered from a kind of charisma fatigue, as it were.

If it was a nightly event, why couldn't I hear it?

And if they weren't speaking in tongues every night, what was stopping them?

One night, after Sofia and I had made love and were still in that drowsy state of sweet somnolence that comes after lovemaking, I found myself suddenly restless.

My mind was elsewhere, and Sofia sensed it. "What is it?"

"I'm listening."

At just that moment the singing at Chapila Grande began.

Sofia cursed softly. "I wish I could stop them. They invade our privacy."

"It's just something they do. Don't be jealous."

"I hate them."

Tonight there was the voice of a woman that I had heard only a few times before. Her singing was harsh and utterly without nuance, a brassy alto voice punching out harmonies to the melody in hard metallic thirds like a metal press, but oddly beautiful.

"I want to go over and talk to them," I said.

"That's dangerous."

Without thinking I said, "I'll go with Alan Klein. He knows the people over there."

What made me say this, I will never know. Sofia's breathing stopped, then started again.

She raised up on one elbow.

"Who?"

"Alan Klein, the North American who came up here to talk to Padre Julio about the *patrulla de autodefensa*. He ate lunch with us. He had a big goofy smile and acted like a buffoon."

Sofia said nothing, but it was incomprehensible that she did not remember Klein. There were not that many people who came to visit us in this tiny village.

"Yes, I remember him," she said finally.

"A classic doofus," I said. I felt more comfortable speaking in English when talking about Klein. "He has something to do with the *patrulla*—I think he talked to Padre Julio about it."

"What did you say to this man Klein?"

"Nothing. Really, nothing."

"Did he ask anything about Chapila Chica?"

"No, actually he didn't. I thought he would, but he didn't."

I babbled on a bit, pretending that I did not notice her silence.

I could feel the fear coming off her. There was an actual smell of fear, a certain body odor. "Why is it so important to know what I said to Alan Klein?"

"The man is a government spy."

I chose my words carefully. "Of course I assumed that," I said, "so for precisely that reason I was very careful. I didn't say anything about you or this village—I mentioned nothing that Klein wouldn't already know."

"Nothing?"

"Nothing."

"But he is a spy. He could make things up."

"Maybe," I said, "but if that is so, maybe it's a very good thing that he likes me so much—he has a very good impression of me. We might be able to use that in the future."

"What did you talk about when you went out on the trail?"

"Religion."

She was incredulous. "Religion? What on earth did you say?"

"I said that all people of faith are trying to serve God in their own way, and that it was terrible that both Chapila Chica and Chapila Grande live in perpetual hostility. I suggested that Big Chapila should have regular communication with Little Chapila, through Padre Julio, of course—but that the two villages needed each other, and we should refrain from doing anything that would add to the animosity that's already there."

Sophia flopped backward and went limp. I gradually became aware that she was cursing at me under her breath. It was the first time I had ever heard her curse in that way; she was cursing not to discharge anger or make a point, but by way of asking God to punish an offender.

I could feel her trying to get control of herself. I held her and stroked her hair.

She did not resist.

After a few moments she stopped cursing. She let her head fall against my chest, and lay very quietly for a long time.

Then she began to laugh.

It was laughter that came from deep within and caused her to shake convulsively. It was the laughter of someone who had learned to laugh without making noise. "Yes, you will save us, *Chico. El Californiano* will save us! You will bring us together!" The fear was still there, but it had become part of her laughter. "*El Californiano* will save us! He will reconcile us!"

"How do you know I don't have the power to raise the dead as well?"

"Shut up!"

Her laughter was choking her.

"Take it easy, Sofia."

Her laughter was so intense and she was working so hard to suppress it that she was asphyxiating. "You will make us all stop fighting! Of course! Don Maitland de la Mancha!"

"Okay."

"You will make us see how wrong it is!"

She was still laughing. Her breath was very short. Her laughter made no sound, but her body shook with it. From deep inside came a wheezing sound.

"Inocente!" She gasped, fighting for breath.

She was laughing so hard I was afraid she was dying. She couldn't stop her body from shaking. The laughter—or crying, or whatever—had become hysterical. So I did what one is supposed to do in a situation like this.

I held her tightly until the storm passed.

And then we slept.

From that moment on Sofia was convinced that we were both going to die. Strangely, that did not alter her obsession concerning the child that we would have. On the contrary, it made the obsession stronger and more resistant to logic. Sofia could not stop talking openly about children and the challenges of parenthood with the women in the village; and they gathered about her every morning to hear what she had to say and to give her their opinions.

I asked Sofia what she would like our child to be like. Her

answers shocked me.

To begin with, our child would have to be a *son*. That was very important to Sofia, this brave Madonna of liberation theology who was willing to risk her life for economic justice in the Guatemalan highlands. Daughters were okay, but let's face it, this might be her only child, and it was important to have at least one son—that is more or less what she told me.

And she wanted a son who was *white*, white enough that he would never be mistaken for an Indian, white enough not only to be a Ladino, but even a North American. Although from the Ladino class herself, she had often been mistaken for an Indian because of her dark skin.

"Aren't you proud of your own color?" I asked her once in the middle of the night. "I mean, your beautiful dark complexion?"

"You know *nothing* about this," she half-whispered, half-hissed in the darkness. She spoke in rapid-fire Spanish mixed with Kekchi and English. "I was the darkest sister in my family…and all of my other sisters had *novios*, men who wanted to marry them. But I never did; nobody wanted me. I was too dark, especially when they saw my sisters—they weren't as dark as I was." She let that sink in. "My father warned me that I would have trouble finding a husband. Nobody wants a woman who is as dark as I am. That was why my father told me to take orders in the church."

"*I* want you. *I* find you desirable, incredibly so. And your complexion is one of the most attractive things about you."

"You're from North America. You don't know any better."

Sofia had noticed people in her own extended family—her male cousins in particular—looking at her as though she were a kind of wraith, or a ghost, a woman of the living dead; and she had heard the cruel whispers about her dark skin. It was as though she were an uncanny reminder of what the family had been before they had become a land-owning family of Ladinos: a guilty reminder of the Mayan blood that ran in every

Guatemalan's veins, a reminder of the Indians who worked and died in the coffee fields that gave the Ladino families their wealth.

And by entering her body, by putting my seed there, I had wandered into this pain-freighted part of her life. Already the color of our baby's skin was an issue, and it hadn't even been conceived.

I hadn't cared about skin color before, but now I *had* to care, because the woman who wanted to conceive my child cared so much about it. She had been hurt by it, wounded by this thing called white skin, and now perhaps we would both be wounded by it. It reminded me again of how little control I had over anything, especially the things I cared most about, especially here in this violent and bitterly divided world, where my own flesh and blood could only be conceived in the contested skin of a civil war.

Chapter Six

Each week brought new reports of disappearances, killings, and massacres of entire villages. Some things were so traumatizing that people refused to talk about them. The rebels won a few victories here and there, usually by ambush; but the government was more interested in destroying villages they thought might support the rebels than in engaging them directly. Throughout the months I lived in the village of Chapila Chica, the Guatemalan army and security services were active in the highlands. It seemed as though Guatemala had fallen into a primal state of sin and death, from which it could be delivered only by more death.

The person most at risk in Chapila Chica was Juan Delmonico. He was in charge of the *patrulla*, the self-defense patrol set up by the army that was supposed to defend the village from attack by Marxist rebels. But of course it wasn't just for self-defense, as far as the army was concerned—they wanted him to go out at night in search of the enemy. They wanted him to set up ambushes, question peasants, and deal summarily with people he thought disloyal to the government.

They wanted a body count.

Failing that, they wanted names of rebel collaborations in the area. For several weeks the lieutenant who had trained the *patrulla* had been insisting that Juan give him a list of people in the area who were thought to be sympathetic to the rebels. Juan had resisted this—there *were* no rebel collaborators, he told them, at least none that he knew about.

Juan told us the whole story at a meeting of the *comunidad de base*, and in the flickering candlelight we prayed for him.

His wife Tani wept.

We were especially nice to Juan Delmonico, once we realized the pressures he was facing. At the *comunidad de base* meetings we deferred to him when he spoke; we stepped aside when we met him or his wife on the path; the woman let Tani collect water first at the spring. We treated Juan like a king who walked among us, and his wife like a queen—two immortals who had fallen unexpectedly to earth and were doing their best to live among us.

We treated Juan Delmonico like a king because he held the safety of the village in his hands.

Sofia was in Guatemala City when Juan spoke at the meeting of the *comunidad de base*. The next morning I went to see Padre Julio. He was busy organizing his primitive system of medical charts and preparing for mass at San Jose del Rio, the market town. I stood in the door of his office while he finished his task.

"I know why you're here," he said.

I said nothing while he finished his task.

After a moment he said, "It's about Juan, right?"

"Yes."

Padre Julio sat down wearily behind his desk, folding his arms on the large plastic panel on the top. He looked like a man who needed a long vacation.

"You have to do something," I said. "You know what the Guatemalan army is. You know how they work."

"Yes, yes."

"Then you must be concerned about Juan."

"Of course I'm concerned about him—he's one of my best catechists."

"Is that the only reason you're concerned about him?"

"I am concerned about Juan because he is a good man, and a man of great faith."

There was a long silence.

"Can't we do something that would make the army lose interest in Chapila Chica?" I asked. "Can't we make them look the other way?"

"I don't think we have any control over that."

"Maybe Juan could tell them that there were rebels around here once, but that they left—that they went to the western highlands."

Padre Julio sighed. "Then the army will want names of people who supported the rebels while they were still operating here."

"Couldn't Juan make up some names?"

"If the army thought the names were bogus, they'd torture him just to make sure. And then they'd kill him."

We sat in silence for a long time.

"There must be *something* we can do," I said.

There was another pause. And then he shrugged.

"Well," he said, "there is one thing..."

"Yes?"

He took some cigarettes out of a drawer.

"Wait a minute," he said.

Padre Julio was one of those Europeans who could smoke the occasional cigarette and not become addicted. He lit the cigarette with a monstrous lighter that he kept in the bottom drawer of his desk. It looked like one of the cigarette lighters that people once won at county fairs in the US. He had to hold it with both hands to make it work.

He inhaled deeply, then exhaled.

"We can't protect Juan," he said, "so he should leave Chapila Chica."

I was glad he was going to be sensible about it. "Absolutely. In fact, he should probably leave the country, don't you think?"

Padre Julio sighed. "Yes, probably."

"There may be another way, but I can't think of it."

"Yes," Padre Julio said, still nodding. "But there's a problem."

"What?"

"He has to *agree* to leave."

"What are you talking about? Of course he'll go—his life is in danger!"

"He doesn't want to leave Chapila Chica."

I was flabbergasted. "You've discussed this with him?"

"Repeatedly. He won't leave. He says he'll never leave."

"Impossible."

Julio sat there looking at me. "Why don't you talk to him?"

"That's crazy. I hardly know him. What would I say?"

Padre Julio took another drag from his cigarette.

A kind of opaqueness had settled over his face, which made it very difficult to tell what he was thinking.

"Tell him you'll take him to the United States with you. Tell him you'll take him to California and help him open a small business. A grocery store, something like that."

I was speechless for several moments. I couldn't believe what I was hearing.

"Are you joking?"

"Tell him there are many people from Guatemala living in California now."

"Really, I'm curious. Are you joking or not?"

But Padre Julio remained silent. I couldn't read his face.

Despite Juan Delmonico's dark and oddly handsome face, my memories of Juan's wife Tani are even more vivid. She was short and squat and had a bad leg, but she also had beautiful eyes, even more beautiful that her husband's. She opposed the self-defense patrol and did not want Juan to be the comandante of it; yet in the event, she accepted it without complaint. In the face of so many powerful forces in the world, she had learned patience.

Once, for example, I'd gone to the village spring to get water, when our pump in the courtyard of Chapila Chica temporarily went dry. I was deputized by Padre Julio to go to the spring and get water in two buckets. Once I got there, I found that the spring was also dry.

Tani was there, waiting.

Not praying, not sleeping, but waiting with the completely focused attention of the Mayan woman at the height of her powers.

I flew into a frenzy of North American purposefulness, insisting that Tani immediately start digging at the spring. I even found a rusty implement nearby, with which I wanted her to dig down to where I thought the water might be. In the meantime, I explained excitedly, I would walk to Chapila Grande to check out their water supply there.

"Come on!" I said. "We can do this!"

I explained it all to her, how we would organize ourselves to handle the crisis of the dry spring.

She sat there, looking at me.

"What are you *waiting* for?" I yelled.

Why was she not rushing to do everything we had to do?

"Get busy!" I commanded. *"Hagala! Hagala ahoramismo!"*

And she laughed a bit shyly, not unkindly.

So I gave up.

And waited with her.

Silently, to maximize my concentration on waiting, because waiting is serious work, involving both physical passivity and boundless faith. In two hours the spring bubbled up and we filled our buckets. She filled hers, and I filled mine.

We waited for the water, and it came.

I have often thought of that afternoon by the spring, when Tani showed me the meaning of her life. She did it all without words. Her life was all about waiting—that was what she showed me. It was not my life, not my meaning, nor would I want it to be; I have no idea whether she was happy or not. But to be shown what a person really is, and to be there with them while they act on it, is a rare privilege.

A few days after the incident at the spring, I ran into Juan Delmonico on the trail that led north to Trotzil Gapachula mountain. I'd just delivered meds to an old man living in a primitive lean-to on the mountain and was returning to Chapila

Chica.

Juan was on a cutoff path that few people used. He seemed surprised to see me but came back to the main path and stood waiting, taking me in with his flat haunted eyes.

"I'm going to the Dog Woman's house," Juan said.

The Dog Woman was a psychotic woman who had suffered from mental illness for many years. I could not imagine what kind of a relationship Juan had with her. "This is not a friendly person," I said. "She may not want to see you."

"We'll see."

"Do you know how to get there?"

"Yes, it's near the little cave on the way to Tzotzil Gapachula mountain, before the fork in the path to the village of Las Espantulas. I've been there before. I have some medications for her from Padre Julio."

I was a little miffed—I had been delivering medications for Julio for months. Why hadn't he asked me to make this delivery?

"I wasn't aware that the Dog Woman took medications."

"She is crazy," Juan was saying matter-of-factly, "so usually she is not able to be friendly. Some days she thinks she's a dog. Other days she believes the devil lives in the big cave at the top of Tzotzil Gapachula mountain, and she stands at the mouth of the cave all day, talking to the devil. On the days when she thinks she's a dog, she is very dangerous."

"Why is she dangerous then?"

He made a little biting motion with his hand. "She bites. So you have to be careful that she does not bite you."

"But she has not bitten you?"

"Not yet."

"How long have you taken these medications to her?"

"I go there often. Perhaps the medication helps her."

For whatever reason, he didn't want to tell me how long he had been delivering medications to her. We were silent for a moment. We were on the trail, but standing in the shade of two large trees.

"Juan," I said, "you must leave Chapila Chica. Padre Julio says you are in danger."

"Chapila Chica is my home."

"You must leave, at least for awhile. You can take Tani with you. Padre Julio can find a place for you to go. He can help you."

He stood looking at me, unsmiling but oddly sympathetic to my confusion.

"Do you want to die?" I asked. "Do you want to Tani to die?"

"I'm ready to die."

"Nobody is ever ready, even if you think you are."

"We have no children." He shrugged. "In one night our children died of a fever. We buried them ourselves. My wife cannot have any more children."

"But you can't simply throw your life away—"

"If the army kills me, maybe they will leave everybody else in Chapila Chica alone."

One heard things like this in Guatemala. I couldn't think of a good reply, which hurt me just as much as the words themselves.

So I let the silence go on.

"Do you still have the weapons for the *patrulla* at your house?" I asked finally.

"Padre Julio told us not to tell anybody where they are."

Clearly it was time to part. I embraced him clumsily.

I stood looking at him, and he didn't turn to leave either.

"You have to leave the village," I said. "Please. Please think about it."

"I want to be buried here."

"I'll take you to California. I'll help you open a business. A small store, perhaps."

He stood looking at me. *"Verdad?"*

"De veras."

He continued to look at me. A smile appeared slowly on his face. "No. Padre Julio told you to say this."

I said nothing.

"Padre Julio told you to say this," Juan said again.

"Why not do it? Come with me to California!"

"My children died here. My mother and my stepmother and my father died here."

I knew he wouldn't leave Chapila Chica. Like me he had a death wish, though a different kind.

"Nos vemos, entonces," I said.

"Nos vemos."

I felt as though there was something more I ought to do or say, but couldn't think of anything.

"Then go with God," I said.

"Then may He go with you, too."

The next time I met with Alan Klein in Guatemala City, I went out of my way to mention Juan Delmonico. I was still upset about Klein's apparent disdain for Juan, and I was anxious to say good things about him. Klein and I were sitting in the cantina. The sun was blazing outside and we were drinking beer directly from the bottle, as we usually did.

"I heard something rather interesting about Juan Delmonico," I said. "Actually, I heard it from Juan himself."

Klein stifled a yawn. "You don't say."

"Try to control you enthusiasm."

"I'll try. How hard, I cannot say."

Klein's stupidity offended me. "Juan Delmonico is absolutely vital to the success of your project, yet you have no interest in him. That makes no sense."

Klein impatiently rubbed his eyes. He looked hung over. "What the fuck are you talking about?"

"You helped to organize a paramilitary organization, a civil self-defense patrol, in a small Guatemalan village. Yet you show no interest in the man who has been chosen to lead the patrol."

"Why should I be interested in Juan Delmonico?"

"He's in charge of the patrol, for God's sake!"

"He's an Indian peasant. They're all alike. He'll do whatever we tell him to do."

"No, you're wrong." I felt my anger mounting, as it always did when I encountered this kind of prejudice. "He's a human being, and you have to motivate him, just like you would anybody else."

"You're a baby, Sutterfield. You have no idea. These people have no ability to think for themselves. They simply can't do it—the idea of initiative, of taking responsibility for something, is something they just don't grasp. They don't get it and they probably never will."

"That's not true."

Klein sleepily confronted me. "Then why hasn't Juan Delmonico made more effort to engage the enemy?"

"Maybe there isn't any enemy. And maybe he thinks there are better ways to win the hearts and minds of the people."

"Get them by the balls, and their hearts and minds will follow."

"That didn't work in Vietnam, and it won't work here."

"Really?" Klein shrugged. "Okay. Give me a concrete example of a better way to win the people's hearts and minds."

"Of course I can." I told him about the medication Juan Delmonico had taken to the Dog Woman of Tzotzil Gapachula mountain. "It was something that Juan Delmonico was in no way obligated to do. He volunteered to take the medications to this pathetic madwoman because she needed it, even though she has a history of assaulting people."

"What medications?"

"I have no idea. But I suspect that it might be psychotropic medication for mental illness."

Klein's eyebrows went up. "Is Father Julio practicing psychiatry these days?"

"I know it sounds crazy." I gave him a brief history of the Dog

Woman, of her fits and delusions, and her physical attacks on passersby. "I have no firsthand knowledge of what kind of medication it was, and for all I know it might be for some physical problem. But given the fact that she's violent, it might be Thorazine, or something like that—some kind of psychiatric medication that might calm her down when she's psychotic."

Klein had been watching me with great interest. "Thorazine, huh?" He laughed. "I know a general or two who could use some of that."

The idea of a Guatemalan general taking Thorazine was amusing, but oddly enough I had heard stories of a general who *did* take it. I had a distinctly uneasy feeling about the conversation we were having. I felt manipulated, but couldn't say how.

"Well," I said, "I can't speak for Juan. But why do you hate him so much? You need him to make the *patrulla* a success."

"Maybe."

"Assuming you want your project to succeed."

"Nobody is persecuting Juan. Being the comandante of the civil self-defense patrol gives him status in Chapila Chica."

"Then why do you think so poorly of a man upon whom the success of the project depends?"

"I'm better off knowing his limitations."

"What limitations?"

"I've said it before, and I'll say it again: Juan Delmonico is purely and simply a dumb Indian peasant. I've been around too many of these people to have any illusions about them."

Now I was really angry.

"I can't believe you, Klein—you pick a guy for a job like this, yet you refuse to trust him. Your bigotry and your elitism make you so blind you can't even recognize your own interests!"

Klein turned sharply to face me. "Who says I picked him?"

"Of course you did. This is your project."

He looked at me for a long time, as though looking at a slightly impaired child. He was not even slightly amused. "I didn't pick Juan Delmonico," Klein said, "the village picked him. But I heard he volunteered first."

"After talking with Father Julio about it."

Klein looked away. "For whatever that's worth," he muttered.

Klein had clearly been drinking for hours before he even arrived in the cantina. Now he took up a theme I had not heard before. We were whores, he maintained, each in our separate ways we had both been corrupted—but I could see only his corruption, and not my own.

Naturally, I labored mightily to disagree.

"The difference between you and me is that I *care* about the people of Chapila Chica," I insisted. "That might seem stupid to you, but it's true. They aren't Marxist guerrillas. They're ordinary people. They just want a better life for themselves and their kids."

Klein was doing his best to match me beer for beer, but he'd been at it longer. Oddly, that seemed to give him an advantage.

"Why are you saying this?" Klein asked. "Do you want to sound good to yourself?"

"I don't want the people of Chapila Chica to get hurt."

"Why would I hurt them?"

"I'm not saying that you *would* hurt them."

Klein seemed to think of something: "Well, what if I did?"

"You damn well better hadn't."

"What if I woke up one morning and decided for some reason that I just wanted to fuck with the people of Chapila Chica?"

"Your job is to protect them."

"What if I had to destroy the village in order to save it?"

Clearly Klein was testing me—everything he said was a test. So now, I thought, I had to up the ante.

"Well," I said, "I guess I'd have to blow your cover."

"Cover? What cover?"

"I'd have to tell the world that you're an American advisor to the Guatemalan army, in direct violation of the directives of the United States Congress."

He must have long ago considered the possibility that I would threaten him in this way because he was ready.

"You do that." He put on his nicest smile. "You tell the world what I'm doing here. And I'll tell the world what *you're* doing. Here you are, a supposedly reputable journalist, writing reports for a case officer of a major intelligence agency." He paused. "I can make sure that the whole juicy story gets into one of the newsweeklies back in the USA. *That* story would appear in print, believe me. It would be a hell of a lot more interesting—*and* more newsworthy— than the boring crap you've been giving me." He stood up. "And once the American media become aware of what you've been doing here, you couldn't get hired on the Weekly Fucking Shopping News of Peoria, Illinois. You'll look like the most disgusting, two-timing snake in the world. Think about it—a journalist who uses his position to spy on his friends! What newspaper would want such a person working for them?"

He got up and went to the door. He stood in the doorway grinning.

"What do you think your friends in Chapila Chica will think of you after they find out you're been writing reports about them for Alan Klein? What will Padre Julio think? And Sofia Mendez?"

He took a pair of dark glasses out of his shirt pocket, put them on, strode back and stood next to me at the bar.

"After the first story appears in *Newsweek*, you'll look like the most worthless piece of shit that ever walked the earth. The radicals on the campuses will hold you up as a prime example of imperialism—a spy posing as a journalist! The liberals will piss and moan about intelligence agencies using journalism as cover. The conservatives will dismiss you as an embarrassment. You'll be seen as an opportunist who would sell his mother for a byline." He paused. "And you know what? I'm not so sure they'd be far wrong."

Klein stood there grinning. With his dark glasses and nasty grin he looked like a grotesque from the depths of some North

American nightmare.

I needed time to think. A long moment passed.

"So," he said, "I will absolutely fucking see you here again."

I stood up—and almost fell down. I wanted to walk out the door of the cantina, but the heat and the light outside was blinding. My drunkenness had suddenly caught up with me.

I learned against the bar.

"The next time you come to Guatemala City," Klein said, "you *will* fucking call me on the telephone and tell me when to meet you."

"Okay," I said.

"And after you call me, you will wait here in this cantina for me, like the self-absorbed, fruity little lapdog that you are. And you *will* give me another written report. And when I tell you to roll over, you will absolutely roll over." He smiled, not unkindly. "I mean that in the nice sense, of course." The smile faded. "Well, sport, what's it going to be?"

I couldn't let him leave thinking I was a loose cannon. That would be dangerous for all concerned.

"Sure 'nuff," I said.

He paused.

"I didn't quite hear you," he said.

"Sure," I said, louder.

"Sure, what?"

"I'm sure that I'll meet you here, any time you say. And I will write what you want me to write."

He walked slowly to the door of the cantina; this time he looked down the street a long time, then back at me. He wasn't as drunk as before. "Looks like we both have a fair amount of shit on each other," he said gently.

"Yes, it does."

To my astonishment he walked over and put his hand on my shoulder. He was smiling at me in a friendly, even solicitous way. It was the first time he had ever done anything like that.

He raised his dark glasses to make eye contact.

"Bygones?" he asked.

"Bygones."

"Mutual respect?"

"Looks more like some kind of stalemate. But maybe that's the same thing."

Klein nodded enthusiastically. "Right. Right. It's absolutely the same thing." He put his glasses on again. "You're okay, Maitland Sutterfield. A little tight-assed, but okay. When people have a stalemate, it is absolutely amazing the ways they can help each other. You wanna be somebody's best friend? All you gotta do is keep your mouth shut. You see? And they can do the same for you. It's a damn good system."

"Is it?"

He turned to go. "Whatever else you say about it, you have to admit it's been around a long time."

A week later I took the bus back to Guatemala City, checked in late in the evening at my little hotel, and rang up the number that I usually called when I wanted to contact Klein. The voice on the message machine was different from the one I usually heard—it was a man's voice, but in a lower register. I left the usual messages, ate a later dinner, and went back to my hotel to wait.

The next day I received no call from Alan Klein, nor did he come directly to the hotel without phoning, as he had sometimes done before. I went out to eat breakfast, returning with US newsweeklies in English. Most of the morning I spent reading and resting in my room.

Still no call from Klein.

Around noon of the second day I called to tell Klein that I had already waited a day and a half for him, and that I planned to leave the next morning. I was feeling vaguely apprehensive and wondered if Klein might have come while I was out. The rest of the day I spent getting meds for Chapila Chica.

That evening, a strange, enveloping sleepiness began to descend upon me, a kind of disorienting fog that abolished thought and feeling. I tried to sleep, but I began to miss Sofia terribly—whenever I drifted off I dreamt only of her, and of making love to her.

I should have been releasing my seed into Sofia's body, I thought, instead of the winding shroud of my gray bedsheets in this cheap heartbreak hotel; but I couldn't stop my juices, they were too hot to stay inside my body. It was as though I was losing Sofia, and could only save her by thinking in endless intimate detail about all the things we did in the middle of the night.

Why was it so important of keep Sofia in mind? Was she in danger? Why was Alan Klein standing me up? Would he ever see me again? Or was he finished with me?

If so, was that good or bad for Sofia and myself?

The morning of the third day I gave up—clearly Klein wasn't going to contact me. I felt frazzled and rejected. I was ready, very ready, to go back to Chapila Chica, where Sofia was even now waiting for me. It was as if Alan Klein was something I had invented to amuse myself, a figment of my imagination, a false memory induced by Guatemala and its atmosphere of danger and intrigue.

Perhaps he was away, out of town, gone on some important business, and would return in a week or two.

If Klein was dead, I wouldn't be sorry, but I'd miss him.

Whatever it was, I suddenly wanted only to be with Sofia, and with the people of Chapila Chica.

I awoke early on that third day. I didn't even try to call Alan Klein—three recorded messages were enough; more than that, and I would start to sound even more pathetic than I already was. Instead I made my way to the place where I would catch my bus to the highlands. The medications for Chapila Chica were stuffed into my backpack, and as soon as the driver let me onto the bus I wedged them securely under my seat. The sun still hadn't risen when we pulled out of Guatemala City.

I drifted into the half-dreaming state into which I usually fell when riding the bus, and instantly my mind was filled with images and thoughts of Sofia. I dreamed of being close to her in total darkness, and the baked-bread smell of her hair and her body; I dreamed of her silent choking laughter in the middle of the night, the way she had of laughing without making noise.

"Inocente," she called.

A judgment on me, but a true one.

"Don Quixote de California thanks you very much," I would say to her, or some such pretentious thing. I think she had not been around that many men that she could tease, men who would laugh with her when she poked fun at them, and she particularly liked that.

And then the laughter would come. I would feel her shaking, swallowing her laughter so that no one could hear, but her body shaking nonetheless.

I wanted her so badly, I could hardly wait.

When I got off the bus, the sun was already in its early-afternoon place in the sky. I was parched with thirst—at the rest stop the little *tienda* had been closed, and I'd drunk only one bottle of beer all day. I started up the trail, my legs stiff with the bus journey.

Then something caught my eye.

There was someone coming toward me on the trail. All I could tell was that it was a woman. She was a good three hundred yards away, and she bobbed as she ran: up, down, up, down.

It was Tani, Juan Delmonico's wife.

It wasn't a good thing for her to run, with her bad leg. The very fact that she was running bespoke a crisis.

She was reaching out to me from far away, as though I could help her keep her balance. She ran with a rolling gait, and I was afraid she would fall—too fast, too fast! She had apparently seen me and was intent upon reaching me, but her bad leg was keeping her from making good time.

I started running in her direction.

She was yelling as she ran toward me, but I couldn't hear her words clearly. She was still too far away and she couldn't catch her breath. It was as though she was articulating words with her mouth, but without enough force from her lungs to animate the vocal cords. Her hands were still reaching out to me.

I looked away for a moment, and when I looked up again she was out of sight. The path dipped down into a gorge, and I was on a level patch on the other side of the gorge. I could still hear her voice, however, or thought I could.

I thought I heard her voice.

I'm coming, I shouted.

I tried to run faster, but my lungs were still adjusting to the altitude, and in a moment I began to wheeze. Oxygen couldn't get to my brain, and I started to feel light-headed.

Then she came back in sight. She was less than a hundred yards or so up the path. I found myself involuntarily stopping to catch my breath. After some seconds I started walking toward her. I didn't really want to run anymore—for one thing, I was afraid of what she was going to tell me. At the same time, I was curious.

Now I thought I could make out what she was saying. It was something about the soldiers.

I noticed how her round body jiggled; it was cruel that she had to run with her bad leg. I had not noticed before how I plump she was. She was breathing hard.

"Soldados!"

At last she stood in front of me, trying to get her breath. I stood there also trying to get my breath. *"Ellos…"* she said.

She struggled to breath.

"Despacio!" I said. "Slowly"

"Los soldados…"

"Who?"

"The army! *El ejercito*!"

When she caught her breath she was finally able to tell me. About twenty infantry soldiers had arrived at her cabin earlier in the day and formed a perimeter around the house. A single man—clearly an officer—had entered the house wearing a ski mask. He spoke to Juan directly, ordering him to follow him. One of the soldiers tied Juan's thumbs together behind his back with wet leather.

"Do you have any idea who the officer was?"

"It was the lieutenant."

"What lieutenant?"

"The one who has been training Juan. The one who first brought the weapons to our house."

"How do you know it was him?

"Juan called him *teniente*."

She was surprisingly calm, but tears streaked her face. I wondered what she said had said when the soldiers took Juan away.

I was surprised they had not taken her also.

"Did they say where they were going with him?"

"*Zona viente base ejercita.* Zone Twenty army base."

We stood looking at each other. I had the thought most likely to occur to anyone in Guatemala in such a situation: *Is it possible that he's still alive?*

"Don't worry," I heard myself saying. *"No te molesta"*

"What can we do?"

A plan began to form itself in the back of my mind. "We'll get him."

"How can we do this?"

"I'm not sure. But I'll do whatever I have to."

She let out a wracking, muffled sob.

She took my hand; and then, as I watched incredulously, she fell slowly to her knees and took my hands in hers.

And she kissed my hands.

There, in the middle of the trail from the main highway to Chapila Chica, Juan Delmonico's wife knelt in the dust, took my hands in hers, and tearfully kissed them. Her damp salt tears burned into my skin. No one had ever done anything even remotely like that before in my life.

I was completely overwhelmed, and so far I had done exactly nothing for her except offer encouragement.

"Tani—" I began.

"Ayudame," she begged, her eyes wide.

Her mouth opened and shut. Her rough lips were still burning kisses onto my hands.

"Ayudame," she kept saying. "Help me."

And I was, I was going to help her, I had to.

"Voy a ayudarte!" I whispered.

Already I had a plan.

I would go to the Zone Twenty army base, and I would personally find out if Juan Delmonico was there. And if he was there, I would stop the soldiers from torturing and killing him. It was the very essence of simplicity, this plan.

And I knew it would work.

It had the one ingredient necessary to make such a plan work in Guatemala at this time: I was willing to die to make it work.

"I'll save him," I heard myself saying. "I'll save him even if they kill me. I'll talk to the soldiers. They'll listen to me."

They would listen to me because I was a white North America who was ready to die.

Today.

That kind of insane fearlessness gives one a particular and impressive strength, and I knew the soldiers would see it. They would see it and respect it. This was what all my dreams and fantasies about Guatemala had been leading up to. Had I not come to Guatemala to die? And was this not at last my opportunity to use that death wish to save a good man's life?

"Do you know the name of the lieutenant who arrested Juan?"

I did not recognize my voice. I was shouting.

"No," she said.

"When did it happen?"

"An hour ago, or a little more."

"Does Father Julio know this?"

"No," she said.

I handed her my backpack. "Go tell him what happened. Go tell him now. Go now! *Que vaya!*"

She hesitated, then turned and started up the path.

I yelled after her, "Tell Father Julio that Juan is at the Zone Twenty army base. And tell him that I've gone to there to find him, and that I'll stop the soldiers from hurting him."

I turned and started running down the trail toward the road.

Chapter Seven

I made my way back to the main road, and vaguely remember standing in the road and flagging down a large truck. I told the startled driver that I had to go immediately to the Zone Twenty army base, because I had extremely important government business there. Later, I hitched a ride in an empty army lorry driven by sullen-looking soldiers who wordlessly motioned me into the back, slowing down just long enough for me to jump out when they turned off the main road. I also remember riding in an old car with a disreputable-looking man in soiled clothes who did not once look at me, or even in my direction.

There was something in my demeanor—a certain wildness around the eyes, let us say—that made people wary. Guatemala was a dangerous place, but nonetheless people picked me up and for the most part left me alone. They took me silently into their cars and trucks, for whatever unspoken reasons, and allowed me to accompany them wordlessly on their journeys.

I told everybody who gave me a ride that I was headed for the regional army base. People were momentarily startled and then frightened; most of them looked away, glancing surreptitiously in my direction from time to time. Probably they were thinking something like this: *Does this man really have business at an army base? Is he crazy? Is he a spy? What could he possibly be thinking?* I was that most unknowable of all beings, a deeply tanned but irrevocably white North American who spoke Spanish and was hitchhiking alone on a mountain road.

People treated me gingerly, with the courtesy due the stranger, but also with the fear reserved for the unknown and unpredictable. No doubt the people who picked me up were as frightened of me as I should have been of them.

The last ride I got was from a man driving a Renault van. This vehicle was unbelievably ancient: at thirty miles an hour, which was apparently its top speed, it exuded the metallic clanking of a tank going into battle. When I told the driver of the van that I was going to the Zone Twenty army base, he told me that he was actually employed at the base himself; he said it was only a few miles away, and that he could give me a ride to the front gate. Soon he turned off the main road, and we passed some signs announcing the army base.

Most of the time, the driver told me, he worked as a carpenter and mechanic at the base. Before I could think of some clever way to extract information from him, he began to ask questions about *me.* When I told him I was from California, he asked me if I knew any movie stars. When I said I didn't, he was silent for several minutes.

"We are almost at the army base," he said apologetically.

"I appreciate your help."

Then he said with great formality, "Before we part I must ask you a question. Please do not be offended."

"I won't be."

"You must promise me," he insisted.

I promised him that I wouldn't be offended, no matter what.

Then he asked the question that was eating at him, "Are you a *turista,* a missionary, or a hippie?"

Because I could not fit comfortably into any of those categories, I thought about telling him that I was a journalist or a writer. But I was wary of startling him, or perhaps arousing some latent prejudice against literary types.

"None of those things," I said.

"Ni modo?"

"Ni modo. Lo siento."

He shrugged and nodded abruptly.

About a quarter of a mile away from the front gate of the Zone Twenty army base, he stopped and leaned across and opened the passenger-side door of his car. He did not look at me, but it was clearly time for me to depart.

"Mucho gusto," he said.

"Igualmente."

I got out, and he slowly drove away.

He stopped at the gate to the army base. There were two guardhouses, one on either side. I watched while the soldiers at the guardhouses waved him through.

It took me a few minutes to walk to the gate.

It should have been dark by then, but I remember it as a kind of twilight—late evening, in other words. Even as I walked toward the front gate I could hear and see the big searchlights on the watchtowers clicking on around the base. That is a sound that one does not soon forget, the clicking of searchlights coming on along a perimeter. There were what appeared to be two reinforced and electrified barbed-wire fences around the perimeter of the base, one in front of the other.

There were two soldiers on duty, one in each guardhouse. They looked at me curiously as I walked toward them.

I had been at roadblocks and guardhouses before, and I knew that it was a good idea to smile, and defer quickly to all requests.

Respect was everything, at such a place.

The two soldiers stepped out of their guardhouses on opposite sides of road that passed through the main gate. They walked toward me at a leisurely pace. I wondered how often it happened that someone approached them on foot. If they were surprised to see a lone civilian approach them in this way, they did not show it.

The road into the army base was paved and in fair condition, wide enough for two-lane traffic. There was a raised crossbar behind of the two opposing guardhouses; behind that there was a very high metal gate that stood open, a gate that I later learned was closed at night.

The soldiers saw that I wanted to walk through the main gate.

They stepped in front of me and looked steadily at me. They

were not frowning, but neither were they smiling.

"I have come to see your commanding officer," I told them.

If these had been American soldiers, I would have expected them to reply with sarcasm: my speech was heavily accented, I had no papers, and I was clearly not Guatemalan. Instead they stared impassively at me, as if I were one more curiosity in a place of many curiosities.

One of the soldiers appeared to be quite old—one eye was white and bleared with some chronic eye condition. "That is impossible," he said as though talking about the weather.

"It is both possible and necessary."

"Who are you?"

"I come from the American Embassy."

"Do you have an appointment?"

"I always have an appointment."

They thought about this.

The other soldier was young, with short-cropped hair that stood up on his head. "What is the name of this man with whom you have an appointment?"

"The general."

Of course, I knew no general at this army base, nor was I even sure there was one; but I was in a desperate mood. I spoke with such authority that the soldiers seemed to believe me, at least for a moment. A moment was all it took—a seed of doubt had been planted.

"What is your name?" one of the soldiers asked finally.

I gave them my card from the wire service in Mexico City. My name was on it. They studied it for a long time. I said my name very slowly, as if it was important that we all pronounce it correctly.

The soldiers gravely took turns trying to pronounce it.

"What part of the United States do you come from?" the young soldier finally asked me in Spanish.

"Soy Californiano," I said.

"Ay!" they said in unison.

They seemed momentarily impressed.

The younger of the two soldiers stayed with me, while the older one returned to his guardhouse.

I heard a muffled telephone conversation.

I made no small talk with the young soldier standing next to me in the paved road. The soldiers were apparently impressed by me. Not intimidated, surely—but happy enough to pass on the responsibility for dealing with me. After all, I was clearly a North American, and in addition to that I was from California, which every Central American knew to be the wondrous place where Hollywood was located.

I heard the ponderous *clunk* of a rotary telephone receiver being set roughly in its cradle. The old soldier came out.

"Come," he said.

The young soldier roughly grasped my arm and steered me forward.

"Will the general see me now?" I asked.

"No," the old soldier said, "he is not here now. But the colonel will see you."

"Who?"

"The colonel. He says he has heard of you."

"What did you say?"

"The colonel says he has heard of you."

I knew no colonel here, any more than I knew a general. Before I could stop myself I said, "The colonel must have been very surprised to hear that I was here."

"How could that be?"

"You mean he wasn't surprised?"

"No. He was expecting you."

We walked in silence.

And that was how I first heard of Colonel Efrain Anibal Montamara, one of the most important men I'd ever meet.

He had an office at the end of a long hall. I was still being propelled along by the younger soldier, whose hand was on my arm. We arrived at the door to the colonel's office and the three of us stepped inside. It was a medium-sized corner officer with a ceiling fan and fluorescent lighting; sitting behind a large desk wedged diagonally in the corner of the office was a tall, gray-haired man smoking a cigarette in a cigarette holder.

He was in uniform and was clearly an officer.

The overhead lighting in the office, like the hall lighting, was yellow-tinted and powerful. It gave everything an oddly comforting yellow luminescence: one had the feeling of being in a submarine, a North American postal facility, or perhaps a dream.

Both of the soldiers came to attention. I could feel the hand of the young soldier tighten on my arm.

The tall officer looked up at us from some papers he was reading on his desk. He did not move.

"The man at the gate," said the old soldier huskily.

He handed the card I had given him to the colonel, who perused it solemnly for a long time. There was the faintest suggestion of a smile around his mouth.

"El hombre a la tranquera," he muttered. *"El hombre a la reja."*

The soldiers shuffled uneasily.

"The man at the gate," the colonel said in English. "Does he have a name?"

His accent was strong but his enunciation sure. *An intelligence officer,* I thought, *recruited and promoted because of his fluency in English.* Almost surely he had lived from some years in an English-speaking country, probably the United States.

For the first time he looked directly at me. He continued to speak in English.

"Are you the man at the gate?"

"Yes. I am that man."

"Are you bearing gifts?"

"*Lo siento.* I bear no gifts."

"No wooden horses?"

"No. I have no wooden horses, and I am not Greek."

He laughed.

He was unmistakably a Ladino, a Guatemalan from the land-owning upper classes. He had blue eyes, full gray hair, and the cultivated aristocratic coolness that was the fashion among Guatemalan army officers at the time. The only thing missing were the tinted glasses; I supposed it was too late in the day for that.

"Do you have a message for me from an embassy?"

"No. I have something better."

"North American money?"

"I would not insult you."

"I would not be insulted if you gave me North American money."

"Then…I wish I was a rich man, so that I had money to give."

Despite the blue eyes, he was dark; but it worked well for him, setting off the pale blue eyes and giving them a piercing preternatural animal quality. All in all, he was quite impressive, although the cigarette holder struck me as a bit much. He reminded me of a somewhat darker version of the now-vanished Hollywood conception of the Latin Lover, as personified by such movie stars as Gilfred Roland and Cesar Romero.

"What do they call you?" he asked me in Spanish.

"You should know. You were the one who was expecting me."

The young soldier holding my arm shifted nervously.

"Yes, of course," said the colonel politely in English, after a slight pause.

"But I can tell you my name, just in case you have forgotten."

"Yes," said the colonel, "why don't you tell me your name, in case I have forgotten."

"My name is Maitland Sutterfield."

At the mention of my name, the old soldier at my side remembered the card I had given him. After some nervous fumbling, he got the card out and handed it to the colonel. The colonel extended his hand and took the card without moving his body. He looked at the card a long time.

"You may go," he told the soldiers finally in Spanish.

The soldiers turned and left us alone in the colonel's office.

Only after they had gotten halfway down hall did the colonel rise slowly to his feet.

"Maitland Sutterfield." Then continuing in English the colonel said, "That is a very unusual name."

"I am from the state of California, in the United States."

"Somehow that does not surprise me."

I paused a moment, but only a moment. "I am a journalist. I live in the village of Chapila Chica, not far from the market town of San Jose del Rio. I work as a volunteer under the direction of Father Julio Domingo, a Jesuit priest who runs a small medical mission."

The colonel waved his hand. "Yes, I am familiar with him, just as I am familiar with you. But you may not know me. My name is Colonel Efrain Anibal Montamara."

I extended my hand. He pretended not to see it. Instead he opened a small box on his desk, took out his card, and put it in my extended hand. As he did so, he bowed, ever so slightly.

Before I could stop myself I bowed also.

"Gracias."

"No hay de que."

The card was elaborate. Along with Anibal Montamara's name were his army rank and various abbreviated words and acronyms that probably had to do with military organizations and awards.

There was another pause.

"You say that you know me," I began.

"Yes."

"I imagine you are familiar with a great many people."

"Yes," he said, "I am the second-in-command for this area, Zone Twenty. Sooner or later I find out about almost everybody in this zone." He paused for effect. "But not all of them come personally to introduce themselves to me."

"No, I imagine not."

"Thank you for coming to see me."

Although he had none of Alan Klein's little-kid enthusiasms, there was something about his manner that reminded me exactly of Klein. It was a certain quality of waiting, a waiting for the other person to give themselves away. He held the good cards, and he was waiting to see how I played mine.

I spotted three metal folding chairs against one wall.

"May I sit down?" I asked him.

"Como no?"

I opened one of the folding chairs and sat down on it. He also sat down—without once taking his eyes off me.

The office was rudimentary, but bristling with evidence of the colonel's sense of himself: there were pictures and certificates of one kind or another covering two of the walls. A fair percentage of them were hung crookedly—perhaps, I thought, because he had only recently moved into this office.

There was a rough and oddly hairy sofa of some kind across the room, but there was a menacing quality about it that made me want to avoid sitting on it. I wondered how many people had sat on that sofa, and how many were still alive. Another part of me wanted to go to sleep on the sofa for a very long time.

"So," I murmured after a pause, "your English is very good."

"I have always spoken it."

"You must have lived in North America."

He hesitated slightly. "I was in the United States." He mentioned the name of a notorious army base in Georgia that trained Latin America officers. "I taught there for many years. It is a beautiful state. Do you know it?"

"Of course."

"Of course you would know it. You are yourself an *estadounidense*."

Guatemalans used that word to indicate a North American from the United States, and not Canada. The subtext was this: people from the United States were cowboys, and therefore a little crazy; the Canadians were assumed to be a bit saner.

"Did you work with the Americans at the Southern Command in Panama?" I asked.

It was pure guesswork on my part, but I could tell by his pause that it was true.

"Yes," he said, smiling. "You've done your homework."

"So have you."

He appeared genuinely perplexed. "How is that, Mr. Sutterfield?"

"You told the soldiers that you were expecting me."

"Yes, I did say that."

"Then you must know I do not work at the American Embassy."

"No. You are a journalist." He indicated the card from the Mexican wire service that the soldiers had given him. "I know that you are a journalist because it says so on your card."

There was a long pause.

I said, "You may also have heard about me from Alan Klein."

"Ah. Do you know him?"

"Did you hear about me from Mr. Klein?"

The cold blue eyes did not waver. "Perhaps."

"And were you truly expecting me?"

"Sooner or later."

He was still fishing for information, and was not about to give anything up. He had stopped smiling, which put me on notice that he was not playing games. But neither was it a game for me: I was here to save a man's life.

"Why were you expecting me?"

"You are in Zone Twenty. This is the district I command. It is my job to know what goes on here."

"So you know my name. But what made you think that we would meet?"

"I knew you would have trouble, and then you ask someone for help. The only thing I didn't know was who you would ask."

"How did you know all these things about me?"

He leaned back in his chair with his hand behind his head, his fingers interlaced. "You are an educated man from the United States. You are a journalist. You are even a bit of a philosopher. And you are living in a small village with a priest, even though you are not a Catholic. All this is unusual. It would be surprising if I did not know about you."

"Why would I come to you for help?"

"Because this is not a natural thing, what you are doing. You are an educated man from North America, living in a poor village in Guatemala. This is not something that usually happens. You must have a reason, but it is not a reason anyone can see. So you must be keeping it secret. If you are keeping it secret, it must be something bad. Therefore you were bound to have trouble sooner or later, and I would probably hear about it." He paused, an abrupt short pause for effect. His cold blue eyes probed my face. "And I was right. Is that not true?"

"But you did not expect me to come to you."

"No. I thought that I would have to send for you."

"But—"

"Instead you came to visit me voluntarily."

"Yes."

"So," he said, the very soul of urbanity, "since you have come all this way, why don't you tell me why you're here?"

I was relieved he was willing to hear me out.

Although his English was for the most part impeccable, I began speaking in Spanish, going back to English frequently to demonstrate that I was aware of his fluency in that language.

I told him that I had come to advocate for Juan Delmonico, a patriotic and loyal soldier of the *patrulla autodefensa civil* in the small village of Chapila Chica, near the market town of San Jose del Rio. Juan Delmonico had unfortunately been arrested by mistake by troops from the Zone Twenty army base. They had been led by a certain lieutenant who had been in charge of training the self-defense patrol at Chapila Chica. Juan Delmonico's wife was hysterical with worry. I had come take Juan back to Chapila Chica so that he could resume his duties in defense of the fatherland.

I knew that the colonel would move swiftly to ensure that justice would be done, so that no embarrassing or compromising circumstances could attach themselves to what had clearly been a most illustrious career. I knew that the colonel was an honorable gentleman (*caballero honrado*), so that speaking one gentleman to another (*de caballero a caballero*) I was certain that he would move quickly to correct this terrible mistake.

The colonel nodded solemnly when I had finished.

"Thank you," he said. "I am indebted to you for talking to me openly and fraternally in this manner. Many things happen in this world. I need to hear all points of view to make a competent decision."

"So you will deliver Mr Delmonico to me immediately."

His eyebrows went up slightly. "Do what?"

"Give me Mr Delmonico immediately so that I can take him home with me."

His expression did not change. He was watching me intently. "I cannot secure the release of Mr Delmonico. In fact I have nothing to do with his arrest."

"But you will find out about it."

He hesitated slightly. "Yes. I will try to find out about it."

"How long will it take you?"

He sat there looking at me with his piercing blue eyes. He was clearly much more interested in me, and the way I spoke, than anything having to do with Juan Delmonico.

So I would have to use that, somehow.

"I want you to find out about Juan Delmonico right now, today," I said, "and I am prepared to wait for you until you do. Because I am not going to leave here until you find out about him, and I am not going to leave here without him. I have good reason to believe that Juan Delmonico is being held on this army base. As the acting base commander, I believe it would be a simple thing for you to find out about it. Let's be absolutely clear about this—I will only leave this army base with Juan Delmonico."

He looked at me a long time.

"That is very interesting," he said. "Why do you say this?"

"That should be obvious. I am very concerned about my friend."

"Why?" He wagged his finger at me without removing his hand from his desk. "Don't pretend that you are his friend. What can you possibly have in common with a poor Indian in a place like Chapila Chica? How could you be friends with such a man, a peasant with a dog's face who cannot even read? What would you talk about with such a man?" He made a small gesture. "You are clearly an educated man. It is not natural for you to care so much about such a person. There must be some other reason you're here. Something you are not telling me."

What exactly did the colonel want to hear? In other words, what did I have to say to secure Juan Delmonico's release? It occurred to me that the colonel might not be saying these things entirely for effect, nor solely to probe for information; he might really believe them, at least in part. He might really believe that I could not possibly care about the life of Juan Delmonico, a peasant with a dog's face who could not even read; and he might believe this with all his heart and mind.

Whatever he wanted me to say, I would say it, if I could only find out what it was.

But right now all I could think of was the truth, *my* truth, however little he might want to hear it. "It is quite natural for me to care about Juan Delmonico," I said firmly.

"I cannot believe this. What do you have in common?"

"He is a patriot and a good man." I launched into a long and passionate defense of Juan Delmonico; but I was careful to combine it with an equally passionate advocacy of the entire self-defense patrol system. "It was precisely you and your colleagues, the officer corps of the Guatemalan army, who originated this system; it depends on the goodwill of the Guatemalan people, otherwise it will not work. Juan Delmonico is simply a Guatemalan patriot, a man of the people, who bravely and graciously volunteered for this important duty. He has served well and loyally. Now he has been arrested by mistake. What would the Guatemalan people think of the *patrulla* system, if people who volunteered for such patrols were not protected by the military? How could the army expect these patrols to succeed?"

"You are an *estadounidense*. What do you care about Guatemala?"

"I care a great deal about Guatemala."

He sat there looking at me. "Yes. You say that. But I cannot believe you. How can I believe you if you cannot explain why?"

"It is written in the Constitution of my country that we are all born equal. The democracy in my country is corrupt and its foreign policy imperialist, but its foundational documents are sound. I don't expect you to believe as I do, but those are my beliefs. As a result of these beliefs, I don't care about a person's class or the family they come from. I don't care if they can read or write, and I don't if they are rich or poor. I don't even care if they have a dog's face. I look at what is inside them—whether they are a good person or not."

He said nothing for a long time.

"There are pretty words," he said finally, "but I cannot believe them. Only a fool or a madman would believe them. And I do not think you are either. You are not telling me the whole truth."

"Someday I'll try to explain more. Now I wish only to take Juan Delmonico back to his village. This is a noble enterprise. I have full confidence in Guatemalan justice and the Guatemalan officer corps. I am sure you will help us."

Again he was silent. He continued to regard me with something like amused interest, but I saw irritation in his eyes as well. It occurred to me that my appearance might be quite bizarre: I had not shaved that morning, and my clothes were dirty. But I had not come to this army base caring how I looked. This was a reckoning, not a performance.

Perhaps the colonel's confusion arose exactly as he said it did; perhaps he simply found it impossible to believe what I was saying.

"How did you find out so much about the civil-defense patrols?" the colonel asked.

"I watched them training in Chapila Chica. And the things I know about them are common knowledge among journalists. The Guatemalan army has given many press conferences about them."

"But not in such detail."

"Well—" I hesitated. "I spent some time discussing it with Alan Klein, the North American advisor."

"There are no North American advisors in Guatemala."

"Then let me put it a different way: I have discussed the civil self-defense patrols at length with my friend Alan Klein."

"Ah, well, yes," he said. "Yes, Mr Klein."

There was a very long silence while we both sat looking at each other. I was beginning to get a sense of how hard it was going to be to get this man to do anything. He held *all* the cards, not just the good ones; and whatever I did or said, the colonel was simple not used to doing what other people wanted him to do.

It was a matter of principle having to do with his status and his rank.

"There is one thing you must understand," I said. "It is very important that you understand this, so I will say it slowly. *I will not leave this base without Juan Delmonico.* You can kill me; you can threaten to kill me; but I will not leave without him."

"Why do you say this?"

"Because I am ready to die."

"I did not hear that. But let's say I did hear it. Why on earth are you putting on this act?"

"I am a desperate man."

"Yes. But *why*?"

I wanted to tell him that I had waited since childhood to come to a Place of Wonders like Guatemala; that I longed to die, because I could not stand to live; and that I had lost the ability to love. I wanted to tell him that risking everything to save Juan Delmonico was precisely the kind of chance I was temperamentally disposed to take.

But no, I wouldn't share that with him today.

"Never mind," I said, sighing. "It is enough, more than enough, for you to know that I am an exceedingly desperate man."

"Desperate."

He began to takes notes on a small pad on his desk. "I…am…an…" He paused and looked up. "What was the word before 'desperate'?"

"Exceedingly."

"How do you spell it?"

I spelled it for him.

"Yes, indeed," I continued, "the man sitting in front of you may appear *exceedingly* normal, but no; he is not normal. He is the very soul of extreme desperation! And we know the stupid and unpredictable things desperate people can sometimes do. Don't we?"

The colonel stopped writing and looked up. "I'm not quite

sure," he said absently.

"Would you like for me to tell you exactly how desperate I am?"

"Yes. Please."

He continued to take notes.

"I am ready to die," I said, "and I am prepared to force the issue in such a way that I will make you kill me, a white journalist from the United States. That is what I am prepared to do if you do not release Juan Delmonico. I will sit down in front of the gate at this army base and stop traffic. But first I will telephone the US Embassy and friends in North America to tell them of my plans."

"Why will you do that?"

"So it will get into the newspapers in the United States."

"I see." He wrote something down. "What else will you do?"

"I will take a weapon from one of your men and start shooting. This will force your soldiers to kill me."

"Or if you cannot take a weapon away from a soldier?"

"I will get one somewhere and attack the base single-handedly."

"Bueno," the colonel muttered under his breath. He continued taking notes. "Is there anything else?"

I was thinking. There were limitless possibilities, I thought, all of them perfectly grandiose. Why limit myself, now that I was making threats? "Or I can take a car and drive through the front gate. Or I can burn myself to death in front of the American Embassy."

"Bueno," the colonel kept muttering.

I cannot remember all the ridiculous things I threatened to do. The thing was, I was ready to die, and I had to make that clear to him.

"So," the colonel said when I was finished, "you will do something desperate, something that will force me to kill you. Is that it?"

"Yes."

He put down the pen with which he had been writing. "Why?"

"Why what?"

"Why are you threatening me in this manner?"

"To make you understand the importance of this, to do something that will greatly advance the cause in which we both struggle. To make you understand that this is the right thing, and in the best interests of Guatemala. You must release my friend Juan Delmonico."

He sighed.

"And if I can't?"

"I will stay here until you change your mind."

He tapped his forefinger slowly on the desk. He did not appear to be amused, but neither did he appear to be upset, surprised or angry. He was simply doing his job. He was doing what he was paid to do; and he was doing it better than most of his colleagues ever could, because of his fluency in English.

"Well, then," he said, toying with his pen, "if this is true, clearly I will have to keep you in custody until this unfortunate matter is cleared up."

"I thought you would say that."

"Then you will not find it objectionable that I must detain you."

"But if you detain me, you must provide me with excellent accommodations. I prefer a room with a view. And a private bath."

"Yes. Of course."

"Don't forget the private bath."

The colonel stood stiffly and pushed a lever on an incredibly old-fashioned wooden intercom that looked like something from a 1930s movie. I half-expected a coy secretary to burst into the room, or a chain-smoking reporter. The colonel barked some orders to nobody in particular, and then stood adjusting his uniform.

Two soldiers appeared. The colonel barked more orders; and the soldiers took my arms, one on one side and one on the other. Although Anibal Montamara was speaking in Spanish, he was speaking in a kind of military idiom that I could not understand, perhaps referring to some discretionary protocol peculiar to his command.

When he was through, he walked past me into the hallway.

"Please excuse me," he said to me in English. "I need to make some telephone calls. Then I will have more information. Will you please excuse me?"

"Only if you release Juan Delmonico," I said.

The soldiers waited respectfully for the colonel to finish with me. He stopped in the hallway and faced me.

"I did not say I would do that," he said. "I said I will make some telephone calls."

"But you will inquire into the matter."

"I will do what I can."

He turned and once again began walking. He was headed for a door at the end of the hallway.

"Gracias!" I called after him. *"Yo lo aprecio mucho!"*

I was truly grateful: I really believed that he was about to free Juan Delmonico. Soon he would be making the necessary telephone calls; very soon he would discover that Juan Delmonico was innocent of the ridiculous charges made against him, and my astonishing Anglo chuztpa would win the day against all odds.

That's what I believed.

The colonel had not killed me outright, nor had he kicked me off the base; wasn't that strong circumstantial evidence that he was thinking about releasing Juan Delmonico into my custody?

I would not allow myself to consider any other possibility.

The soldiers put me in a cell facing a grassy square, where I remained for the next twenty-four hours. There was a wooden bench along one side of the cell and a single woolen blanket. The flying cockroaches were content to stay inside the crevices running along the wall on the other side of the cell from the bench where I slept. After about an hour I was taken out by two soldiers about to go off duty, who escorted me to a small latrine with a hole in the floor that served as a toilet.

I was apparently the only person being held in the quadrangle. My guess was that these cells—I counted sixteen of them—were for soldiers awaiting disciplinary hearings, or perhaps visitors from other military units. I did not see many soldiers around. Most of the troops appeared to be off the base.

The worst thing about the cell at first was the smell. Other prisoners had urinated against the walls, and at first the stink of the urine was overpowering. The stench gradually grew less objectionable, however; I was surprised at how quickly I got used to it.

I was taken out at midnight by two soldiers who took me to the latrine before allowing me to exercise in the moonlit square. I was surprised by that, and grateful. Two soldiers asked me about California. Our conversation was in Spanish, but there were a surprising number of Americanisms in their vocabularies, sometimes in English and sometimes translated directly into Spanish. I wondered where they were picking up the American idioms.

Television, I supposed.

"Are you from Hollywood?" one of the soldiers asked me as I exercised.

I told him I had been there just before coming to Guatemala.

"Do you see many movie stars?"

"Not many. About one a week."

"Who do you see?"

I rattled off the name of every celebrity I could think of. "Elizabeth Taylor, Gregory Peck, Bob Hope, John Wayne—"

One of the soldiers got excited. "John Wayne?"

"Oh, yes."

"He is a good one."

"Oh, yes."

There was a pause. I had the soldier hooked now.

"How often do you talk to him," he wanted to know, "and what do you say?"

"We talk about Guatemala," I said, wanting to see how far I could go with it. "We talk about the civil war in Guatemala."

"No, *gringo,* this cannot be the truth."

"*De veras,* we do."

"No, *mano,* you are joking with me."

"No, truly. John Wayne's wife is Hispanic, from a Mexican family living in California, and he is concerned about the spread of communism. We discuss the war against communism in Latin America. He says *el Ejercito de Guatemala* cannot defeat the communist revolution here without help."

"What?" said the other soldier. "What does he say?"

Neither of the soldiers bothered to whisper any more, they were so excited. Our voices were echoing around the quadrangle.

"John Wayne says that the Guatemalans will never win the war against the *subversivoes* without help. And he is a good friend of Ronald Reagan, the President of the United States."

I had them completely hooked now.

"Yes, we will," said the first soldier. "Of course we can do it alone."

"Without the North Americans?"

"*Si, se puede.* We can do it without help."

"Everybody needs help sometime."

"We have our own methods."

The two soldiers guffawed.

"Tell him this," the first soldier said after a pause. I couldn't tell from his tone whether he was in earnest, or simply playing along. "Tell this to John Wayne the next time you see him. Tell him that it can be done—tell him we can beat the subversives without any help from him."

"Okay," I said. "I'm sure he'll be glad to hear that."

The sun was just coming up the next morning when the soldiers came to take me to the office of Colonel Efrain Anibal Montamara. He was on the telephone having an intense conversation that had not quite reached the shouting level, but was getting close. The colonel looked up, clearly irritated.

"It's the North American," one of the soldiers said.

"I can see that."

Anibal Montamara muttered something to the person he was talking to on the telephone, then put him on hold. For the first time he looked at me. "What did you think of your room?"

"Very nice."

"I'm glad you liked it."

"I particularly liked the flying cockroaches."

"Ah." He shrugged. "They, too, must live the life."

"Of course."

"I will talk to you in a moment. In the meantime I must finish this telephone call." He got up and brushed past me. To the soldiers he said in Spanish, "Stay with him here in my office."

"Si, mi colonel," one of the soldiers said.

As the soldiers waited awkwardly with me there was no easy conversation about movie stars. Their fear of the colonel was palpable. It had nothing to do with respect—it was fear, pure and simple.

And, I suspected, they were just about to go off duty. I heard the colonel enter another room down the hall. I can't remember exactly how long he was gone, but it couldn't have been more than ten minutes. I assumed then that he had gone to use the telephone, although I had no way of really knowing that. He could just as easily have gone down the hall for a cup of coffee. I forced myself to stop thinking about it—the less I knew about his activities at this army base, the better.

I heard his footsteps coming back down the hall.

As he came back into the room, the colonel was briskly rubbing his hands together.

"Bueno," he said to his soldiers. "You may leave us alone now."

"Si, mi colonel."

The soldiers left. The colonel turned to me.

"I have solved the problem!" he announced. He was quite pleased; he sat down behind his desk and beamed at me. "I have inquired about the man who was arrested at Chapila Chica."

"You mean Juan Delmonico."

"Yes. That one."

"And?"

"He was not a patriot after all. He was a subversive and a criminal. He was helping the communists."

I was dumbfounded. "What are you saying? That can't be true!"

"Sit down." The colonel gestured toward a metal folding chair. "We are very *exacting* about these things." He emphasized the word *exacting,* as though he wished to impress me with his vocabulary in English. "Yes. Very exacting indeed."

"Juan is a patriot. You're making a mistake."

I had no desire to sit down. If the colonel thought he was going to get away with selling me this bill of goods, he was very much mistaken. It was another dodge, another attempt to pass the buck, another excuse to keep from releasing Juan Delmonico.

"Oh yes," the colonel was saying, "we definitely have proof. Do you think we would not investigate such a thing? Juan Delmonico was giving the rebels medications. He went to the house of a certain woman who lives on the path to Tzotzil Gapachula mountain. She is called the Dog Woman by the people who live there."

"I know of her."

"She is a communist. Juan Delmonico would leave the

medications at her house, and the rebels would pick them up." Once again he gestured toward the metal folding chair. "Why don't you sit down?"

I felt like I was about to faint. He could only have gotten this nonsense from one source, I thought, and that was Alan Klein. But why?

"Alan Klein is making up these accusations," I said. "I know he must be telling you these things. Klein has an agenda—for some reason he hates Juan Delmonico. You can't arrest a man just because Alan Klein made up some crazy stories about him!"

"Klein is a usually reliable source." The colonel rolled the two words around on his tongue. "A *usually reliable source*. Isn't that what you journalists call such people? Alan Klein is such a person. We investigated it, and it was true. Juan Delmonico was giving medications to the *rebeldes*."

"I tell you, you can't believe what Alan Klein tells you! He's lying to you. Lying is what he does for a living!"

"But we have investigated, and the reports were right. We found medications at the Dog Woman's house."

"Of course you found medications!" I shrieked. "They were goddamn psychotropic medications! Juan Delmonico was taking them there to calm this woman down!"

Again he shook his head.

"No, no. Why would anybody waste such medications on such a woman? Besides, there were many other things—antibiotics, bandages, leg braces. There were too many other things to count."

Leg braces? That was impossible—there had been no leg braces in the medications I had brought up from Guatemala City. I had never seen a leg brace in all the time I had been in Guatemala. If a brace was needed in the highlands, somebody would have to figure out a way to make one.

A kind of despair began to come in on me. Nothing I could say was going to do any good. Yet I *had* to think of something: Juan

Delmonico's life was in my hands.

I briefly considered taking the colonel hostage. I was not armed, and the colonel was wearing no sidearm that I could see. Perhaps he only wore one in the field. Or perhaps he never wore one. In any case, there were many witnesses— including one civilian, if one included the custodian who had dropped me off a mile from the gates—who had seen me come onto the army base.

I had to think of something.

"My colonel," I said, "I see now that it is especially important that you release Juan Delmonico. By releasing him, you will save his life. And you must release him not because I say you must, but because honor demands it. You will understand when I tell you the secret work that I do."

His ice-water blue eyes did not blink. "I would be very interested to hear about this secret work. Exactly what are you talking about?"

"I am a special contract employee working with the American Embassy." I was careful not to claim that I was a case officer, which would imply that I was on salary. "My field is intelligence. I collect information about people who are helping the communists."

Anibal Montamara sighed. "There are many people collecting information in Guatemala. And they all have different reasons."

"But not many people doing the work I do."

"And what is that?"

"I work directly with the CIA." I pronounced it *see-ya,* the way the Latin Americans did.

"But—" He frowned, appearing to recall something he had heard a long time ago. "Aren't military advisors prohibited by the American Congress?"

"Yes."

"So how can you be doing this kind work?"

"My work is completely covert."

"I see."

But his blue eyes did not waver, nor did his expression change.

"No one knows about it except yourself, and the man to whom I report," I continued.

"And who would that be?"

"Alan Klein."

He was momentarily startled. "Who?"

"Alan Klein."

"Ah," he said politely. He waited just long enough to make the next question sound proper. "And what do you do for Mr. Klein?"

"I write reports for him."

"Reports?"

"About Chapila Chica."

"Why do you write such reports?"

"Mr. Klein and I are both soldiers in the war against communism."

"I'm sure the reports are very interesting to Mr. Klein." He paused. "And what else do you do?"

I was momentarily confused. "Isn't that enough? I gather information for the American government, damn it! I am a soldier in the war against communism, the same war you are fighting! I live in Chapila Chica, and I know everything that happens there; and I can tell you that there is nothing subversive going on in that village! I know from my own direct experience that Juan Delmonico is in no way a *subversive!*"

"I am sure it is all very helpful."

I was not getting enough through to him. "But doesn't this demonstrate to your satisfaction that I am a loyal friend of all those who are fighting against communism? I am part of the struggle against the enemies of civilization, and that is the same struggle in which Juan Delmonico is engaged."

"I think you are mistaken."

"He is not a *subversivo*—he is a warrior fighting against communism!"

The colonel shrugged. I was getting used to his shrug. "People write reports all the time about each other. They do it for many, many different reasons. How can I be sure about your motives? I have no idea why you do what you do. I am not even sure why Alan Klein does the things he does. It has nothing to do with the matter at hand, which is the traitorous actions of a coward."

"The reports I've written must count for something!"

The unblinking blue eyes remained fixed on my face. The only emotion the eyes betrayed was curiosity; but at the same time the colonel was beginning to smile.

I did not trust his smile.

"Alan Klein," he murmured. "Did he promise you money that he did not pay you?"

I was surprised at how defensive this question was making me feel. "I am paid very little by Alan Klein," I said.

"But did he perhaps promise to pay you more?"

"He promised to get some of my journalism published."

"Did he do so?"

After a pause I said, "No, not yet."

"Well, then—" the colonel said triumphantly, "you have no complaint except that you have not received the money that Alan Klein promised you. Alan Klein was dishonest with you—but perhaps that happened because of your stupidity. That does nothing to convince me that I should take you seriously."

I said nothing. My body felt cold.

"They mean nothing, the reports you wrote," the colonel said harshly. He did not sound like a man making a judgment, but rather a man alluding to a situation he found distasteful. "I have heard about your reports from others. They are worthless!—absolutely worthless!"

Had he really heard about my reports written for Alan Klein? Was it possible that he had read them? I doubted it.

But why did he refer to them at all?

"Maybe I could write reports for you," I heard myself saying.

He looked at me with something like incredulity. "I do not need your reports."

There was no mistaking the contempt in his voice.

"There must be *something* I could do for you," I said, my voice cracking slightly.

The colonel seemed momentarily shocked. I was, too—I hadn't expected to find myself groveling in quite this manner. But I didn't care; I would do anything to get Juan Delmonico off this army base and out of the clutches of the military.

There was a long silence.

"Well," the colonel said finally.

His ice-cold eyes continued to fix me with their unblinking feral blueness, but there was a qualitative change in his expression; now he was mulling something over. What had I set in motion behind the lunar chill of those blue eyes?

"There is something I want to show you," the colonel said.

He began to rummage in a bottom drawer of his desk.

He sat suddenly upright, and appeared to be thinking. Then he wheeled about on his chair and proceeded to search in the middle drawer of a tall metal file cabinet behind him. Although I could not quite put my finger on it, something in his demeanor had changed radically.

He was very alert, very focused. It was very important to him, whatever he had in mind.

At last he found what he was looking for—and having done so, he turned slowly toward me. On his face was an expression I had not seen before. It was cool and very contained, but he was trying too hard to suppress a certain excitement; behind the cool eyes and carefully noncommittal smile, I sensed the presence of an obsession.

He held a manila folder. From it he took a few sheets of paper and sat looking at them. "Have you seen this?" he asked. He handed me the sheets of paper. On them was a badly printed newsletter. At the top of the first page was title, *El Pueblo*. It was clearly a political publication; it was full of the revolutionary slogans typical of the Marxist-Leninist Left at the time in Latin American. I read just enough of it to see that it was the publication of an organization that purported to have a base in the highlands, an organization that claimed to be engaged in armed struggle. It was filled with typographical errors, much of it was too faint to even read, and it was so poorly printed that it was hard to make sense of it.

I did not brother to read much of it. The rhetoric of political radicalism does not interest me: promises of a bright tomorrow, the glorious future that all would enjoy one day—*the people united, can never be defeated!*—left me cold. The glorious dreams of most political radicals have as much chance of coming true as I have of being elected Pope by the College of Cardinals in Rome.

"So?" I asked.

He leaned forward. "It is an underground newspaper printed in the area of Chapila Chica. A *radical* newspaper."

I was astounded. "Don't joke with me."

"This is no joke." He leaned forward and jabbed at the papers in my hand with his forefinger. "I promise you this is no joke."

I looked again at the hideously printed newsletter. It was absurd that such a thing would be produced for a readership around Chapila Chica, or any of the other villages in the vicinity of San Jose del Rio; to begin with, there were only a few people in the entire area who could read. And this was nothing like a newspaper, but only a badly printed newsletter.

"Most of the people around Chapila Chica can't read," I pointed out, "and this wretched thing is in Spanish. Most of the people around there speak Kekchi. How on earth could Kekchi-speaking people understand a newsletter in Spanish?"

The colonel shrugged. "I didn't say it was distributed in the area around Chapila Chica. I said that it was printed there."

"And distributed where?"

He shrugged. "We aren't sure."

"Well, speaking as a journalist and editor, it certainly doesn't appear to be a publication with a very large subscription base."

He did not smile. "What does that mean?"

"That it is probably not being read by very many people."

"Well—" He took the poorly-printed pages back from me. "I must make sure that people can never read it. I must stop it now."

"So...?"

"I must find the printing press and destroy it. When I find the people who own this press, I will find the most radical subversives in the area."

"What does that have to do with me?"

I thought about it—but not very long.

I had come here to rescue Juan Delmonico, I would do or say anything to accomplish that goal. I took it as given that there was nothing even remotely approximating a printing press in the area around Chapila Chica. But I would promise the colonel anything, if it would cause him to think about freeing Juan Delmonico.

"If I agree to your terms," I said, "you must release Juan Delmonico into my custody, so that I may take him back to Chapila Chica."

The colonel's eyes neither blinked nor wavered. "Juan Delmonico has nothing to do with you. You will help me find the printing press in order to save your own life. You claim to be a contract employee of the US Embassy who is fighting communism, but you can only do that if you have my protection. There are people who want to kill you; and if you do not help me find the printing press, I may not be able to protect you."

So that was it—his ace in the hole.

The casual way he delivered the threat made me suspect that he was bluffing, but I would promise anything to free Juan Delmonico.

"What will you do if I cannot help you?"

The colonel shrugged. "I can only protect you if you understand my situation."

"And if I help you find this printing press you are looking for, you will protect me?"

"Exactly."

"And you will release Juan Delmonico?"

"No. I cannot do that."

I leaned forward and put my hands on his desk. I was still sitting. "No, my colonel," I said in a low voice, "you will not kill me. You are bluffing. I am a citizen of the United States, and I have no connection to the rebels and no sympathy for them. You would not dare kill me. Even if the station chief in Guatemala City were to order my death, you would not do it. That would be the job of the CIA itself. If you did it, there would be too many questions, especially since I am not an activist of any kind." I paused just long enough to check out his response. My words were getting through. "So don't threaten my life. That would be a big mistake. And I don't think you like to make mistakes."

He shrugged slowly, this time with an almost feline delicacy.

"There are many things," the colonel said, "that can happen to an *estadounidense* in this part of Guatemala. There are rumors in these mountains about Americans who kidnap children. You will forgive me for mentioning this, but one hears these rumors." That much was true—I had heard these same rumors myself. "Two months ago a mob attacked an American tourist woman in the plaza of a city not fifty kilometers from Guatemala City. They were convinced she was a kidnapper. They beat her up and left her for dead."

"I heard about this incident. It is entirely deplorable."

"Indeed."

"I was impressed by the fact that the police and the soldiers did nothing while the woman was being beaten."

"Then you will know that I am serious,"

"So," I said, "if I do not help you, you will arrange for something unfortunate to happen to me."

He frowned. "I am merely saying that there are limits to what

I can do. I will extend my protection to you only if you agree to help me."

"If I help you find the printing press the rebels are using?"

"Yes."

"I have already agreed to help you with that," I said patiently, "but I have also made it clear that I will not leave this place without Juan Delmonico."

There was the beginning of respect now in the eyes of icy blue, but the irritation remained.

"You want something from me, and I cannot give it to you. Then why are you here? What do you want of me?"

"Are you upset?"

He ignored the question. "Why do you want to create problems for both of us?"

"I wanted to start this day in the right way."

Indeed, it was early. What was Anibal Montamara doing here in his office so early in the morning? His presence could explain the rough woolen blankets on the sofa—most likely he had worked late and slept on the sofa. Perhaps he was the duty officer, and had to stay on the base all night.

"I *must* secure the freedom of Juan Delmonico," I said. "I will not leave without him."

"I cannot release him."

"I demand it. And I demand that you release him now."

He shook his head slowly. His faint smile had come back, but it was tinged with impatience. "It cannot be done."

"Si, se puede."

"Fool!" He was almost pitying. *"Inocente!"*

There was something calculated and mean-spirited about the way he said the word *inocente.* It did not seem to be entirely accidental that he had used that word, although of course it had to be.

But I could not let myself think about that. Instead I said, "I will not leave this army base without Juan Delmonico."

He sighed and shrugged abruptly.

"In that case I must once again find a place for you to stay."

"I certainly hope that once more you are able to give me a room with a private bathroom," I said.

He was just able to control his temper.

"Of course you will have a room with a private bathroom," he said.

The colonel stood and barked something into the intercom, and a coarse, otherworldly voice answered him with words I could not understand.

The colonel released the lever on the intercom with a snap.

He straightened his uniform with several quick little jerks. "Of course you can go to the room with a bath," he said. "Anyone can go to the room with a bath. We are humanists in Guatemala, fully cognizant of human rights, especially those of the press, but we are not paternalists."

"Nobody expects you to be."

He was still angry, and my sarcasm did not help.

"We are not paternalists in Guatemala," he was saying, "but we are humanists. That is well known. All informed people are aware of it."

I bowed slightly.

"I am your sure servant in these matters," I said in Spanish. "I place my trust in the honor of the Guatemalan officer crops."

The soldiers put me in the same cell facing the grassy square, where I remained for the next seventy-two hours. Once again I was taken out every eight hours to go to a small latrine with a hole in the floor that served as a toilet. Twice daily I was given beans, rice and warm soup in a tin cup. I was glad they were giving me soup instead of water: at least the soup had been heated, and was therefore less likely to make me sick.

The soldiers who stood guard outside my cell were getting used to me. I wondered why they were there at all. Did the colonel think that I was some kind of closet Houdini; a gifted escape artist who was likely to break out at any moment? It was far more likely, I decided, that they were there simply to impress me.

I was of great interest to the soldiers, who talked about me as though I was not present. Perhaps they talked so candidly in front of me because they thought I did not have long to live. Or perhaps I was so exotic to them that they saw no reason not to discuss me as though I were a creature from another planet. One soldier maintained that I was a North American attorney; another said that I was the husband of a pop music star in Hollywood; still another believed that I was the leader of the communists in North America.

They were strangely deferential to me.

Why? I couldn't figure that one out, given who I was and the situation I was in.

What else had they been told about me—and by whom?

Once I overheard one of the soldiers talking about me while I was in the latrine. "You see, he talks to himself. Did they not say that he does this?"

"Yes," I heard the other soldier say, "but many people talk to themselves. You do it yourself in the morning. I hear you often."

"Yes, but I do it to wake myself up."

"Perhaps he's still dreaming when he talks to himself."

"Yes," said the other soldier sarcastically, "maybe we're still dreaming too."

I was inside the latrine when I heard these things. I came out of the latrine just in time to see one of the soldiers make a circular motion next to his head, apparently to signify madness. Did he think I was mad?—or was he simply taunting his comrade? I couldn't tell.

When they saw me looking at them, they giggled.

The only person I could think of who might have suggested that I was mad was the colonel. I did not mind that. He was less likely to have me killed if he did not think I was responsible for my actions.

"He was awake when he was talking to himself," one of the soldiers said as they took me back to my cell. "You saw it. He was fully awake."

The other soldier said nothing.

Later, after they had taken back to my cell, I howled like a wolf. I could hear them listening outside. The flying cockroaches on the other side of the cell stopped their rustling and grew very still. The soldiers outside were completely silent. I kept up the howling for a good long time. If they were going to think me mad, I thought, I would damn well give them the sounds of madness.

The second night in the cell I lay awake remembering all the things that had brought me to Guatemala. At times I fell asleep and dreamed, so that the two states, remembering and dreaming, merged seamlessly together. I thought of my childhood and the stories I had read, the stories of King Arthur and the enchantments of the Arthurian world. I remembered the dreams of my youth, the dream of a magical land, and the Place of Wonders where I would find the Holy Grail, the loving cup of youth and eternal regeneration.

I thought of the dream that I had often had as an adolescent, in which people spoke in a magical language of chivalry and honor, and how that language had turned out to be Spanish, the language of Cervantes. I dreamed of my divorce in San Francisco, how I had traveled south and crossed the border, and my job at the wire service in Mexico City. I dreamed of how I had first come to Guatemala, and how I had found the village of Chapila Chica—or perhaps it had found me, I no longer knew which it was.

Why had I sought out a land that was in the midst of a brutal civil war? Was I so conflicted emotionally that I had to find a country that was tearing itself apart? Historically, the wars in which the Guatemalan army had participated had nothing to do with honor, and everything to do with mass murder and oppression of the Mayan nation. So what had I intended to prove by coming here—that I, too, could be tortured and murdered?

Who was I trying to impress?

Why had I come here?

It had something to do with death, of course. On one level it was about seeking death; but perhaps it also had to do with getting to know it, and not being quite so overawed by it. Many people did that—it was said to be one of the secrets of achieving mental health, not to mention spiritual peace. Of course, coming to Guatemala was all about my own emotional needs.

But so what? Had my death wish not served me well? Did I not have a chance of saving Juan Delmonico's life precisely because I was willing to risk my own? Call it bravery or call it being a damn fool, in my own mind I still thought it the best strategy, even though there was no guarantee it would pay off.

In my own mind there was every indication that the colonel was even now arranging to have Juan released. The colonel was desperate to find the rebel printing press, the keeper of the rebel word; but the colonel needed my help to find it, he needed my eyes and ears in Chapila Chica. And he would not have my help until he released Juan Delmonico—that was the deal, was it not? Furthermore, Colonel Efrain Anibal Montama had seen that I was completely unafraid of death, and that condition had spoken to him. I was sure of it.

My gamble would work. Juan would be free.

Once in the middle of the night I thought I heard a volley of shots from automatic weapons. Afterwards I heard some orders being barked. It seemed to come from very far away, from the other side of the army base.

Then I heard nothing.

There was no general alarm of any kind, nobody in my part of the base was stirring. After the shots and the orders everything was very quiet.

So I went back to sleep.

The third day I was given a single tortilla with my soup. I cannot remember being hungry once, all the time I was there. But my trips to the latrine were far and few between; and I soon found myself urinating against the far wall of the cell. I had not bathed or shaved for many days now, and I began to experience that odd sense of disorientation that one has when one is hot, dirty, unshaven, and separated from human contact. I withdrew into myself, into my dreams and daydreams.

That night the darkness was a long time coming; it seemed to take forever for the sun to set, as though my dreams were impatient to visit me. My mind became incredibly active even before I fell asleep, before I slipped fully into a dreaming state.

This night the dreams were very different than the night before.

In this night's dreams, the third night of my second confinement, I was honored by a visitation from my great-great-great uncle, the redoubtable Algernon Sutterfield, who was killed in 1835 in the state of North Carolina; killed in a duel because of this opposition to slavery. It had been Algernon Sutterfield who in the 1820s had founded the first *Southern Messenger* (the first of many publications with that name) in North Carolina, using it mainly to promote his antislavery ideas. He went largely unknown during the 1820s, except for the sizeable Quaker population in the Piedmont area of the Carolinas, which approved of his antislavery stand and supported his publications.

In the 1830s, however, any discussion of the morality or immorality of slavery became a sensational inconvenience in the American South; and therefore discussion of it was no longer allowed by the planter class. Throughout the southern states the antislavery newspaper editors and writers were murdered, driven out, or silenced. This form of state terrorism came later to North Carolina than elsewhere, because of the longstanding antislavery tradition in the Piedmont; but the forces of the Slave Power were inexorable. It was finally in 1835, at a time when all the other antislavery newspapers in the South had already been silenced, that the time of reckoning came for Algernon and his radical newspaper.

An entire succession of slaveholders from the eastern part of the state committed themselves to eradicating Algernon Sutterfield, deciding that each of them would challenge him to a duel until one of them prevailed. This assembly-line approach to the code duello was, in the event, unnecessary: the first slaveholder to meet Algernon on the field of honor had no difficulty in besting him. Algernon took a bullet clean through the chest, and although to witnesses he appeared to bleed very little, he was dead within the hour.

In my imaginary conversations with Algernon, I had always pictured him as a swashbuckling figure, a journalistic *D'Artagnan*, as it were, a kind of ideological freebooter willing and even anxious to risk his life for an idea of justice or honor, or even for some favorite theological or philosophical conceit. But this night, in a dark cell on a Guatemalan army base, he did not come to me in that way.

Rather he came to me as a bleary-eyed newspaper proprietor, as opposed to a musketeer out of Dumas, with the pockets of his printer's apron full of type and his spectacles slipping down over his nose. Interestingly, his own eyes were red with sleeplessness, although he appeared to me as I was actually sleeping. It was not the first time Algernon Sutterfield had spoken to me in my dreams, but I had never seen him so clearly before, nor had he assumed a form quite so human, nor so compelling.

"Maitland, good fellow!" he half-crowed, half-drawled, not

without affection. "Well now." He was staring at me over his spectacles. "My grand half-sir, what kind of trouble are you in now?"

In his right hand he casually held a book.

I knew which book it was. It was a book some Sutterfield had written, which had to do with the history of the Sutterfields from their beginning in the tangle of fishhooks that were the families of Virginia and Anglo-Dutch New York. The book had long since been lost, but there were still Sutterfields living who had read it and even some who talked about it, and who purported to know what it meant and where it was hidden.

"Don't judge me, Uncle Algernon," I said to him.

"Why would I judge you, nephew?"

"Because I have not yet died with honor; I have not even died."

"You will. Be sure of that. Your time will come."

There was almost always a kind of Socratic dialogue when Algernon was in my dreams; one of us would ask the seemingly reasonable questions, the other would supply the seemingly self-evident answers. But as in all dreams, as in some of the dialogues of Socrates himself, the important things were in a kind of code.

"Your time will come," Algernon said again.

"Perhaps," I said, "but what if it doesn't come in time?"

"Meaning?"

"A joke."

He smiled. "Tell me why you joke, Maitland."

"I'm joking because I might die when I'm awake. That's why people joke." But I felt no fear, only a vague niggling irritation.

"Not very likely," he said gently, as though to cushion me from a great disappointment.

"If I do not die, I am afraid my friend might die."

"But that is different," he said with what impressed me as great wisdom, "although death can happen at any time, and there are many kinds of death."

"Why do you come to me tonight?" I wanted to know.

"Because you need me."

As I say, my great-great-great uncle had often visited me in my dreams. He was as many different people as he needed to be. Today he was full of manly cheer, but worried. Algernon had come to me, not because I was in some prosperous and ideal situation, but because I was a stranger in a dangerous land.

"I'm glad you're here," I said.

"I'm here to congratulate you. There is no more noble enterprise than the defense of a friend. Even if—*especially* if—you are not successful."

But I was convinced that I would be successful, that my insane gambit would have a sure and certain outcome, that the colonel could not help but release Juan Delmonico, because he needed my help; and I quickly apprised my ghostly ancestor of that fact. "The colonel wants my help, and I told him I would give it to him. In return, he will release my friend. Or at least I believe he will."

"But what if your gamble does not work?"

"It has to work. I must save my friend's life. Help me do this, Uncle Algernon."

I addressed my great-great-great uncle like an old friend, but as a member of my family he was also a legend. I had heard many stories about him when I was growing up, of his genius as a newspaper editor; of Sherwood House, the mansion where he lived with his beautiful wife and daughter, in modern times transformed into offices for a gaggle of ambitious attorneys; and of his various eccentricities. Once he had gotten kicked by a mule and lost the power of speech for six months, but when speech returned, he was an even better writer than before. Ever afterwards, he had been the recipient of occasional waking visions in which he saw angels, historical characters, and many unearthly creatures whose full raiment could not be adequately described—and what was most amazing, I thought, was that almost all the people and animals in his visions were *friendly,* and none threatening or frightening. Some of the doctors in my family had looked back at him from the 20th century and speculated that perhaps he suffered from temporal lobe epilepsy, which could conceivably have triggered the visual hallucinations; but his visions had been a great comfort to him—a kind of free entertainment, a private theatre with a cast of thousands, as it were—in his lonely struggle against slavery in North Carolina.

Tonight Algernon was *my* vision, *my* comfort. In my dream-bound state it was as though by being in my dream, he was in the cell with me.

"Ah," said my ever-friendly ancestor, as he paced up and down the vales of my dream, "you do not lack bravery—I can see that. Your bravery is a form of foolishness, but bravery is almost always foolishness anyways—yours is just a slightly purer variety of foolhardiness. But you lack understanding of your opponent's mind and heart. You do not see the one thing that can defeat him, this ferocious colonel of yours."

"And what is that?"

"He is obsessed by honor. Honor is the thing that haunts him, day and night. He wants more than anything to be what you would also like to be, and neither of you are—Christian princes with perfect social skills and impeccable taste. He would like to be an old-world kind of aristocrat who knows instinctively how to handle every situation, from a pitched battle to an unexpected flirtation by the wife of a friend. Neither of you will achieve that, of course. You are both too clumsy, both of you lack social skills, and both care too much. You care too much about how you look to yourself; he cares too much about how he looks to other people. But that is still his great weakness—his desire to embody honor, and to embody it definitively in a single lifetime."

"Can he be worse than any man in your world?"

"He is completely evil," said Algernon my spectral uncle, "but I have known men who are likewise bad through and through.

Do you think slaveholding was a kind of harmless hobby or vocation invented by a few rich insecure men who had nothing better to do? It was a brutal system of pure evil: it got into one's blood and nerves. It changed everything."

"Why did they do it?"

"To become rich quickly. And then to pretend to be aristocrats, patricians in a country home, with a long driveway in a grove of trees, a beautiful garden and a small park. They thought they could do in one generation what it had taken every great family in Europe and the British Isles at least three generations to accomplish."

"Did it work?"

"No, because the means they used defeated them; anything based on human bondage can take people in only one direction, toward moral collapse and aesthetic vulgarity. In Europe they had at least a dream of service. In the American South, wealth was used for vanity and gaming—different games for the men than for their bored and angry wives, but gaming nonetheless."

"Then how must I defeat the colonel?"

"You must challenge him in the one area where he can be hurt. Real honor is forever beyond him, because no truly honorable man would accept a commission in an army that habitually rapes and murders civilians as a matter of policy. But he cannot let himself see that. In the meantime, he is being eaten alive by his desire to be an honorable man. So attack him there—at that point where he wants to be what he cannot be."

"Attack his honor?"

"No, attack the fact that he desires honor more than anything, but can never have it," said my great-great-great uncle Algernon, "but do it in a way that he does not expect. Do it with actions, not with words." Algernon was already fading. "I believe your last name is Sutterfield, is it not? Then you must already know that you are a natural-born prince of the quixotic gesture. Find some impassioned yet preposterous gesture, something your colonel cannot resist, that holds up the mirror to his cowardice. Make your move in a way that paralyzes him...and once you hook your fish, haul him in; give him an opportunity to prove his honor in the only way acceptable to you...by releasing your friend—"

"How can I do that?"

"You will know how, when your time comes."

And he was gone, my mysterious great-great-great uncle.

And I awoke.

On the morning of the fourth day of my second imprisonment, just as it was getting properly hot in my cell, I was taken to see the colonel. Two soldiers came to get me. I could hear them talking outside for a long time before they even turned the key in the lock.

When they opened the door the bright sun blinded me.

"Then colonel wants to see you," said one of the soldiers. "The colonel wants to see you now."

He spoke slowly and deliberately in Spanish, as though repeating commands in a canine training school.

"You have not asked me if I want to see *him*. What if I do not want to see the colonel?"

"He does not have to ask you," the soldier pointed out with great dignity. "He will see you whenever he wants to."

I had to concede that this was probably true.

I sat on the wooden bench in my cell but did not stand. I did not look forward to stepping out into the blazing sunlight.

"Yes, he will see you," the soldier said after a pause. "He will see you now."

"Then perhaps this is my lucky day."

I got up and staggered out of my cell, easing myself into the blinding sunlight.

I was very stiff—partly, I suspect, from dehydration. My body ached and I was covered with the film of dirt and sweat that one takes on after days of not bathing. They had not been giving me much soup, and I did not drink the water they gave me, for fear of getting sick; and I tended to drink the soup slowly, so that my body could assimilate the maximum amount.

The sun hit me like a hammer.

This was at a much lower elevation than Chapila Chica. There was no hiding from the sun. To get a bad sunburn in this place was to die; it was something that an Anglo had to be careful about. Luckily, I already had a very dark tan.

A second soldier stood a short distance away from the door to the cell. Both soldiers wore dark glasses. Sunglasses were big that year in Guatemala; sunglasses and muscle shirts and bracelets and epaulettes and various kinds of camouflage gear. Also cigarettes: every male who could afford them seemed to be a chain-smoker. American cigarettes were the favorite.

After I had gotten used to the sunlight—it took almost a full minute, standing there swaying slightly with my hands over my eyes—the soldier farthest from me gestured with his automatic rifle for me to follow him. I fell in behind him; the other soldier fell in behind me. We went single file into a door at the far end of the quadrangle, and down a hall. We were not speaking. Our footsteps echoed down the hall in front of us.

Anibal Montamara was waiting for me in his office. I was impressed again with how dark his face was: his cold blue eyes gleamed like turquoise bound in leather. His uniform was already dark with sweat under his armpits, and today he was wearing lightly tinted glasses; I had the impression that he had just come in from outside.

"Mi colonel!" said one of the soldiers.

They saluted and left. There was long silence.

"Mi colonel," I murmured finally.

"Did you expect someone else?" asked Colonel Efrain Anibal Montamara. He put a cigarette in his cigarette lighter and slowly lit it. He stood there looking at me. "Did you expect someone else to be in my office?"

"No," I said.

"Did you sleep well?"

"Very well. Except there was no bath."

"Pardon?"

"I asked for a room with a private bathroom."

He laughed; then suddenly cursed.

"And if I had you shot, what would you ask for?"

"A grave with a bathroom. A mausoleum with a bathroom." At this he smiled, but crossed himself quickly. "I am a North American," I continued, "and we are very clean. With us cleanliness is a kind of religion. Don't ask me to be something I am not."

"Of course."

We were both standing. He motioned for me to sit down.

"Of course," I said.

I clumsily unfolded a mental folding chair and sat. He sat down behind his desk. I could smell myself: it was the high cheesy ripeness of someone who has not bathed for days and has been sweating a great deal.

"I smell like a pig," I murmured.

"Ah yes," Anibal Montemara said, letting himself down in to his chair, "I am sorry about the room with a bath. I could not give you a room with a bath. There were none available."

"You do not have to apologize."

"It is an explanation, not an apology."

"*Yo lo aprecio mucho.* I appreciate it very much."

"Was it a good room otherwise?"

"Very nice. Especially for the flying cockroaches."

"Ah yes." He shrugged very gently and appeared to be thinking about that; and I found myself wondering if he had even been in such a cell himself. "Well—as I have said before, they, too, must live the life."

"As we must all live."

We were silent a long moment. The first-floor office was getting hot. There was some king of air conditioning in the building but it did not seem to be working well. In the late evening it had been hot, but not as stifling as this.

The colonel fanned himself. "I apologize for the heat."

"It's not as hot as my cell."

"No," he said thoughtfully, "I suppose it's not."

We were silent again.

"I have thought many times about you the last few days," he said.

"I have been here four days in all. Four days and four nights."

"Yes, four days and four nights," he said, "and during much of that time I was wondering what to do with you. But I also knew that it was you who chose to stay here."

"Because I will not leave without my friend Juan Delmonico."

His brows furrowed. He looked genuinely bewildered. "That is what you said. But do you see now?—Do you see that I can do nothing for you?"

I was honestly dumbfounded. In my heart of hearts I had not doubted for a moment that he would release Juan Delmonico, or help him in some way.

"What do you mean?" I said, my voice beginning to rise. "You are a colonel in the Guatemalan army! You are evidently the acting duty officer on this base—you are in charge! Juan Delmonico is being held here. What do you mean, you can't help me?" I was getting breathless. "Of course you can help. Start by finding out where he is!"

He spread his hands. "But you see, there is a problem. Even if I knew where he was, I couldn't release him."

"Why not?"

"He is a traitor and a coward who gave medical assistance to the enemy."

He sat with his hands folded serenely in front of him on his desk.

On his left were two gunmetal gym lockers. For the first time I noticed books on top of the lockers. The colonel was watching me carefully as I looked around his office. In spite of myself it occurred to me again how handsome he was, according to a certain standard of Latin American professionals of late middle age.

From far away came something that was not quite a scream, but a prolonged human yelp; then silence. I could see his eyes narrowing behind his dark glasses. Still we were silent.

"You will not help me find Juan Delmonico," I said, "so how do you expect me to help you find the printing press of the *rebeldes*?"

"You must find the answer to that yourself."

"So you will accept my help in finding the printing press—"

"I have already made that clear."

"—so in return you must release Juan Delmonico."

He looked genuinely surprised. "As I said before, I can't do that. And I'm really getting tired of having to explain that to you."

Perhaps, I decided, the colonel really thought I was going to help him find the rebel printing press whether he released Juan or not. That would make it a matter not of bluffing, but of self-delusion. There was a fine line between the two things his world, but they were definitely not the same thing. The more I thought about it, the more it seemed likely that he had talked himself into believing that I could indeed find this printing press.

"I can't release this man," he said again, opening his hands as if to show me there was nothing inside them, "and you know very well that I can't. How many times do I have to tell you?"

"Then I won't help you locate the printing press."

"Yes, you will."

"Why?"

He tilted back in his chair and looked at me. "Because of your great dedication to the struggle against communism. I have complete faith in you. You have told me yourself that we are brothers in the struggle against the same enemy."

I was silent. There was nowhere I could go with that.

"Let Juan Delmonico go," I said. "Please. Juan Delmonico is a patriot."

"I cannot do this."

"Then I will not leave without him."

"Are you ready to die?" he asked without missing a beat.

"Absolutely," I said without hesitation.

"But you see," the colonel said after a slight hesitation, "I do not really believe that. That is what you are saying, because you are behaving like an actor in a play. You said this before, and I did not believe you then. This is like playing a part in a theater to you. Maybe everything is a theater to you. But I do not really believe that you are ready to die for a skinny peasant with big ears; a man who cannot even read, who is a traitor to his country."

"The only way you can find out for sure is to kill me."

"No," Anibal Montamara said after another pause, "there is another way. I will send you away."

"And kill Juan Delmonico?"

He shrugged slowly, and turned his hands palms up. "I have nothing to do with that."

I remembered my recent dream and the conversation with my great-great-great uncle Algernon Sutterfield.

"You are the one who is an actor in the theatre," I said, "because you are not a true gentleman. You want more than anything else to be a gentleman, but you are not." The specific words I used were *caballero honrado*. "You think you are an honorable gentlemen…that is what you think!—an honorable gentleman!"

"You are insane, and becoming more insane each day."

"But it is only something that you *pretend* to be," I continued, "because you know very well that it is not true. And because you know, you must pretend to be a gentleman every day of your life! Do you not get weary with the pretense, imagining in your mind how you must look to someone else? Because if I can see through it—if even I can see that you do not have the honor of even a simple man like Juan Delmonico—cannot everybody else in the world see the same thing?"

The colonel said nothing, but I could tell I was getting through to him. How many people had been able to address him in this way? Not very many, I was certain. The only reason he was allowing me to continue was probably his curiosity—he wanted to see what I would say next.

"You do not even know what the word gentleman means," I said.

"Is that so?" He was speaking English again. "How do you know all these things?"

"Because I am a gentleman, and have always been a gentleman."

He began to laugh. "A North American cannot be a gentleman. You have no gentlemen there. You have rich Jews and capitalists and movie stars and people who inherit money. You have businessmen and corporations. You do not have the spiritual capability to be a gentleman."

"Our wealthy families define the word patrician."

"Patrician," he said slowly, thinking about it while he rolled the word on his tongue. "*Patricio*. But that is not exactly a *caballero*."

"Have you not heard of the southern part of the United States?"

He nodded reluctantly. "Yes, I have lived in one of your southern states."

"Then you will know that it is a land that has produced the truest gentleman in all of the Americans." He lifted his hand to argue the point but I paid him no mind. "My family came directly from Britain three hundred years ago, and in Britain we were knights of the realm. We were rich squires who were given great titles. Do you think that I do not know what a gentleman is?"

He laughed incredulously. "This is a joke."

"No, I'm not joking now."

"Next you will say you were educated in England."

"Of course I was," I said without hesitation, raising my voice.

"Next you will tell me you went to Eton."

"Exactly." Madness was upon me. I breathed deeply and projected my voice, an actor trying to reach the last row. "Am I the only Etonian you have ever encountered in your deprived existence on this planet? Shame, palpable shame and dishonor, that you would not know this scapegrace son as a true Etonian when you see him! It's all in the way we carry ourselves, don't you see?"

"What are you talking about?"

I couldn't stop myself. I raved on at length about an imaginary Etonian ethos—how different it had been in the days of Orwell and Connolly, the deplorable modern tendencies that were sapping the strength of the upper classes, the daily life of an Etonian punctuated by wild escapades in London; and so on *ad infinitum*. As I was yoiking up this bizarre nonsense I was actually shouting.

Anibal Montamara didn't know what to make of it.

"And you, sir—you!" I continued. "You and your comrades…whores, pimps and racetrack touts! What on earth do you expect to gain by all this pretense? What on earth would you do if the Queen came to visit?" I leaned forward. "I'll bet you don't even have a dress uniform!"

"You're mad."

"Quite. But do you deny that your officer corps lacks even the pretense of a dress uniform?"

"Of course I have a dress uniform," he said stiffly.

"I doubt it, sir."

"I have one."

"I can hardly credit that, sir, unless I see it with my own eyes."

"What do you mean?"

"Show it to me!"

I could tell that he was debating whether to throw me out of his office at once, or wait and see what I did next. Again, curiosity got the upper hand.

"I do not have to show anything to you."

"Lies!" I said. "Do not compound your lack of grace by lying about what can only be earned! Of course you do not have a dress uniform! No Guatemalan army officer has a dress uniform!"

"Every Guatemalan officer has a dress uniform!"

"An unthinkable calumny!"

"My dress uniform is hanging in one of the lockers behind me."

"You do not help yourself by prevarication, sir!"

The colonel frowned. Clearly he did not understand what I was up to. Nor did I, at that point—I was simply making it up as I went along.

"You are completely mad," he said. "The heat of the cell has driven you mad. You North Americans are too delicate."

He stood up and spun a combination lock once, twice, and finally three tunes; and opened one of the gym lockers to his left. There was a white uniform handing on a wooden coat hanger. I saw a little gold braid hanging from an epaulette.

"See?" he asked. "My dress uniform. Are you satisfied?"

"Don't be silly! You don't even have gloves!"

He poked around in the locker. "Of course I do!" He withdrew the gloves and a gold-tipped swagger stick. The color of the gold on the swagger stick matched the gold braid on the uniform. "There," he said somewhat smugly, laying the gloves and the swagger stick on the corner of the desk, "what do you call *these?"*

It was then—and only then—that I knew what I had to do. It was just as my great-great-great uncle Algernon had said: *You will know when the time comes.*

And the time had come.

"If you do not release my friend," I said, stepping up to the desk to a place directly in front of Anibal Montamara, "my honor will be vilified beyond a point at which words could no longer suffice to make it whole and clean. I will have to demand satisfaction!"

He blinked. "What are you talking about?"

"I will have to meet you on the field of honor."

"What?"

"I will challenge you to a duel if you do not release my friend."

"A duel?"

"Duelo."

He stood there looking at me. What I was saying seemed to hit him.

All at once he began to laugh. Colonel Efrain Anibal Montamara threw back his head and roared with laughter; and in it I heard the laughter of all the powerful of the earth as they beheld the madmen, the fools, and the idealists they were so willing and able to crush underfoot.

"Yes," I muttered to myself, "it is a joke. But it is not a joke that either of us will soon forget."

He continued to laugh.

I picked up the gloves lying on the corner of his desk. In so doing, I dislodged the swagger stick, and it fell off the desk, its gold point clacking leadenly against the tile floor. The colonel's eyes followed the swagger stick which was probably much more valuable than the gloves. He was at the point of bending over the retrieve the swagger stick—but evidently there was something about the way I was handling his gloves that made him pause.

"Give me the gloves."

"Call for your soldiers, coward."

"Give the gloves to me!"

"I will not." I continued to hold them firmly in my right hand.

"You must call your soldiers before I will give you your gloves."

He took my measure. He saw that I was serious—and pushed the lever on his ancient intercom and barked a command. Two of his soldiers arrived at his office door holding their rifles.

"Thank you," I said.

"Now that my soldiers are here, would you please give me the gloves?"

"No."

"Then my soldiers will take them."

"First I must do something—something very important." I brandished the gloves slightly. "Now that your soldiers are here to witness it, I must challenge you."

"Challenge me?"

"To a duel."

"You are completely mad."

"And so are you."

He looked away, in the general direction of his soldiers. It had almost surely occurred to him by this time that I was about to do something that would embarrass him. He glanced back at me just in time to see me strike him full across the face with his gloves. I put my whole body into it, swinging as hard as I could. The sound of the gloves hitting his face made a soft but satisfying *thwack*.

I cannot adequately describe the colonel's reaction.

There was a sharp intake of breath, and an almost feminine shudder: and then the lunar blue eyes fixed me with a stare of hatred. He stood there looking at me. There was reddish welt across his dark leather face.

I threw the gloves down on the desk.

"Duelo," I said very loudly, almost yelling, making sure that the soldiers could hear it. I continued to speak loudly in Spanish. "I challenge you to a duel in the presence of soldiers in your command!" One beat, two. "If you do not fight a duel with me, you will be forever dishonored—your honor has been impugned

beyond the ability of words to redeem it!"

He opened his mouth to speak, but couldn't.

Then in English he said, "Now I really will have to kill you."

"Then we must meet on the field of honor!" I chirruped happily. I said it twice, in both English and Spanish.

The two soldiers at the door were horrified.

"A duel to the death!" I shrieked. "I demand satisfaction!"

I said it several times in Spanish, just to make sure that the soldiers understood it. There was no question that they did—on their faces was a horror beyond the power of words to describe. It was the worst nightmare of every enlisted man in the Guatemalan army: to personally witness the deliberate dishonor of a ranking officer, and to carry that away with them in memory. That made them complicit with the dishonor itself, simply by witnessing it. I wondered how they would talk about it later, and how word of the incident would make its way around the base.

This time I was in the cell for a full week. On the morning of the last day—the eleventh day I had been on the army base—two soldiers came to get me. They deposited me outside the front gate. They said nothing to me and I asked them no questions. It took me about ten minutes to walk to the main road, at which point I started hitching rides. Again, I do not remember very much about how I got to the trail to Chapila Chica, any more than I remember how I got from Chapila Chica to the base. I got rides from people; I looked like a disheveled madman; and nobody talked to me any more than they had to.

Nor did I talk to them.

If Juan had been released, I fully expected him to be waiting at his house, or perhaps he would meet me on the path to Chapila Chica. If the army was determined to keep him, I knew exactly what I would do. I would organize an international human-rights group that could call attention to Juan's imprisonment. I had reasonably good organizing skills, and I was a North American, which meant that I could set up the headquarters of the group safely in the US or Mexico City. I would make it my life's work to obtain the release of Juan Delmonico. It would give my life meaning.

It would not be such a bad thing. It would allow me to do something concrete about the massive violations of human rights in Guatemala. I would organize people both inside and outside Guatemala; *Guatemaltecos* and *Norteamericanos* working together for a common cause. We would not be silenced.

I was looking forward to it.

I was sleeping in the cab of a deuce-and-a-half truck with no windshield and a truck-bed full of lashed-down chicken coops when I suddenly realized that we had overshot the trail to Chapila Chica. There was something wrong with the driver's brakes, so it took him a long time to stop; and it took me a good half hour to walk back to the deserted buildings on the main highway where the path to Chapila Chica began. I started up the trail feeling (and no doubt looking) like a wraith of death.

I had been on the trail only about an hour or so when I saw Padre Julio coming toward me. He did not wave at me, although it was clear that he saw me.

Apparently somebody had seen me on the path, and told him. For some reason I was not surprised to see Padre Julio, although I had no idea what he was doing there. He was apparently making good time; and then suddenly he stopped—he simply stopped and waited for me to come to him, without walking toward me.

He was wearing a hat and he did not stop to take off the hat and wipe his face, as he usually did.

He looked exhausted and shaken.

I was wheezing badly from my asthma as I approached him. I had gotten used to the asthmatic wheezing, and in any case my lungs had made an adjustment to the lower elevation of the Zone

Twenty army base. I half-expected Padre Julio to comment on my bearded face and overall filthiness. But he did not.

"What happened to you?"

"I was a prisoner on the army base."

"Are you alright?"

"I'm alive."

He paused.

"Something terrible had happened here." His voice was shaking in a way I hadn't heard before.

"You'd better tell me," I said.

"There was a massacre. The village of Chapila Grande was destroyed by the army. The people were all taken out to a field outside the village. They were all killed. The only survivors were two children who were visiting relatives at San Jose del Rio."

I stared at him.

"But Chapila Grande is a pro-government village," I pointed out reasonably. "The soldiers have absolutely no reason to attack it."

"I know. Nobody understands it. But it happened."

"When?"

"Two days ago."

For a moment I thought I was dreaming, back in my cell.

"Tell me exactly what happened," I said.

"The soldiers marched everyone in Chapila Grande to a place outside the village and killed all of them. They left the bodies in the sun. People were coming from all the villages in the area to look at the bodies. The men from Chapila Chica dug a long ditch, and we buried them in a mass grave. The vultures were everywhere."

"No," I said.

"Yes. That is exactly how it happened."

"But it was *your* village that the army hated," I pointed out again, the very soul of reasonableness. "It was Little Chapila that the army suspected of helping the rebels, not Big Chapila."

"The army did not touch Chapila Chica. Some of the families of Chapila Chica are hiding in the caves of Trotzil Gapachula mountain. They are preparing to leave for Mexico. A guide is coming from the west to help them."

"And the people of Big Chapila?"

"Everyone is dead."

"Everyone?"

"Everyone. I will show you the mass grave where we buried the people."

Try as I might, I could not think of any reason why Padre Julio would lie to me about this.

"Are you sure about this? The army did not attack Chapila Chica?"

"They did not come near Chapila Chica."

"There must have been a mistake."

"Yes."

And then it hit me—if Chapila Chica was safe, Sofia Mendez was also safe. Thanks be to God, my beautiful Sofia Mendez was safe!

But why wasn't she out here, to meet me?

And then—only God can help me with this—I laughed. What a horror show! The black comedy of it! Chapila Grande, the village of pious government collaborators, had been wiped out by government troops! "They supported the government, yet the army slaughtered the entire village!"

Father Julio looked at me as though I were mad, as indeed I must have been. I could hardly wait to hear what Sofa thought of all this.

"Where is Sofia?"

"Maitland," he was saying, "listen to me."

"I need to talk to Sofia."

I couldn't form any opinion about the astonishing news, or even believe in it completely, until I talked to Sofia about it.

"No," Julio said.

"Did she go back to Guatemala City?"

"No."

By now the dread was setting in. I did not like the desperate look in Padre Julio's eyes.

"Where is she?"

Maitland, he was saying patiently.

He was trying to tell me something, but all I could think about was that I wanted to talk to Sofia.

"Where is Sofia?"

His face was white.

"I need to tell you something," Julio said.

"Then tell me."

He stood there in the sun getting whiter and whiter and more deathlike. He took my hands in his; his hands were shaking.

"The afternoon of the massacre, Sofia went to Chapila Grande to talk to the people. She thought they might have seen you. She was there when the troops arrived." Father Julio put his hand on my shoulders as though to keep me from falling. "Sophia was killed along with the others, Maitland. I gave her last rites, and I helped to bury her body with the others."

Chapter Eight

After the massacre (*la violencia*, as the people around San Jose del Rio called it), I did not go back to the village of Chapila Chica but instead took up residence in the deserted village of Chapila Grande. I camped out in a small house with two rooms, a kitchen and a bedroom, one of the few wooden houses in the village; the others were mainly concrete-block buildings. In this house had lived the woman from the California church who had originally converted Chapila Grande to Pentecostalism. I had the feeling that she had just stepped out and might soon be coming back, so I left everything in the house exactly as she left it.

During the day this wooden house was hot, but not as hot as the other houses. At night I slept on the floor in the kitchen on a pile of old blankets, under which I placed a canvas ground cover. When it was cool at night, I wrapped myself in a single green comforter for warmth. The comforter, which was cheap and satisfyingly old and dirty, looked like it might have been a gift from the village's Pentecostal mother church in California. It was the kind of item one might have bought at a discount store in the San Joaquin or Sacramento valley, at K-Mart or Target, perhaps, or a Wal-Mart on some lonely stretch of Highway 99.

In fact, a lot of things in this strange little house had a discount-store look: pillows and pillow-cases, plastic-rimmed mirrors, cheap tapered candles by the box, gallon containers of Dr. Bronner's liquid soap. Over the back door was a rough canvas lean-to under which the woman who lived here had probably bathed, using water from the river; the ground there was bare and dark and smelled of liquid soap.

I wondered what had gone through the mind of the California missionary when the soldiers ordered out of her house. She must have suspected that something bad was about to happen. She might even have suspected that they might not be coming back for some time—that they were about to be temporarily relocated, perhaps.

But a massacre?

No, that made no sense, given Chapila Grande's unqualified support of the government and the army.

The thatched hut next door had been torched, the only house in the entire village that had been burned. That was strange, to say the least—I never did find out why that house had been burned to the ground, and all the others spared. Perhaps people had tried to hide inside, and the soldiers had burned them out. Or perhaps one or two of the soldiers had casually started to burn the houses, and their commanding officer had abruptly ordered them to do something else.

In any case, the smell of burnt thatch was very strong, even inside the house where I slept, strong enough to give me asthma almost every night. Still, I made no effort to clear away the charred remains of the burned house, because I liked the smell. It made me feel closer to the destruction that had occurred on the day when Sofia died—and therefore closer to Sofia.

It was deep night when Padre Julio first came to see me. Why he came over in the night I do not know—perhaps he wanted to make sure I was there. I had been in Chapila Grande ten days or so, and I still couldn't sleep; I was sitting at one of the two unstable chairs at the kitchen table when I heard someone coming. It was two or three hours before dawn, and the little house had cooled down nicely; I had a single candle burning, and the pale moonlight outside was so luminous that it cast shadows. Because it was preternaturally quiet in the deserted village, and because the noise level was so low—and also because my hearing had become strangely acute—I thought I heard Padre Julio when he was still a long ways away, when he was still on the path that wound around the outcropping of rock and dropped into the village.

The footsteps stopped just inside the village. I really didn't want to go to the door, didn't want to talk.

"Maitland?" he called out. "It's Padre Julio."

I knew it was Padre Julio, but I said nothing.

"Can you hear me? Look, I know you're there."

"I'm tired," I called back finally. "*Cansado*."

"I have to talk to you."

I got off my rickety chair and went to the door.

Padre Julio was standing in the pale moonlight; he was unshaven, and there was a stricken look on his face. He was wearing his clerical collar but no hat, which meant that he intended to get back to Chapila Chica before the sun came up.

"You shouldn't be on the trail alone at night," I said.

"Maitland?" He tried to smile. "Is that you?"

The front door was broken but screened, and there were some cloth sacks hanging over it to cover a small hole in the screen. I pulled them aside so he could see me.

"It's me. Come on in."

He took his time coming inside the house, and when he did he stood looking at me in the light of the single candle. "You look terrible," he announced.

"Looking terrible is an important part of my new monastic rule."

"Yes, well—" He paused. "I'm here because I'm concerned about you."

"That's your problem, not mine."

"I can see you're growing a beard." He took a step closer. "Do you bathe or change your clothes?"

"I can bathe in the river when I feel like it."

"That's not what I asked."

"Some people are meant to live away from the world."

"And mortify the flesh?"

"Something like that."

He took a deep breath and shook his head.

"I wanted to make sure you're alive," he said, looking around the room. "What are you eating?"

"Beans."

I explained to Padre Julio that I lit a fire once a day to cook a pot of beans, and I ate the beans throughout the day. I also had rice, just in case I got tired of eating beans; but I had almost no appetite, so the beans were usually enough.

"Do you have everything you need?"

"Yes, thank you."

Julio went to the broken screen door and looked out at the silent village in the darkness, then back at me. He shuddered. "This is madness. You can't stay here."

"I just want to be left alone."

"The soldiers might come back to Chapila Grande."

"I don't care. I hope they do."

Overnight I had become the most important citizen of Chapila Grande, because I was the only citizen of Chapila Grande.

"I have news about Juan Delmonico," Padre Julio said.

"Is he dead?"

"Yes."

"I thought so." I sat down on one of the two unstable kitchen chairs. "Come on in, then. I'd better hear all of it."

Julio came into the kitchen. The moonlight came in through the door, but I let the single candle burn. "I guess I've been waiting for you to come and tell me that Juan is dead."

He looked around. "Can I sit down?"

"You can if you want to."

"Do you usually sit at the table?"

"I can do anything I want to. I'm the only person home."

He sat down slowly on the other chair at the table in the kitchen. For the moment I remained standing.

So, I said, "Tell me about Juan."

"His body was found by some peasants."

"How did he die?"

"Killed with a machete. Most likely he was killed by the same soldiers who took him into custody."

"Any idea when?"

"My guess is that they killed him the same day they took him. His body was found near San Jose del Rio, near a camp that some soldiers set up in an abandoned house near the river."

"Had he been tortured? Mutilated?"

"A patch of skin had been pulled off his back. Except for that, he wasn't mutilated. He didn't appear to have been tortured. The skin may have been scraped out after he was dead. There's no way to know." He paused. "It's my guess that the soldiers never had any intention of taking him to the army base. Probably they had orders to kill him right away."

"It happened quickly, then."

"He was buried six days ago in the San Jose del Rio churchyard," Father Julio continued, "and I officiated at the funeral."

"Did anybody come?"

"Many people came to the funeral."

"I didn't know about it."

"Would you have come to the funeral if you'd been invited?"

"No."

"It was felt that you were already in some danger, and we didn't want to expose you to any additional danger. So you weren't told."

A moment's silence ensued. "Is that all?" I asked.

He shrugged but kept his eyes on my face. "Some of the people in the district are afraid of you. Some think you are psychotic. Many say they can't trust you."

I kept waiting for the bad feeling, the feeling like a trap door opening in the bottom of my stomach, but I felt nothing. I could have been a piece of volcanic rock lying at the bottom of the ocean.

"Where is Juan's wife?"

"I'm arranging for her to leave the area." He shifted slightly in his chair. "As long as I'm here, do you have other questions?"

"Questions about what?"

Julio cleared his throat. "Do you want to know what happened here in Chapila Grande?"

"All the witnesses are dead, aren't they?"

"There was a survivor who lived long enough to tell us about it."

My heart jumped, and my voice didn't work at first. "Was the survivor Sofia?"

"No," he said quickly, his voice also catching slightly. "Sofia was gone when I arrived."

"Did she tell you why she wanted to go to Chapila Grande?"

"Something about their hymns—she wanted to talk to them about their hymns. And for some reason she thought they might have seen you."

So, I thought.

Then a strange thought occurred to me, which was that it might help Padre Julio to talk about how it happened.

"Okay, tell me what you know about the massacre," I said.

I put my hands on the table and waited.

"Everybody in the village died at the same place. None of the people died in their houses—they all went with the army as soon as they were ordered to do so. At first they had no reason to believe that anything bad would happen."

"Then?"

"The soldiers ordered the men to dig a long ditch. Then soldiers told them they were going to bury ammunition in it, but the villagers guessed that they were lying. They stopped digging when the ditch was only a foot deep. They demanded to know what was going on."

"And then?"

"The soldiers lined them up and shot them, and they fell backwards onto each other. The soldiers left them that way."

I knew about the massacres of the Guatemalan army. I knew what they did, and how they usually did it. The ghastly details interested me not at all, any more than knowing what every man, woman and child in the gas chambers of Auschwitz did after the pellets were dropped. Since the villagers of Chapila Grande were human, I was reasonably sure they were quite hysterical when they were being killed.

Or maybe not. It made no difference.

Now it was over for them: which was the very best thing about being dead. Once you were killed, you no longer cared about how the killing was done. The fascination with grisly details was part of a world to which the dead no longer belonged. So why should I worry about it, if I didn't like grisly details? I was closer to the dead than the living right now, and would be for some time.

But there was one particular thing, a certain thing, that wouldn't go away until I asked about it. "Were the woman raped?"

"There was no rape. The women were not separated from the men at any time. The troops seemed to be in a hurry. They seemed to be under orders to kill everybody as quickly as possible, and leave the area. Maybe they were afraid of an ambush, although I don't know why they would be."

I did not disbelieve what he said, but neither did I believe him. As long as there was one chance in a billion that he wasn't telling the whole truth, I felt that the fix was in. *It's all public relations anyway,* I thought. *All playacting.*

"Was anybody mutilated?"

"No."

He was still answering too quickly.

Couldn't he just take a little more time? I wondered. *Doesn't he realize how phony he sounds?*

"Well, thank you," I said. "Thank you for that thoughtful report."

"For what?"

"A spirited yet restrained performance. That is what I would write if I were a drama critic."

"What the hell are you talking about?"

"A thoroughly spirited performance, that was at the same time skillfully understated, implied rather that acted out in plain view. All done by an actor who was not at all inhibited by the disadvantage of having to play himself. That is what I would write in my review of your performance."

"Maitland," he said, "whatever you're doing to yourself, stop it."

"I can't."

"Why not?"

"I'm in the throes of a spiritual breakthrough."

I explained it to him. It was a startlingly simple proposition: the world was evil, but as long as I *knew* it was evil, and I had the strength to hate it, I was not completely evil myself. I would strive daily; I would do whatever I had to do, to hate the world and everything in it—starting with myself.

"That's quite a vision," Julio said. "What does it accomplish?"

"It gives me a moral compass, a moral philosophy."

Padre Julio shrugged and sighed deeply. He did not seem inclined to protest. "I'll be back in a couple of days. We can continue the discussion then."

"Don't bother."

"I can't just leave you here alone. You're a raving maniac."

"I'm doing my best."

He sighed and shook his head. "Is there anything I can do for you? Anything?"

"Yes, there certainly *is* something you can do for me," I said, the very soul of sweet reason, "and you can do it now. You explained *how* the massacre at Chapila Grande happened—now let's talk about *why*. Chapila Grande supported the government. So why did the army kill everyone in a village that supported them?"

"I don't know. Nobody does."

"The army must have had a reason. What *could* have been their reason? *Was* there any reason?"

"It's a complete mystery."

"Somebody must know something. Things like this don't just happen by accident."

Padre Julio said nothing.

After a long time he went to the front door and stood there looking out through the screen.

"It happened so quickly," he said. "The soldiers didn't even stop to burn the houses, you know. It was as though they were retaliating for something that had just happened, as though they had just been ambushed. But how could that be? The troops hadn't been fired on. They had nothing to retaliate for."

"Did this village ever help the rebels?"

"Never."

"Did anyone in this village every publicly oppose the government on any particular issue?"

"Never. This village always supported the government, even before they converted to Pentecostalism. Nobody in this village was ever involved in any kind of political opposition, much less armed struggle. It is well known that Chapila Grande always supported the government, even when the village was still Catholic."

"That's what I heard."

"It was Chapila Chica that was always the radical village, the subversive village. The Pentecostals in Chapila Grande even tried to incite the army to attack Chapila Chica—they said we were communists. So why did the army attack Chapila Grande, why did they kill *them*, and not the people of Chapila Chica? Nobody can figure it out."

I continued to live in the little house in Chapila Grande. All the time I was there I felt exactly like a house guest, however disorganized my thinking was, as though I were housesitting for a person who would soon return. The woman who lived there had stepped out for a few moments or a few weeks, and I was taking care of her property, waiting for her to come back.

I was also waiting for my beautiful Sofia Mendez; but the new world she was in had its protocols. Sofia had gone to Chapila Grande, and never come back. Didn't that make them friends for all time—comrades, even—in the great ecumenism of death?

Perhaps I would not be able to see Sofia again until the Pentecostal missionary from California formally introduced us, since Sofia had been killed with her. Only then—after the woman from California had formally clarified their difficult relationship—would I be able to make love to Sofia again. Then we would make love in the schoolhouse, but the schoolhouse would be in Chapila Grande.

I woke up at nights wanting Sofia, reaching out to her, but finding only myself.

When Sofia was alive, I had lain next to her, waiting each night for the Pentecostal singing to begin; and now that I slept here in Chapila Grande, where the singing had begun, I waited for it even more impatiently. There were times when I heard it, at first not as voices but as memories. Then when memory faded I waited patiently for the singing to begin in the field outside the village, because that is where I thought of them as being, even though the field held only their remains.

The most important part of this notion was not just that I imagined the villagers of Chapila Grande returning, but that if they returned from the dead, we —Sofia and myself—would join them. We would live in Chapila Grande in the new schoolhouse we would build. We would join the little community of worshippers in Big Chapila, and they would teach us to sing. And we would be safe, *because the singing would protect us.* This delusion I believed with all my heart, that we would be absolutely and totally safe, Sofia and myself, *as long as we learned how to sing.*

That was my obsession. It was as good as any other obsession, I thought.

Each night I waited for the Pentecostals to sing, and after a time I *did* hear them singing, at first only a few times. And when it began, I felt that Sofia and the others were on their way. It might take her a long time to get here, but she was headed home.

I knew it was an auditory hallucination, but I had never heard anything more beautiful, so I wanted it to continue. And yes, sometimes the songs came from the killing field outside the village, but it also came from other directions, so I was not upset by that. The singing was my connection to the dead of Chapila Grande, but also to Sofia, because she had come here from another direction to meet with them. Now they were together.

Each night I waited excitedly for the singing to begin, however faint and distant it might be; and it happened sometimes that if I began to drift off to sleep and heard the singing, I felt that I was back in Chapila Chica in the schoolhouse, lying next to Sofia and just beginning to hear the singing that would make us safe, because when people were singing they were not killing or being killed.

Some nights—quite often, in fact—the singing filled my dreams. And then I would sit up abruptly, trembling and awakened; sometimes the singing would fade as soon as I awakened, but on a few occasions the singing went on all night, and I lay drifting in and out of sleep, listening to the passionate beauty in the night air.

I was never afraid because I was letting it all happen. It was my special project.

But other times all I could hear were the sounds of the wind, or one of the big cats that haunted this part of the mountains; and Sofia still had not come. Some nights I heard the wind, the cats, and the singing all together. Some nights the singing was constant and powerful, like the soft but rhythmic *shhhhhhhhhhh* of a tide that rose and fell on the mountain, a ghostly, hallucinated echo chamber collapsing dreamily into its own slow-motion wavelength.

I was amazed by how the singing filled my nights; and I was even more amazed at how it comforted me. It was proof (the singing voices were proof) that the people of Chapila Grande were still here; and if they could sing, Sofia could sing too, and she would be with them.

The second time Padre Julio came to visit me I had been dozing all morning, and it was almost noon. The heat in the kitchen was overwhelming. My sleep had been disturbed, too full of auditory hallucinations and strange images to provide much rest; but I did not want to awaken yet. I wanted to see what would happen next in the psychotic borderland into which I had drifted.

I heard the crunch of footsteps and rolled off my pallet and went to the door. It was Julio, all right. He was wearing a floppy hat I hadn't seen before. He took it off and stood shading his eyes with it. I could not see him very clearly in the bright light.

"Good morning, Maitland," he said. "Can I talk to you?"

"It's too early to talk."

He looked at his watch. "It's almost noon."

"I decide when it's early and when it's late. And I don't get up until I'm ready."

"Please?"

On an impulse I stood away from the door and made room for him to come inside. He came in and stood looking around the kitchen, until I motioned for him to sit down. We sat on the two infirm chairs and sat looking at each other across the kitchen table.

"Could you stop staring at me?" I asked.

"Sorry."

No doubt I did look terrible, by any standard, and I was also irritated from being awakened. "Why did you come here?"

"I wanted to ask you to come back to Chapila Chica with me."

"I don't want to come back to Chapila Chica," I said.

"Why not?"

"I'm closer to Sofia here. But Chapila Chica would remind me of Sofia when she was alive. The schoolhouse would remind me of what it felt like to make love to her. I can't handle that."

He sighed, then nodded.

Of course he had known that Sofia and I were lovers, everybody had known that. But it seemed somehow wrong for him to acknowledge it so quickly and so easily. I wanted to go back to the time when everyone was pretending that it was secret. If it could be a secret again, perhaps Sofia would be safe, and everything would be okay.

"What are you going to do?"

"I'm waiting for the second Pentecost."

"Meaning?"

"The second coming of the Pentecostal missionary from California."

He continued to look steadily at me. "I want you to come back to Chapila Chica for a very special reason. I want you to come back to guarantee our safety."

I was trying to make sense of what he'd just said, but I was drawing a blank. "Meaning what?"

"Remember that I told you that many people in Little Chapila would be leaving for Mexico? Some have already left, but others are staying. That's what I want to talk to you about. Alan Klein came to see me yesterday. He told me that the soldiers at Zone Twenty will never bother Chapila Chica if you are living in the village."

I was astounded.

"Did Klein tell you why he believed that?"

"He said that an officer at Zone Twenty told him so. This officer interrogated you and decided that you were insane."

I made it a point not to show any reaction. "That wouldn't stop them from killing me," I said, "and it certainly wouldn't stop them from killing the rest of you either."

"They don't want to kill an American unless they have to. Therefore if you come to stay at Chapila Chica they will not attack us. Alan Klein told me this. He said I should personally ask you to come back to Little Chapila. Just by being there, you could guarantee the safety of the village."

I thought about it but decided against it. It sounded too much like one of Klein's ugly jokes.

"No," I said, "you cannot trust anything this man Klein says. He will say anything, just to watch your reaction. He will say something on one occasion and something completely different on another occasion. I don't know what he's up to now, but you can't take anything he says seriously."

"How do you know so much about him?"

"Never mind."

Julio said nothing for a long time. "I'd still like you to come back to Chapila Chica."

"Maybe," I said, "but you must do something for me first."

"What?"

"You won't like it."

"What is it?"

"You must perform a marriage ceremony."

His eyes widened. "A marriage ceremony? What are you talking about?"

"For myself and Sofia Mendez."

This, too, had become an obsession since I had learned of Sofia's death. Did not the nuns symbolically marry their Lord, who had been put to death and then miraculously resurrected, and then taken up to Heaven?

If that were true, why couldn't I marry my dead girlfriend, who had made me so happy in the middle of the night?

Padre Julio was looking at me with disgust and disbelief.

"Sofia is dead, Maitland," he said slowly. "What are you talking about? I saw her body."

"I need to marry her anyway. I want to stand above the place where she is buried, and I want you to marry us."

"I don't want to hear another word of this."

"Then forget about me coming back to Little Chapila."

"This is absolutely insane."

"Absolutely."

He was starting to be angry with me. "You acknowledge that? That you are psychotic to have such thoughts? That this conversion is complete madness?"

"Of course."

"Then why are we having it?"

"Because some kinds of madness make more sense than most sanity."

Padre Julio was having difficulty being patient with me. "Sofia is *dead*, Maitland!"

"That is exactly why I want to marry her. Because she *is* dead." He was staring at me, so I continued, "It would be the simplest marriage you have ever performed. We go to the field outside the village where the people of Big Chapila are buried. We would stand on the mass grave where she is buried, you and I. You say the words from the prayer-book; and she and I will be married, and it will be over."

He sat there looking at me. "Are you testing me in some way?"

"No."

"I was afraid of that. No, I don't believe you are."

"I said I wasn't."

"Why do you want this? Really?"

"I believe she was pregnant when she died."

I could see this made no sense to him, and I wasn't surprised, since it made no sense to me either. It was simply one more obsession that had sprung up and been endlessly elaborated in my dreams. To make things right, I had to marry Sofia.

"This is worse than madness," Padre Julio was saying, "because for one thing, it is incredibly disrespectful to Sofia Mendez, and you are insulting the hell out of me too. What kind of California madness is this, that you would make fun of the sanctity of marriage? What you suggest would not help you, and it would not help Sofia. Everything has been forgiven. That is why Christ died for us, so that we would not have to torture ourselves with such things."

I shrugged.

"If you will not marry me to Sofia, I will not come back to Chapila Chica."

Father Julio looked at me for a long time. I gathered that he was beginning to realize exactly how crazy I had gotten. Or perhaps, despite my denial, he thought I really was testing him—that I was proposing such an act of sacrilege precisely because it was unthinkable, and would drive him permanently away.

And wasn't that one reason I was proposing it?

I was silent too, while he thought about her. There was nothing oppressive about our silence; it came naturally, like the underbrush that was already starting to creep in upon the village of Chapila Grande and cover the sides of the cinderblock houses.

"You must have loved her very much," he said finally.

"No, I didn't love her—I *couldn't* love her."

He stared at me uncomprehendingly. "Then why—?"

"I was emotionally incapable of loving Sofia when she was alive, because I thought she could hurt me again, like my wife hurt me. But now, now that she is dead, I love her."

"But not before."

"No, not before. I couldn't love anybody then."

Julio sat looking at me.

"How long have you known this?"

"Since I came to live here in Chapila Grande."

"So now that Sofia is dead—"

"Now that Sofia is dead, I love her." I paused. "You may

laugh, if you wish; you may judge me—certainly you judge me to be insane, that much you have already said. But I never thought I would love anybody again. I've waited all my life to love someone this much."

"I'm not laughing at you."

"But you *are* judging me."

"No," he said wearily, "I don't even judge you— you can't judge a madman. You're not guilty by reason of insanity."

"Then you will understand that I have to commit myself in this way, by marrying her, in front of God and at least one person."

"Marriage is a sacrament. It's not meant to be used as some kind of California psychotherapy."

I shrugged.

"Suppose," I said, "just this one time, it *is* some kind of California-style psychotherapy. Why not make the most of it?"

"It is unhealthy. Too many Americans are involved in this kind of self-indulgence. It's narcissism in the name of love."

"So is most religion."

"It wouldn't be good for you. It isn't even good for you to think about it. Any secular person could tell you that, much less a priest."

"It is a very simple proposition," I said. "If you do what I ask of you, I will come back to Chapila Chica. You will have your California hostage to guarantee the safety of your village—at least according to Alan Klein. If you don't do what I ask, I won't come near Little Chapila. It's as simple as that."

"Maitland—"

I stood up.

"Marry me to Sofia Mendez. We will stand on the earth above her grave and you will say the words."

"You are suffering from major depression," he said, getting up to go.

"Think it over!"

"There is nothing to think over," he said.

He left the door hanging open. I had taken away the rough sackcloth that had been hanging on the door; without the extra weight, what was left of the door would not swing closed. I could see Julio walking the path that led to the main path that went to Little Chapila. From behind he seemed to walk with a considerable weight on his shoulders—he had developed a noticeable stoop, I thought.

Something about that made me laugh.

Of course it wasn't right, to laugh at his anxiety. But that was one of the prerogatives of madness, one of its many privileges, to laugh at the perplexity of others, even their suffering, as long as one was similarly prepared to laugh at one's own suffering.

The name of the woman who had lived in the small wooden house where I now stayed was Kalisa Brun. She was a missionary from a loosely organized Pentecostal denomination in the San Joaquin Valley of California, and an honest-to-God Pentecostal preacher, although she probably hadn't been ordained. I discovered these things by going through her belongings in the house. I did not judge her, because the reasons for judging the Pentecostals was gone, now that she was dead and everybody in the village was dead too.

It would have been easy to judge Kalisa Brun, because I thought she was a fanatic. Yet she *had* left California to come here to live. I wondered if there were many liberal Episcopalians who would do what she did, leave their homes and come all the way to Guatemala to minister to poor people in a forgotten village on a mountain. Not many, I decided.

I got to know Kalisa Brun well, living in her house. It was clear that when the soldiers had ordered all of them out of their houses, she had left very suddenly taking nothing with her. She had simply walked out the door and went with everybody else in with village to the place where they would die. People ordered from their homes by soldiers do not take things with them: they leave in a state of confusion and die in a state of shock, and they leave things in their houses exactly as they were in the moments before they were taken away.

Evidently Kalisa had been washing dishes when the soldiers arrived; half the dishes were finished, and half waiting to be washed. Two wooden tubs—dark soapy water in one and rinse water in the other—stood silently on the rough ledge under her cabinets, waiting like ghostly witnesses for the task to be completed.

I left the dishes alone.

Then one day I finally washed them. It was a huge effort, because in so doing I acknowledged that Kalisa Brun herself would never finish the task. Thereafter I ate daily on a single plate that I washed before and after every meal. Everything else I left exactly as I found it, except those items that I absolutely needed to survive.

There were sacks of rice and beans in a cool dugout in her back yard—enough, I estimated, to live on for six months or more. I put away my hiking boots and took to wearing some discarded sandals I had found by the trail leading to the killing field. All the clothes that I cared to wear I spread out on Kalisa's bed: a pair of jeans, another pair that I had converted to cutoffs, three T-shirts, a few pairs of underwear. I knew that I would never sleep in the bed itself. Kalisa's bedroom was too small to accommodate my tumultuous dreams.

Although I refrained from doing so at first, eventually the time came in my madness when I rummaged through Kalisa's private things. What I was looking for, or what I thought I would find, I do not remember. There were letters and a sparse, poorly written journal in a box under her bed; and yes, I did discover a few things about Kalisa that I never would have guessed. I learned, for example, that she was a keen amateur naturalist with an impressive knowledge of the local flora and fauna, after finding a notebook under her bed full of sketches and notations about local plants, flowers and insects. Everything Kalisa wrote was in English except for a few of the notes about local plants, which appeared to be in German.

In a square plastic pocketbook in the closet I found photos of her with what appeared to be family members.

There was something odd about the family. Although I found a German passport with Kalisa's picture on it, the family members did not look at all German: their clothes seemed Eastern European (her mother wore peasant blouses in several of the photos), and their facial expressions were tense and defensive. According to an entry in her journal, Kalisa's parents had been pre-war followers of the educational philosopher Rudolf Steiner. But her family members did not look at all like pioneering educators; there was no lingering trace of the free-thinking *Goldenen Zwanziger Jahre* in the way they stood huddled together in the photographs, nor did they even look like prosperous German patriots. I decided that the photos had been taken somewhere in the rubble of Europe after the Second World War, but probably not in Germany.

The family looked like people with a secret.

There were, to be sure, letters in German from her mother—letters without envelopes, letters with the tops and corners broadly scissored off; tops and corners on which, I suspected, there had originally been letterheads and printed addresses. It was impossible to tell what part of the world the letters had come from.

I wondered if Kalisa Brun had communicated regularly with the Pentecostals in California after coming to Guatemala, and whether they were now wondering why she hadn't written—and I wondered also if they knew of the terrible fate that had befallen her and her Pentecostal converts in the Guatemala highlands.

But despite these mysteries, I found evidence of no scandalous secret vices among Kalisa Brun's personal effects, no closeted sins and no scarlet letters. She had come from Europe to California with an American serviceman as a husband and opened a successful restaurant on Highway 101 near Salinas; leaving her husband she had then found her true church in Pentecostalism. Likewise she had found her true self here in the Guatemalan highland village of Chapila Grande—a self that had no other purpose than singing and celebrating God's love in the speaking of tongues. As she made clear in her journal, she had chosen this simple, out-of-the-way life because it was exactly what she wanted.

She belonged here.

Which was one reason, I suppose, why I kept feeling that she would surely return.

Increasingly, I slept through the morning, arising early in the afternoon to go to the spring where I got water. After getting water, I would cook beans and eat them. Afternoons and evenings I spent lying in a hammock I had set up under a tangle of trees in the backyard of a cinderblock house near the edge of the village. I set up a latrine on a path that had once gone to a rock quarry and had since been overgrown.

One day I was too sick to go to the hammock on the edge of the village, but instead slept through the day on the ground cover spread on Kalisa Brun's kitchen floor. It was hot in the house, but I had picked up a strange fever which had gotten worse the night before, and I simply didn't want to get up and move around. I didn't awaken until that evening, when it was just starting to cool off.

I awoke to the sound of knocking on the remains of the screen door.

"Go away," I croaked.

"Open up and come out with your hands up!" said a loud voice outside the door in English.

"I'm too sick."

"I'm a friend, damn it! Open up, already, or I'm coming in."

I pulled the dirty green comforter over me. I knew who it was by now. "What kind of friend are you?"

"A better friend then you deserve, idiot."

"What do you want?"

"I'll tell you after I come in."

The door opened and Alan Klein stepped into the kitchen.

"Get the hell out of my house, Klein," I muttered. My throat was swollen and tender and it hurt to speak.

"This isn't even your house, pal."

"It is now."

From the stealthy way he stepped into the kitchen, I could tell her was wondering if I was armed.

I sat up slowly.

He was the same as I remembered him from before.

He still had the same boyish grin, the same blustering manner and the same contemptuous sarcasm. He wore a webbed Sam Browne belt on which two canteens jostled. His expensive khakis were dirty and soaked through with sweat, but retained their telltale creases: they had either been pressed, or he had taken to wearing the polyester kind worn by television journalists. He had the fashionable two-day stubble that he often cultivated, but as before he sported an expensive haircut—and there was nowhere in Guatemala where a man could get such a good haircut. He must have gotten it in Mexico City, I decided.

"I don't want whatever you're selling," I said. "I'm fresh out of American money."

"I'm not selling anything."

"You're always selling something," I said.

Klein sighed patiently. "Is that any way to talk to a friend?"

"Don't pretend to be my friend. I really don't like that."

"I can't help it."

It was true—in his own mind, he really *was* my friend.

I got up slowly and sat at the kitchen table. My head was

throbbing with the fever I had gotten, and the heat inside Kalisa's kitchen hadn't helped any. "Damn it, Klein," I said, "I'm not even awake."

"Wake up, then."

"I really don't want to be awake. What's the point?"

Klein nodded in a businesslike way. "I'll get back to you on that. I never have figured that one out myself."

"Wait for me outside," I said sharply.

Whenever he came around it meant that he wanted something. But despite my throbbing head, I could not help but remember—as he himself reminded me from time to time—that I was a stranger in this dangerous land, and I might need his help someday. Bottom line, I had to talk to him. He could always find me if he really wanted to, even if I were wild man living in a deserted village populated by dead people.

Klein was saying, "It's too damn hot in here to sleep, you know. Are you okay? Are you sick?" He unhooked one of his canteens and handed it to me. "God, it's a good thing I came up here to see you. You can't be left alone for a moment."

I took a pull of water from the canteen. It tasted clean and good, unlike the water I had been drinking. He took it back gingerly. I knew he would not drink from it now—which was probably why he brought two canteens.

"Do you feel better now? Are you okay?" When I did not answer he turned toward the door. "Take your time, pal. I'll be outside."

I got up slowly and went to the place where I kept my water. My body was aching, but not as badly as it had the night before. I threw some of the water on my face; the water came from the river and it was quite warm. I felt like drinking some, but it had been standing in one place too long.

I opened Kalisa's kitchen door. Klein was waiting for me outside. It was strange to see someone standing in the dusty abandoned courtyard in the middle of the village.

"What time is it?"

"Almost seven o'clock in the evening."

"My God."

I shook my head—I was still groggy.

He clucked nosily. "This can be very serious. I would have thought you'd know that by now. Heat prostration is one of the—"

"It has nothing to do with heat prostration, Klein. Besides, I like feeling like this. It's part of my plan. I will get sick any time I want to. I *like* getting sick. It has nothing to do with you."

We stood looking at each other.

Behind his officiousness and his stilted adolescent grin he was, as always, watching me carefully.

"You play the fool very well," he said.

"I suppose you are going to say that I play it well because it comes naturally to me."

"It *does* come naturally to you. In the world of fools, you're a star."

I exited the house and turned wordlessly and started walking toward the river. Klein followed about ten feet behind me.

"Is that why you came to see me?"

"That's it, actually," he said. He was still walking a few paces behind me. "You're a total idiot, but you are an idiot without any hidden agendas. You are an idiot solely for the sake of being an idiot. That makes you a totally American idiot."

"And you like that."

"Yes."

"Fuck you very much."

We were silent until I reached the river.

It was much cooler near the river, although it was often swarming with insects. Tonight the insects were not too bad.

I squatted down by the river and looked into the current. The water was muddy but there were places along the river where it was clear; clean enough to wash clothes and even clean enough to drink. The best water, the water I usually drank, came from the spring about a quarter mile down the river; but sometimes the spring was dry and the natural rock pool beneath it would be scorched and dry. Then it was necessary to drink from the jars of water that I kept in Kalisa's kitchen. The longer the water sat around, the more likely it was to make me sick.

Klein sat on a rock above me. His legs hung over the edge of the rock.

"Do you have news?" I asked.

I heard the crunching of his Sam Browne belt as he unhooked a canteen again. "I just wanted to see how you were doing."

"You wouldn't come up here just to check on my health. That's not the way you operate."

I turned to face him, and there was a pained look on his face. "Why do you have such negative thoughts about me? Okay, I'm a bad man. Is that what you want to hear? Sure, I'm no angel—but am I *always* a bad guy? Why can't I do something nice every so often, maybe just for the fun of it?"

"You're always looking for a way to use people."

He was smiling again but he still had a pained look on his face. "Do I talk to *you* that way?"

He stood up on the overhanging rock and abruptly put his hands on hips. It was such a stylized gesture that I couldn't help laughing.

"You look like you're about to do a John Wayne impression," I said, "either that or Mae West."

"Doing what?"

"You're always performing, Klein."

I squatted down by the water again. The insects were getting worse. I wore no insecticide, but the bites of the insects did not hurt.

I imagined what it must have felt like to be among the people of Chapila Grande at that last moment when they were being pierced into death with automatic weapons, standing in rows just two or three hundred yards to my right, the bullets stinging them like bees, the little bites of the entrance wounds fading into the longer bleeding moments as they tumbled slowly backwards onto each other and became the big sleep, the long sleep, the forever sleep.

Back into the cradle, endlessly rocking.

Back to Mother Night, the mother one who came before the earth goddess and her difficult marriage to humankind.

"What the hell is going on with you?" Klein asked.

"I'm going crazy, that's what I'm doing. It is my right, and it is something that I want to do. In that sense you could say it is a *planned* madness. It is every bit as calculated as the most rigidly conceived performance art. And it will go on exactly as long as I want it to go on."

"Congratulations for being so predictable."

He came down from the rock and squatted down a few feet being me.

"Watch out for the insects," I warned him. "The closer you get to the river, the worse they get."

"I'm wearing insecticide."

Truly, the insects seemed to be leaving him alone. Klein was always prepared, always ahead of the game. The insects were biting the hell out of me. But it was a kind of power, to let the insects bit and not to feel it. Best of all was to feel the bite and know that it was painful, but not to care.

"They found Juan Delmonico," I said.

"You mean, they found his body."

"Yes."

"And there was a church funeral."

"Yes."

"I'm told that a lot of people came to the funeral."

I did not reply. We were silent for awhile. There was something I had to ask Klein.

"Did the colonel give the order to kill Juan Delmonico?" I

asked him finally.

"Which colonel?"

"Don't fuck with me."

He shrugged. "Okay, I presume you mean Anibal Montamara."

"The same." "Did Anibal Montamara order the killing of Juan Delmonico?"

"Hard to say. Maybe."

"Likely?"

"Honestly, yes. I mean, the order had to be approved by him. So yes, you could say he was involved in the death of Juan Delmonico. He certainly must have known generally how it was going to occur. And afterward he probably got a report from the troops who did it, or at least heard about it from another officer."

"How sure can you be?"

"I'm not sure of anything. There are a million different channels here in Guatemala. There is civil war going on, and every little military or intelligence unit has its own protocols. It could be a unit that wasn't even in his chain of command—it often happens that way. Personally, I suspect the colonel was in on it from the beginning, at least in part."

We were silent a long time.

"What about the massacre?"

"I don't know. Maybe he wasn't directly involved, at least in the beginning. But he probably has guilty knowledge of it."

I was strangely touched by his unexpected used of the legal term *guilty knowledge*. I wondered where he had picked that up—perhaps an attorney, or a law textbook?—or from some interdepartmental hearing into his own questionable activities?

"All right, let's say he was only partially involved. But why was he involved at all? Why would he want to massacre a whole village?"

Klein began to smile.

"Some ornery guy slapped him across the face with his own

gloves. Then this same character challenged him to a duel, right in front of his own troops. For a guy in the colonel's position that was an intolerable insult. He went ballistic; he had to do something right away to prove he wasn't a total weenie."

"Wait a moment." I was trying to take this in. "You're saying that this happened because I humiliated him?"

"That's right, pal."

"Because I challenged him to a duel?"

"It wasn't just a challenge to a duel, although that's crazy enough. You did it in front of his own men." Klein was looking at me steadily. "Anibal Montamara, fight a duel with *you*? Why should he waste his time fighting a complete idiot? Please. Of course he's not going to do that."

"Instead, he orders the massacre of a whole village."

"Or maybe he just gives the green light to something that's already been planned."

"It still results in the massacre of a village."

"He's got to do something, doesn't he?"

"But why Chapila Grande? *Chapila Grande was a pro-government village*. If he wanted to retaliate against me by destroying a village, why didn't he order the destruction of Chapila Chica, the village where I was staying? Why destroy Chapila Grande?"

Klein shrugged very slowly and stood up.

"That part is driving you crazy, isn't it?"

"Yes."

In the deepening dusk I could not see very much, but I thought I saw something in his eyes when he looked at me. I could have sworn that what I saw in his eyes was pity.

"There is only one person who can answer that question," he said, "and that is Colonel Efrian Anibal Montamara himself. Only he can say why it happened that way."

"Then I must ask him."

"Okay, but you might not like the answer."

Damn, I thought.

But Klein was right. Only Anibal Montamara had the answer.

Chapter Nine

By noon of the following day, I was at the entrance of the Zone Twenty army base, having hitchhiked there one last time to see Colonel Efrain Anibal Montamara. I was there because I had a question to ask the colonel—I needed to know why the people of Chapila Grande had been killed by his soldiers, and also my beautiful Sofia who happened to be visiting there on the day of the massacre. I didn't understand how such a thing could happen, because the people of Chapila Grande had always supported the government. It just didn't make sense that the army would massacre an entire village of its most vigorous supporters. If anybody knew why, it would be Anibal Montamra.

So there I was, walking slowly toward the gate to the army base.

The gate was open and there was no traffic. It was early morning, but I could see one soldier in each of the two guardhouses just inside the gate. I was sure the soldiers could see me coming, and as I walked toward them I wondered what I would say to them and what they would do to me.

Both soldiers stepped slowly out of their guardhouses, one on each side.

The soldiers at the gate were different than the ones I had encountered before. It seemed from the way they looked at me that they had been given my description. One of the soldiers trotted past me, then turned to face me. He raised his rifle as though raising a hand in greeting, paused long enough for me to cower, then brought the butt down hard. As I turned away the reinforced metal part of the stock cut into my back.

I fell to my knees.

"What did you do *that* for?" I asked him, genuinely aggrieved.

"Vamos."

He held his rifle at chest level and motioned with a quick jerk of his chin for me to walk ahead of him. I got up and we proceeded to the other side of the guardhouses. His partner searched me thoroughly, then disappeared into the guardhouse to use the telephone.

It did not take long for him to get his orders.

The first soldier pointed brusquely in the direction toward which I was to walk. It was already getting hot. The fever that had been haunting my body was still with me, and I found it difficult to concentrate on putting one foot in front of the other. The soldier following a few steps behind whacked me smartly on the shoulders with his rifle butt whenever I did not walk fast enough.

Thus was I once again directed to the colonel's office.

It was like a recurring nightmare that one forgets during the day, but is always there, waiting for the dreamer to go back to asleep. But I had to penetrate to the heart of this dream—I had to know the truth about the massacre of Chapila Grande. It made no sense, because Chapila Grande had always supported the government; and I refused to believe that so many people would die without a reason. Why would the Guatemalan army wipe out a village that supported everything the army did?

It was the same corner office, the same desk. Behind it sat the same Colonel Efrain Anibal Montamara.

He had gray-tinted sunglasses on, and he was smiling. He was still smiling when the soldier standing directly behind me landed a blow squarely on one of my shoulders with the stock of his rifle. I stumbled forward and landed face-first on the sofa facing the colonel's desk; the rough cowhide reeked of alcohol and cigarettes. As my face hit the sofa I also got a whiff of another smell—the faint, barely discernible scent of human fear, the fear of people who could not control their bodily functions.

"Thank you," the colonel was saying in Spanish to the soldiers who had been whacking me with their rifle butts, "thank you very much for bringing the famous journalist Maitland Sutterfield to me in such a quick and efficient way."

"Si, mi colonel," barked the soldiers.

They looked at me anxiously, then at the colonel, then left.

"Bastards." I sat up slowly on the cowhide sofa. "What the hell did they do that for?"

Colonel Anibal Montamara paused to light a cigarette.

"Maybe it was something I said to them when they called me."

"What did you tell them?"

"I told them that you were the madman from the North American who has been living in an abandoned village. I told them you had been known to steal the body parts of infants to sell in North America. I told them that you could not be killed because you are a North American, but not to worry about how roughly they handled you. I will suggest that they hurt you more the next time you show up."

He took a deep drag from his cigarette. He watched me with his cold blue eyes. "They know exactly who you are, Maitland Sutterfield. Everybody on this army base knows who you are."

"Do they know that I insulted you in front of your soldiers?"

"Yes."

"Do they know that I challenged you to a duel?"

"Yes. Everybody knows that."

There was a subtle change in the colonel, I thought. The eyes, if anything, were icier and colder in their feral blueness: he stared at me with something close to pure loathing. Yet two or three times I had discerned a nanosecond of hesitation before he answered my questions.

"And so," I said, "because I humiliated you in front of your soldiers, you told them could have a little fun with me, right?"

"I said absolutely nothing about having fun. If I had wanted them to have fun I would have ordered them to have fun."

He'd made his point, so I turned to the business at hand. "I've come to ask you a question about the massacre at the village of

Chapila Grande."

"That doesn't surprise me. But I may not answer you. Please don't make me angry." He rapped softly on his desk with the hand in which he held his cigarette. "I can have you killed at any moment. And I may do so, regardless of the consequences to me. Do you understand that?"

"I'm not surprised to hear you say that."

"Does it not make you afraid?"

"No. It might make me afraid later, right before I die. I can't really say." I continued somewhat officiously, "You see, colonel, I really *want* to die, but I am too cowardly to do it myself. I'm waiting for someone like you to do it for me. If you *do* decide to kill me, I'll let you know when the hour of death finally arrives, exactly how I feel about it."

"Yes, please do." Anibal Montamara was looking at me from behind his gray-tinted sunglasses. "Some think you're brave, some say you're crazy. I believe you are both."

I was restless. I was here to discuss the death of innocent people, and instead we were throwing verbal sliders.

It was time to get to the point.

"I believe you gave the order to kill the people of Chapila Grande." I spoke in English because I wanted to be absolutely sure I was saying exactly the right thing.

He shrugged. "Why would I order that?"

"I don't know. But the massacre was done by uniformed soldiers."

He shrugged. "No doubt these were Cubans dressed up as Guatemalan-army soldiers."

"Cut the crap."

We sat looking at each other.

"Is that what you want? Cut the crap?"

His voice was soft.

"Yes," I said.

"All right," he said, breathing deeply. "Let's cut the crap. I might have had something to do with the death of a great many people in this military zone."

"What do you mean, you *might* have?"

"I don't always know."

"You don't know?"

"That is correct," the colonel said, "because a soldier doesn't always know about the people that he kills. And even when he does know, he doesn't always know exactly how it happened. And why should he? It may not be his responsibility to know about it."

"But you know the intention. You either give an order, or you don't."

"What I mean," he said, leaning forward and lowering his voice, "is that I never would have even heard the name of certain villages such as Chapila Chica and Chapila Grande if it had not been mentioned to me. The name came up in certain conversations regarding the security of this military zone—do you see what I'm saying? Somebody had sufficient reason to take action. In this case perhaps they felt they could hardly do otherwise. So there was a plan. I may have heard about it, and I may not."

"You can't remember?"

"I can't remember now." He laughed harshly. "Would it do any good to remember? No. I don't think so."

I imagined myself holding a cigarette in a cigarette holder exactly the way he did, inhaling and exhaling at exactly the same time he did, a relaxed but perfect mirror image of the colonel. If I could *be* the colonel, would I know his secrets?

And if I did, what would I do about it?

"*Somebody* gave the order," I said.

"Right."

"And you may have had something to do with it."

He hesitated slightly. "Yes, yes, I suppose so."

"But you can't remember."

"Not at this moment."

"And of course there are no written records."

He considered this. "Actually, there are some. Most are in code. They are all secret. No one can see them but me and a few others."

"Why don't you consult those records to refresh your memory?"

"And what good would it do? Would it bring back the dead?"

"It would establish the truth."

He leaned forward. "Would the truth bring back the dead?" he said again.

"No," I said, "but we can honor the memory of the dead, and honor what they did on this earth by protecting the living from people like you."

"People like me?"

"People like you."

"Ah," said the colonel softly, "yes, there it is." He paused a very long time. "And how could they be protected?"

I sat there looking at him, and he at me.

"I'm not sure," I said.

The interview wasn't going well. I was here to discuss the most difficult question of my life—the massacre at Chapila Grande—yet here I was, sitting in the office of this mass murderer, talking about philosophical issues.

"Why were the people of Chapila Grande killed?" I asked. "Just tell me."

"I would have thought you would have figured that out by now. A smart man like you."

"Just tell me."

He spoke slowly, like an adult speaking to a small child. "You insulted me. You gave me an intolerable insult in front of my soldiers."

"And?"

"Your insult forced me to take action. When a man is insulted in that way, he must take action. And it must be strong action."

"So—"

"I took action."

I thought of my great-great-great uncle Algernon, who had appeared to me in my dreams and advised me to challenge the colonel's honor. Could he have foreseen such an outcome to his advice, or was this a part of a game plan that only the dead could see?

"But why Chapila Grande?" I asked. "Chapila Grande was loyal to the government. It was Chapila Chica that was always supposed to be the radical village. Why Chapila Grande, and not Chapila Chica?"

"You will not believe me if I tell you."

"Try me."

"I swear you will not believe me. I do not believe it myself."

"Tell me what happened."

The palms-down hands came up suddenly in a palms-up gesture, accompanied by a sharp exhalation of breath. "Very well. You want the truth. I owe you nothing, but I will tell you the truth anyways." He adjusted his gray-tinted glasses carefully. "This is the only time I will ever talk about this. If you tell anyone, I will deny it. And they will not believe you anyway."

"Tell me," I said.

He waited a long time before speaking.

"I cannot remember exactly the sequence of events. You may not believe that, but it's true. All I can remember is that a decision had been made to destroy Chapila Chica. People had been talking about it for a long time. At first people were saying we should relocate the village, and then people were saying they were too far gone, they should be killed along with their priest. One thing people agreed on: if the rebels were to have a base around here, it would be in Chapila Chica."

"There are no rebels in Chapila Chica."

"Not now, perhaps, but if the rebels were ever to find support in this area, it would be in the village of Chapila Chica. It is well known that the priest at Chapila Chica is a *subversivo*. You saw yourself a copy of the radical newspaper printed in the area. In any case, I did not plan the attack. There were people who wanted to destroy the village, and it was getting harder for me to ignore these people." I said nothing, and after a pause he went on, "When you went insane and struck me in front of my soldiers, I gave the order to go ahead. Little Chapila would cease to exist, and no one would be allowed to settle there in the future."

I said nothing.

"The soldiers were transported in two-and-a-half ton trucks up the mountain road until they reached the path to Chapila Chica," the colonel continued. "They disembarked and started up the path. Then—" He paused. "Something very strange happened."

"What do you mean, something very strange happened?"

"They took a wrong turn. They did not follow the maps, or perhaps the maps were wrong. And they went to the wrong village. Somehow the soldiers in this operation ended up going to Chapila Grande instead of Chapila Chica."

He hesitated.

"And what happened then?"

"They followed their orders, which were to destroy the village, but...it was the wrong village. They thought it was Chapila Chica, but it was Chapila Grande."

"What did you say?"

"I said that it was a mistake. The soldiers were supposed to destroy Chapila Chica. But they made a mistake." A wheedling tone came into his voice, as though I was uniquely qualified to appreciate the desperate humor involved. "You see, the captain had orders to destroy Chapila Chica, but he didn't know the terrain. So he took the wrong turn and they went up the wrong path. And because he took the wrong path, he ended up destroying the wrong village...he thought he was destroying Chapila Chica, but he was destroying—"

"Chapila Grande."

We sat looking at each other. I could not believe that I was in the office of this army officer and that he was telling me these things, because they were unbelievable. I was already wondering how anyone could live with something like this, or even if they wanted to try. But there was no doubt that he was telling the truth, because what he was saying was not something anyone would ever invent. But how on earth a person could make an adjustment to this particular truth, I did not know.

"It is true that Chapila Grande was a village that supported the government and the army," the colonel continued. "Its people were loyal patriots of the fatherland. Therefore, it goes without saying that it was a terrible tragedy that they had to die. A terrible mistake was made. But simply being sorry does not bring them back to life. And in the end their death served the national purpose."

"How?"

"It created bodies. That is always the purpose in a civil war. You kill many people, and you make sure that people in the area have a chance to see the bodies. We are talking here about civilians. When other people in the area see the bodies of ordinary people, if frightens them more than anything else, because they see that it could happen to them, even if they are not themselves combatants. Once they have seen the bodies, they are usually very compliant."

He leaned forward to make his point. "Please try to understand me. I am talking about the function of dead bodies. You destroy a village to create dead bodies. You kill *everybody*—men, women and children. And everybody in the neighborhood of the village comes to see the bodies. It sends a message that the army will do *anything* to defeat the rebels. It shows people that if we have to we will keep killing civilians until every Indian in the highlands is dead."

He leaned backward in his chair. There was a moment's

silence.

"The really important thing is the dead bodies," he reiterated, "because if you have enough dead bodies, it doesn't make any difference what kind of people they were when they were alive. It doesn't matter if they were pro-government or anti-government, good people or bad people. Once they're dead, they've dead."

"Dead," I heard myself murmuring.

"Yes. And they have to be in a place where many people can see them. It is better if there are many woman and children. The object is to create terror. And if enough people see the bodies, people will feel the terror. If there are many woman and children, they will know that even woman and children are not safe. That's all that is important. It doesn't matter who the people are. Please believe me. I have thought about this a great deal."

I feel like I was about to pass out. "Yes, but the people of Chapila Grande were on your side."

Colonel Efrain Anibal Montamara shrugged. "I have already pointed out that this is a tragedy. If I was in a position to change things, I would do so. But I am not in such a position. And now that the massacre has happened, I must in all honesty tell you that the dead bodies of Chapila Grande served the purpose just as well as the dead bodies of Chapila Chica. They are dead, and they will always be dead; and the people in the neighborhood of San Jose del Rio saw them just after they'd been killed. And now the people of the region will be much less likely to help the rebels, if they have any choice in the matter, because they are afraid they will be killed too. That is what is most important, regardless of where the dead bodies came from. I'm sure you will agree that there is a kind of simplicity to it."

He was clearly enjoying the state of shock I was in.

"And the original order was to destroy Chapila Chica?"

"Yes."

"And Chapila Grande was destroyed by mistake?"

"Yes. Chapila Grande was destroyed by mistake."

"Are you sure?"

"I am absolutely sure." He paused. "Perhaps it was because the two villages sound so much alike—Chapila Chica, Chapila Grande. Who can be sure? Maybe the field officer confused the two villages. Or maybe he got faulty directions from someone he met on the trail. Who can be sure? The villages were not on any map—there are no maps for villages that small. What is certain is that this commanding officer truly thought he was destroying Chapila Chica."

"Why didn't he ask the people of Chapila Grande themselves?"

"People in such a situation will say anything. How on earth could he believe them?"

"It was a whole village of men, women and children!"

"Yes. *Que lastima*. What a pity. Sorry about that." The colonel's shrug was slow and expressive. "*Sorry about that*...is that not what soldiers from the US said in Vietnam? I met many of those same soldiers when I was teaching in Georgia. Americans are always sorry, but everybody knows how the world really works. If you want to blame anyone, blame me. But you know very well that what happened to Chapila Grande was your fault."

He was waiting for my reaction.

"Are you saying that it was my fault that the people of Chapila Grande were massacred?" I asked.

"I am saying that if you had not challenged me to a duel in front of my soldiers, it would not have happened—at least not at this time. You slapped me in the face and challenged me to a duel. You did this in front of my soldiers. That was unacceptable. I had to take some kind of very strong action. You left me no choice."

"No," I said, "you cannot say this. You had a choice, and you ordered the massacre."

"Ah, but you had a part in it. I wouldn't have done anything at that time if you had not struck me in public."

"And because of that—"

"And because of that, yes; I did what I did."

I was struck dumb. The silence went on and on.

"If that is the truth, or even part of the truth, I would rather be dead," I said finally.

"Are you really ready to die?"

"Yes," I said after a pause.

He leaned forward so his words would have the maximum effect. "*Cut the crap,*" he said slowly and distinctly.

"What?"

"*Cut the crap.*"

I could not speak.

"Are you going to kill me?" I said finally.

"No," he said, "I don't think I will kill you, Maitland Sutterfield. Not right now. I don't think I will do that. Not on this army base."

"Why not?" I asked.

"You will kill yourself someday, either that or drive yourself crazy." He leaned back in his chair and laced his fingers behind his head, looking up at the ceiling. "Furthermore, I do not want to kill a North American unless I have to. As you said once before, it is really the responsibility of your own CIA—or at the very least your state department—to deal with American civilians who interfere with the foreign policy of the United States. If I were to do that, it would create unnecessary problems for me. So I will not be doing that, Maitland Sutterfield. The people in the San Jose del Rio region have seen enough bodies for the time being."

"But I'll write about the massacre at Chapila Grande. I'll contact the North American and British newspapers, and I will make sure that the world finds out about it."

"Then Chapila Chica will cease to exist. Many of the villagers at Chapila Chica are coming back to their homes, I'm told. I could make their priest leave the country simply by talking to his bishop. Once their priest is gone, it would be a simple thing for my field commanders to kill off every last person who comes back to the village of Chapila Chica. Perhaps I could kill them off one by one." He paused. "And that is exactly what I will do if you make trouble for me." He paused again. "I don't really want to do that, because I already have too much to do, and it would not accomplish much. But I will do it if you force the issue."

So he had me. He seemed poised and ready to continue the conversation, but I had nothing left to say.

"All right," I said finally, "I won't write any stories about the massacre at Chapila Grande. But I want you to promise me that you will leave Chapila Chica alone forever."

"I will not make promises to you."

I remembered what he said during my first interrogation. "I will help you find the printing press," I said, "the secret printing press that the rebels are using to print subversive material in Zone Twenty."

His eyes narrowed. "The press?"

"You know the one. You showed me something the rebels printed with it."

Now it was his turn to ponder my words.

"Tell me a little bit more," he said finally.

"You have told me that certain things are being printed by the rebels in this zone. I can't confirm this independently, but you told me this, and I believe you. You want to capture this rebel printing press: I'll try to help you find out where it is. All you have to do is leave Chapila Chica alone."

He was hooked. The phantom printing press was clearly an obsession with him.

He nodded once, emphatically. "Yes, of course I'll leave Chapila Chica alone."

The agreement had come far too quickly, it seemed to me. Perhaps he had discussed the printing press with Alan Klein and had expected my offer. But I didn't really care—all I wanted was his verbal agreement. He could break the agreement any time he chose, but it was something.

Or so I thought.

"Good," I said. "It's our contract. Our Faustian pact."

"Our what?"

"A Faustian pact is a profane but binding agreement, made with the devil. Somewhat like a marriage, I would say."

He looked momentarily alarmed—he even looked around to see if anyone had overheard me. I suspected that he did not quite understand what I meant by a Faustian pact, but it was my reference to marriage that made him especially uncomfortable. The idea of two men participating in anything that could be compared to a marriage was not something he wanted to think about.

"You are truly mad," he said finally.

"Thank you," I said.

So I left him.

This time no guards harried me with their heavy rifle butts: I was a free agent, a lone pilgrim making my way back to my mountain, back to my madness. I had expected to die, but Anibal Montamara had refused to kill me. Instead he had given me the truth, a slow-acting poisonous truth designed to kill me a little at a time. It made no difference that he was a psychopath in a uniform. The truth was still the truth, and it could kill you no matter who gave it to you.

For the second time I found myself hitchhiking back to Chapila Grande from the Zone Twenty army base.

It was evening by the time I got back to the place where the path to Chapila Grande began. I found the path and started up it in the twilight. I met no one, although the high grass and the jungle were alive with animals. For a moment I allowed myself to hope that one of the big cats would come after me. But as always, they did not want me; it was as though my self-disgust was a protective bubble that I carried everywhere.

The village of Chapila Grande was waiting for me.

None of the dead had returned to their houses. The village was absolutely and totally still: not so much as a single wild animal—not so much as a solitary snake—had taken up residence in the underbrush that was growing between the concrete-block houses. I kept on walking until I reached the field outside the village. I had already been to this field many times, and I had no trouble finding the long ditch where Sofia was buried.

The mass grave just outside Chapila Grande had not remained fresh for long—already it was overgrown with vines and underbrush. In a matter of weeks it would be completely covered. When the rainy season came in a month or so, it would sink lower and be completely obscured except for a slight depression in the earth around the edges.

I had seen other mass graves in Guatemala. They had been pointed out to me by those who knew where they were located. There was always the slight depression in the earth, the little sinking line around the edge that marked the place where the bodies lay. Once the dirt was dug and the bodies planted, there was never quite enough of the original earth to bring it permanently back up to the level of the ground around it. Perhaps that was because the actual composition of the dirt changed, once the bodies were in it.

I stood over the mass grave where Sofia lay with the people of Chapila Grande, and confessed my love to an image of her in my mind, until I began to feel the presence of her near me. I confessed my love to her while the twilight world bore witness.

And what I said to her went something like this:

"I love you. I didn't love you when you were alive, but I love you now. Now that you are gone from me, I love you as much as any man has ever loved anyone."

There was no sound.

"Tell me what I should do," I said.

There was only silence and the moonlight.

"Should I kill him?"

Then there were only the moon, myself, and the memories. The memories came together and she was there; and for a very long time they were more real than anything in the world.

I did not sleep for three days and nights. At noon on the fourth day I fell asleep. That night I was still sleeping, but I awoke when I heard the footsteps of an intruder. It was a spooky night, full of ghostly little gusts of wind that nudged the trees. There was even a little mist blowing at treetop level, lit by a half moon.

The footsteps stopped outside my door. "Maitland," the voice said, "come on out. Come on out right now. I need to talk to you."

It was definitely Padre Julio's voice.

I got up slowly, and took my time pushing open the broken door. "What is so important that you have to come here at this hour?"

Padre Julio had grown a neatly trimmed beard over the last few weeks, and in the moonlight one could not tell if it was white or grey. "I couldn't sleep," he said.

I was a little taken aback. "That's a common problem."

"To be frank, I'm afraid for the people of Chapila Chica."

"What makes you think Chapila Chica isn't safe?"

"We *will* be safe," Julio said, "if you come back to live in Chapila Chica. That is what I have been told. They will not kill the rest of us as long as you are there, because they do not want to kill an American if they can help it. That's what I've been told."

I stepped out the door and stood on the cement block that was my front step. The night was cool. "What do you think? Do you think it might be true, what you have been told?"

He hesitated.

"Yes," he said finally, "when different people keep telling you the same thing over and over, it's likely to be true."

"Or it's something that some powerful people want you to believe."

"Anyway, you will not come back to Chapila Chica, so we do not even have that measure of protection."

We were both silent for a moment.

"You know what you can do to get me to come back to Chapila Chica," I said.

"You want me to marry you to—a dead woman."

"Yes."

"What you require of me is madness, still you insist that I must do it."

"Yes."

He turned abruptly away from me and looked at the deserted houses of Chapila Grande. The moonlight from the half moon seemed stronger now, and the mist I had seen earlier at treetop level had disappeared.

Padre Julio muttered something. It sounded like he was praying for forgiveness. Whatever it was, it was quite intense.

"All right, you win," he said in a low voice.

"What?"

He turned back toward me. His aristocratic features were stern, but even in the silver light I saw the concern and compassion on his face. Even when he was distraught, the compassion and the undercurrent of pity was always there.

"All right, you will have what you want, even though it is madness," he said softly, looking me directly in the eye. "You will have your marriage to Sofia." I was impressed that he did not flinch from the word *marriage*. "You will have it exactly as you wish. Please let me know what you want me to say. You must write it down, every word of it. If you write it down and I read from it, the sin will not be as great. I will read it as a poem written by a madman driven insane by the death of a loved one." He paused. "I have never done anything like this before. But I'm certain that God loves you, Maitland, and I'm equally certain that God loves Sofia too." He shuddered suddenly, and closed his eyes. I could see how hard it was for him. Then he took a deep breath, and was once more the confident, educated, well-bred Castilian.

"Tell me—when you want me," he said. "I am completely at your convenience in this matter."

Padre Julio went to San Jose del Rio for two days, then came to Chapila Grande in the middle of the night. This was the night we'd agree on. There were no clouds and no breeze, as though the mountain itself was preparing to be a respectful witness. Nor was there any preening triumphalism in the moonlight, no golden ripeness of noon; this was a night thing, and not the orthodoxy of the day. The moon was silver and the moonlight that illuminated the small world of Chapila Grande was also silver, and there was a dry heat in the air that tasted like cool metal.

It was almost midnight before Julio arrived. He found me sitting on the step of the little wooden house waiting for him.

"Good evening, Padre Julio."

"Don't call me that tonight."

"Isn't that your title?"

"Call me Julio," he said sharply.

We proceeded to the mass grave outside of town. In the weeks since the massacre it had become overgrown. We stopped at the edge of the long ditch and I handed him a paper with some words I had laboriously composed. I had used a Catholic prayer-book—two, in fact—but also phrases from Anglican liturgy; I had even lifted a phrase or two from the prayer-book of King's Chapel in Boston. I'd changed the wording in certain places, partly to better express what I wanted to say, but also because I knew it would make it easier for Julio. Some of it I simply made up out of whole cloth.

"You want me to read the words?" Julio asked.

"Yes. Is there enough light?"

He waited as his eyes adjusted to the silver moonlight. "Yes," he said finally.

Julio had insisted that I write down everything I wanted him to say. As for myself, I had memorized everything.

"Well," he said, looking down at the paper I had given him.

Under our feet lay the hopes and dreams of a village, whose people in their last breathing moments had experienced something not so different from the apocalypse they preached; they were Pentecostals whose last and most fervent *glossolalia* came not from a visitation of the Holy Spirit but from the penetration of live bullets in their bodies. Who could say whether they saw, as the light of Tzotzil Gapachula mountain faded for each of them, the millennial glory they had sought in worship?

"They died bravely," Julio said, as though reading my mind.

"That's an incredibly Spanish thing to say."

"They showed no fear. They were singing when the end came."

I tried to imagine it, but I couldn't, so I banished the images from my mind.

"It doesn't surprise me that they were singing," I managed to say.

"Their faith lifted them up at the last moment. I don't believe that God forgot them, or that God will ever forget them."

We pushed though the underbrush to the center of the long ditch. It looked very different than it had a month or two ago—in fact it looked different than I remembered it from just two days before. I could see how such places became forgotten. Already it was hard to tell exactly where the place of burial was, except for the slight depression around the long rectangular ditch. I had to look for it a long time in the moonlight to see where it was.

"Well," Julio said.

He unfolded the paper I had given him and looked at it for a long time.

"Dearly beloved of God...." he read.

For a moment it looked like he was going to have difficulty with it. He paused and then started reading again.

"We are gathered here in the sight of God, and in the midst of this—" he paused, "...this village, to join together a man and a woman in matrimony."

He paused a long time and then continued.

"Marriage is an honorable estate, instituted by God in the time of man's innocence. It is not therefore to be taken lightly or unadvisedly; but reverently, discreetly, soberly, and in the fear—"

Again he paused.

"...in the fear of God."

His voice had started to waver. He cleared his throat.

"Do you know of any impediment why these two people may not be lawfully united in matrimony?"

"No," I said.

"If you know of any, do so now confess it."

"I know of no impediment."

I felt the heat rising up through my feet: not the heat of rotting flesh, but of passion remembered perfectly, of desire perfectly resurrected, where all the lines of love and memory converged—past moments restored in love's body.

"Maitland Sutterfield," Padre Julio said, his voice barely whispering now, "will you have this woman to be your wedded wife? Will you live with her in your heart after God's ordinance, and all the ordinances known to humankind, in the estate of matrimony?"

"I will."

"Will you love her, comfort her, honor and keep her memory, in sickness and in health, in good times and bad times, in sorrow and in joy, in life and in death; and forsaking all others, keep her memory alive in you so long as you live?"

"Yes, I will."

"Who gives this woman to be married?"

"This earth of Guatemala," I said.

God help me, I knelt.

"Born of a woman," I said, reciting the words I had written, "you had only a short time to live. You worked for the Kingdom here in this world, and were cut down. I send my heart down to you, into the earth for safekeeping; take it from the unforgiving light of this world into the soft and loving shadows. As the earth gathers us out of the earthly light into the passion of this moment, let me be with you."

"And so I commit myself to you: earth to earth, ashes to ashes, dust to dust; in sure and certain hope of resurrection, while you that sleep in death will live in my memory, the memory of your husband; as each daily memory puts asunder that mighty working, whereby death is liable to subsume all things unto itself."

I cleared my throat.

"I, Maitland Sutterfield, take you, Sofia Mendez, to be my wife, to hold in memory from this day forward, for better or for worse, for richer or poorer, in sickness and in heath, to love and to cherish, until my death restores us once again to each other; and to that end I pledge my promise."

I paused.

"I endow you with no worldly goods, not even my poverty: but with my memory I promise to keep you safe, as long as I and my memory of you shall live."

There was a long silence.

I felt satisfied and happy—so happy, in fact, that I wanted the moment to go on forever.

"I love you, Sofia," I said, as though she could hear me perfectly through four feet of earth.

It made such good sense, it seemed so natural, to kneel there and talk to Sofia. Why would anyone pray to a god they had never seen, when one could talk to a woman in whose arms one had experienced the gift of sexual healing, the love medicine that heals the wounds men have?

Julio was praying softly. "Lord, please, forgive this...episode..."

Like mine, his voice was also shaking.

"Understand," he was saying.

We were there for a long time. Finally Padre Julio turned abruptly and left. As he walked away, the underbrush tore at his trousers as though the dead were pulling at him to keep him from leaving them. I was relieved it was over, and very happy, because I felt that Sofia would understand perfectly if there were anything left of her soul; and it would make her happy wherever she was. Furthermore it gave me the connection with her that I needed, because now that I had the connection forever I could leave Guatemala if I had to.

As deeply unsettling as it clearly was for Padre Julio, not even he could not miss the logic of what I'd done. Sacrilege it certainly was—but who else had attempted to honor even *one* of those who slept in the mass grave outside Chapila Grande? Who else had visited this place and said words of *any* kind? When the world did not want to remember innocent people murdered by cruel and ambitious men, only madmen were left to mourn, that was the simple arithmetic of it.

Surely Julio knew that. Wasn't it for that reason that he had stood there with me, against his will and better judgment, best man and witness to my insanity?

It may also have been for that reason that he later found himself deeply affected by what we had done. He had made what I thought was the right decision, but in retrospect I believe it was at this time that he began to experience certain unmistakable problems, both of faith and problems regarding the nature of his ministry, which grew worse because of the political changes being imposed upon him and his village. Lost and crazy as I was, from that moment on it was not I who was in the greater danger, but Padre Julio Domingo.

Chapter Ten

Julio Domingo did not come to see me for almost a week—and when he did, he said nothing about moving to Chapila Chica. That surprised me, because he had made such a fuss about it before; so the next time he came to visit me in Chapila Grande, I asked him if anything had changed. Did he still want me to come back to Chapila Chica, and by so doing to ensure the safety of village?

"It seems that Chapila Chica is in less danger than I thought," he said a bit uncomfortably.

"Who told you this?"

"Someone who knows."

"Klein?"

"Yes," he said after a pause.

Klein was always one step ahead of me, I thought. "What *exactly* did he say?"

"He said the army had already accomplished its goal, and that there was no need to kill any more civilians in the area."

I felt a chill. "My God. Those are exactly the words used by Colonel Anibal Montamara. Or words to that effect."

"Are you surprised by that?"

"No."

We were sitting at the table in the kitchen of my little house in Chapila Grande. It was almost dawn; Padre Julio was on his way to the main road, where he had arranged to catch a ride to San Jose del Rio.

Since the priest who had disappeared had not been replaced, Padre Julio had to go there regularly to do pastoral work.

"Klein also said that you made a deal to help the colonel find some kind of printing press. He said it would ensure our safety, at least for as long as you keep up your end of it."

"Or pretend to."

"So you *did* make some kind of deal."

He waited for me to respond.

"It's true," I said, "as far as it goes."

I told Padre Julio about my deal with the colonel; I would help him find a certain printing press, which Marxist rebels were supposedly using to print some kind of underground newspaper.

"What will the colonel do?"

"He agreed to make sure that Chapila Chica is not attacked."

Padre Julio groaned. "Where will you find such a printing press?"

"I won't. There is no such press. It is nothing more than a horrible little newsletter, and probably comes from another part of the country entirely."

"Did you see the publication?"

"Yes, and it's practically unreadable. I doubt if more than a handful of people have even seen it."

"What will you do when you can't produce the press?"

"I'll keep stringing him along, if he contacts me. I'll give him false information that will make him think I'm on the verge of finding the press."

He rolled his eyes. "My God, haven't you learned anything?"

"I suppose not. Aren't you going to thank me?"

"No, I'm not going to thank you. I'm not at all sure that this game-playing doesn't put Chapila Chica at greater risk."

"You don't really believe that."

Padre Julio paused. "No, I suppose not. To be perfectly frank with you, Alan Klein was quite reassuring. He seems to have a lot of input with the colonel."

"That's good, I suppose."

The thought of the two of them together made me sick to my stomach.

"Klein also seemed to enjoy the idea of you making deals with the colonel. Or trying to."

No doubt, I thought, Klein got a kick out of my pathetic

attempts of influence Anibal Montamara. What a treat, what a bonanza of unsolicited entertainment I had turned out to be—a deranged American of unparalleled awkwardness (and a quintessentially arrogant journalist at that), playing grab-ass with one of the most treacherous wolves in a country of wolves!

"What a wonderful guy," I said.

"In fact," Padre Julio said, a certain weariness having crept into his voice, "Klein postured himself as the savior of Chapila Chica. Instead of simply threatening me, he presented himself as someone who would intervene with Anibal Montamara to save my village, as long as I do what he wants me to do."

Padre Julio's voice was flat, the vocal equivalent of a thousand-mile stare.

"That's absolutely Klein's style," I said, "to make veiled threats while simultaneously offering to intervene to save you. And praising himself for doing so."

"Yes."

"Well..." I said. "Thank God for small favors. At least Chapila Chica is safe."

"No," Julio said. "I do not thank God for small favors. Klein made a deal with me, just the way you made a deal with the colonel. But Klein's deal was a little different. He told me that I must stop all the organizing of *campesinos*. I must keep a very low profile. No more studying the New Testament in the *comunidad de base*; no more rural cooperatives to bargain collectively for the price of corn from the milpas. No more support for social justice, period. Nothing that would cause the army and landowners in the area to think we were in any way *subversivos*."

"In other words, there must be no more advocacy for social justice, no more trying to improve the standard of living for the highland Indians."

"Yes."

There was a long pause.

"Well," I said.

There was another long pause.

"What will you do?" I said.

"What *can* I do?" His voice was bitter. "They've won. The landowners and the army have shown us that they are willing to massacre civilians in the villages to keep what they have. They've made their point. The army made their move long before the rebels were strong enough to protect us."

You should have known better, I thought, *than to think that the Guatemalan army would not commit mass murder, or that anybody could protect you.*

But I said nothing.

There was probably nothing I could say that Julio Domingo had not already thought of himself.

One day I set out on the trail toward Tzotzil Gapachula mountain to visit the cabin of the Dog Woman, who had disappeared the day of the massacre and had not been seen since. I had a theory that she was hiding out in the bush and would someday return. But where exactly did she stay and how did she get by?

I wanted to talk to her.

In my madness I had the bizarre idea that we had something in common, something that we desperately needed to discuss—the fact that we were both mad, perhaps, and that we therefore needed to exact some clever territorial and emotional division of labor.

I had gone about half a kilometer down the path when I ran into Miguel, the small man who had first accompanied Sofia and myself on the path to Chapila Chica. He was carrying his machete in a crude handmade wooden sheath. He stopped dead in his tracks, put his hand on his machete, then bolted. Apparently he did not recognize me—or perhaps he just didn't trust me. He stopped about fifty feet or so down that path and looked back at me.

"Pescado?"

That was the nickname he had given me, because I helped him catch fish in the river. It took a moment to remember that. "Yes, it's me."

"You aren't a ghost?"

He asked first in Kekchi, then in Spanish.

"*No soy espanto*. I'm not a ghost."

He walked slowly back to the place where I stood waiting.

He was wary, but no longer afraid. "Padre Julio said you were alive," he said.

"He was right."

Miguel shyly reached out to touch my beard, and then my tangled hair. "Yes," he said, with a puzzled grin, "you are alive."

"Yes, yes, it's me."

We stood silently for a moment. "How are the people of Chapila Chica?"

"They are alive, too, those that are still there."

"Padre Julio tells me that things are not the same. He believes that the people of Chapila Chica do not have the same hope as before."

"Hope?" he said with the same puzzled air. *"Esperanza?"*

"Hope that if you celebrate the sacraments you'll go to Heaven. Hope also that the people in the highlands will get more money for the corn they grow, and that someday the rich landowners will give the people more money for their work. Hope that there will be social justice in Guatemala."

I immediately regretted using the words *justicia social.* It was easy for me, a North American, to use such words. But for Miguel, a Guatemalan peasant in the early 1980s, it was dangerous to even acknowledge that such words existed. For him, the importance of such words consisted entirely in the amount of risk he assumed in using them.

"No," he said after a long pause, in the same noncommittal tone, "we have lost the revolution in Chapila Chica. That is what Padre Julio told us."

I was dumbfounded. "He said that to you?"

"Yes."

"Did he say this to the others at Chapila Chica?"

"He said it to the entire village. Do you think he is right?"

"Yes."

"What did the people say?"

"Many people are leaving now. Many are going to Mexico."

For the area around San Jose del Rio, the revolution was indeed lost, even if the only revolution that Padre Julio wanted was a peaceful transition to a slightly better life. The army had made its move, and the people of Chapila Grande slept in their mass grave; and the people of the area were thoroughly terrified. Social justice, even the mildest and most reformist kind of social justice, would have to wait for another day, another decade, maybe another century.

"Lo siento," I said. "I'm sorry."

He looked at me. "Why do you say you're sorry? You did nothing wrong."

"I am sorry the world is not a better place. I am sorry that the United States destroyed democracy in Guatemala in 1954, and that it has been supporting military dictators even since. I'm sorry that Guatemala is such a cruel place, even though it is beautiful, and that you cannot make it a better country in your lifetime."

"You must leave these mountains," he said without hesitation. "The things you say now are dangerous."

"Yes, I know I should leave. But I can't."

"Do you want to die?"

I had been asked this question so many times by *Guatemaltecos* that by now I was completely accustomed to it. Miguel did not mean it as a joke, a rhetorical question, or a disguised warning. He was simply curious—if I wanted to die he was no doubt prepared to find that unfortunate, but not incredible.

"Maybe so," I said. "What's wrong with that?"

There was pity in his eyes. He looked at me a long time.

"Vamos a ver," he said. "We'll see."

"Yes, we'll see."

He was looking into my eyes as though looking for answers.

"Que sera, sera," I said after an uncomfortable pause.

He laughed as though hearing a favorite witticism, which it may well have been. Perhaps he found the words especially comical because they came from the lips of an Anglo from North America. Most likely he understood that by invoking such a hapless cliché I was making a dark joke, and that I was letting go of this part of my life because I no longer had any control over it. To this day I do not know why he found it so funny. He was laughing as though he thought it a clever remark of great wit and originality.

"Que sera, sera!" he barked happily, his eyes crinkling.

I continued to hang out—perhaps living is a bit too grand a word for what I was doing—at my little house at Chapila Grande. The abandoned village was almost overgrown by now, and I made no attempt to clear away the brush. I concentrated only on keeping a couple of paths cleared, especially the ones that led to my latrine and to the spring where I got water.

I hoped that someday, if they had any decency at all, the charismatic church in California that had sent the missionary Kalisa Brun to Chapila Grande would erect some kind of monument, when everything was safe, to memorialize the people who had died there—a historical marker, as it were. I just hoped they would have the presence of mind to use Spanish and Kekchi on the historical market, and not just English.

I wondered if in her last moments on earth Sofia had been praying. I wondered if she thought about the child we had been trying so hard to conceive; I wondered if she thought, however fleetingly, of me. I would give any earthly possession to know what she said to the people of Chapila Grande about their hymns, and why she wanted to talk about them; but I would never know what she thought at the hour of her death and I wouldn't try to guess. Because that way—very clearly and simply—lay madness. I was already mad, but I knew that if I thought too much about the reasons why Sofia came over to Chapila Grande on this particular day, the madness would get worse, and I would become more insane than I already was.

I was around the bend, beyond the pale; a man without a country, a culture, or a world. Like most North Americans, I had been taught that I could write my own ticket—I could have almost anything I wanted, as long as I wanted it badly enough. That is what people grew up believing in the US.

While I had never believed completely in that dream, vestiges of it had remained.

Now all had fled, laughed out of court.

The reality, I now saw, was that everyone functioned inside their own sphere of helplessness. It was a great concept: not only did it reduce the zone of responsibility; it also reduced the blame zone to almost nothing. One was not responsible for the way the world worked, and therefore not responsible for ameliorating its dangers; neither was one to blame for its horrors.

Not one tiny bit.

It wasn't heroic, but it made tons of sense. The world was lost, but for just that reason I didn't have to care.

Whatever happened, happened. *Que sera, sera!*

It was so simple, every morning I woke up laughing.

I no longer cared, so nobody had to care about *me*.

But there was one person who cared about me, and that person was Julio Domingo, who visited me regularly. At first his visits were somewhat perfunctory, but before long they became an almost daily event. Padre Julio was in crisis too, it turned out—and the demons with which he was wrestling had a distinct family resemblance to my own.

Julio thought I was traumatized, and needed to talk; but so did he, because—although he might have denied it—he was similarly traumatized.

No doubt his own need to talk came as a surprise to him.

We suddenly had so much to talk about that we had to see each other no matter what. Padre Julio started showing up almost every day. He talked about the loss of his social-justice vocation; I babbled endlessly about myself and my preoccupation with death. I woke up each morning wondering when Padre Julio would visit, and thinking about all the things I wanted to say to him.

We became obsessed with each other's demons, and all the intelligent things we could say about them.

We met in the back yard of the small cinder-block house where I had strung up a hammock. I suggested to Padre Julio that we engage in a private chess tournament that would go on every day through the months of April and May, the winner to be the person who won the most games out of fifty. May, we both knew, would be the last dry month before the rainy season began.

In my madness I thought of our chess competition as a private joust to determine the unacknowledged king of the mountain. "The loser will be sacrificed before the rains come," I told Padre Julio, "a ritual sacrifice that will ensure a good corn harvest from the milpas after the rainy season. It's not as good as getting a better price, but it's something."

After a couple of weeks, each of us had lost an equal number of games. Whether he won or lost did not seem to affect Padre Julio as much as it affected me. That did not, however, cause him to play with any less concentration than I did.

And naturally, while we played, we talked.

Padre Julio said he would have to disband the present cooperative he had organized in Chapila Chica and the villages around San Jose del Rio, and the thought of doing so was devastating to him.

"For the first time in two thousand years, the Church was able to see the necessity of social justice," he said. "It was in front of our noses all the time, don't you see, right there in the scriptures. What did we think Jesus was talking about, when he talked about building the Kingdom? What did we think he was saying, when he said, *Thy will be done, on earth as it is in Heaven*? At last we could finally see what he was really talking about. *The Kingdom of God begins on earth*. Heaven must begin here, or not at all."

"No more pie in the sky?"

"No more pie in the sky. You need to eat the pie now, because if you don't, you'll never recognize it in the afterlife." He glanced up at me and then looked quickly back at the chessboard. "Actually that is a very good way of expressing it, although it may seem like a joke to you. But just when the Church is forced to see the truth of it for the first time, and we start putting it into practice in the real world, we are stopped dead in our tracks."

"That often happens in the real world."

"That is the tragedy of the twentieth century. We were stopped before we were able to get really started."

Liberation Theology was under attack, not just from the landowners and the military, but from the Vatican. Priests were being forbidden to participate in "politics," which meant anything that the conservative bishops and their rich landowning friends didn't like. It was a particularly harsh setback for the Jesuits. They had embraced the idea of Liberation Theology with an enthusiasm not seen in Roman Catholicism for many years: and then, before the idea could be put into action and tested, the counterattack from the landowners and the military and their conservative allies in the Vatican had begun.

In the meantime, the peasants that had welcomed the idea of social justice as a practical applied Christianity had been left exposed. There was an armed revolution lead by Marxist-Leninists who cared neither for the Church nor for the cost in human life that such a revolution would exact; and this revolution gave the landowners and the army a convenient excuse to murder and terrorize those peasants who simply wanted a little more money for their corn.

The Christ of social justice would be driven back onto the crucifix on the walls of the churches, where his dangerous ideas could be silenced once again. The peasants, the Indians who had for a brief season welcomed him into their homes, their fields, and their base communities, would be crucified in his place. By machine guns, by machetes, by mutilation, by torture, and by mass rape, they would die horribly at the hands of the army and the security agencies, supported by the money-worshipping North Americans.

Julio stopped having *comunidad de base* meetings in Chapica Chica. His lay catechists were told that a change was under way, and that from now on they would concentrate on celebrating the sacraments. Social justice was no longer a central concern of the Church in the San Jose del Rio region. The Indian peasants in Chapila Chica and the area around San Jose del Rio would have to accept the harsh social world into which they had been born, and the church would retire to its traditional role—emphasizing the miracle of God's grace and the rewards of a wondrous afterlife.

Padre Julio had severed all connection to the United Committee of Farmworkers, the rural produce cooperative with which he had been working.

"It's just as well," I said, "since there's a civil war going on. The army sees such rural cooperatives as just another political front of the rebels, you know. The landowners are obsessed with maintaining their privileges. Anything that challenges their profits will automatically be seen as communism."

"To want justice for the people does not make you a communist."

"You will never convince the Ladino class of that."

We had just come back from the river, to the leafy backyard behind a house on the edge of the village where we talked, played chess, and occasionally dozed off to escape the heat. Today, in the late afternoon, the shade of the extraordinarily thick trees that sheltered the backyard was deep and cool.

The shade felt good.

"Then just talk about human rights," I said.

"That is also impossible. The landowners deny that the peasants have any rights to begin with. Talking about human rights reminds the landowners and the army how they have always stayed in power, by violating the peasants' human rights. If one even mentions human rights for peasants, one might as well go ahead and organize them into rural cooperatives. The risk would be the same, and they would have more to gain."

Overnight, the village of Chapila Chica had lost its identity, Padre Julio complained. But there was a part of me that felt that perhaps it had never been a particularly good identity to begin with. Maybe it had all been playacting, people getting misty-eyes over some trendy new version of Christianity that had no more chance of working than the traditional aspects of the faith that were already dying out. What had been accomplished?

Nada. Another blind alley, more broken dreams.

"The villagers of Chapila Chica look at me," Padre Julio continued, "as though any moment I will start talking again about building the Kingdom of God on earth, so that they can talk about it once again. They would love to talk about it the way we once did, but we can't. The fact is, this generation of *campesinos* will not be able to win even the smallest increments of social justice. To talk about it would only make them aware of what they have lost."

"Maybe that would be a good thing. To talk about what you have lost, I mean."

He shook his head. "Losing social justice is a bad thing, and once you start talking about the bad things in Guatemala, you cannot stop. There is so much of it."

"Then you simply must find a new way of seeing things as a priest—some new vocation, some new spiritual truth."

"Justice for the people was at the heart and soul of what I did. We were going to sell our corn for a higher price, because we were going to bargain collectively, together with people in other villages. Having a little more money for your children is a very concrete thing." He was silent a moment. "The people were also looking forward to getting something for themselves without resorting to violence. That may sound abstract, but it's not. It's something they wanted."

We were both silent.

"And now," Padre Julio said, "every time someone mentions the corn we are growing, the people in Chapila Chica automatically think about the price we were hoping to get. But we won't get it. And we can't even talk about it because it's dangerous now; so people fall silent. They look at me, and they seem to be asking me what happened to the thing we had looked forward to for so long. And I have no answer for them. I can't even tell them how I feel about it."

"Why don't you call a meeting and clear the air? Explain to them why you can't work with the United Committee of Farmworkers anymore."

"I can't," Julio said, "because there will be some who are ready to die rather than to give up the dream of social justice, and I do not want to encourage them. Nor do I want to split the village into two warring camps. So it is better that they continue to wait for me to bring the subject up, and that I continue to say nothing. That way they will slowly realize that the discussion is over."

He did not come back for a week.

The next time I saw him, Padre Julio came over in the middle of the night. I got up from my pallet on the floor and lit some candles; I had candles placed all around the kitchen of the little wooden house. I did not suggest that we play chess, because it was clear that something was wrong. I sat at the table and Padre Julio sat down in the candlelight across the table from me.

He was wearing his clerical collar, which seemed oddly out of place in the middle of the night. He was also unshaven.

"Did I wake you?" he asked.

"I was dreaming."

"Yes, I heard you talking in your sleep before."

I was happy to see him, despite the lateness of the hour. I told him about my dream. "I was playing chess with a skeleton, yet I couldn't get the skeleton to play. So I started yelling at him."

"Where was I in the dream?"

"Why should you should be in my dream?"

"Aren't I the person who usually plays chess with you?"

"Only in the real world."

His speech was pressured and his eyes were red, and they moved restlessly around the room. He was so agitated that for a moment I thought he might be about to have some kind of convulsion. He was smiling, but his smile was frozen and self-deprecating, as though he were an actor who had forgotten his best moves. He was normally a very sophisticated and self-possessed man, so it was very strange to see him this way.

"How important am I in the real world?" he asked suddenly.

"What do you care what the world thinks?" I asked this with some irritation. I had always thought of him as being supremely unconcerned about what other people thought of him.

"No, no, no," he said softly, "I'm not talking about what the world thinks. I'm talking about what *you* think."

"About what?"

"What I do as a priest."

I looked at him, sitting there across from me. By now I was definitely starting to wake up.

In the ghostly candlelight, he reminded me of old photographs of Miguel de Unamuno in 1936, before his death in Salamanca. Padre Julio was the quintessential Latin intellectual, the one who told you what part of Spain his grandparents came from and what titles they had, but insisted with equal vigor that he had no social pretensions to defend. People like him, and people who wanted to be like him, peopled the universities and thronged the political Left in the Latin American countries by the thousands; a fair number had already succeeded in getting themselves killed, some with great flair and imagination.

Many more would die in the years to come.

"You are typical of a certain type," I said. "You truly want to give suffering people some relief. The problem is that you confuse your courage with your ability to achieve your goals."

"Like you?"

"I have no courage, and I have no goals."

"But you are not afraid to die," he said.

"I am afraid to die, and I am afraid to live, afraid of the dark and afraid of the daylight—and that cowardice will end only when death becomes the only way left open to me. But I do not have the courage to kill myself. Instead I hope somebody will do it for me."

"Why?"

We sat looking at each other in the candlelight. "I don't know for sure," I said, "but from earliest childhood I was fascinated with death and destruction. I thought of little else. I was not interested in learning how to live with distinction in a world in which people kill each other. The point, as I saw it, was only to die with distinction."

"Do you still believe that?"

"Not as much as before."

"What is left for you to believe in?"

"Very little."

Padre Julio's eyes were bright in the candlelight.

"Would the world be better off without people like me?" he asked suddenly. "If all the priests in the world were gone, would it be a better place?"

"This sounds like an exit interview."

"Maybe I'm getting there."

I groaned. "Look, you have every right to experience whatever dark night of the soul you wish, but by what right do you ask me to analyze you, and ultimately to judge you? I really didn't have the energy to pull it off."

"Try."

"Okay," I said, "I'll be brutally frank. There's something about you that confuses me. Clearly you think that the world can be improved—but if you truly believe that the world can be made better, why do you bother with faith in the next world?"

"Because justice and faith complement each other. The world of social justice is a right-handed kingdom. It is direct, and moves directly to correct a problem. But the problems people have are never quite as straightforward as they seem. The spiritual world is a left-handed kingdom, where everything is indirect—paradoxical, if you wish."

"And?"

"They go together," he said simply.

"Well then," I said briskly, the optimistic American solving yet another problem, "you have nothing to worry about. You have lost your vocation for social justice, and you can no longer operate in the right-handed kingdom. *But you can still operate in the left-handed kingdom*. You still have your faith in God. That's more than a lot of people have, right?"

Padre Julio was leaning forward with his face in his hands. I could see that he was unraveling, because the tears were starting to come through his fingers.

"All right, I can see you're hurting," I said, "but what's wrong with a priest having faith?"

"What's wrong," he said with a sharp enunciation that made

the words sound like bullets punching a tin surface, "is that I don't believe in the same things anymore. I just don't believe that God can help us in Guatemala. Not now."

"What?"

"I have no faith, or at least not the kind I ought to have. I don't think I have for a long time. Now do you understand?"

As Padre Julio told the story, it had been building up for a long time, but he knew the exact moment when he stopped believing completely. (Or rather, the moment when he could acknowledge that fact to himself.) The week before he had gone to the market town of San Jose del Rio to say mass. He stayed overnight in the crumbling rectory next to the church. On the second day he was approached by a soldier who wanted to say confession. What followed had been completely traumatizing, so he was desperate to talk about it to me. He framed in as a third-person story that happened to someone else, but it was painfully clear that it had happened to him.

The soldier had a red nose and comically large ears, with a certain staring quality in his eyes typical of those who had endured head wounds. He was in excellent physical shape, unlike most of the Indians in the highlands. He made his request with a kind of exaggerated deference that felt dangerous to Father Julio.

He wondered if the soldier had been sent to kill him.

They entered their separate sides of the confessional, which was old-fashioned and ornamented on top with crude brass cherubs and seraphim, and which reminded Padre Julio of a time machine from any number of Hollywood movies. They sat behind thick velvet curtains that were as old and odoriferous as time itself; there had been no electricity since early afternoon, so they used candles.

It began like any other confession, with the soldier speaking in the childlike rote voice in which men often confessed. (It was the women who liked to relive their sins during confession, Father Julio had discovered, whereas the men were often terrified of them.) But this was not like most confessions. This soldier was talking about a military operation that involved the killing of civilians.

With a start Padre Julio realized that the soldier was talking about the massacre of a village.

"What was the name of this village?" Padre Julio asked sharply.

"Some called it Chapila Chica, and some called it Chapila Grande," the soldier noted, "but it was actually very small. I don't know what the right name is."

"What did you do?"

"We killed all the people; all the men, and the women and children too." Before Julio could say or ask anything, the soldier exclaimed, "We were ordered to do it. We had to follow orders!"

The soldier claimed to remember little about the massacre. Nor was he particularly bothered by the morality of killing civilians, in the way that he understood morality; it was all part of his work, and he was only following the orders of his commanding officer. But he wanted to confess, he said, because he had started to wonder if perhaps his commanding officer might not have ordered the massacre of the wrong village; and he had begun to suspect that he might, for that reason, be in a state of sin.

Padre Julio questioned him closely about the massacre.

He kept his voice calm—he didn't want the soldier to bolt. The soldier was clearly trying to cooperate, but nonetheless Padre Julio got the feeling that he was concealing something.

"You must tell me everything that happened that day," Father Julio told the soldier. "You must confess to every specific act that was sinful. Then we will talk about the events that led up to the killing."

"They said it was Chapila Chica, but I think it may have been

Chapila Grande." He thought about what Padre Julio had just said. "Why do we have to talk about everything that happened?"

"It will help in your redemption if you can understand what happened, and why they happened."

"How will it help?" the soldier asked. He was stone-cold sober and quite calm. "I want to confess."

"Then you must tell me everything."

"I am telling you everything I can remember, Padre."

"No. There is more that you are not telling me."

Then, and only then, did the soldier show signs of what Father Julio at first assumed was remorse. The soldier bent forward and put his clenched fists against his forehead.

"*Ahhhhh, Padre,*" he was moaning, rocking slowly back and forth.

"I'm listening."

The soldier's words were muffled by his arms, which by now covered his face. "There is something I have not told you. I am afraid to tell you because you will think I am crazy."

"Is it true? Are you crazy?"

The soldier began to cry. "Yes, Father, *soy loco*."

When the soldier had finished crying, he got down to business. He talked about certain things that happened during the massacre at Chapila Grande: specifically he talked about the one thing that happened that he could remember with absolute clarity. It also happened to be the one thing he wanted to forget, but couldn't stop remembering. It concerned the death of two women in the village.

When the people were marched out to the killing field outside the village, the villagers had begun to sing their Pentecostal hymns. Two women sang louder than the rest. One was energetic and brave and went out of her way to comfort the others. The other was white and had a fierce expression on her face and spoke Spanish with a strange accent. Some of the soldiers thought the second one might be a European.

Certain soldiers wanted to rape them, but the white woman sang so fiercely that they were unable to do so. The other woman stood beside her and held her hand and sang with her. During the killing the two women sang like possessed beings. The soldiers ordered them to stop, but they wouldn't; instead they sang louder. The soldiers shot them, but they still wouldn't stop singing; many different ways they tried to kill them, but nothing seemed to work. They filled their bodies with bullets and hacked at them with machetes, but they wouldn't die.

Nor would they stop singing.

As they lay on the ground the singing became weaker. The soldiers were frightened.

Only when they decapitated the white woman did she stop singing. Then, and only then, would the other woman stop singing.

She died soon afterwards.

Father Julio saw that the soldier was deeply shaken.

"If you are truly sorry, God will forgive you," Father Julio told the soldier who had come for confession. "There is nothing that God cannot forgive. If you are truly sorry in your heart, God has already forgiven you."

"Thank you," the soldier said, "but there is something else."

"What is this other thing?"

"I cannot stop the white woman from singing. She is not really dead. Somewhere she is alive, because I can hear her singing every night when I want to sleep."

Padre Julio spoke carefully but with great passion.

"You are not at all concerned about this woman. You are concerned only about yourself—you are concerned that you cannot sleep."

The soldier looked at him uncomprehendingly. "Yes, Father."

"You are only sorry that her singing is causing you to lose sleep, causing you to suffer, is that not true?"

"Yes, Father."

"Then you are really not concerned about her suffering."

"Yes, Father."

Padre Julio leaned forward. "Can you not see that this is the root of your problem? Only when you feel the pain of this woman can you really forgive yourself! Only when you die with her can..." He started to say, *Only then will God forgive you.* "Only then can you find the peace you are seeking! Can't you see that?"

"Yes, Father!" the soldier shrieked. "Every night! How can anyone sleep when they have to listen to something like that? If I can't sleep, I will die!"

Padre Julio took a deep breath.

"What do you think I should do to help you?" Padre Julio said, not without a certain satisfaction at the soldier's terror.

"Please talk to the white woman. Ask her to stop singing."

"From what you have told me, it is clear that she's dead."

"You must talk to the white woman," the soldier said without missing a beat. "I know that God will forgive anything. I believe that God has already forgiven me. But the white woman will never stop singing until she forgives me. Until then she will sing every night when I want to sleep." The soldier put his fingers through the grill that separated them in the confessional and gripped it tightly. "Can you help me? Can you make the white woman stop singing?"

"What will you do now?" I asked Padre Julio after he told me that story.

I felt that it really was a kind of exit interview, in more ways than one. But of one thing I was sure—it was time for him to leave Guatemala. But when I brought it up he wouldn't answer me.

From that time on, I asked him about his plans every time he came over to play chess. "What will you do? Will you stay in Guatemala?"

"I have no idea."

"Too many things have happened—you can't go on here. You

will have to leave Guatemala."

When I first said this, he did not reply.

Then, over a period of about two weeks, he began to speak in generalities about the future. Although he probably didn't realize it, he was still traumatized, which caused him to speak in a oddly light-hearted way. "Life is like learning how to play a musical instrument and playing a concert at the same time, don't you think? Every day is a concert for which there is no rehearsal. In retrospect, one sees how a rehearsal could have helped, but in daily life we are always reading the notes for the first time."

"In what part of the world will you present your next concert?"

"One isn't sure of the venue."

"In other words, you have no idea where you're going."

But about leaving Guatemala, there wasn't much doubt. At a certain point we started to speak of leaving as if it were inevitable—whatever home truths Guatemala was supposed to teach us, we had already learned. It was time to make a graceful exit, conduct a strategic withdrawal, and start looking for the keys to the highway.

Neither of us awoke one morning convinced that we should make a decision one way or the other. The decision seemed to have been made for us: the fact that we would have to leave Guatemala felt both fated and unavoidable. Too many bad things were happening, and you had guilty knowledge of too many of them, and then you were on the *lista*, the death list, and you had to leave. The lucky ones were those who became aware of what was happening before they got on the list.

Because Padre Julio's pastoral duties now included San Jose del Rio, he was finding it almost impossible to get to the capital to pick up medicines and other supplies. A seminarian staying at the church in San Jose del Rio had done it a few times, but he had gone back to Guatemala City, so Padre Julio asked me to do it.

I was supposed to drive into Guatemala City and pick up supplies from a list I'd been given. I'd get a big load of medications, along with certain foods and dry goods from the non-governmental organizations and the church warehouses, in preparation for the rainy season. Hopefully, I would be able to do it every week until the rainy season started. I had a good general idea where to pick things up in Guatemala City, since I had often gone there with Sofia, mainly to pick up medications.

Julio stopped by one morning to give me instructions for proceeding, knocking on my broken screen-door before dawn. I got up and let him in. Although I would normally have been sleeping, I had been awake on my pallet on the floor for some time.

Padre Julio was on his way to San Jose del Rio.

"I'll be celebrating Mass this afternoon and evening," he said, "and once again tomorrow morning. I'll be hearing confessions tomorrow until early afternoon."

There was enough predawn light for me to see his face. "Doesn't the loss of faith make it harder to celebrate the Eucharist?"

"On the contrary—I enjoy it more," Padre Julio said. "I couldn't go on like this indefinitely, of course, but in the short run I like it. Now I am celebrating the last meal of Jesus the condemned criminal, not God. And it really *was* his last meal, because there would be for him nothing except death by public execution."

"Why do you want to remember this particular condemned criminal?"

"Because he was teaching a new way of life, a way of life universally ignored by Christians in every time and place."

"I wouldn't go around broadcasting that insight, if I were you."

He shrugged.

"I have lost whatever faith I had before," he said, "and in a way I'm glad of it; but that doesn't mean I should cause everybody in these mountains to lose theirs. There is no hope for justice now, so faith is all they have. I refuse to take that away from them."

"Sit down," I said, "and tell me what the hell you want me to do."

He sat down at the table.

Since the death of Sofia Mendez and my defection from Chapila Chica, he said, it had become very hard to get the things he needed, especially the medications he dispensed.

He gave me a detailed list of the supplies he needed, which also contained the addresses of the places where I could pick them up. I would have to drive through the early-morning hours and pick up the supplies during the day, and start driving back to Chapila Chica later that same day.

"Are you sure you can handle this?"

"If nobody else is available to do the job, I'll have to."

"Indeed," he said solemnly.

His bishop was loaning him a *cuatro*, a small truck with four-wheel drive. It would be driven to the partially abandoned village where the trail to Chapila Chica left the main road; the *cuatro* would be driven there late at night on Wednesday, and would be left there unattended. Thursday morning I was to make my way to the truck, which would be parked under a certain tree near the main road, and drive it to the capital.

"The key to the *cuatro* is struck in the ignition," Padre Julio said. "You will have to start the truck by connecting certain wires underneath the dashboard."

He took a long time explaining how to connect the wires.

I was thinking about the way he kept looking at my unkempt hair and beard. "I'm not a very respectable-looking guy. Your friends at the church warehouses may not like that."

"Then stop feeling sorry for yourself and clean yourself up," Padre Julio said briskly. "To begin with, shave your beard off—I assume that you still remember how to shave. I will cut your hair in a few days."

He went out the door, and I stood in the doorway watching him. He was about twenty feet away when I called out.

"Padre Julio!" I said.

He came back and stood patiently in front of me.

"Tell me one thing," I said. "Will I be picking up anything that might end up in the hands of the rebels or that could help them in any way? In other words, is there anything that could be considered contraband, anything that could get me in trouble with the army or the government security agencies?"

"No." He frowned and started toward the trail.

I didn't like the peremptory way he had dealt with my question.

"Wait a minute!" I yelled. He stopped and turned back halfway. "Tell me or I won't go!"

He was smiling, but in his attitude there was undercurrent of impatience bordering on hostility. *You're too late,* I thought I heard him mutter under his breath.

"What do you mean by that?"

"You are in absolutely no danger. There will be no proscribed articles, no contraband of any kind in these supplies."

"Don't lie to me," I said. "I want to know about it, if there is anything that could get me I trouble."

"Don't worry."

He turned and started walking away.

"You are in no danger, I promise you—no more than anybody else."

I went to the main road to get the *cuatro* on Wednesday evening, while the sun was still up, but it wasn't there. It wasn't until I was climbing back up the trail that I remembered that the truck was supposed to be left there very late Wednesday night, and that Padre Julio had advised me to come early Thursday morning. I returned early the next morning.

The *cuatro* was there.

I got the vehicle started and let it warm up. Although it was small, the engine throbbed like an eighteen-wheeler. It burned diesel fuel, the pleasant stink of which reminded me of my hitch-hiking times. Eighteen-wheel semitrailers were the best rides on the road, and I had done a fair amount of time sitting in high cabs talking to weary truckers.

Keep talking to me, kid, the long-haul drivers would say.

I got on the road toward the capital, hitting thirty miles an hour on the smooth stretches and staying at about fifteen to twenty miles an hour most of the time. The road was as rough as any in Guatemala, mined with axle-killing potholes every two or three feet. There were only a few vehicles on the road, mainly the deuce-and-a-half transport vehicles preferred by the Guatemalan army. I passed a couple of parked four-wheel vehicles with tinted glass. I could not see the faces of the occupants.

I got to Guatemala City safely and started rounding up the supplies.

Many of the agencies and NGOs that were on Padre Julio's written list were the same ones I had visited earlier with Sofia Mendez. Being in the same places I had visited with Sofia aroused strong feeling in me that I had difficulty controlling. The feelings were passionately sexual, with a kind of extraordinarily bittersweet nostalgia attached to them, a nostalgia not only for the lovemaking Sofia and I had done together, but everything that we could have done.

Most of the people at the NGOs, church warehouses, and international aid agencies did not recognize me from the times I had come with Sofia because I looked different now. They tried not to stare at my long hair and wild beard.

The love for Sofia that I carried around inside me was burning a hole in my chest. It was better than the emptiness that I had felt before, but it was dangerous, because I was so full that I could not hold it. What if somebody accidentally burned themselves on its hard acetylene flame?

I went to the NGO where Sofia usually got most of her antibiotics and pain medication.

"Hey, where's your girlfriend?" murmured a young Canadian. He did not look up from the clipboard he was consulting. "Couldn't she make it today?"

"No," I said.

"Busy?"

"I'm very busy."

The young Canadian spent a long time making a note on the papers held by the clipboard, which lay flat on his desk. Finally he looked up and smiled. "Well, tell her hello for me."

The Canadian turned to a Belgian relief worker and began speaking in French to him. I used a hand-truck to take the cardboard box of supplies I had been given outside. There was another four-wheel drive truck coming up the narrow street. I could still hear the Canadian speaking in French to the Belgian relief working in the office I had just left.

From an office on the second floor of the building I heard someone speaking in German. The voice went on for a long time and then it would stop for a few moments and then start in again. Perhaps, I thought, he was talking on the telephone. I put the supplies in the truck and got the truck started.

By mid-afternoon, I had finished getting the supplies.

I was relieved, since that meant I would avoid most of the traffic later. I headed out of the city.

I started picking up elevation as soon as I got onto the pothole-riddled road into the mountains. It was incredibly hot in the *cuatro*, even though Guatemala City had been okay. I could not stop thinking about the children that Sofia and I could have had. It had seemed like a dream when she was alive, but now I had a special interest in trying to imagine what their faces would have looked like. I pulled over at a little roadside *tienda* and drank a beer and ate some tough barbequed meat, but the thoughts would not go away.

The heat was also driving me crazy.

I got back on the road and tried not to think about the sex Sofia and I had together, but I couldn't stop. My body was so aroused that it was almost like being with her again in the darkened schoolhouse. Combined with the heat and the beer, the desire that was sweeping through me made me feel suddenly disabled, to the point where I had serious doubts about whether I could control the vehicle on the winding mountain road.

But I kept driving.

Even the steering wheel and the floor gearshift were hot; they left gritty black stains on my hands, and my forearms had turned pitch black from resting them against the steering wheel. When I accidently touched the metal dashboard, it burned my hand. I simply wanted to get the drive over and park the truck and store the most important supplies in the little wooden house in Chapila Grande, and go to sleep in my hammock on the edge of the village. Tomorrow I would go down before sunup with a couple of people from Chapila Chica and get the rest.

I was about ten kilometers from the trail of Chapila Chica when I lost control of the vehicle.

I was driving too fast, of course, and bouncing up and down in the sweltering cab like a cork in a storm surge. As far as I could tell, this truck had never possessed anything even remotely like a safety belt. I hit a sharp curve and felt the road start to shift away from me. That was a terrible feeling in this part of the mountains, because there was no shoulder to swing around on, and the road had a tendency to crumble when one got too close to a gorge. I tried to compensate by twisting the front wheels in the opposite direction, but it was too late.

The *cuatro* went over on its side and started sliding sideways down the hill. The descent was slow and dreamlike. The gorge was not a steep one, and the truck was buoyed up by thick underbrush as it slid slowly down the hill. I was conscious during the whole thing, hanging onto the steering wheel for dear life, although I struck my forehead on it. As the truck came to rest on its side against a tree, the windshield popped out. It popped out whole, then broke against the steering wheel and shattered around me into many tiny pieces.

Everything was absolutely quiet.

The cab of the truck was filled with shattered glass. I wondered if the truck could be seen from the road above. I was not hurt particularly badly and felt no pain, but I was covered in blood from glass cuts from the broken windshield; and it was hard to move in the cab of the truck without cutting myself further on the broken glass.

Then I heard the zopilotes.

Zopilotes, the vultures of Guatemala, do not often announce themselves with any of the sounds one normally associates with birds. They make themselves known with a certain insistent rustling of their wings that one hears when they begin to gather in groups, waiting for their next meal. It is a soft sound, but a chilling one, a sound that one does not soon forget.

Buzzards feed on the dead, of course; the newly dead, the dead that have been dead a long time, and the living that are about to die. Zopilotes will eat anything that looks to them as though it *ought* to be dead—in other words, anything that is vulnerable. They are everywhere in Guatemala: I had gotten so used to them that I no longer noticed them. It was not unusual for zopilotes to follow people walking on the roads and trails of Guatemala, waiting for them to topple over and furnish them with an easy meal.

They were particularly disposed to follow North Americans. Perhaps it was because we dressed so differently from the Mayan-speaking people of the highlands, or were so much taller than most of them, we were not perceived by the zopilotes as human beings at all, but as another species entirely. Or perhaps there was a tentative quality about the way we moved, a sense that we were not quite at home, that made us look as though we might stumble into situations that would make us easy prey.

As I'd just done, unfortunately.

I was laying absolutely still in the cab of the wrecked truck—I had the crazy idea that if I did not move, I would bleed less—and I looked out of the hole where the windshield had been and saw a zopilote perched on the hood of the truck. Another zopilote joined him. I could hear the wings of the others rustling quite clearly now. I gathered that there were many of them: a third zopilote hopped lazily onto the hood of the *cuatro*, and there seemed to be others behind them in the trees. They were definitely aware of me inside of the truck—otherwise why would they be sitting on the hood?—but in my demented state it seemed that they wouldn't look directly at me; and somehow that was especially threatening.

"Can't you see me, you ugly bastards?" I taunted. "Look at me! Why don't you *look* at me?"

The zopilote nearest to me on the hood of the *cuatro* casually poked his head in through the big space where the windshield had been, and lunged at my stomach and tried to tear open my belly with his hooked beak. I could hear myself screaming loudly. I saw the hook on the beak as it went for my stomach, and I struck it squarely on the side of the head.

It withdrew its heard from the cab.

Zopilotes had an instinct to tear open the stomach of their prey and eat the spilled entrails. It was for this all-important move that the zopilote had the hook on the end of their beaks. By tearing out the entrails of their prey they ensured its death, and by feasting on its entrails, they did not even have to wait until it was dead before feeding on it.

I had seen the zopilotes tear open the stomachs of their prey many times. They did it with a lightning-quick jerk of the head and a slight but muscular twist of the hooked beak. It was like a snake striking. Sometimes the quick head would jerk at the stomach and the entrails seemed to spill out even before the zopilote finished the swift twist of the hooked beak.

They were incredibly fast.

I had vision of how it would look when the zopilotes got my stomach opened. I would have to sit there looking at my own entrails, and I would not have the slightest idea what to do with them. Then I would have to try to stop the zopilotes from grabbing at them with their beaks and eating them one by one.

I heard myself screaming.

My screams were from very far away and from right inside my head at the same time.

The three zopilotes on the hood of the truck were briefly joined by a fourth. When the fourth zopilote tried to squeeze past the three that were already there, they flapped their wings and pushed him away; I could see the scaly red legs of the zopilotes very clearly. It was said that they vomited up a special chemical that covered their bodies and allowed them to stand around in the entrails of their prey without getting infections on their wings or legs.

The faces of the zopilotes were absolutely nonexistent, because in place of a face they all had the amazingly useful hooked beaks. I noticed that they were all jerking their head sideways, as though practicing the killing move they were going to make when they got my stomach in the hook of their beaks and were twisting it open.

The same zopilote that had come after me before tried again. He stuck his head lazily through the broken windshield. I turned my body as he struck: his beak hit my ribs and tore at them. Then the second zopilote stuck his head through the windshield. Thereafter my memory of what happened is a bit sketchy.

I remember that one of the zopilotes actually got my stomach in his beak and was turning sideways, trying to twist it open, and at that point, in my mind's eye, I saw my own entrails falling out.

There were far too many of the zopilotes now, but I was resisting wildly, trying to smack the vultures at the moment they stuck their heads through the windshield. Language had fled: I had nothing to say to the zopilotes that a scream could not communicate much more effectively.

One of the zopilotes went for my eyes.

It was then that some men driving by on the road above saw the truck and heard my screaming and came down into the shallow gorge and chased the vultures away. Horrible to relate, I remember clearly that the men were laughing. Perhaps they were laughing because they were shocked to find me alive. Or perhaps it was because they did not want me to feel ashamed that they had heard my screaming. Perhaps they were so rattled that laughing was the only way they could deal with it.

"Zopilotes," muttered one of the men.

The men laughed uneasily.

The men were positioning themselves to pull me out of the cab through the space where the windshield had been. They wanted to make sure the truck would not slide further down the hill.

"Tienen hambre," said another man. "They were hungry."

They all laughed.

When the men pulled me from the cab of the *cuatro,* I was drenched with bodily fluids. My face was wet with blood and tears, my body leaked sweat and blood, and my pants were drenched with urine; and there was a taste in my mouth that was different from anything I had ever tasted before.

I got word to Padre Julio but did not go and see him. Nor did he come to see me for several days.

Padre Julio sent some men from Chapila Chica to pick up the supplies from the cab of the truck. Most of the supplies were okay, I found out later, although a bottle of alcohol had been broken. Other men came from San Jose del Rio and pulled the truck back onto the road. It took them a long time—well into the night, I was told—to get the engine started again. Afterward it ran with no perceptible problem, although there was no money to replace the broken windshield and the fenders had to be taken off to allow the front wheels to turn without obstruction.

I had no broken bones, and I healed quickly. There were scars on my stomach, rib cage, and forehead.

After the experience with the zopilotes I decided to leave Guatemala as soon as I could. But I had to say goodbye to Padre Julio first, there was no getting around that. I figured he'd come around sooner or later, if only to see how I was doing after my experience with the *cuatro* and the zopilotes. I decided that I'd spring the news on him the next time he visited me.

Then I would leave.

He finally showed up one night at two o'clock in the morning, knocking on my door. I opened the door and there he was, carrying two bulging bags with a large backpack on his back. I knew immediately what he was doing and what he was going to tell me.

"You were so right, Maitland," he said breathlessly, "it really *is* time for me to leave Guatemala."

"Damn," I said, "you beat me to it."

"We need to talk."

"Come on in," I said.

There was a fair amount of moonlight in the kitchen of the little wooden house, but I lit a couple of candles anyways. I motioned for him to sit down, and he sat on one of the two wobbly chairs at the kitchen table. The candles kept guttering out, and it took a long time to light them so that they continued to burn.

"Why do you always show up at night?"

"It's cool, and it's not that far from Chapila Chica."

I sat down from him at the kitchen table. "So you're leaving."

"Yes, yes." He seemed very happy. "It's time, just as you said."

I had not anticipated that Padre Julio might get the drop on me in this way. Here I was, patiently waiting from him to show up, so that I could make my little speech about how I had to leave Guatemala, and then take my bittersweet leave; and here *he* was, doing *his* goodbye, before I could even say anything!

I felt like an actor being upstaged by a friend.

"Are you really awake?" he asked.

"Yes, thank God."

"Nightmares?"

I nodded. I had been dreaming about the zopilotes.

I had clearly heard the ominous rustle of their wings as they got together to finish me off. They wanted to open up my stomach and stand in my entrails and eat me like roadkill. Once I got sufficiently awake to understand that the zopilotes were not in the kitchen with me, I could not find my way back to the same deep sleep. When Padre Julio knocked on my door, I had been laying there on my pallet on the kitchen floor with my eyes open.

Padre Julio could hardly contain himself. His hands were shaking. "My God, I'm really leaving!—It's hard to believe!"

I could think of nothing to say. Now that the time had come, all I could think of was all the things I had always wanted to talk to him about, but hadn't had the chance.

"When are you leaving?" I asked finally.

"I'm on my way now."

"Where are you going?"

"A safe place. Someone is waiting for me back on the main trail."

"Will I see you before you leave?"

"No. This is the last time I'll see you."

The weirdness of it hit me. I started to laugh. "How the hell can you do this to me? I was just about to leave Guatemala myself, and now you come and beat me to it!"

"It's not a competition, Maitland."

"No, it certainly shouldn't be, but it feels like it."

"Like the old joke, 'Don't leave me before I abandon you?'"

"Yeah, I suppose so, something like that."

But for him, it was simply time for him to go. That part I believed.

"I'm going too," I said evenly. "I was only waiting to say goodbye to you."

He raised his eyebrows. "When will you leave?"

"Tomorrow morning."

"Where will you go?"

"Back to San Francisco."

There was a long silence.

The two remaining kitchen chairs had gotten so rickety that I had stopped trying to sit on them, but tonight we were putting our full weight on them. Both chairs swayed perilously, but Julio did not seem to notice.

"Where are you going?" I asked.

He smiled in the candlelight, and I could tell he was wondering how much he should tell me.

"East Germany. I will be attending an important conference that will attempt to educate the world about the crimes committed by the Guatemalan government. It might also bring us a little closer to peace in Central America."

I should have seen this coming, I was thinking, or something like this. "And after the conference?"

"I'll be staying in Europe. I'm going to write a cultural history of psychoanalysis, and why it was so important to several generations of Americans and Europeans. I'll be receiving a small stipend while I do the research and write the first draft."

"Where will you do your research?"

"Central Europe, Germany and Austria."

"The lands that gave us Doctor Freud."

"And Karl Marx and Albert Einstein."

"And Adolf Hitler," I said.

"Yes," he said, "that's why I want to go there, not just because of the origins of psychoanalysis. I want to study it in the larger context of a breakdown in morality in Central Europe. Germany in particular is a haunted place. I want to interview the ghosts."

Haven't you encountered quite enough in Guatemala? I felt like asking. Instead I said, "Hopefully you have already learned something of value here, and will learn more there."

"All the major witch-burning went on in the German-speaking lands that were influenced by Martin Luther. It was there that the legend of Faust arose, and it was there that the Holocaust happened. If you want to know about evil, the pure heart of it, that's where you must go."

"Have you spoken to your bishop about all this?"

"Yes, at length. As I mentioned, I'll be receiving a small stipend from the Church."

"Just remember during all this that there's more to German-speaking culture than Nazis and the Holocaust."

"Yes," he said, "but it's not the music, the theatre, the literature, and the scientific research that haunts us today, but the Holocaust."

"Does it haunt you personally?"

"I want to find out about evil."

"In yourself or in the world?"

"Both," he said.

"Well—you'll find both kinds in the East German workers' paradise, I'm sure."

He did not quite understand. "There is nothing evil about seeking justice for the poor."

I realized it was too late now for this kind of discussion, but I wanted to put in a cautionary note, now that I knew where he was headed. "What is evil is to believe that the East Germans can help the Guatemalan people find justice. It would be a great temptation to believe that."

He dismissed this with quick, barely discernable gesture. "You don't have to lecture me about the communists, Maitland—

I know what their agenda is. But sometimes we have to make common cause with those who are misguided. The world is in the midst of great changes, and we have to stand with the oppressed."

I said nothing for a long time.

"How did you hear about this conference in East Germany?'

"A group in Mexico City contacted me about a conference on national liberation movements, and invited me to attend. They explained that it is being held in East Berlin, but is not exclusively for Marxist-Leninists. It is open to all people interested in the oppression of indigenous peoples."

"Will you have time to study the history of psychoanalysis?"

"That's my plan," he said rather mysteriously, adding, "It is always conceivable that I may stay in Europe as some kind of permanent liaison with one of the human-rights groups. In any case, I'll start my study of psychoanalysis in East Berlin, and go to West Berlin when I'm ready."

"Don't you think the people of East Germany are oppressed, too?"

"If they are," he said very clearly and succinctly, "and I can see that they are, and they have the will and the courage to struggle against their oppression, I will help them in their struggle."

I was silent. He had it all figured out. *Perhaps you'll get the martyrdom you want so badly after all,* I thought; but I didn't say it, although later I wished I had. Instead I said, "Do the people of Chapila Chica know you are leaving?"

"No. And there's no reason for them to know. All I want them to know is that Padre Julio went to San Jose del Rio, and was then called to Guatemala City by his bishop, and afterward found it necessary to leave the country. That is what they'll be told. They won't be surprised. They've seen it all before."

"Have you discussed your loss of faith with your bishop?"

"No," he said. He added, "It would be helpful politically, you see, if I continued to wear the Roman collar a bit longer."

"Your bishop won't be so inclined to let you wear it, once he finds out you've gone to East Germany."

"Yes. Well." Padre Julio hesitated. "He'll be given a particular point of view about my visit to East Germany. He has the strange idea that I can help the Jesuits by talking to certain people there. In any case, he will not want to defrock me—that's a process that takes some time, and it is always embarrassing to the church. He would much rather that I voluntarily give up my vocation myself, and formally petition to be released from vows. It's also much easier for the Vatican that way."

We were both quiet for a long time.

I wondered if Padre Julio had any idea what he was getting into. But he didn't seem to care; and it occurred to me that perhaps he was every bit a self-destructive as I was, but that his self-defeat took a different form than mine. Perhaps the arc of his failure had a slower velocity, a longer and more studied parabola and a better learning curve with a bit more dignity in the bargain, as it bore him downward. Self-destruction could look very much like heroic idealism to those who didn't know what to look for.

We both stood up, as if on cue.

"Do you have any idea what you're doing?" I asked.

"I have been very candid with the group in Mexico that is arranging my trip. They know that my participation is strictly nonpolitical—that is, humanitarian. They have assured me that the East Germans are comfortable with that."

He had made up his mind. This was the way Padre Julio wanted to leave Guatemala. He was happier than I had seen him for a long time. I knew him well enough to know that whatever he did, he would ultimately find a way to do it that was not morally reprehensible. I was simply questioning his knowledge of the world, or rather that part of it that he would be entering. It would be a hall of mirrors, which could easily become hell on earth for a man of honor.

But I couldn't interfere.

I took him in my arms and hugged him tightly, kissing him on both cheeks in the Latin way. I had often rehearsed it in my mind, deciding I would wish him goodbye in just this way that was so very Latin, and therefore so appropriate; and just as I kissed him on the cheek the second time, I happened to remember what Che had written in one of his letters to a comrade: *I embrace you as tightly as your manhood will allow. . .*

Padre Julio put his hand on my shoulder, and stood looking at me in a way that I could not read. "I wish we could make a miracle together."

"That is beyond me."

"That doesn't keep me from wanting one."

"No," I said.

I had the feeling that he thought I was doomed, while I had exactly the same feeling about him. There was so much that we didn't know about each other, and so much to say—about that and everything else—and so few seconds left, that it was no use belaboring it.

We released each other.

"Are you walking to San Jose del Rio right now?" I asked.

"Yes. I will be there most of the day tomorrow."

"I'll walk with you."

"No, please don't. It would be better if you didn't."

I had the feeling he was protecting me, so I agreed to let him go on alone. "When will you actually leave the country?"

"Tomorrow night."

He had waited until the last moment to tell me. Good security, that. It would not be right to ask him which route he would take out of the country. Perhaps he did not yet know himself; perhaps he would simply make his way to Mexico City, and would be contacted by his friends once he got there.

"I believe this is goodbye," I said, because it was true, and I could think of nothing else.

"Yes," he said. "It's goodbye."

"There is so much more to say."

"There is never enough time to say everything," he said, "and probably that is the only thing we can ever say anyway."

"Unless we meet again. Then we'll say everything."

"*Until* we meet again."

"*Auf Wiedersehen?*" I asked.

"*Auf Wiedersehen,*" he said.

I lay down again on the unkempt pallet on the kitchen floor. I did not care that it was only a pile of dirty rags, because I knew I wouldn't be alone. The candles had guttered out, and the moon's glimmering yellow light was coming through the trees into the kitchen, and it was the same yellow light in which I dreamed; which was why I knew I wouldn't be alone.

No sooner had I laid down on my pallet on the floor than I slipped into my otherworld of dreams, a world thronged with ghosts of people dead and alive. When I awoke the kitchen was bathed in yellow light, and there was a figure of a woman standing in the light, reaching out to me. It was my beautiful Sofia, and she was standing about ten feet away from me.

I always knew Sofia would come.

I was dreaming, but my eyes were open, so Sofia came to me right there in the kitchen.

She was standing on the other side of the table, as though she had stepped out for a moment and just come back. She looked exactly as she always had. With the stitched and tailored *huilpa*. The designer jeans. The little chain on the wrist.

And the black hair.

And the black hair—the beautiful, luxurious black hair that I wanted to eat like cotton candy.

And the thick fruit-ripe lips, and luscious welcoming hips.

And the black eyes, looking at me, and the beautiful floating smile, smiling at me, smiling, smiling, smiling.

Smiling, forgiving, smiling, forgiving.

Chico, she was saying, or at least that is what I thought she was saying.

Sofia?

Chico, she said again.

I'm right here.

It was as though our voices were traveling through water.

Where are you?

Where could I go, in this sea of love?

She was gently undulating, in a way that told me that neither of us were in control. Yet there she was, big as life.

Te amo, she said. *Te quiero*.

At this point our words became every language in the world, including English.

I love you too, I said.

You will die anyway.

Is that why you came, to punish me?

No.

Did you come to forgive me?

No.

Why did you come?

Wait.

Sofia, I said.

I waited, just as she asked me to. Was she trying to teach me something about eternity in this yellow light? My body was beginning to respond to her, as though the yellow light was made of sexual feelings, and I had to feel sexual desire to be in it. Or maybe my body throbbed because it was the only way I could be with Sofia forever.

How long would Sofia have to wear her favorite outfit, the designer jeans and a stitched and tailored shirt in the style of the multicolored *huilpil*? How long would she have to wear the same outfit in eternity?

Don't go, I said.

Sofia raised her hand as though reacting to me.

I love you, I said.

Yes.

You're my wife. Can you hear me?

Yes, but you're alive, Chico.

I'm trying to die.

You can't die, and you can't live.

What can I do?

You must be brave, and do the two things you fear.

What are those two things?

You must love another woman. If you don't, you will insult me and every woman who ever lived.

What if she won't have me?

Love her, my husband.

What will happen to me if I can't love again?

Your ghosts will bury you.

Will I be buried alive?

Worse than that, but I cannot tell you how much worse.

What is the second thing I have to do?

Tell the people in your country what they have done to us.

They will not listen. They are a cheerful and optimistic people, and they do not like unpleasant truths about themselves.

They took our freedom in 1954. They made us live like dogs. You must tell them what they have done to us.

They will never believe it. When you tell them about this, they become silent. This Silence goes everywhere. They are a family with secrets.

Then write this book.

What book?

You know what book.

Already she was beginning to fade away, and the glimmering yellow light was also fading.

I was suddenly desperate.

Don't go! I said.

Don't forget me, Chico.

Don't go!

Write it, Sofia said.

Her voice was already distant.

And she was gone, and the yellow light was gone, and I was alone.

I left late that morning. I didn't take much. I gathered what was left of my asthma medication and my clothes and my spiral notebooks and put them in my backpack. I took my leather pouch with its travelers' checks, tied it to my belt with leather thongs, and stuffed the pouch into my underpants. I put my boots on, and as I left the little house I used a wooden doorstop to wedge shut the broken door from the outside. I went to the mass grave outside of town and said goodbye to Sofia, although I knew I would be taking her with me. Then I went down the mountain on the main trail and waited on the main road. After about an hour someone stopped and gave me a ride to Guatemala City.

It was not until much later that I heard from some journalists about Colonel Efrain Anibal Montamara. This was long after most of the people of Chapila Chica had left the village, either for Mexico or the market town of San Jose del Rio.

After I left Guatemala, Anibal Montamara had continued to be obsessed with finding an underground printing press, the same printing press that he had questioned me about at the Zone Twenty army base. God only knows where he first got this idea—all I could find out for sure was that he continued to believe that there was an underground printing press being used to print a rebel newspaper, and that the press was located somewhere in the area around San Jose del Rio. And he was determined to find it.

Ultimately he did find it, but not in the way he expected.

He began to go out in the field himself, taking company-size army units with him, doing regular sweeps of the villages around San Jose del Rio, systematically interrogating, torturing, and terrorizing people in an effort to get information about the secret printing press that he believed to be in the area. The people knew nothing, because there was no such press.

The rebel command took an increasing interest in his activities. They conspired to plant further tantalizing information, stories that could not quite be confirmed or denied or even traced to their origins, stories that indicated that there *was*, in fact, a printing press secreted in the area; and Anibal Montamara swallowed the bait hook, line and sinker.

He redoubled his efforts to find the press.

Finally Anibal Montamara received a report—fabricated by the rebel command in Mexico City—that the elusive printing press had recently been hidden in the abandoned house of the Dog Woman: the psychotic woman who had once lived on the path that led from Chapila Chica to Tzotzil Gapachula mountain. The colonel quickly put together a command of rangers equivalent to a small battalion from the base at the Zone Twenty army base and transported them in two-and-a-half ton trucks on the main road to the path that went to Chapila Chica. There the trucks were parked and the troops went immediately to the abandoned house on the trail to Tzotzil Gapachula mountain.

The Dog Woman's house was still there, although it had partially collapsed. At first the lieutenants of Colonel Efrain Anibal Montamara could find no clear indications of human use or habitation, but then they found a telltale pile of cigarettes nearby. Anibal Montamara excitedly ordered his troops to search the part of the house that was still standing.

And there, wrapped in an oiled tarpaulin, was a little printing press. It was a very old press, the kind that had to be laboriously operated by hand. It looked like it had been used recently. There was still wet ink on one of its ancient plates.

The colonel excitedly called for a helicopter.

The soldiers laid the printing press on the oiled tarpaulin in the shade of a tree and stood looking at it. The soldiers were expressly forbidden to touch it: Anibal Montamara intended to take it back to the Zone Twenty army base and take it lovingly apart, piece by piece, in a new lab that he had set up next to one of the interrogation rooms near his office. As strange as it seemed later on, he apparently told one of his lieutenants that he intended to dust it for fingerprints.

The helicopter from the Zone Twenty army base arrived.

Colonel Efrain Anibal Montamara, assisted by his troops, carefully lifted the printing press onto the helicopter, still wrapped in its tarpaulin. Anibal Montamara could hardly wait to get back to base and show his commanding officer, an influential general who was also an old family friend, what he had lately and so luckily discovered. It promised to be a defining moment of his career. The colonel darted about, shouting out commands; and when the press was properly secured in the helicopter, he boarded the aircraft.

The pilot lifted off with the colonel and few others.

The rest of the unit stood watching the helicopter gain altitude. The plan was that they would make their way back to the trucks and drive back to the base.

The helicopter was making a wide circle to go back to the army base when it happened.

According to people who saw it, the helicopter turned into a bright orange fireball. The sound of the explosion reached the area around San Jose del Rio five seconds later. People ran out of their houses to see parts of the orange fireball, all that was left of the helicopter, fall slowly into a gorge. Its remnants were scattered over a large area.

All the body parts had been consumed by zopilotes by the time the patrols from the Zone Twenty army base got there to investigate.

These things happened because one of the rebel commands in Mexico City had decided that Colonel Efrain Anibal Montamara had become an insufferable irritant. According to their information, he had been responsible for the massacre at Chapila Grande; as a result, it was decided that they would terminate his influence in the area by terminating him personally. Obsessed with finding a nonexistent printing press, he had given the rebels the means to do it.

A small, obsolete printing press was found in Guatemala City and was taken through a laborious route to the area around San Jose del Rio. A rebel commander had been sent from the western highlands to plant a small but powerful explosive device inside the press.

After the rebel operation, the few remaining people of Chapila Chica scattered, leaving for other villages and to places they had prepared near Tzotzil Gapachula mountain; many found their way to the refugee camps in southern Mexico. When the soldiers from Zone Twenty army base arrived to take revenge on the village, there was nobody left to kill because everybody was already gone.

If you have enjoyed this book, why not tell other readers by posting a review on your preferred booksite. Recent bestsellers from Roundfire are:

The Bookseller's Sonnets
Andi Rosenthal
The Bookseller's Sonnets intertwines three love stories with a tale of religious identity and mystery spanning five hundred years and three countries.
Paperback: 978-1-84694-342-3 ebook: 978-184694-626-4

Birds of the Nile
An Egyptian Adventure
N.E. David
Ex-diplomat Michael Blake wanted a quiet birding trip up the Nile – he wasn't expecting a revolution.
Paperback: 978-1-78279-158-4 ebook: 978-1-78279-157-7

Blood Profit$
The Lithium Conspiracy
J. Victor Tomaszek, James N. Patrick, Sr
The blood of the many for the profits of the few… *Blood Profit$* will take you into the cigar-smoke-filled room where American policy and laws are really made.
Paperback: 978-1-78279-483-7 ebook: 978-1-78279-277-2

The Burden
A Family Saga
N.E. David
Frank will do anything to keep his mother and father apart. But he's carrying baggage – and it might just weigh him down...
Paperback: 978-1-78279-936-8 ebook: 978-1-78279-937-5

The Cause

Roderick Vincent

The second American Revolution will be a fire lit from an internal spark.

Paperback: 978-1-78279-763-0 ebook: 978-1-78279-762-3

Don't Drink and Fly

The Story of Bernice O'Hanlon Part One

Cathie Devitt

Bernice is a witch living in Glasgow. She loses her way in her life and wanders off the beaten track looking for the garden of enlightenment.

Paperback: 978-1-78279-016-7 ebook: 978-1-78279-015-0

Gag

Melissa Unger

One rainy afternoon in a Brooklyn diner, Peter Howland punctures an egg with his fork. Repulsed, Peter pushes the plate away and never eats again.

Paperback: 978-1-78279-564-3 ebook: 978-1-78279-563-6

The Master Yeshua

The Undiscovered Gospel of Joseph

Joyce Luck

Jesus is not who you think he is. The year is 75 CE. Joseph ben Jude is frail and ailing, but he has a prophecy to fulfil…

Paperback: 978-1-78279-974-0 ebook: 978-1-78279-975-7

On the Far Side, There's a Boy

Paula Coston

Martine Haslett, a thirty-something 1980s woman, plays hard on the fringes of the London drag club scene until one night which prompts her to sign up to a charity. She writes to a young Sri Lankan boy, with consequences far and long.

Paperback: 978-1-78279-574-2 ebook: 978-1-78279-573-5

Tuareg

Alberto Vazquez-Figueroa

With over 5 million copies sold worldwide, *Tuareg* is a classic adventure story from best-selling author Alberto Vazquez-Figueroa, about honour, revenge and a clash of cultures.

Paperback: 978-1-84694-192-4

Find more titles and sign up to our readers' newsletter at http://www.johnhuntpublishing.com/fiction.

Follow us on Facebook at https://www.facebook.com/JHPfiction and Twitter at https://twitter.com/JHPFiction.

Most titles are published in paperback and as an ebook. Paperbacks are available in physical bookshops. Both print and ebook: editions are available online. Readers of ebooks can click on the live links in the titles to order.